TAKE DEAD AIM

by

DON WADE

Sleeping Bear Press

Sleeping Bear Press

Sleeping Bear Press
310 North Main Street
P.O. Box 20
Chelsea, MI 48118
www.sleepingbearpress.com

Printed and bound in Canada.

10 9 8 7 6 5 4 3 2 1

Library of Congress Cataloging-in-Publication Data

Wade, Don.
Take dead aim / by Don Wade.
p. cm.
ISBN 1-58536-037-6
1. Golf—Tournaments—Fiction. 2. Intelligence officers—Fiction.
3. Assassins—Fiction. I. Title.
PS3623.A34 T35 2002
813'.54—dc21
2001008215

For Julia, Ben, Darcy, and Andy

ACKNOWLEDGMENTS

I owe a huge debt of gratitude to Danny Freels, my editor at Sleeping Bear Press, who read the early chapters of this book and immediately became the story's biggest fan and supporter. He went to Brian Lewis, Sleeping Bear's publisher, and urged him to publish my first run at fiction (if you don't count an endless stream of expense reports over the years). Happily, Brian trusted Danny's judgment and gave him the go-ahead to do the deal. In the months that followed, I have come to totally trust Danny's judgment as well. He has been a patient, wise, thoughtful, and most of all, a deeply caring editor. For this, I thank him and thank all the good people at Sleeping Bear as well—especially designer Felicia Macheske for creating the fine cover, and publicist Kolleen O'Meara for her valuable assistance.

Chris Tomasino was my agent at RLR Associates when I first started on this book, and her support, criticism, and loving attention to the story and the devils that lay in the details are greatly appreciated. So are the support and advice given me by Bob Rosen, Jonathan Diamond, and Jennifer Unter of RLR. Thanks to all of you for all you've done over the years.

Finally, thanks to Julia and our kids, Ben, Darcy, and Andy. Writing a book—especially a piece of fiction—can become an all-consuming monster. There are a lot of sacrifices a family has to make, and mine made them without complaint.

They truly believed.

This one's for them.

CHAPTER ONE

If life had taught Tom Quinn just one thing, it was that if you live in New England long enough, eventually everything evens out.

The winters can be brutal, and longer than the dearly departed Cardinal Cushing's weekly pleas for his favorite charities. Not for nothing were the Pilgrims a stern and often dour lot.

Spring can come and go and you might never notice it. For a few days, a hint of it will linger softly in the air. Then a March storm will rip up the coast, sending local television reporters out into traffic to report breathlessly that, yes indeed, blizzards produce lots of snow. The spring snows play hell with the daffodils, but they always lend a special air of hope to Opening Day at Fenway.

Summers in New England? Splendid days scattered here and there around the hot and humid Bermuda highs. The answer? Go to the mountains or join the Kennedys and the crowds and head for the Cape—the all-natural Hilton Head with New York City's traffic.

Then there is the fall, and it makes all the rest seem, for a time at least, tolerable. Days dawn sharp and clear, then soften with the rising sun. Leaves, even late in the season, grace the world with defiant flickers of reds and golds. All set off by waters that spark and flash in an afternoon's fading light.

When you get out and play on one of those utterly sublime days, you know you're stealing one from the calendar. That's how Tom Quinn felt when he walked off the 17th green at Kittansett. That, and a certain melancholy, for as he grew older he missed those long, easy days when he was a kid just playing a game at places like Kittansett and Myopia; Charles River and The Country Club.

Kittansett sits hard by Buzzards Bay, across from the Cape on a peninsula in the next-to-nothing town of Marion, Massachusetts. It is what it has always been, which is a secluded, almost unknown, seaside course—one of the best in America. Kittansett hosted the Walker Cup in 1953, which was after hickory shafts disappeared but before anyone really cared about a match between a bunch of Anglo-Saxons separated only by an ocean and a common language. Give or take a few hurricanes that have washed over the place, and not much has changed at Kittansett since then.

"How do we stand, Pres?" Tom asked, as he and Pres Elliott walked toward the 18th tee.

"We pushed the front and that birdie just put you 1-up the back and the match," Pres said, as he marked the scorecard.

Prescott G.B. Elliott was one of Tom's oldest friends. They'd known each other since they were kids, dominating junior tournaments around Massachusetts in the '60s. He was all Yankee—Middlesex, Harvard, The Country Club, Kittansett, and the Financial District. Tom, who was Boston College from birth, liked him anyway. In fact, they were like brothers. Their early rivalry had forged a deep and abiding bond. They had bummed around Europe playing in tournaments right out of college—the happiest days of Tom's life. They had been best man at each other's weddings and when Tom's marriage fell apart, Pres and his wife, Annie, were there for him, no questions asked.

"That was a lovely shot back there, Tom," his caddie said as they headed for the next tee. "You've not lost your touch. Neither has Mr. Elliott. I can't believe it's been 40 years since I first set eyes on you two going at it down here. I would never have picked you to be friends all these years later. Not with the wars you two had. Oh, they were beautiful to watch. Of course, all us caddies were pulling for you, what with you being one of us and all. There's not been two like you since."

"They were fun, weren't they?" Tom said, placing his arm lightly on the small of the old man's back and helping him up the short set of worn wooden steps cut into the side of the tee box. "And I did notice that you wore your lucky sweater."

"Well, of course I did," he said, brushing his hand along the front of the old, gray crewneck he wore over a faded, plaid flannel shirt. "I had to for the coming back of yourself. Now don't let up—and mind the wind."

The wind. The 18th at Kittansett was a fine par 5, but like most holes on seaside courses, everything depended on what the wind was doing. If there was no wind, the hole lay down and was there for the taking. Most of the time, though, there was wind and more often than not, it was a hard wind to gauge. Out-of-bounds ran down the right side of the hole and tall, thick rough and bunkers protected the left side. The wind, which seemed stronger as the sun sank lower on the horizon, was gusting from right-to-left off the water.

Tom pulled his driver from the bag and walked to the right side of the tee, to give him the best angle into the fairway. While some players started the ball out into the wind and let it drift back, he liked to start the ball out in the center of the fairway or green and curve it back against the wind. He always figured that gave him the biggest margin of error. Besides, he had checked the pin on 18 when they teed off on the adjacent first hole and knew it was cut to the left side of the green, behind a deep bunker. Hitting his approach from the right side would give him the most possible green to work with.

He set his Titleist Pro V1 on the tee, and then turned it slightly to the right, so the logo would be at five o'clock. He'd focus on hitting the logo, which would help ensure that he didn't hit the ball from the inside, causing a draw. He set up to the ball with a slightly open stance, took one more look at the trees to gauge the wind, and then took the clubhead straightaway from the ball. His one thought was to keep his left wrist firm at impact, to prevent a hook. The ball was hit solidly and about 200 yards off the tee it began cutting back against the wind, landing in the right-center of the fairway, about 270 yards out.

"Good drive, T," Pres said, as he bent over to tee his ball. Pres had a new Titleist driver and he had driven the ball beautifully all day. He lined up his shot from behind the ball, aimed down the right rough, and hit another good drive. The wind caught it and moved it left, into the center of the fairway.

"Good swing, Pres," Tom said, as they headed off the tee. "You get that from the 'Driver of the Month Club'?"

"You've got to start trying this new stuff, Tommy," Pres said, putting the tee back in the pocket of his worn, beige corduroys. At 6'2", he was a couple inches taller than Tom, and wiry. In fact, except for a few wrinkles and a little less reddish-blond hair, his looks hadn't changed that much over the years. Tom had decided that aging gracefully is one of the benefits of never having to worry about money.

"Someday maybe, but not on a CIA salary," he said.

They reached their drives, but from the back tees neither could go for the green in two. The key was leaving a full sand wedge and the best angle into the pin. Pres hit first, and his 2-iron left him in a perfect spot about 90 yards from the hole. With a 1-up margin, that was all Tom was looking for. Just play it safe. Play the odds. You don't need a great shot most of the time. You just need to avoid the bad ones. Just like his job. Any day that's not a bad day is a good one.

Maybe the shot was too easy. Maybe it was because he let his mind drift off to work. Whatever the reason, he got lazy with the 3-iron and never finished off the shot. The ball started down the middle of the fairway, was hit by the wind, and kicked sharply left. Now he faced a tough lob up over a bunker. If he was in the fairway he had a chance. If he was in the rough he was looking at a six. If he got lucky and found the bunker, he could at least spin the ball and stop it near the hole. But he knew he didn't deserve a break like that after such a stupid play.

Pres was away. At 93 yards and downwind, it was a perfect sand wedge for him. He caught it cleanly, but the wind took some of the spin off the ball. It hit, checked once, and then released, rolling some 15 feet past the hole. Good for a five, maybe a four, but he had probably taken six out of the picture.

Tom drew a good lie in the fairway. That, and the 1-up cushion he had to play with, was the only good news. The bad news was the deep bunker between him and the hole. He had to clear that or the stroke was history. To get it close he had to land the ball in the fringe, hope the grass would kill it, and let it trickle down to the hole. That gave him about three square feet to land the ball. The safe play was to forget the hole, get the ball on the fat part of the green, and play for a five.

"What kind of putt does he have?" Tom asked his caddie.

"Dead in," the caddie said. "All he has to do is get it started. He's still a good putter, sir. Figure him for a certain four."

Tommy pulled out his sand wedge. It was an old Wilson Staff, a JP II. The sole had been worn down over the years, which made it easy to lay the blade open and slide the clubhead under the ball cleanly. Rust had pitted the clubface, which helped put spin on the ball. Tom knew he could get the ball up quickly and land it softly—if his nerves would let him.

"Screw it," Tom said to the caddie. "I've got a shot to play with. I'm not gonna give this to him."

"Five bucks says you don't get it within 10 feet, Tommy," Pres said.

"You're on," Tom said.

He made a couple practice swings, and then set up over the ball. He laid the clubface wide open, opened his stance and aimed left of the flag. He lowered his hands and set them behind the ball. He took one last look, not at the flag, but at the spot in the fringe where he needed to land the ball. He took the club away from the ball with a quick, almost sideways cocking of his wrists, and then flicked the clubhead under the ball with his right hand. The ball shot quickly into the air, rose over the bunker, and landed softly on the apron. It rolled toward the hole, curving to the right as it lost speed.

"It's in, sir," the caddie said, quietly.

"You bastard!" Pres yelled.

But the ball hit the high side of the cup, spun out and picked up speed as it turned out of the hole. It finally stopped eight feet from the cup.

As Tom walked to the green to mark his ball, Pres finished lining up his putt. The caddie was right. The putt was dead straight. Pres set up over the ball, and addressed the ball off the toe of his putter, an old, dinged-up Bullseye—the same putter he'd used since he was a kid.

Hitting the ball off the toe of the blade helped kill the speed.

The putt was pure. It started on line and never left the hole.

"Good four, Pres," Tom said, bending down to replace his ball. He carefully set the words, "Pro V1," facing the hole, right on the target line. That was where the two halves of the cover were joined, and gave the truest roll. It was a small thing, but it helped improve the odds. Always play the odds, he thought.

The ball wanted to work left at the hole but he needed to hit it firm. *One putt to win the match. Two for a tie*, he thought.

"What are you thinking, sir?" the caddie asked as they studied the putt from behind the ball.

"If I die the ball at the hole, it's a right edge putt," Tom said. "If I hit it hard, I can't give the hole away."

"Don't give the hole away, sir," the caddie said softly. "A shot as good as your little pitch there deserves a four. And sir, remember that the grain is growing toward you at this time of the day. Be firm with it."

Tom set up over the ball and lined the face of the worn Ping Anser at an old pitch mark six inches ahead of his ball, right on the line. His eyes traced the line to the hole and back to the ball. He slid his hands slightly forward to start the stroke, and then hit the ball, making sure that his hands led the putterhead into the ball. He watched the ball as it ran up the slope toward the hole.

Pushed it, he thought, as the ball headed toward the right edge of the hole, where it lingered for a second before falling into the cup.

"Great up and down, Tommy," said Pres, taking the ball out of the cup and flipping it to his friend. "Let's go have a pop."

Tom, Pres, and their caddies walked off the green and Tom handed his ball, glove, tees, and ball marker to his caddie, who placed them in the bag.

"I'll clean up your clubs for you, sir," the caddie said.

"They're fine," Tom said, pulling two $50 bills from his wallet. "Just leave the bag over by the pro shop. It was great to see you again. It brought back a lot of pleasant memories. You take care of yourself now and I hope I see you in the spring."

"Thank you very much, Tommy," the caddie said, shaking Tom's hand. "I'll look forward to it. Maybe we'll win then, too."

After changing their shoes, Tom and Pres sat out on the porch of the old, gray-shingled clubhouse. The clubhouse was officially closed for the season, but Pres came up with a bottle of Mount Gay rum, a couple of small bottles of Schweppes tonic water, and a bowl of ice.

"No lemon?" Tom asked, as he pulled a dark green windshirt over his head, and ran his hands over his short, gray-black hair.

"These are perilous times," Pres joked. "The Democrats rule. We all have to make sacrifices."

While Tom poured two strong Mount Gay and tonics, Pres checked the scorecard.

"Good round, T," he said. "As little as you play, 74 is a great score. Cheers."

The drink went down smoothly, with the burning of the rum cut by the sweetness of the tonic. The alcohol and the warmth of the late afternoon sun combined to ward off the gathering chill. Tom felt himself relax. Even a casual game with his oldest friend brought out all the old tension and nervousness. He loved the game but it was never really fun. It never had been.

"Now, you didn't come all the way up here just to nick the Elliott fortune," Pres said, lighting a cigar and then sliding a $50 bill across the table to Tom. "What's going on?"

"We need you to help clear some assets for us," Tom said. "You know the drill."

"How much?" Pres asked.

"About 30 million," Tom said, instinctively looking around to make sure they were alone. "Three equal units. The first within a couple weeks. The rest when certain contingencies are met, probably within six months."

"We can do that," Pres said, slowly rubbing the ash from the tip of his cigar against the edge of the table. "We'll run it offshore, through the Caymans or through one of the big insurance companies in Bermuda. Either way, it's a no-brainer. I'll need to know which bank, the account numbers—the usual."

"You'll have them this week," Tom said.

"I don't suppose you can fill me in on any of the sordid details," Pres asked.

"No," Tom said. "We're cutouts on this one. But for this kind of money, I'm pretty sure you don't really want to know."

"Okay, Tommy but I've got to level with you," Pres said, pouring some more rum into the large, plastic cups embossed with a blue scallop shell, the club's symbol. "I have a feeling that this isn't about just running some money or playing a little golf. What else is on your mind?"

"I don't know," Tom said. "I'm losing my edge. Maybe it's me. Maybe it's the Agency. Maybe after all these years any job would get old."

"I can see why toppling democracies and propping up third-rate dictators would eventually lose its appeal," Pres said.

"Yeah, and don't forget the thrill of teaching torture techniques," Tom said. "Seriously, I mean before, we used to have a mission. We had to beat the bad guys and we did it. We beat the Russians. We broke up those groups of fanatical bastards that hit New York and the Pentagon. What's our job now? Trying to keep drugs out of the hands of America's dustheads? Making sure we know just how many millions of North Koreans are starving this month? Or maybe we should try to figure out how many more traitorous assholes like Aldrich Ames are still lurking around Langley. For what? So they can get a lifetime pass in one of our cozier prisons?"

"Well, you could take the long view," Pres said. "Peace can't last forever. There's bound to be fun and games again soon."

"Right, and by the time that happens the Agency will be so hopelessly screwed up that we won't be able to get out of our own way," Tom said. "Do you know what we had to go though last month? Sensitivity training."

"Seriously?" Pres laughed.

"Yeah, 16 years of Jesuit education and I had to have three women from the Anti-Defamation League come in and teach me how to get in touch with my inner feelings. Your tax dollars at work."

"A kinder, gentler CIA," Pres said, swirling the ice around his cup. "I know I'll sleep better tonight. Look, you're not getting any younger. You don't have a life. Even if you had a life it'd be fucked. You beat the bad guys and all you have to show for it is a government pension and a pissy little 401K. My offer is still open. Take the jump."

"I don't know, " Tom said. "We've been friends for a long time. I don't want to even consider this if going to work for you is going to change that."

"Going to work *with* me," Pres said, draining his glass and crunching down on an ice cube. "There's a big difference. Now let's get going. Annie's expecting us by 7:30 and she's invited one of her friends to dinner."

"Not again," Tom said.

"She can't help herself, Tommy," Pres said, as he threw his arm over his friend's shoulder. "You know how married women are. They can't stand to see a guy who's single and happy. It's too threatening."

"Anyone I know?" Tom asked.

"Nah," Pres said. "Missy or Muffy or Buffy or something. Some friend of hers from The Country Club whose husband hit it huge with an IPO and bailed on her. The good news is that she doesn't look like the winner of a claiming race. The better news is that she got the membership. Marry her and we're a lock in the Fall Member-Member."

"Sounds like a variation on a familiar theme," Tom said. "Didn't we try this before, for about five unhappy years?"

"Yeah, but you're older and wiser now," Pres said. "Besides, we've toughened the membership policy. We've hit our quota of micks. It's probably the only way I could sneak you past the admissions committee. C'mon, let's go."

As they drove away from the club, the sun was setting on Buzzards Bay. Pres was on the phone to Annie, telling her they would be late. Tom turned to his right and stared out the window, across the gentle expanse of Kittansett. He thought back to the first time he'd made that drive. He had won that day, too. He had beaten Pres at his own game and on his own course. Their picture made the papers the next day. Pres had the easy smile of a winner who just happened to lose that day. Tommy had the trophy and the smile of a kid who had won but hadn't lost his doubts.

All these years later, nothing had really changed.

CHAPTER TWO

If you take the Green Line out from downtown Boston, past Symphony Hall and the great museums and through Brookline Village, you come to Boston College—a sprawling, stone testimonial to the power of Irish Catholicism in America.

In the small, provincial world that is Boston, the natives never tire of telling people how their city is Oxford, Cambridge, and the Sorbonne all rolled into one for the price of a token on the "T." In truth, in the small, provincial world that is Boston, only two schools really matter—Harvard and Boston College.

MIT, Boston University, Northeastern and all the rest are all well and good, but if something important happens in Boston—in politics, finance, journalism, commerce, or the arts—it's a safe bet that the fine, soft hands of Harvard and Boston College will be guiding the decision—either with subtlety, or muscle, or both.

In 1972, on the verge of graduation and his 22nd birthday, Tom Quinn looked into his future and saw a hopeless muddle.

A high number in the draft lottery had kept him from a guided tour of Vietnam and he never once felt guilty about missing that.

The law seemed attractive for a while, but for every Elliot Richardson and Archibald Cox there were a thousand squalid, pathetic little ambulance chasers and bagmen hanging around Beacon Hill and City Hall.

He had a cousin high up at the *Globe*, which had become a great paper under its editor, Tom Winship, but the idea of spending his life getting quotes from the likes of "Dapper" O'Neil and Louise Day Hicks never held much appeal. Why quote people who can't even read what you write, he figured.

Teaching? Maybe, but then who wanted a job as a glorified parole officer?

Pres's father kept making noises about banking. Tom's parents kept making noises about listening.

He'd been thinking about the Peace Corps. He kept telling himself that it appealed to his best instincts. What it really did was give him some breathing room and got everyone off his back. Naturally, Pres thought that was the single dumbest thing he'd ever heard.

"Let me understand this," he said after one of their regular Thursday afternoon squash games over at Harvard. "We have a chance to go around Europe playing all these great courses and you want to go to Guate-fucking-mala and teach the natives about flush toilets. Am I missing something?"

Pres was right, naturally. What Tom really wanted to do was just go to Europe and get golf out of his system. Of course, there was the matter of his bank balance, which was one trip to Suffolk Downs away from zero.

It was with a certain amount of dread, then, that he steeled himself for yet another meeting with his career counselor, Father Francis Murray. Above everything else, BC's Jesuits despised muddled thinking—especially after four years of their best efforts—and Tom had pressed Father Murray to a point of despair that, as he was quick to point out, it was not only a sin but also an insult to God.

His curiosity was piqued by a call from Father Murray asking Tom to meet him late in the afternoon at the Common, across from the State House. Tom took the Green Line in, got off at Park Street, and started the short walk up the hill. The air was crisp and cold, and the wind coming off the harbor gave it a sharp edge. He turned up the collar on his overcoat and adjusted his blue and maroon striped scarf.

The Common was alive with people heading home from work and shoppers trying to finish up their holiday shopping. A small front had moved through earlier in the day, dropping a few inches of snow. Not enough to screw up traffic but just enough to blanket the Common and mask the inevitable grime and litter of a city winter. As he passed the great fountain off Tremont Street, where the Hari Krishnas and other street people loitered when the weather was warm, the lights strung around the Common and the Public Garden for the holidays were turned on. Up on Beacon Hill, the golden dome of the State House glistened in the clear night air, set against the starry, ink-black sky. It was Chamber of Commerce time, the stuff of thousands of postcards.

As Tom made his way up the granite steps that led to Beacon Street, he saw Father Murray leaving the State House with a man he recognized as State Senator Jim Finigan. The two had grown up in neighboring three-deckers in a working class section of Cambridge, a short distance but a world removed from Harvard Yard. Finigan, who had graduated from BC just after the war, was the college's fixer in the State House.

Tom's first thought was that Father Murray had arranged a meeting with Finigan to help set up a state job for him when he graduated. Government as employer of last resort was, after all, a long and cherished tradition in Massachusetts. But the priest had insisted that Tom wear a coat and tie, and it was unlikely that it was for "Knocko" Finigan's benefit.

The two men stood and talked for a moment at the base of the State House steps, then shook hands. Father Murray spotted Tom, waved, and carefully made his way through the traffic backed up on Beacon Street. Knocko Finigan turned left and headed for the bar at the Parker House to get on with the real business of governance.

"Hi, Father," Tom said. "I didn't know the archdiocese provided house calls for absolution. Was this an individual confession or did you let the whole bunch off the spiritual hook?"

"Ah, Thomas," the priest said. "So young and yet so cynical. It seems that some of our good neighbors in Brookline don't see the wisdom of our expansion plans. Our dear friend James has agreed to help their elected representatives overcome their doubts. Come along now. It's a lovely evening for a walk."

Father Murray had been injured during World War II, and while he rarely spoke about his wounds or his service in Europe, the Purple Heart, Navy Cross, and other service medals he kept in a small display near his desk spoke volumes for his courage and patriotism. Tom did know that a bullet had smashed into his right leg and the injury forced him to walk with a cane and a noticeable limp. As they turned and headed back down the steps to the Common, Tom gently took the priest's arm at the elbow, to make sure he didn't slip on an ice patch and fall. The priest smiled but said nothing.

As they reached the last step, there was the sound of sirens and seconds later a series of police cars, their blue lights reflecting off the neighboring buildings, pulled in front of the old Park Street Church.

"Let's go have a look," the priest said.

By the time they reached the church, a crowd had gathered. A group of antiwar protesters had taken to the church steps and chained themselves to its doors. Apparently they had splashed blood, or at least something that looked like blood, across the doors. The dozen or so protesters were chanting, "Stop the bloodshed! Stop the killing! Stop the war now!" Just as the first lights from the television news crews flashed on, a young man pulled out his draft card and set it aflame. The protesters cheered. Some people in the crowd cheered, too. Tom wondered what Father Murray was thinking at just that moment.

"It's a horrible thing, this war," the priest said, as if reading Tom's mind. "It's destroying us. We're destroying ourselves over it. Come along, I've seen enough."

They walked for a while in silence. After a few moments, Tom asked the priest what he thought about the demonstration.

"It's their right, of course," he said, with a sigh of resignation. "But it's awfully easy to be self-righteous with a deferment tucked away in your vest pocket. You?"

"I don't know Father," Tom said. "When you ask yourself what we win if we win, I don't think it's worth it. The protests? I'm not much on protests. I think most of the guys I've seen at demonstrations are just trying to get lai..., uh, get a date for the weekend. Call me a hopeless romantic."

They walked on, slowly. A strong gust of wind swept down off

Beacon Hill and Tom turned slightly, trying to shield the priest from its full force. Off in the distance, the bells and carillons of the neighboring churches began to ring, signaling the start of the six o'clock services.

"Tom, I've been giving a lot of thought to what you might do when you graduate," Father Murray said. "Have you ever seriously considered government service?"

"Well, Father, as you know I've been thinking about the Peace Corps," he said. It was a wink and a nod answer. Truthful as far as it went, but a little like going to confession and saving lying for last.

"Yes, and that's very admirable," the priest said. "But I'm thinking about something you might be a little better suited to and find a bit more interesting. Thomas, during the war I volunteered for a group called the Office of Strategic Services. Have you ever heard of it?"

"Sure, it was the original CIA," Tom said.

"That's right," the priest said. "After the war, I went into the seminary but a lot of the fellows stayed on. Some of us have kept in touch over the years, and every so often if we have someone we think might fit into the Agency, we pass his or her name along. Do you understand what I'm getting at?"

"Yes, Father," Tom said. "At least, I think I do."

"I've had my eye on you for a while now and I think you know that I have a special affection for you," Father Murray said, pausing to avoid the people waiting to cross Charles Street and enter the Public Garden. "I passed your name and your background to a friend at the CIA. They've checked you out and would like to meet with you. If you're interested, we can go ahead. If not, this conversation never took place. Okay?"

Tom felt a chill of excitement run through his body. Maybe the fog that had closed around his life for the past few months would, at last, begin to clear.

"I'm interested, Father," Tom said. "I'm a little surprised but I'm definitely interested."

"Good, I thought you might be," the priest said as they made their way through the entrance to the Public Garden. "My friend's name is Brendan McDermott. He's waiting for us over at the Ritz-Carlton."

"Brendan was with me in France when I got this," he said, tapping his leg with the cane. "We were in a small town, Conde-Sur-Noireau, on the River Orne just inland from the Normandy beaches. We were working with the Resistance, preparing sabotage operations for the D-Day invasions. We were there to blow up the rail lines so the Germans couldn't get new troops to the beaches. Someone tipped off the SS. I caught two rounds from a Luger. One shattered my knee. German patrols were everywhere. Brendan could have cut and run. Instead, he got me to a safe house where we hid until the invasion. I owe him my life."

"Did you ever find out who betrayed you?" Tom asked.

"Yes, it was the sister of one of the Resistance fighters," the priest said. "She was a collaborator, in love with an officer in the SS."

"What happened to her?" Tom asked.

Father Murray stopped and looked straight into Tom's eyes. Then he turned and leaned against the railing of the bridge that ran across the lagoon where the swan boats cruised in the warm weather. For a few moments, he watched the people skating in the moonlight. There was the sound of blades scraping against the ice, kids laughing and shouting and, in the distance, the sounds of the city. A few couples walked past, sharing the most beautiful and romantic spot in Boston. Father Murray turned slowly and looked at Tom.

"Life is about making choices, Tom," he said. "War is about making terribly hard choices because the rules—whatever you think they might be—don't apply. She made the wrong choice."

The priest turned away and looked back at the skaters.

"Peace is a wonderful thing, Tom," he said, without turning around. "But like all wonderful things, it comes at a very dear price."

Tom put his hand gently on the priest's back.

"C'mon, Father," he said. "I'd very much like to meet your friend."

CHAPTER THREE

Riviera has always held a special niche among the golf clubs in Los Angeles. Los Angeles Country Club had the old money. Bel-Air had the Hollywood elite. Hillcrest had people who couldn't get into other clubs because they were Jewish, or in show business, or both. And Riviera had golf history.

The course has hosted the Los Angeles Open, on and off, since 1929. Ben Hogan won the U.S. Open there in 1948. It's held two PGA Championships. *Pat and Mike*, starring Spencer Tracy and Katherine Hepburn was filmed there.

The club is just off Sunset Boulevard, about halfway between Beverly Hills and the Pacific Ocean. In the '20s, '30s, and even into the 1940s it was in the middle of nowhere. Now it sits nestled among some of the most exclusive and expensive real estate in America.

None of this mattered to the man sitting alone in the top floor restaurant at the Holiday Inn on the corner of Sunset and the 405 Freeway. From his table, he could look south and watch the early evening traffic inch its way out of the city. North or south, it didn't seem to matter. The traffic barely moved. Looking west along Sunset it was the same story, compounded by a series of traffic lights that seemed to work at random. In the reflection, the orange light from the setting sun captured the pale green intensity of his eyes and the streaks of blond in his sandy brown hair. Lost in thought, he didn't notice the waitress approach his table.

"Would you like to order?" she asked.

He turned away from the window and looked at the woman. She was attractive, in her mid-20s, he supposed. But like so many young women in America—and Great Britain, for that matter—she seemed determined to sabotage her looks. The purplish streaks in her harsh, angularly cut brown hair nearly matched her dark lipstick. The excessive makeup around her eyes was jarring. The odd collection of rings that pierced her ears and the small tattoo on her left arm, just above the wrist, completed the picture. A college student, perhaps, but more likely a would-be actress.

"Yes," he said, running his eyes down the menu. "I think I'd like some fish. The Coho salmon, is it fresh?"

"Swam right down from Seattle this morning...at least that's what they told me," she said, with a delightful conspiracy in her voice. "No, seriously, the fish is usually a pretty safe bet."

"Fine then, I'll have the salmon, grilled but not charred," he said. "And instead of the mango-ginger chutney, would it be possible to get a béarnaise sauce on the side? Possibly with some vegetables, steamed but still firm."

"No problem," she said. "Would you like another vodka?"

"Thank you, no," he said. "But some wine perhaps. One from your state would seem appropriate. What about a chardonnay? A Cakebread, perhaps?"

"You're not from here, right?" she said, picking up the menu.

"No," he said. "London. I'm just over combining a little work with a holiday. I'm with the BBC. By the way, is smoking allowed in your restaurant?"

"Smoking? Here? In the People's Republic of Los Angeles?" she laughed. "You're not from London. You're from the moon."

"Ah, yes," he said, closing the box of English Ovals. "Never mind that simply breathing the air here is enough to kill you."

"What are those?" she asked.

"They're from England," he said, holding out the stylish white and red box. "Quite mild, actually. Please, take one."

"Hey, thanks," she said, pulling one from the box. "I'll sneak it on my break. Be back in a flash with your wine."

He studied her as she walked away, and then returned his gaze to the endless string of automobile lights that stretched off into the distance. The traffic was a complication he hadn't considered, and he wondered if it was like this on the weekends as well.

"I'm taking a chance," the waitress said, suddenly back at the table, "but I think you'll like this one just as much as the Cakebread. It's a Lindemans from Australia. Every bit as good and they're giving it away over here.

"I think you'll find it amusing," she said, perfectly catching the pretensions of a sommelier. "It is understated in its first impression, but it lingers. The more you savor it, the more you'll appreciate it."

She uncorked the wine, and poured an inch or so into his glass.

"It's very good," he said after taking a sip. "Here, please try some."

"Sorry, it's against the rules," she said, filling his glass.

"Do you always follow the rules?" he asked.

"It depends," she asked. "Some rules are more stupid than others."

"Yes, well you're quite good," he said. "Far too good to be wasting your talents in a place like this," he said.

"Anyone who can read the *Wine Spectator* can pick a wine," she said.

"No, I meant your impression of a wine steward," he said.

"I'll send you my reel," she said. "I think you'll find *it* amusing, too."

"I'd love to see it," he said.

"Are you serious?" she asked.

"Absolutely," he said. "We're always looking for new talent. I'm here for a few days. Leave it for me. By the way, is the traffic always this bad? I have to go over to the Riviera Country Club on business but I wasn't counting on this mess."

"On weeknights, yeah," she said. "Of course, this weekend, with the tournament, it'll be really screwed up. I live over by the course. It's going to be a horror show. It is every year."

To his surprise, the meal was actually quite good. The salmon steak was thick and moist and grilled to perfection. The béarnaise was perhaps a bit on the bland side but it blended well with the fish, and the vegetables were extraordinary. All in all, remarkable for an otherwise unpretentious hotel whose greatest attraction was its spectacular view of the longest parking lot in southern California.

He signed his check, billing it back to his room, and leaving a generous tip. When she returned to pick it up, she had a timely offer for him.

"Listen, the people I'm renting from are at the desert for the weekend," she said. "Most people that live around the course take off during the tournament. They don't want to hassle with the crowds. If you want, you can park at my place and walk over to the course. Here's the address and phone number."

She wrote the information on a slip of paper, in big, looping handwriting.

"Thank you," he paused, reading her name. "Terry. Perhaps I'll take you up on it."

He carefully laid the paper inside his billfold, finished the last bit of wine, and walked to the bank of elevators. The restaurant, which had been nearly empty when he'd arrived, was almost full. As he waited for an elevator, he reflexively gazed across the room and noticed the waitress stealing a glance at him as she took an order from a table near the bar. He smiled slightly, entered the elevator, and headed for his room.

The next morning dawned bright and clear. It was early, not quite seven, but as he stood on his room's balcony, he could look down on joggers and bikers making their way along Sunset Boulevard. He could hear a woman giving the three-day weather forecast on the morning news. The weather, she chirped, was going to be dry and hot for the next three days, with Santa Ana winds blowing out of the east. He reentered the room just in time to see the news anchorman—remarkably vapid, even for the breed, he thought—congratulating her, presumably for single-handedly producing such wonderful weather. Then he presented the day's beach report. Well, at least the important news was out of the way. Now the city's vast millions could get on with their lives.

He had just finished shaving when room service brought his breakfast, along with complimentary copies of *USA Today* and the *Los Angeles Times*. He scanned the front pages of both. *USA Today* gave its usual quick bytes of news, but the biggest story was a phone-in reader survey about the upcoming Valentine's Day and how people could improve their love lives. *Ah, America*, he thought.

On the bottom left-hand corner of the *Times* was a small article headlined: "State Dept. Officials Cite Breakthrough in Anglo-Irish Talks." The subhead read: "Key IRA Officials Drop Demands and Agree to Meet British, Unionists in Dublin."

"Not bloody likely," he muttered, opening to the jump to finish the story. A few minutes later he knew he had to place a call to his contact in Ireland, and soon, since there was an eight-hour time difference. Almost as an afterthought, he took the sports section and tore out the starting times for the day's first round of the Los Angeles Open. He wanted to be sure to get to the course in time to see Mr. Peter Brookes—Britain's biggest sporting celebrity and the finest golfer in the world.

When he reached his car in the rear parking lot, he looked around before opening the trunk, just to make sure no one was nearby. If one of Los Angeles' thousands of gang members happened to steal this car, he'd have hit a bloody jackpot. In his bag was a 9-millimeter Glock automatic pistol armed with bullets that expanded on impact. The damage from these bullets was nightmarish. The entrance wound was small, perhaps a half-inch round. The exit wound was the size of a man's fist. Stashed under the rear seat, unassembled, was a sniper's rifle he'd picked up from his contact when he arrived in town. The barrel of the rifle was detachable and the two halves could be quickly and easily screwed together. The stock and grip of the rifle were made of a very hard but light plastic, and the firing mechanism was incredibly precise. Any identifying markings had long ago been blotted out with acid, just as they'd been on the Glock. The rifle held just three 30.6 heavy-grain rounds at a time—but in the kind of work this weapon was designed for, there was seldom an opportunity for even a second, let alone a third, chance. It was designed to kill—quickly and from a distance—and then allow the shooter to escape without detection. A few days earlier, he'd driven into the mountains east of the city and test-fired it. He wanted to get a feel for the gun and calibrate its sight. It was an impressive weapon...and it was a pity that, with any luck, by Monday morning it would rest deep somewhere out on the floor of the Pacific.

He drove out of the parking lot and headed west on Sunset. After a few minutes he came to Brentwood, a wealthy enclave made famous—or infamous—around the world by the O.J.

Simpson murder trial. Idling at an intersection, he noticed a series of shops and restaurants to the left, with a bank of pay phones isolated off to the side, under a canopy of trees. When the light changed, he wheeled his car to the left and found a parking space in front of a small grocery market. He pulled a piece of paper with a phone number from his wallet, walked across the lot to the phones and placed the call, billing it to a prepaid phone card— which made tracing the call back to him impossible. After just a few moments, he heard the familiar, double short rings of a phone somewhere in the U.K.

"Belfast Trading," a man's voice answered quietly, with a soft, Irish accent.

"Is the game still on?" he asked, scanning the street.

"Yes," the Irishman replied.

"I saw a story in the paper..." he said.

"Don't believe everything you read in the bloody papers," the Irish voice came back, firmly. "Have you made contact yet?"

"Today," he replied. "Very soon today."

"Fine, then get on with it," and then the line went dead.

He replaced the phone and drew the box of cigarettes from his slacks. Pulling a cigarette from the box, he tapped it firmly against the metal of his lighter, lit it, then took a long drag and checked his watch. It was now almost 10 and the outdoor tables were filling with people—mostly in their 20s and 30s, he supposed. What did these people do all day, he wondered. Just how much shopping and exercising could you possibly do? He could understand the women. Most were probably married, and probably to a husband on wife number two, three or four. Or better yet, maybe they were divorced and cashing big alimony checks every month without having to provide even the minimal conjugal duties. But the men? What sort of mindless existence was this? It gave one pause.

The sight of these people, many still in their tight, Lycra exercise clothes, drinking overpriced coffee with their friends, brought his mind around to the whole awful O.J. Simpson business. Surprisingly, it had been given huge amounts of coverage in London. He didn't quite understand the fascination. O.J. Simpson starred in a sport that was all but alien to Great Britain. And he was no Olivier as an actor. One thing was certain: Raines knew that whoever killed the late Mrs. Simpson and her friend was an amateur. A professional killing would have been clean, neat, and quick. Small caliber rounds to the base of the skull. Death would be instantaneous. No, whoever butchered these two people acted in a rage—and for all the people he had killed, Graham Raines had never killed out of anger.

He left Brentwood and followed the signs to the tournament. The girl was right. Traffic was going to be nightmarish on the weekend. Parking would be worse. Fortunately, he arrived early enough to get a spot in the driveway of a house close to the club— for an exorbitant $25. As he walked toward the club, he studied the location of the police officers on duty. There were just a handful. Most of the security appeared to be private—Rent-a-Cops, as they called them in the States. No worry there, he thought, but the police were likely to be out in force on Sunday.

The clubhouse was enormous—a rambling, beige, stucco affair capped by an orange tile roof. The building probably dated back to the 1920s, when the club had opened. It overlooked the course, which ran along the base of a canyon. The canyon walls rose steeply on either side, and were lined with expensive houses that also offered clear views of the course.

After buying a ticket that was good for the entire tournament, he picked up a program featuring a detailed map of the course. Peter Brookes had an 11 A.M. starting time. That meant that he would be playing the televised holes on the back nine when the cable network began its broadcast at 1 P.M. With any luck, Raines thought, he'll have a similar time Sunday.

As Raines rounded the corner of the clubhouse, he heard an announcement from the first tee.

"Fore, please," the first tee announcer said. "We'd like to welcome two old friends of this tournament. Ladies and gentlemen, the 11 o'clock starting time. Playing first, from Kingsmill, Virginia, the winner of the 1988 and 1989 U.S. Opens and the winner of 17 PGA Tour events, please welcome former Ryder Cup Captain Curtis Strange."

The gallery, which was packed into the walkway between the clubhouse and the tee, applauded warmly. From one of the clubhouse balconies, a fan yelled: "Curtis, you still the man!"

On the tee, Strange touched the bill of his cap and gave the gallery a slight nod and a small, tight smile—actually, almost more of a grimace. He studied the shot from behind the ball, and then walked into position. He waggled the club crisply a couple of times, cocked his head and glanced down the fairway that stretched maybe a hundred feet below the tee, and then hit his drive. The ball soared out against the blue sky, with the downtown Los Angeles skyline as a backdrop. Strange watched its flight for a couple seconds and then, sure that it would find the fairway, he bent down and picked up his tee. He acknowledged the applause with another small nod and slightest of smiles.

"Now on the tee, from Austin, Texas, the winner of the 1984 and 1995 Masters and 17 PGA Tour events, please welcome another former Ryder Cup Captain, Ben Crenshaw," the announcer said.

Like Strange, Crenshaw acknowledged the applause with a tip of his cap and a small nod. He addressed the ball, but unlike Strange, he barely waggled the club, instead moving it back and forth over the ball with a slight movement of his wrists. At the same time, he constantly moved his feet, working them into position as he stared down the fairway. Finally, he turned his head slightly to the right and began his swing. Unlike Strange's swing, which was somewhat short with a lateral movement from side-to-side, Crenshaw's was long and flowing. The ball tore off the clubface and started toward the middle of the fairway, but it soon began to hook and was headed for the out-of-bounds stakes. But Crenshaw got lucky. As he looked on anxiously, the ball landed and took a big bounce to the left where it struck a teenage couple that were walking along, their arms around each other, oblivious to anything but themselves. The ball bounced off the boy's leg and rolled back into the fairway.

Back on the tee, Crenshaw shook his head in disgust, swiped the tee out of the ground, muttered something under his breath, and slid the driver back into his bag. He stood there for a moment, practicing his takeaway, and crossed his arms. Then he stole a glance at Strange, who rolled his eyes and broke into a wide smile. Crenshaw began laughing, too.

"Gosh darn it," he said to Strange, as he pulled off his hat and ran his hand through his graying blond hair. "Just once I'd like to get a break on this hole."

The gallery's laughter was interrupted by the announcer.

"Finally, the last member of this pairing, from London, England, the #1 ranked golfer in the world, please welcome Peter Brookes."

It was the first time Raines had seen Brookes in person. Unlike both Strange and Crenshaw, who seemed surprisingly slight, Brookes had an athlete's build. He was tall, probably 6' 2" or so, Raines estimated, with enormous shoulders and a thin waist. He weighed around 200 pounds and his thick, black hair and angular features served to accentuate his dark eyes. Indeed, his eyes were almost eerie and were the man's most remarkable feature. They were cold, betraying no emotion or feeling. "Assassin's eyes," one writer had called them in the volumes of background material Raines had studied. Whatever Raines might have lacked in understanding the game of golf he more than made up for with his keen sense of human nature.

Yes, Raines thought. *Quite right on that account.*

The gallery's reaction was polite but subdued. Raines had read that American golf fans—like his fellow players—respected Brookes but didn't much care for him. He was cool, aloof, single-minded, and both utterly self-confident and self-consumed. Perversely, the British fans were drawn to him for those qualities—and because he did what so few Britons had done for a very long time—dominated a sport without even the slightest hint of apology.

Brookes was meticulous. He nodded slightly and briefly raised his hand in acknowledgment—without even so much as glancing at the gallery. He gazed intently down the fairway, carefully adjusted his glove and addressed the ball. But then, at the last moment, he stepped away and tossed a few blades of grass into the perfectly still air, watching them drift softly to the ground. Then he repeated his entire routine from behind the ball. Raines noticed that Strange and Crenshaw exchanged expressionless glances.

Finally, back in position over the ball, Brookes carefully checked the position of his feet—slightly closed—then took the club slowly away from the ball. Unlike Crenshaw and Strange, whose swings had a natural flow to them, Brookes's swing seemed mechanical, moving from points A to B to C. But it was effective. The ball bored straightaway into the air and then seemed to rise, like a jet leaving the runway. The sound was different as well.

Crisper. More precise. The ball reached its apex and then, ever so slightly, drifted to the left and dropped softly, landing in the middle of the fairway, well ahead of both Crenshaw and Strange.

As the gallery applauded the three men, Brookes quickly picked up his tee and headed down the hill. He disdainfully held out his driver for his caddie—as his caddie struggled to catch up. Crenshaw and Strange and their caddies followed. Somehow, Raines suspected, that's how it would be all day.

Raines checked the course map. He was only interested in the closing few holes, the ones that would be televised on the weekend. The 18th hole played back to the clubhouse, and ran along the base of the canyon. He walked down the long, winding cart path that ran from the clubhouse down to the course. When he reached the bottom of the hill, he turned right and walked down the right side of the 18th hole, a long par 4. Towering eucalyptus trees lined that side of the hole, and the canyon wall, covered with thick, wild shrubbery rose up from the left rough. Running along the top of the hillside was a series of expensive houses. Any one of them would be well suited for his purposes.

As he walked along, he noticed where players' drives landed, and how long each group had to wait to hit their drives and second shots. The hole was difficult, particularly the long second shot into the green, which held up play.

Raines checked his watch. It was now slightly past noon and although it was Thursday, the course was already surprisingly crowded. If the weather held for the weekend—as was predicted—the place would be a veritable mob scene when Brookes arrived on the last hole, especially if he was in one of the final groups. Raines was counting on chaos and confusion to help cover his escape—after the assassination of Peter Brookes.

The two problems he faced were clear: he had to devise a plan for getting into one of the houses on Sunday and then make his way though the traffic and past the police after the shooting. Neither would be easy.

But he got lucky. While he sat in traffic on Capri Drive, he noticed a Federal Express deliveryman approach the front door of one of the houses overlooking the golf course. *Of course*, he thought, *what better way to gain entry to a house?* And surely in Los Angeles there must be any number of places that rent costumes—

a FedEx deliveryman's uniform, for example. As he drove slowly down Capri and back around toward Sunset, he also wrote down whatever names and numbers he could read on the mailboxes.

The rest of the day was spent gathering his disguise. After just a few phone calls, he found a shop in West L.A. where he could get a FedEx uniform, and he got a box that would hold his rifle from a nearby FedEx shipping center.

When he finally returned to his hotel room early in the evening, the message light on his phone was blinking. His first thought was that the newspaper story had been accurate and Belfast was calling him off. There was, for a moment, a bit of relief. He didn't have any qualms about killing Peter Brookes, but he knew this was far from an ideal situation. He still needed to plan an escape route and judging from what he'd seen today, nothing seemed very promising.

He picked up the phone and pushed the keys to retrieve his message.

"Hi Mr. Archer," said the woman's voice, using the assumed name he'd registered under. "This is Terry Gardner, the waitress you had last night—whoops, that's probably not the best way to put it—anyway, I didn't know if you were going to the tournament tomorrow or not, but if you are and you want to park over at my place, I just wanted to tell you that we have a pool and you're welcome to come in for a swim. I'll be around there most of the day. And I do have that reel you offered to look at. Well, that's it...oh, and thanks for the big tip last night. That was great."

Raines replaced the receiver, went to the honor bar near the television, filled a glass with ice and poured himself a double Finlandia. Then he slid open the glass door to his small patio, and pulled a chair out into the warmth of the fading sunlight. He took a sip of the drink and lit a cigarette. Exhaling, he took another sip and considered Ms. Terry Gardner and her offer. A swim tomorrow might be just the thing he needed to take the edge off some of the stress he was feeling. A swim and who knows what else.

Friday dawned hot and dry and according to the newspaper, the winds out of the mountains were to be subdued. This was quite good news for the people fighting the wildfires that had been flamed by the Santa Anas—fires that, while troublesome, apparently weren't nearly as bad as last year's torrential rains and horrific mudslides, at least according to the perky little couple bantering away on the morning news. And this was a place where people moved for the weather?

Raines checked Thursday's tournament scores. Justin Leonard led with a 67, largely made possible by chipping in four times and holing a shot from a bunker. Two players were in at 68 and Peter Brookes had shot a 69 despite the condition of the greens that, he allowed later to the press, were not up to his considerable standards.

When his playing companion, Curtis Strange, had been asked about Brookes's comments he said, "Aw, I don't know what he's complaining about. We all had to putt on 'em didn't we? Besides, they kinda reminded me of greens over in Britain. He should be happy—for a change."

Brookes, Strange, and Crenshaw would go off at 1 P.M. today. Conversation would be limited in that pairing, Raines imagined.

The later starting time gave Raines a chance to drive down to Long Beach where, if all went according to plan, he was scheduled to leave the rifle with the captain of a commercial fishing boat late Sunday night. When the boat set out for its run early the next morning, Raines's rifle would be on board. A couple of hours out to sea, it would be slid quietly overboard. By then, Raines would be on a British Airways flight for London—and his account in Zurich would be richer by £500,000.

Raines drove south on the 405 Freeway. A half-hour later he passed the exits to the Los Angeles Airport. Thirty minutes later he turned off onto the 710 Freeway to Long Beach. The city was a dreary, industrial port that had long since seen its best days. The poor were everywhere. It was as depressing a place as he'd seen since he arrived in the States.

He stopped at a gas station and asked directions to the pier where the trawler was docked. As far as Raines could tell, the attendant could barely understand English, let alone speak it. The other attendant wasn't much better. Finally, in frustration, one of the men went inside and came back with an old, wrinkled street map.

"Ees good map, si?" he said, smiling proudly and handing the map to Raines.

"Bloody Third World country," Raines hissed as he handed the man a dollar and drove off.

Finally, owing as much to luck as to the filthy, outdated map, he found the pier and the abandoned warehouse where he was to leave the rifle in an unmarked box along with $1,000 in small, well-worn currency. He never would actually see the ship's captain and the ship's captain would never see him.

By now, the sun was high in the sky and, with no wind it was well into the 80s. Raines pulled the expensive Sea Island cotton sweater over his head, folded it precisely, and placed it on the rear seat of the nondescript rental Ford. Then, checking the map, he made his way back to the freeway and headed north, well pleased to be leaving Long Beach, California.

Traffic was inexplicably jammed up on the 405, and by the time he reached Riviera it was after 2 P.M. As he turned left on Capri, he was stopped by a pair of security guards.

"No parking here, sir," said one of the guards. "There are shuttle buses from Pacific Palisades High School. Just keep heading that way on Sunset."

"Yes, well I'm actually here to visit a friend," Raines said, coolly. "Here's her name and telephone number."

Raines handed the guard the slip of paper from his billfold. The guard went over to a nearby table, called the number, and returned to the car.

"That's fine, sir," the guard said. "Miss Gardner is waiting for you. It's down on your right and the gate will be open. Have a nice day."

"Thank you, officer," he said. "And you have a nice day as well."

He reached the house—a handsome, white-stucco building that had the feel of an old, Spanish mission to it. It was surrounded by a tall wall, and as he turned into the driveway he noticed the elaborate black iron gates closing smoothly behind him. The driveway went past the house and turned to the left, into a courtyard that sat between the main house and the guesthouse, where he assumed the girl lived. One thing was clear already: Terry Gardner wasn't paying the rent on her waitress salary.

He got out of the car and heard her call from behind a thick hedge entwined with bougainvillea.

"I'm in here, by the pool," she said. "The gate's around by the side of the cottage."

He entered the pool area and was temporarily blinded by the harsh sunlight reflecting off the blue water and the bright, white concrete pool deck. As his eyes adjusted to the light he saw the girl seated on a wicker chair at the far side of the pool, painting at an easel. She was wearing bikini bottoms, a faded, blue denim work shirt and an old baseball cap turned backward to let the sunlight reach her face. Her dark hair was still wet and combed straight back. Patches of water spotted her shirt.

As he walked toward her he was struck by how very different she looked from the first time he'd seen her. Without makeup, she was much more attractive. *Terribly attractive*, he thought. Her eyes seemed to pick up the blue of the pool, and a ridge of freckles ran across her cheeks and the bridge of her nose. Moreover, without the heavy slather of dark lipstick, her lips were far more delicate that he remembered. Mercifully, she'd even removed the series of rings from her ears.

"A painter, are we, Miss Gardner?" he asked.

"A struggling artist, Mr. Archer," she replied.

"Yes, well aren't we all, Miss Gardner," he said.

"Some more than others," she said, "And please call me Terry."

"If you'll call me Graham," he said, moving behind her slightly to look over her shoulder at the painting. It was actually very good, a watercolor of the garden that framed the cottage's bay window. "Your work is lovely. And so is this property. Have you lived here very long?"

"A little over two years, since I moved out here from Ohio after college," she said, laying down her palette on the grass and wiping off her brush on a rag. "The owners are friends of my family. He made a fortune when he sold his company about 15 years ago and moved out here to work at the corporate headquarters. They're great people. They let me stay here for next to nothing. I just kind of keep an eye on the place when they're gone. They travel a lot on business, mostly down to Mexico and South America, so there's never any hassle with privacy."

"So Los Angeles is your American Provence—you moved here for the light, as it were," he said.

"Hardly," she said, walking to the side of the pool and running her hands through the water, before splashing some on her face. "Like everyone else, I'm here trying to break into the business. I was a drama major at Ohio State but there's not much of a movie industry in Ohio. So, here I am."

That, at least, explained the invitation, he thought. She may have found him interesting, perhaps even attractive—but not as interesting and attractive as she found his supposed connection with the BBC and the possible break it might offer her career.

"And I'm glad you are," he said. "Thank you for the invitation and the use of the driveway. You were quite right about the parking here. It's every bit the disaster you said it would be."

"Well, you don't have to worry about that," she said. "I've got to work the lunch shift tomorrow but I'll give you a pass card that opens the gate. You can put it on that table if you leave before I get back. Do you want to take a swim?"

"I'm afraid I don't have a proper suit," he said. "One doesn't think of swimming in England at this time of the year and I didn't have a chance to stop and buy one this morning."

She looked at him with a crooked grin and shook her head.

"There's a pile of suits in the pool house over there," she said, pointing at a small bungalow tucked away in the shade at the corner of the yard. "I'll get us some iced tea. See you in a minute."

The pool house was dark, warm, and musty. As he entered he searched for a light switch, finally finding a chain attached to a single, overhead bulb. The poolhouse, it turned out, was actually a small apartment—perhaps a caretaker's quarters at one point. There was a shower, toilet, and sink—all marred with varying degrees of rust stains—and a small bed covered with piles of towels and an odd array of old swimsuits. Clearly, no one had lived here for a very long while.

He found a suit and slowly began to undress, clearing a space for his clothes on the bed. Through the window, he watched the girl set the glasses of iced tea on the table. Then she removed her cap, ran her fingers through her hair, and slowly shook her head to loosen the matted-down hair. She next removed her shirt and laid it across the back of one of the pool chairs. When she turned and walked toward the pool house, he caught his first full glimpse of her. Her legs were long and perfectly formed—narrow at the ankles and knees, but smooth and muscular. Her hips were narrow and there was just the slightest hint of weight at her waist. Her breasts, while not large, were full, round, slightly upturned and made all the more attractive by the shine of the tanning oil that glistened in the sunlight. Her shoulders were quite broad and her arms sinewy. Perhaps, he thought, she had been a swimmer as a teenager.

As she approached the side of the pool, she looked over at the pool house window and squinted into the sunlight, trying for a sharper view. Then she ran her fingers, slowly, along her inner thighs, adjusting the material away from her skin. Next, she reached up and slightly cupped her breasts, pulling the bikini's cups inward more toward her breastbone. A moment later, she dove gracefully into the air, sliding smoothly into the water, where she surfaced seconds later and began an effortless yet powerful freestyle.

He wondered, for a second, if that little display had been for his benefit, then finished changing and looked at his reflection in the mirror. He felt he was in quite good shape for a 46-year old. Regular workouts had kept his body in trim. His hair, while flecked with gray along the temples, was cropped short but still full. His face bore almost no wrinkles. Only a nasty, purplish scar on his left shoulder revealed anything about his past. He picked the white, Ashworth golf shirt up from the bed, put it on, and headed for the pool and whatever might present itself for the rest of the afternoon.

She surfaced just as he approached the side of the pool and pulled his shirt back over his head.

"Well, check out the bronze bod of an English god," she joked, sarcastically, smoothing the water off her face with both hands. Her eyes covered the length of his body and then returned to his face. "C'mon in. I promise you it'll be warmer than anything you'll find in London."

Well yes, hopefully, he thought and then dove in.

For a long time they exchanged small talk as they slowly circled one another in a sort of ballet. Every so often he caught himself stealing a glance at her breasts—and every so often she caught him doing it. If it bothered her she didn't let on...and if it bothered her he'd be astonished. Finally, he decided to play a card.

"So, what sort of actress are you?" he asked, reaching over and sliding a shock of her hair back off her face.

"Comedy's my favorite," she said, arching her back and gliding into a backfloat. "I'm not neurotic enough for serious drama. Of course, neurosis is what this town is big on—in case you hadn't noticed."

"Neurosis is at the heart of show business, whether it's here, London or New York," he replied, gliding alongside her. "You seem well-enough balanced. Why get involved in it?"

"Why are you involved in it?" she asked, righting herself and gently treading water.

"For the money," he said. "Strictly for the money. Besides, I'm on the programming end. We develop and purchase programming for the BBC. I don't have to deal with the so-called artists."

"So you're here to do some programming deals?" she asked.

"In part," he said. "And in part to talk about co-venturing a sports series with one of your networks, which is what brings me to this frightfully boring golf tournament. I'd prefer to sit and watch the grass grow at Riviera than watch one more bloody minute of the golf itself."

She glided to the side of the pool, and lifted herself out of the water. As she did, the bottom of her suit slid off slightly. She stood up and walked a couple of steps toward the table before pulling it back up. She returned with her glass of iced tea, sat on the edge of the pool, and offered him a drink.

"The tape you mentioned? Do you have an extra copy?" he asked, gliding closer to her. "I'd like to have some of our production people view it and offer an opinion."

"You're sweet but I'd really like you to see it first," she said, bending down and running her hands across his head. "You might decide I'm awful and not want to waste anyone's time."

"I doubt that," he said. "I'll tell you what. We'll watch the tape after dinner tonight. You decide where we should go."

"I can't tonight, Graham," she said.

"Well, tomorrow then," he said.

"I'm sorry, but I'm toast tomorrow," she said. "There's a group of us that mentor some girls from South Central. We've had a long-standing plan to take them out sailing. I just couldn't back out."

He reached and took her hands, pulling her toward him. She slid slowly into the pool and wrapped her legs around his hips, leaning back against the edge of the pool. He put his arms around her waist and ran the fingers of his right hand along the elastic waist of her bikini. With his left hand he pulled her closer to him, until her breasts pressed against his chest. He kissed her, softly. She pulled his head toward her and kissed him deeply. She lowered a foot to the pool bottom and moved her thigh against him, then rocked forward and pressed herself against his hip. As they kissed, he reached down and pulled her firmly against him, and then he began sliding her up and down against his hip until she began the rhythmic grinding herself. She kissed him even more deeply, and her left arm squeezed him tightly around the neck. He reached behind her neck and unslipped the knot holding up the bikini top, and then leaned back and pulled the top away from her body, tossing it aside. He leaned over, cupped her right breast in his hand, lifted it toward his face, and then kissed it, softly at first and then harder.

She let out a cry, held herself harder against his hip, and then a moment later, pushed herself away, breathing deeply.

"Not now," she said, burying her face into his neck. "I can't now."

"Why?" he asked, running his hand along the back of her thigh. "There's no one around for God's sake."

"No, there isn't time," she said. "I have to go. I don't want to rush this. Please try to understand. Call me tomorrow night. I should be back around 10ish. Promise?"

"I'll try," he said, with an edge of annoyance in his voice. "But I can't promise."

"No promises then," she said, pressing her hips against him and kissing him fully. "You're welcome to stay for as long as you want."

And with that she lifted herself from the pool, put on her shirt and started toward the cottage.

"Here, you forgot this," he said, holding up the top of her bikini.

She leaned over, took the top, and kissed him again.

"Thanks," she said. "I thought you might want to keep it as a trophy."

"You don't get the trophy until you've made the kill," he said, then slid under the water and tried to swim off his frustration.

After she had been gone for a half hour or so, he went into her cottage and scoured the kitchen for a set of keys to the main house. Just as he expected, it didn't take long to find them. She had stuck them away in a coffee mug, along with the code for the security system.

He let himself into the house and made his way into the kitchen. Spotting the telephone hung over the large counter, he meticulously searched the nearby cabinets for the family's phone list. He finally found a worn, green leather address book and searched it for names with an address on Capri Drive. He found two, and jotted down the names and phone numbers. After carefully replacing the book, he left the kitchen and began to investigate the rest of the first floor. Tucked away in an extension off on the right side of the house was an exquisite office, paneled in dark walnut and decorated with rare and expensive Cecil Aldin hunting scenes and cascades of photographs that traced the history of the family. He went through the desk drawers looking for another address book but came up empty. He was about to leave when he spotted an electrical cord running from behind a cabinet. He opened the twin doors and discovered a computer.

He hesitated to boot it up. The system might keep a record of when it was accessed, but then who would suspect that anyone had been in the house over the weekend? Besides, it didn't look like a particularly sophisticated unit and by the time anyone discovered the files had been opened he'd be on holiday somewhere far removed from Los Angeles. Let the girl try to explain who might have been dicking around with the old man's computer.

He turned on the computer. It made a gentle hum, beeped, and then the screen turned a royal blue and presented a series of file options. Good. No entrance code was needed. He studied the options, and clicked on a program called "TeleMagic." The program asked for a three-letter ID. He searched the top of the desk and came across a stack of mail addressed to Mr. Edward J. Seaton. He tapped in EJS and hit enter. The file opened and a menu offered another series of files. He moved the mouse and clicked on the file marked "Personal." Up came an alphabetical listing of names, addresses, phone numbers, names of family members, birthdays, anniversaries, and other minutiae. He paged down through the file. It was a gold mine. Every neighbor on Capri was listed. He quickly printed out all the information. Later, he would compare it with the list of houses overlooking Riviera that he'd written down earlier. Then he shut down the files, turned off the computer and, after taking one last look to make sure nothing was out of place, left.

He spent Saturday trying to work out the details of his escape. He would park at the girl's house and, with any luck, he might get away before the police set up roadblocks on Sunset. He figured that once he made it to the 405 Freeway, he was safely away. Studying a map, another option was to try to reach the Pacific Coast Highway and head south. To do that he'd have to wind his way along the myriad of side streets through Pacific Palisades to Santa Monica. The police couldn't possibly block off all the streets. The danger was getting caught up among the thousands of people hurrying to leave the course. He knew that the longer he spent in the area, the higher his risk. He could always hide the rifle and disguise somewhere on the property and just stay with the girl until the police left the area. Still, the ideal solution was to flee, so for much of the afternoon he drove around, trying to find the safest route to the Pacific Coast Highway. By the time he was finished, he had dismissed the idea as an invitation to disaster.

Early in the evening he stopped at a place along the beach called "Patrick's Roadside Pub." It was crowded and noisy and he was sure that he wouldn't be noticed or remembered. Following dinner, he walked along Santa Monica beach and tried to collect his thoughts. After a while, he stopped and sat down in the sand, leaning back against a lifeguard stand. He lit a cigarette and watched the ships sailing south, toward Long Beach. He hoped that, with any luck, he might be heading that way tomorrow night. After a while, the temperature began to drop and he decided to leave. When he reached the hotel, he phoned the girl. To his relief, there was no answer. He left a message on her machine. It was 9:20. By 10:00, he was asleep, but it would be a fitful night's sleep. It almost always was.

He awoke the next morning and checked the weather forecast. It called for partly cloudy skies but with strong, gusty winds moving ahead of a winter storm off the Pacific. He called the girl and apologized for not meeting her the night before, claiming the jet lag had caught up with him and he'd decided to go to sleep early.

"A better offer, more likely," she said.

"No really, I'm awfully sorry," he said. "I'll make it up to you tonight. What time will you be back to your house this afternoon?"

"Brunch service ends at two, but there's a private party a few of us have to work," she said. "I'll try to sneak out early, but I probably won't be back much before five."

"Well, take your time," he said. "I wouldn't want you to jeopardize your career."

"This isn't a career," she said. "This is cruel and unusual punishment. See you soon."

After his usual breakfast of tea, yogurt, and sliced fruit, he packed and then began making a series of phone calls, going down the list he'd lifted from the Seatons' computer. He came up empty with his first three calls, getting answering machines that offered nothing in the way of useful information. On the fourth call, a man answered. He apologized, said he had a wrong number, and hung up. On the next call he got lucky. A woman with a strong Mexican accent answered.

"Hello, yes," the woman said.

"Mrs. Cunningham? Mrs. J.P. Cunningham?" he asked.

"No, Mrs. not here," she said.

"May I speak with Mr. Cunningham then?" he asked.

"No, Mr. not here, too," she said.

"I see," he said. "When do you expect them to return?"

"Who is this calling?" she asked.

"I'm very sorry, this is Federal Express—the delivery company," he said. "We have a package we need to drop off but we wanted to make sure somebody would be there this afternoon."

"Mr. and Mrs. no be here today," she said. "They gone for many days. Rosa be here for you package."

"And you're Rosa?" he asked.

"Si, me Rosa," she said.

"Fine, Rosa," he said, checking his watch. "One of our men will be by, say, around twoish."

"That's okay, Rosa be here," she said, and hung up.

He checked the sports section again, just to be sure of the starting times for the final round of the tournament. Peter Brookes, tied for the lead, was in the last group, scheduled to tee off at 11 A.M. If they played in four hours, they would go off the air at 6 P.M. New York time.

He went to the lobby and placed a long distance call from a phone booth, billing it to the prepaid calling card. There was a momentary silence and then the familiar double rings. He was about to hang up after several rings, when a man answered.

"Belfast Trading."

"Delivery will be made this afternoon," Raines said.

"What time?" the man asked.

"Roughly 2:30, my time." Raines said.

"Good luck, then." The Irishman said.

"Yes, quite," Raines said, and hung up.

When he returned to his room, Raines lay down on the bed, closed his eyes, and ran though his plan. Were there any problems he hadn't anticipated? The traffic, certainly, but he did have options. The Mexican maid? No, it would be at least until tomorrow before anyone found her or even missed her. The girl? Well, he simply hoped she wouldn't prove to be a problem. If so, he'd deal with her when the time came.

He checked out of the Holiday Inn, paying by cash and traveler's checks. When he arrived at the girl's house a short time later, he was relieved to find she already had left for work. He quickly removed the rifle, disguise and other material from the trunk of his car, and retreated to the pool house. There, he pulled off his shirt and put on the FedEx deliveryman's shirt he'd bought at the costumer's shop, tucking it into his black slacks. He pulled a dark, V-neck sweater over his head, and then slid off his tasseled loafers and put on a pair of black athletic shoes. Putting the FedEx cap on completed the disguise, even if it made him feel slightly ridiculous when he saw his reflection in the mirror.

He checked the time. It was now almost a quarter past one. He'd have to hurry along. He pulled the Glock from his bag and checked to ensure the clip was full, and then slid it tightly into the grip until it clicked. He pulled back the cocking mechanism, and a bullet snapped sharply into place. He clicked on the safety and put the gun into the black leather pack he would strap around his waist. He also put in two additional ammunition clips, as well as a roll of metallic duct tape and a small, portable television. Finally, he put in a small box of cartridges for the rifle and a disposable syringe.

Next, he opened the long FedEx box and carefully laid the pieces of the rifle along the bottom. To one end, he placed his carefully folded sports shirt and to the other end, a yellow cashmere sweater. If he had time, he would change into them afterward. Either way, they would cushion the pieces of the rifle and keep them from sliding about in the box.

Moving quickly now, he removed a plastic case containing two brown contact lenses from his bag. Leaning close to the mirror, he carefully placed them in his eyes. He knew that people, if pressed by the police, were likely to remember his green eyes, but were less likely to recall rather common brown eyes. And if they did, so much the better.

Finished, he thought, as he lit a cigarette, inhaled deeply and exhaled the smoke through his nostrils. The hit of nicotine worked quickly to settle his nerves, which were being worked upon by the adrenaline. Still, that nervousness was a good sign, he knew. It heightened his senses. His hearing was more acute. His eyesight sharper. It was as though he could even sense danger through his very skin. The feeling was like that of a young child, walking home through the woods in the dead of night for the first time. Fear bordering on terror but exhilarating just the same. There was nothing in life to match it, really. Not sex. Not gambling. Not sport. Nothing. It was the pure, unbleached thrill of the hunt—and now the hunt was finally on.

He tucked his belongings under the small bed and covered them with some old towels. He looked out the door to make sure the girl hadn't come back. Then he made his way out across the pool area, through the hedge, and around the far side of the house, away from the driveway. He pulled the cap low over his eyes, and exited through the front gate and onto Capri. Across the way and three houses down was the Cunningham house. He glanced at his watch. It was 1:35.

He crossed Capri and fell in behind a group of people walking toward the Riviera clubhouse. At the Cunningham house, he peeled off and headed up the walkway to the front door. As he did, he heard the sound of engines overhead. He looked up and saw an enormous blimp pass directly above.

The woman who answered the door was short, barely more than five feet tall and a bit on the heavy side. Her black hair, flecked with streaks of gray, was pulled straight back off her forehead and held in a bun. Her face was heavily lined and weary. He guessed she was in her 50s, perhaps a bit older.

"Is this the Cunningham residence?" he asked, politely.

"Si," she said, poking just her head and shoulders past the door, which was only slightly ajar.

"You must be Rosa," he said, trying to sound as friendly as possible. "I believe we spoke earlier. I'm from the delivery company."

"Si, we speaked," she said.

"Splendid," he said. "Well then, here's the package for your Mr. and Mrs. You just need to sign for it. While you're signing, I wonder if I might use your loo."

She looked at him skeptically.

"Been fighting the bloody trots all day," he said, as he clasped his right hand over his stomach and bent over slightly. "I'm afraid it's rather an emergency, Rosa. Your bathroom, please?"

He was quite sure she didn't understand half of what he was saying, but after pausing for a moment, she opened the door and motioned for him to enter, pointing to a bathroom just off the foyer.

"Bless you, Rosa," he said. "You're a dear. I won't be a minute."

He entered the bathroom, pulled on a pair of disposable rubber gloves, then shut the door, and quietly turned the lock to the right. He unzipped the small bag and pulled out the Glock, being careful to leave the safety in place. From another room, he could hear Spanish being spoken from a television.

After a minute or so, he quietly opened the door. Rosa was in an adjacent room, and he walked up behind her and wrapped his left hand over her mouth. She tried to scream, but the sounds were muffled. He moved the gun around in front of her face so she could get a good look.

"Rosa," he said. "You must keep very still and nothing bad will come to you. Do you understand?"

He could feel her shaking.

"Do you understand, Rosa? Nod yes or no, please."

Her head moved up and down, tentatively. She began to sob with fear.

"Are you alone, Rosa?" he asked. "Are you here by yourself, nod yes or no."

Again, her head moved up and down.

"Fine, Rosa," he said. "I'm going to remove my hand now and I want you to promise me that you'll behave. Do you understand what I'm saying?"

Again, she nodded. He slowly pulled her head to the left, turning her body so she faced him. Her dark brown eyes pleaded to him. He grasped the back of her head with his left hand. He pulled his right hand toward his face. Holding the Glock, he moved his index finger off the gun and placed it gently against his lips, signaling silence. He locked his eyes on hers, and consciously tried to make them seem soft, almost friendly.

"Now Rosa, I have a job to do and I do not wish to hurt you in any way," he said. "I will not hurt you if you do as I say. Do you understand, Rosa?"

"Si," she said, her voice shaking with fear. "You rob Mr. and Mrs?"

"No," he said, checking his watch. It was now 1:45. He pointed the gun in the direction of the sound from the television. "Rosa, is that your room?"

"Si, Rosa's room," she said. "Please, no hurt Rosa."

"No, not as long as you behave properly," he said. "Come along now, let's go to your room."

She walked, unsteadily, across the main room and down a narrow hallway. He kept his left hand on her shoulder until they entered the room, where he moved away to close the wooden, slatted blinds. He then turned on a table lamp and motioned for her to sit on the bed. Again, her eyes pleaded with him.

"Please, not do bad thing to Rosa," she said, making the sign of the cross and clasping her hands together in prayer.

"No," he said. "I'll tell you exactly what I'm going to do. I'm going to take this tape and bind your hands and feet. Then I'm afraid I must place some tape over your mouth so you cannot call out. Then I'm going to give you an injection to help you sleep. It will all be quite painless, I promise you."

He tore off two lengths of tape and placed them over her mouth. Then he lightly bound her hands and feet and gently laid her out on the bed, with her head elevated slightly. He noticed rosary beads on her night table, and handed them to her. This seemed to comfort her, and she began to pray, working her fingers along the worn, wooden beads. Then he pulled the syringe from his bag, took off the plastic protective tip, and slowly pushed on the plunger until a stream of clear liquid shot from the needle. He took her arm, found a plump vein, and injected the drug.

"Sweet dreams, Rosa," he said, as her eyelids fluttered shut over her tear-drenched eyes. He turned off the light and left Rosa to her prayers and her soap opera.

He returned to the main body of the house and methodically began checking for the best place to set up. The patio and pool area were out of the question. Too exposed. The kitchen might work. It offered good sight lines down to the tee, but a small stand of thin trees were a problem. They swayed in the gusting winds. He checked two other rooms before reaching the master bedroom at the end of the hall. It was enormous, with a huge bed, a television, a vast array of exercise machines and, most importantly, a master bath that opened through sliding glass doors to a large Jacuzzi deck ringed with a tall, thick hedge. The deck offered a clear view of the golf course below. He found a hole in the hedge, and dragged the metal and glass patio table with its large umbrella over to the spot. He would be hidden from almost any vantage point. It was now 2:05.

Back in the master bedroom, he quickly opened the FedEx box and turned on the television to the golf telecast. He listened as he carefully assembled the rifle.

"We've had beautiful weather here all week, Ben," the announcer, Tim Prince said, "but as we come down to the closing holes of this year's Los Angeles Open, we'll be very lucky if we don't get some tough conditions. As you can see from our blimp shot, there's a storm front approaching quickly off the Pacific. The winds are already picking up."

Raines looked up at the television. It showed a thick, black line of clouds out over the water. Outside, the wind was starting to gust strongly, moving even the large branches of the eucalyptus outside the windows.

"Timmy, we may get out of here before the rains hit, but these are hard winds to play in," said his partner, Ben Ward, as the cameras panned to a line of trees swaying in the winds. "The air is very heavy coming off the ocean and there's no way to predict when a gust is going to hit. The heavier the air is, the more the wind affects your shot. Plus, the wind gets down in this canyon and swirls around in the trees. It's like the back nine at Augusta. I remember losing here one year in conditions like this. It forces you to guess, and I guessed wrong on an approach and buried my ball under the lip of a bunker. It's tough."

"Who do you like in these conditions?" Prince asked.

"You've got to go with experience, Timmy," said Ward, who had been a top player in the '50s and '60s before becoming a respected teacher and golf analyst. "I like Peter Brookes. He's played a lot of his golf in Europe where you get this kind of weather. So much of playing in bad weather is mental. That's why a player like Tom Watson is so good in it. He's as mentally tough as they come. He has a perfect attitude for adversity. The tougher it gets, the more he likes it because he knows the rest of the field is going to back off. Brookes is the same way. With a two-shot lead, he knows they have to come and get him. I like his chances."

"Okay, let's go back out to 16 and pick up the leaders," Prince said.

Raines finished assembling the rifle. The barrel fit tightly, as did the silencer. He carefully attached the small, powerful scope and tightened the two small screws that held it in place. He tested the firing mechanism several times before inserting the small, three-bullet clip. While quite light overall, the weight of the stock's rubber pad balanced the barrel and the silencer. The firing mechanism, clip and small pistol grip, centered the overall weight of the weapon. Now all he could do was wait.

• • •

Jake O'Banion was having a nearly perfect afternoon. The long-time producer and director of the network's golf coverage was where he loved to be on a Sunday afternoon: sitting in the production truck with a wall of monitors in front of him, a group of ego-sensitive announcers cowering at his every word out on the course, and a great leader board keeping millions of viewers stuck in front of their televisions. All that and an unlimited expense account, a huge salary, and virtual immunity from the petty hassling of the suits back in New York. What could be better?

Well, maybe an announcer with half a brain out on 16.

"You fucking imbecile, watch the monitor!" O'Banion screamed into his microphone, his words going directly into the earpiece worn by Andy Clarke, a former tour player now, inexplicably, in his third year as an announcer for the network. "Don't talk about shit that the viewers can't see. You're the dumbest white man on the face of the earth."

Clarke went blithely on.

"The 16th hole is a 170-yard par 3 that plays directly toward the Pacific Ocean..." he said.

"Move the fucking microphone away from your mouth," O'Banion shouted. "You're popping your 'P's. C'mon, get in the God damn game."

Poor word choice by O'Banion. It was like a Pavlovian signal to Clarke, a Born-Again Christian.

"This magnificent hole is a perfect example of how the architect, George Thomas, took this splendid piece of land God created and was inspired to fit it to man's temporal needs..." Clarke went on.

"I'll kill you," O'Banion growled into his microphone, after slamming his hands down on the console. "I will personally—personally—feed you to the fucking lions. I don't want to hear one more word about God, his kid, Casper the Holy Ghost, or anything else. If people want religion, let 'em watch that fraud Jerry Falwell. Throw it to 17."

"While we're waiting for Peter Brookes to select a club, let's go to Clive Wolcott on 17," Clarke said.

As Clarke finished speaking, Charlie Walsh, O'Banion's longtime number-two man punched a button on the console that switched the on-air shot to Justin Leonard on 17.

"God help him," O'Banion said, in mock prayer. "He knows not what he does."

The crew in the truck erupted in laughter.

"Well, I must say that the wind, which had been just the merest zephyr, well, it has suddenly become quite fierce," Wolcott said, in a rich, English baritone. "These fellows who started late have really gotten the worst of it, I'm afraid. It will take a brave soul to bear up to this, I'd say. And, on the subject of brave souls, here's Justin Leonard's little wedge shot to this bearish par 5."

The on-air monitor showed a face-on shot of Leonard from a camera in the fairway.

"Stand by four," O'Banion said to Charlie Walsh.

Leonard took one more look at the green, then took the club back and hit a three-quarter punch-wedge, driving the ball in low to keep it under the wind.

"Roll four," O'Banion called. Walsh slid a switcher and the on-air monitor showed the ball landing on the green, bouncing once, twice and then checking up just inches from the hole.

"Cut back to mini-two for a reaction shot," O'Banion said, sharply.

The on-air screen showed Leonard, tamping down his divot with his wedge, and then looking up to the large gallery lining the fairway and acknowledging their roar with a smile and a small wave.

"Let that reaction play out, Clive," O'Banion said quietly into his microphone.

Through the speakers in the truck, the roar washed over the small room.

"Steady old boy..." O'Banion said with an exaggerated British accent, as the noise subsided. "...and now go."

"Well, there's a shot across the bow of Mr. Peter Brookes," said Wolcott. "And don't you for one moment think he doesn't know that this battle is well joined. I rather favor Leonard's chances if he can get in with a birdie on 18. It is looking very gloomy out over the ocean..."

"Clive, throw it to 16," O'Banion said, after watching Brookes's tee shot on the bank of monitors. "His Royal Highness just blew it into the right-hand bunker. As they say, 'He be fucked.'"

"...and perhaps, very gloomy for Peter Brookes, who has found trouble lurking on 16. Let's go back to Andy Clarke," Walcott said, seamlessly.

"Good job, you beautiful Limey bastard," said O'Banion, his interest picking up as the play came down to the closing holes. "Andy, just set up that Brookes hit it into the death bunker on 16, and that with Leonard's birdie on 17 we're looking at a two-shot swing and a tie. And don't forget Dexter Bradley. If he makes two on 16 he's only one back. He could reach 17 in two with that wind coming off the ocean. If we don't mention him the critics will be all over us tomorrow. I'm going to put up a leader board. Talk us out to commercial on my count..."

O'Banion punched up the first page of the leader board.

BROOKES	—10	15
LEONARD	—9	16
BRADLEY	—8	15

O'Banion turned off the switch that opened his mike to Clarke and turned to Walsh, seated next to him.

"We've got a two-minute hole until Brookes reaches his ball," he said, pointing to the wall of monitors. "He's still back on the tee trying to figure out where his dick was on that swing."

"He left it with that blonde we saw him with at Bel-Air last night. What about Leonard's drive?" Walsh asked, looking up at the monitor picking up the feed from the 18th tee.

"Big fucking deal," O'Banion said. "He hasn't missed a fairway in two weeks. He's not going to miss this one. Andy, wake up. Let's go. And five, four, three, two and...we're away on commercial."

"We're clear," said Walsh.

O'Banion opened his microphone to all the announcers.

"Alright, listen up you guys," he said. "We've got a live one here. The world's greatest player versus the best America can cough up this month and the new Great Black Hope. A huge storm brewing off in the Pacific. A clash of Titans...aw, fuck all that stuff. Just keep up the intensity. Timmy and Ben, we're coming to you off the break. Give me one page of leader board and some stuff from Ben on getting into the clubhouse first with a number. We're back in one minute. Timmy, I'll count you in."

• • •

Up on the hillside, Graham Raines finished weighing down the patio table and umbrella against the rising winds. Then he returned to the bedroom and switched the television to the Weather Channel. The local radar showed the leading edge of the storm just offshore, and the forecaster was predicting it would reach land within the hour. The storm, he knew, would be a mixed blessing: it would make his already-difficult shot even more complicated. On the other hand, a driving rain would add to the chaos, and make his escape considerably easier. He lit a cigarette and called to see if the girl had returned to the cottage. He let the phone ring until her voice came on the answering machine, and then clicked off. He turned the television back to the golf, just as Peter Brookes prepared to play his bunker shot from behind the 16th green.

• • •

"The good news is that he has a decent lie," said Andy Clarke. "The bad news is that no matter how well he plays it, he can't stop it close to the hole. He missed it in the one place you can't afford to miss it on this hole—an inexcusable mistake for a player of his caliber."

Brookes hit a good shot, sliding the clubface neatly under the ball and landing it softly just over the crest of the bunker. But the ball took off, ran past the hole, and came to rest on the collar of the green, against the first cut of rough. Brookes lashed his wedge through the sand, then tossed the club at his caddie's feet, took his putter and walked toward the ball. The veteran cameraman, Bobby Wren, framed a tight close-up of the caddie's face as he glared at Brookes in disgust.

"Asshole," his caddie, Speedball, said, to no one in particular— except to the several million or so viewers watching around the world who could read lips.

"That's Mr. Asshole to you, Speedball," O'Banion laughed. "Good work, Bobby. Stay there and pick up Brookes's putt then jump over to flank the landing area on 17. Give me a close-up of Brookes's ball. I want to see what kind of lie he has."

The ball had come to rest snugly against the collar of rough surrounding the green. Brookes addressed the ball with the leading edge of his sand wedge lined up with the center of the ball, then gave the club back to Speedball and took his putter, a new Ping model. Wren panned down to a close-up of the ball and the putter head, which Brookes had turned so the toe of the putter faced the ball.

"Andy, throw it to Ben," O'Banion said into his microphone. "Bobby, stay with that shot."

"Ben Ward, this is kind of a risky shot at this point in the tournament, don't you think?" Clarke said.

"Andy, he doesn't have to hit the ball a long way," Ward said. "All he wants to do is make solid contact. You wouldn't do this with a putter with a smaller head, like a blade putter, but this isn't a bad play. Even if he misses it slightly, he'll probably leave it below the hole. What he doesn't want is a downhill putt on this green. It's too spiked up. I like this play."

Brookes played the ball well back in his stance, off his right foot. He set his hands ahead of the ball, even with his belt buckle.

Without breaking his wrists, he drew the club back, and then hit down firmly on the ball. It popped into the air, settled on the green, and began rolling smoothly. As it neared the hole, the gallery's roar increased until the ball came up inches short, and they groaned and then broke into applause. Brookes ran his hand through his hair and shook his head in disbelief. After giving the gallery a small wave, he tapped his ball into the hole and walked briskly to the side of the green. He and Leonard were tied at nine-under. Now it was Dexter Bradley's turn.

Bradley was the biggest story in the game. In part because of his remarkable talent, in part because he was black and promised to be the next Tiger Woods, and in part because of his remarkable life story. He had come from a poor family and started caddying when he was 12. His mother, who dragged him—almost literally—to the golf course that first day, didn't know much about golf but she did know that any place that kept her son off the streets, earned him a little money, and let him see rich people up close couldn't be all bad—or bad at all.

Almost from the first day, he was fascinated by the game. The club's professional, sensing that enthusiasm, made sure he got to caddie for the better players who, in turn, encouraged his interest. Soon, he was winning all the caddie tournaments. Then he moved on to junior golf, where he dominated at every age level. When he graduated from high school, there was an Arnold Palmer Scholarship waiting for him at Wake Forest.

By the time he graduated—with honors—he had dominated amateur golf. When he turned pro and joined the Tour, the expectations were enormous, and none higher than his own. He won early and by the age of 24 he was a genuine celebrity bordering on becoming a legend.

"This is a huge opportunity for Dexter Bradley," said Andy Clarke. "He's about 12 feet below the hole. It's not a hard putt, but at this point in the tournament, there really aren't any easy putts. This is for a birdie that will tie him for the lead."

Bradley took his time looking the putt over, then set up over the ball and was ready to hit his putt when there was some commotion in the enormous gallery surrounding the green. He backed off momentarily, then set up and put a good stroke on the ball.

"It looks good...it's right on line if he hit it...Yes, sir!" Clarke exclaimed.

The gallery roared and several people raced toward the 17th tee. O'Banion punched up a shot of Leonard walking up the 18th fairway to enormous applause from the spectators.

"Justin Leonard has always been tremendously popular at this tournament, hasn't he, Ben?" Tim Prince asked.

"I remember seeing him play in the U.S. Amateur when he was a kid and you just had a sense that he was going to be a special player," Ward said. "I wasn't surprised when he won the British Open. He's got a game that will hold up for a long time."

"Good work, boys," O'Banion said. "Alright Clive, your turn. Leonard is in the fairway on 18. Bradley's making his move. Brookes has his back to the wall. It's nut-cutting time in La-La Land. This is for God, Queen, and Country. Go, Clive."

"Let's go to Clive Wolcott on 17," Prince said.

"Well now, young Master Bradley has absolutely crushed his drive, easily the longest of the day. He can definitely reach this bearish par 5 in two, but this is also when Peter Brookes is the most dangerous, I reckon," Wolcott rumbled, as the viewers watched the Englishman prepare to drive on the 17th. "I well remember the first time I saw him, at the British Boy's Championship, lo those many years ago. I was struck even then by his rather fierce determination under pressure. His is the blackest of hearts when he thinks he might be denied his just due."

Wolcott's timing was impeccable. He finished speaking just as Brookes lashed his drive.

"Well, well, well, now you see exactly what I mean," Wolcott said, as the camera followed the ball as it bound down the fairway. "He's quite remarkable in his ability to rise magnificently to the occasion. He's like the old British bulldog I should say. Once he gets his teeth into the meat of it, there's no letting go. I must say, I rather admire the old boy."

• • •

After watching Brookes hit his drive, Raines took the rifle off the bed, checked to ensure the first round was locked in place, and went out onto the deck. The air had gotten heavier and the smell of rain was in the air. Out to the west, he could see sheets of rain approaching. It was just a matter of minutes before the storm hit. He turned on the small portable television and set it on the table, adjusting the antenna for the best reception. He heard a roar from off to his left, and turned up the sound on the television.

"Another remarkable approach shot from Justin Leonard, Ben," said Tim Prince. "How many times have we seen him do that this year?"

"Timmy, confidence breeds confidence in this game," Ward said. "He's always been a good player but now maybe he feels like he has something to prove with so many good young players coming along—and the more he proves it, the better he plays. The great players learn how to feed off success. I think he makes this putt and then goes quietly. He's done what he needs to do. You can't control what the other guy does."

"And now the rain is starting, Ben," said Prince. "That makes Brookes's and Bradley's jobs much tougher."

"Exactly," said Ward, crisply. "I like Justin's chances."

Raines positioned himself under the umbrella, protected from the rain and sheltered from the winds by the hedges. He rested the rifle on a mound of towels and aimed through a hole in the hedge. He carefully focused the sight on the far marker on the 18th tee until it came sharply into view. He glanced at the small screen on the television, which showed Brookes standing in the 17th fairway. His caddie stood next to him, straining to hold an umbrella over Brookes in the gusting winds.

"You've got 241 to the front edge and 160 to carry the second bunker," the caddie said. "The pin is 17 and 11 from the left side and you've got 10 yards over the left-hand bunkers."

"I like seven, Speedball," Brookes said.

"Seven it is," the caddie said. "Don't baby it, either."

Brookes pulled the 7-iron from his bag and walked into the ball. Just as he prepared to hit, the wind seemed to turn and quarter off his right shoulder. The rain came down harder. Brookes backed off and took another look at the shot.

"Clive, he won't hit this shot until he's ready," said Ward. "If you watch the great players, they all have a routine that they follow, right down to the split second, no matter what the conditions.

Snead and Nicklaus did that better than anyone I ever saw. You could set your watch by them."

Brookes got back over the ball, took a practice swing, and started the 7-iron out over the right rough, drawing it back into the right side of the fairway, taking the bunkers on the left side of the fairway out of play, and giving himself a perfect angle into the flag. Over on 18, the crowd let out a loud roar as Leonard made his birdie, taking the lead.

"Leonard?" Brookes asked his caddie.

The caddie looked over at Bobby Wren and mouthed Leonard's name. Wren nodded and flashed all five fingers of his left hand twice. Leonard had finished at 10 under.

"Yeah, 10 under in the tent," the caddie said.

The caddie reached into the large side pocket of the golf bag and pulled out a clean, dry white towel and a waterproof Slazenger windshirt. He handed the shirt to Brookes and then carefully hung the towel from the ribs of the umbrella.

"How's the glove?" he asked Brookes.

"Fine for now," Brookes said. "I'll take a dry one on 18."

Bobby Wren scrambled to get into position for Dexter Bradley's shot. Bradley's drive had gotten high into the air and was swept down the fairway by the strong winds racing ahead of the storm. The ball hit on a slight downslope and took a big jump down the fairway.

"You've got 223 to the front and 17 back to the hole," his caddie said. "Big wind behind us. I don't know, Dex. It's kinda gusting and there's a lot of trouble hangin' around this green."

Dexter Bradley turned and looked back toward the Pacific.

"Lots *more* trouble when that storm hits," he said. "I'd rather take my chances here."

"A four would go a long way, Dex," the caddie said.

"Three would go a lot further," Bradley said as he pulled a fairway wood from his bag.

"I like that thinking," Ben Ward said. "He's got to know that Leonard is in at 10-under and with the storm coming up, he's got to figure a three on 18 is a real long shot. If he pulls this off, he's got a chance at making three and taking the outright lead or at least a four and a piece of the lead. If he doesn't, he's not going to win— and winning is all this young man cares about."

Dexter Bradley set up to the ball, aimed toward the right side of the green, and closed his stance. He swung the club back slowly, anchoring his feet and coiling his upper body. He lashed into the ball and it ripped off the clubface, soaring into the air and steadily turning to the left. It hit in front of the green, jumped once into the air and began running toward the hole. From the moment the ball left the clubface, the gallery began to roar. As it grew closer to the hole, the roar became louder and louder. When it finally stopped, some six feet from the flagstick, Bradley responded by pumping his fist in the air and giving his caddie a high five. The scene was electric.

The intense pressure was now squarely back on Peter Brookes but he appeared to be emotionless as he strode intently up the fairway. When they reached Brookes's ball, the caddie paced off the distance from the nearest sprinkler head and then double-checked the number against his well-worn yardage book.

"I've got 86 to the pin," the caddie said. "We had 83 yesterday. It was just a good, smooth 60-degree wedge."

"No, in this weather I'd have to hit that too hard. The ball might slide up the clubface. We need to get this back to the hole."

Brookes pulled the towel back from on top of the irons, reached down and placed his right hand on the sand wedge. He hesitated for a moment, squinting up toward the flag that fluttered inconsistently in the wind, then fanned through the irons in the bag until he pulled out the 8-iron. The caddie looked at him briefly, then pulled the bag onto his shoulder and stepped away.

Brookes made a practice swing, took another look at the green, and then moved into position. He closed his feet slightly and played the ball back in his stance, with his hands even with his left thigh. He made a three-quarter backswing, clipped the ball cleanly off the wet turf, and made an abbreviated finish with his swing. It was a soft swing and the ball took off low to the ground, driving through the wind and rain. It landed on the front edge of the green, bounced once, twice, three times, then began running smoothly toward the hole. As the ball lost speed, it broke left, and finally came to rest some 10 feet short of the hole—right behind Bradley's.

"Ben, talk to me about that shot," Jake O'Banion said into his microphone.

"That's the kind of shot you learn to play in Europe because of the weather," the analyst said. "Over there, they play a lot more along the ground. Here, kids only learn how to put the ball up in the air, so they're at a disadvantage in wet, windy conditions. A guy like Peter Brookes plays the game the way Hogan and Nelson and players from Texas did in the old days. My hat is off to him. He's a complete player."

They reached the green just as Bradley finished marking his ball. Since it was directly on line with Brookes's putt, he waited for the Englishman to indicate which side he needed to move his coin. Glancing up the line, Peter Brookes said, "Left, please." Brookes then marked his ball and flipped it to his caddie. Speedball cleaned it carefully and handed it back. Brookes glared at him before he replaced the ball on the green. A nearby microphone picked up their conversation.

"Get a new book," Brookes said to the caddie. "That yardage was off."

"Can't be. It was right all week," Speedball said. "Let's forget about it and make this putt. It's a ball outside right if you die it at the hole. Everything wants to move toward the ocean. If you hit it hard, don't get it outside the hole."

Brookes leaned over again, looking at the line, then began to rise and move toward the ball.

"I'll put it on the right edge and die it at the hole," Brookes said. "If I miss it, I don't want to look at anything nasty coming back. I'll take my chances on 18."

Brookes got comfortable over the ball, made two practice strokes as he stared at the hole, then wiped the putter blade across one leg of his trousers. When he was ready, he nodded slightly and the caddie, who was holding the umbrella over him, moved away from the ball and out of Brookes's vision. The Englishman took one last look at the hole and hit the putt. The ball had no sooner started to roll toward the hole, when a strong gust of wind came from the left. It was just enough to slow the ball and keep it from breaking into the cup. It came to rest on the edge of the hole and a moan rose from the gallery packed in tightly around the green. Brookes bent from the waist and slowly raised the putter until the shaft came to rest against his forehead. He closed his eyes tightly in frustration and then walked up and tapped the ball into the hole for a par. A shot back with just one hole remaining.

Dexter Bradley took his ball from the caddie and set it on the green. He and his caddie lined up the putt. They paused for a moment while the caddie raised his hand and asked the gallery to settle.

In the production truck, Jake O'Banion wanted a reaction shot of Peter Brookes in a window when Bradley hit his putt. He got more than he bargained for. As Bradley addressed the ball, Brookes asked his caddie a question, then turned back and called to Bradley.

"Dex, hold it," he said.

Bradley looked up and backed away from the ball.

"Did you move the ball back a clubhead before you replaced it?" Brookes asked.

Bradley looked over at his caddie. The caddie looked stunned, and shook his head from side to side. Bradley looked back at Brookes, nodded, remarked his ball, then replaced it correctly.

"That's what makes golf unique, Timmy," said Ben Ward. "It's the last gentleman's game."

Dexter Bradley made his putt for eagle and jumped into a tie with Justin Leonard. As he walked to the next tee, he caught up with Peter Brookes.

"Thanks, man," he said, placing his hand on Brookes's back. "That was big."

"No," Brookes said. "I want to win, but I don't want to win that way. I'll get you here."

As Raines watched Dexter Bradley putt out on the small television screen, he gently clicked off the safety and sighted the rifle down to the tee box. The gallery raced to get a good position to the right side of the tee. The back of the tee was hedged in by shrubs and wild plants and the left side was roped off. He watched as security guards opened a hole in the gallery for Brookes, Bradley, and their caddies. The gallery applauded as the two players walked onto the tee, stone-faced and resolute.

Speedball placed the bag in front of him, took the umbrella from Brookes and handed him a fresh, white glove. Brookes dried his left hand on the towel hung inside the umbrella, then meticulously put on the glove, taking special care to fit it snugly over his fingers and smoothing any wrinkles from the palm.

Dexter Bradley had the honor and tore a drive down the left side of the fairway into perfect position. The gallery roared their approval and he acknowledged it with a smile and a wave.

Now it was Brookes's turn. He pulled the headcover from his driver and handed it to the caddie, then took the driver from the bag and teed up his ball, oblivious to the noise from the gallery. The caddie moved back to the side of the tee, next to Bradley, blocking Brookes's view from any movement in the gallery that might distract him

Up on the hillside, Raines carefully aimed the rifle at the center of Brookes's back, at a spot just to the left of the spine. He would aim for the heart, knowing that if he missed even slightly, the damage from the collapsing, hollow-point bullet would be fatal as it tumbled and tore through the man's body. He felt the small beads of perspiration forming along his upper lip and brow, and forced himself to take deep, slow breaths. As Brookes settled into position, Raines's last thought was to squeeze off the round with a slow, steady pressure on the trigger. There could be no quick movements, no last room for doubt.

He focused intently on a small spot on Brookes's windshirt and slowly exhaled. At the very last second, just as he'd barely begun to squeeze the trigger, he was aware of the wind gusting in the trees off to his right. The rifle fired with a quiet, barely audible, thupping sound as the silencer muffled the shot. At that very split second, he saw Brookes step away from the ball and turn to the right, to check the wind in the trees along the hillside.

The bullet tore into the caddie's abdomen, just below the rib cage. Thrown backward by the bullet's impact, Speedball let go of Brookes's bag and it crashed to the ground. For a moment there was an eerie silence, then a woman in the gallery looked at the figure lying at her feet, saw the blood begin to spurt from the wound, and screamed. Soon people were running in panic, shouting in horror. Some sought cover amid the shrubs behind the tee. Others ran back toward 17, seeking shelter in the tall trees. At first, Brookes didn't realize what had happened, but then he quickly dove onto Dexter Bradley, knocking him to the ground and shielding him with his body. In a matter of seconds they were surrounded by Bradley's private security guards and plainclothes policeman — with guns drawn. They were quickly hurried from the tee.

Down in the production truck, there was chaos as well. Bobby Wren's down-the-line shot of Brookes preparing to hit had been on-air. When he heard the woman scream, he turned the camera to his right and saw the caddie sprawled on the ground. Then he saw the blood spreading across the front of the caddie's white golf shirt and bib and his experience as a news cameraman—and his instincts—took over. He focused on the dying man, as everyone around him panicked. Across the world, millions of people watched the last moments of the caddie's life drain before them.

"Bobby, what the fuck is going on down there?" Jake O'Banion shouted into his microphone.

"Speedball's shot," Wren said calmly into his small headset. "I don't know from where. Didn't hear a thing."

"Jesus," O'Banion said softly, and then took control, calmly barking orders. "Get me a wide shot from that flanking camera back up on the hillside on 18. Bobby, stay with the kid. I'll go to you when they get some help down there. Stay down and stay put."

He opened his microphone to all the announcers.

"Listen up," he said, without a trace of nervousness in his voice. "We've had something happen down here on 18. We're not sure what it is. Nobody—and I mean *nobody*—says anything unless I tell you to. Timmy, I'm going to you and you say just what I tell you. There's been an incident on 18. We're trying to find out exactly what happened. Apparently one person—a caddie—has been injured. We don't know how or how seriously. Stay with us for more information as it develops."

As Prince repeated what O'Banion had told him, sirens could be heard in the background. Viewers saw the huge gallery race back toward the clubhouse as the rain began to fall harder, in wind-driven sheets.

"Where's the goddamned blimp?" O'Banion said to Charlie Walsh.

"Headed back to Santa Monica airport," he said. "The winds were too much."

"Get him back over here," O'Banion said. "I want some over-heads. I want to see what the fuck is going on here."

O'Banion looked up at the wall of monitors flickering in front of him. The camera set on the hillside behind the 18th green was following an orange and white EMS truck as it raced, lights flashing, down the 18th fairway toward the tee. A police car followed closely behind it.

"Get me that shot of the EMS guys," he called. "Timmy, we still don't know what happened for sure. Police and medical crews are on the scene."

Back on the tee, Bobby Wren kept his minicam trained on the caddie, knowing the shot would never get on the air. Blood now drenched the caddie's shirt and a pool spread out on the grass and drained down the side of the tee. After the initial panic, a man and a woman—doctors, Wren thought—had tried to help the caddie. It was no use. He gasped for breath but could only cough up gobs of thick, dark red blood. They tried to comfort him and stop the bleeding.

Wren steadied the camera with his right hand and ran the fingers of his left hand in front of the lens, trying to signal O'Banion or Walsh in the truck.

"Yeah, Bobby," O'Banion said.

"He's gone, Jake," Wren said.

"You're sure?" O'Banion asked.

"Jake, I've seen dead guys," he said. "Speedball never had a chance."

Just as Bobby Wren finished speaking, the EMS team and police escort reached the body. Wren never flinched. The police forced people back as the EMS technicians worked feverishly on the caddie, blocking Wren's shot. A few seconds later, three men took the sponsor's banner that had hung behind the tee, and held it around the caddie and the EMS team, shielding the body.

"Bobby, you're on live, but if those guys move I don't want to see the body," O'Banion said. "If this kid has a family I don't want them finding out about this from us."

On the console in front of Charlie Walsh, a light began to flash on a telephone. He answered it and then handed it to O'Banion.

"New York," he said. "Some producer from the evening news."

"O'Banion," he said. "Yeah, a caddie was shot on the 18th tee. Worked for Peter Brookes, the British guy. Dead, we think. No, you can't go with that. Why not? Because we can't confirm it. Don't they teach you guys anything in journalism-fucking school? Yeah, Dexter Bradley was in that group but he wasn't hurt. How the fuck do I know if he was the target? Okay. In two minutes we'll go to the studio in New York and your guy will feed it back to Timmy for an update. Who's anchoring your news? Okay. Hey listen, just remember what I said. This is my call. We're not confirming anything yet. A caddie was shot. His condition is unknown but believed to be serious. Are we on the same page? I don't want any surprises from you guys."

He hung up the phone and opened his microphone to the 18th tower.

"In about two minutes we're going to lead the evening news," O'Banion said. "They're going to go on early because of this. Unless we get some official confirmation—and that means unless you hear it from me—all we're saying is that a person believed to be a caddie for Britain's Peter Brookes was shot and wounded. His condition is unknown but the wound is believed to be serious. There are no reports of any other injuries..."

"Jake, Tom Black from the tour staff just came in here and told us it's really bad, probably fatal," Prince said.

"Until you hear it from me, it's not official, do you understand?" O'Banion said. "Now, I want you to fill for a couple minutes then you'll throw it to some fluff named Susan Greer who's anchoring in New York. They'll do a tease and maybe show some footage of the shooting, then come back to you live for an update. Watch your monitor. We may get the blimp back over here for an overhead of 18 and all the police and EMS stuff. Okay, now take a deep breath and stay with me. You okay?"

Prince looked pale, but he nodded grimly at the camera. As he did, the light on the truck phone began flashing again. Walsh answered it.

"You've got to be fucking kidding," he said, slamming down the phone and looking over at O'Banion.

"Your pal Glaser in sales," Walsh said. "The sponsor wants to know if we can stop showing their banner on 18."

"Fucking suits," O'Banion said.

"Jake, the blimp's back over the course," Walsh said, pointing to the wall of monitors. "The winds are pretty rough. They're not sure how long they can stay up. The pictures are going to be pretty shaky."

"Okay, tell them we're going to try and open with Timmy in a split screen with New York, then go to their overhead," O'Banion said. "I want them to give me a pretty tight shot of the tee area and then open up to show me the hole and the surrounding area. I'll talk them through the shot."

The shot from the blimp showed police officers fanning out along the hillside to the left of the hole. Roadblocks were set up on either end of Capri and the gallery was being moved away from the 18th tee and back toward the clubhouse. Down on the tee, Bobby Wren again signaled the truck by waving his fingers in front of the camera's lens.

"Yeah, Bobby," O'Banion said.

"Jake, they've got a priest with him now," Wren said. "The cops are blocking me off, but it sure looks like he's getting the Last Rites."

"Stay there and give me whatever you can," O'Banion said. "See if you can get me a shot of the cops going up the hill."

O'Banion had four camera shots to work with: Bobby Wren's shots of the police scrambling up the hill, with guns drawn; the flanking camera on the 18th fairway, which could give a close-up of the tee and pan the entire fairway; the blimp, for as long as it could safely stay in the air; and the hard camera in the announcer's tower on 18. He had to watch a monitor with the network's feed from New York, and he had to make sure his announcer's comments matched the images on screen—without either one going over the line of what he believed was in good taste. And he had to do it instinctively, without any time to plan or react. It was live television and it's what he did better than anyone else in the business.

"Timmy, 30 seconds and we go to New York...I'll count you in at 10...Set up VT1, I want to roll Bobby's first reaction shots early ...New York, once you throw it to Timmy you follow my lead. I'm going to give you Timmy on-air with an update, we'll switch to a scene-setter and maybe an overhead if we can hold the blimp...I've got some cop stuff...hold on, it looks like they're putting the guy in the ambulance...take camera two on VT2...Timmy we're away to Susan Greer in 10...watch your monitor and listen to me...okay New York. We're ready when you are...and five, four, three, two and we're away."

Then he leaned back in his chair, held his face in his hands for a moment, and then stared blankly at the wall of flickering monitors.

"Jesus," he said softly.

. . .

Moments after the shooting, Raines had already left the house and calmly, but quickly, made his way to the girl's cottage. When he saw the bullet slam into the caddie, he shoved the pile of towels into the pool. The chlorine would destroy any powder residue and the water would remove any fiber or hair traces. He methodically broke the rifle down and put the pieces back in the FedEx box. He stuck the Glock automatic back into his waist pouch, turned off the television, took it back inside, scanned the bedroom to make sure everything seemed in place, then left through the front door.

It was strangely quiet when he walked outside. Small groups of people were walking down the street, but their heads were down or hidden by umbrellas, seeking shelter from the driving rain. It wasn't until he was safely through the gate and behind the walls of the estate that he was first aware of the sirens, their screams quickly growing in both number and intensity. He cut through the front yard and around the far side of the house. He ducked into a stand of shrubs and removed the FedEx sweater and hat, jamming them into the box. When he reached the rear of the house, he looked over at the cottage. The lights were out and the girl's car was not in the turnaround. For a moment, he thought about trying to leave, but the intensity of the approaching sirens convinced him it was too late and too risky. He'd have to wait it out with the girl.

Checking one last time, he strolled around the heavily wooded side of the yard until he reached the pool house. He pushed open the door, carefully slid the box under the bed, and quickly finished changing his clothes. Then he looked at his reflection in the small, dirty bathroom mirror. His face glistened from sweat and as he bent over to splash some water on his face, he heard a car door shut in the driveway. He quickly turned off the light and headed for the cottage.

He met the girl just as she came through the gate and they entered the cottage together.

"Did you hear what happened?" she asked. "It was on the radio. Somebody was shot at the tournament."

"Yes, it happened just as I was leaving the course," he said, and as he did, he could hear the nervous tremor in his voice. He hoped the girl wouldn't notice. "Bloody awful thing. Christ, it's frightfully cold. You wouldn't have any scotch, would you?"

The girl dug an old bottle of Johnny Walker Red from one of the kitchen cabinets. She wiped away the film of dust with a towel, then handed him the bottle and a glass.

"Ice?" she asked.

"No, neat is fine," he said. "Would you mind if we put on the television? I'd like to see if they have any news on the shooting."

"Sure, I'll get it on my way upstairs," she said. "I want to get cleaned up. Are you okay?"

"Sure, fine," he said. "Just a bit shaken by it all, I suppose. You go on."

Once she left, he removed the waist pack and hid it in a closet. Then he cracked open the bottle and began to pour the whiskey into the glass. As he did, his hand shook ever so slightly, causing the bottle to clatter along the rim of the glass. He grasped the bottle with both hands, poured three fingers of scotch, and quickly downed it. The whiskey burned against his throat and then stung again when it reached his stomach. The smell of the peat filled his nostrils and he gave a small shudder as his body reacted to the alcohol. He poured more scotch into the glass and took another, smaller, drink. He rolled the warm whiskey around in his mouth before slowly swallowing it. It was already beginning to take the edge off his nervousness. He lit a cigarette and moved to the small living room, bringing the whiskey with him, and turned his attention to the news.

All the local stations were broadcasting from the golf course, having broken away from their regular programming. He changed channels quickly, trying to get the most recent information. CNN was the first to announce that, based on information from police, the caddie was indeed dead on arrival at the hospital. The reporter, citing a "high police official," said there were no suspects or motives. Police, the reporter continued, were searching the area and had set up a series of roadblocks around Sunset Boulevard.

Raines reasoned that the roadblocks wouldn't be up for long. Too disruptive. He also figured the police would almost certainly come by asking questions. Maybe they'd just go to the main house and overlook the cottage. No problem, either way. If they come back here, we're just a couple sitting out the weather with a midafternoon toss in the bedroom. Certainly nothing suspicious about that. Still, there was the problem of the rifle. And the girl.

Minutes later, she came back downstairs. Her hair was still wet from her shower, and she had combed it straight back off her forehead. She wore a pair of jeans and a tight white T-shirt with a Union Jack across the front. What she clearly wasn't wearing was a bra.

"How nice of you to come to attention for the flag," he said.

She smiled and blushed slightly.

"I wanted to make you feel at home," she said, sitting next to him on the couch and taking a sip of the whiskey. "Are you better? It must have been awful."

"Still a bit frazzled, I'm afraid." he said, pouring more scotch into the glass. "I suppose you Americans get used to this type of thing but not us."

He took another drink and handed her the glass. As he did, he noticed that she was staring into his eyes, with a quizzical look on her face.

"Is something wrong?" he asked, running his hand gently along her cheek.

"Well, this is kind of silly, but one thing that I remember from the first night at the restaurant was your eyes," she said. "They were the most beautiful, intense green I'd ever seen. I guess it must be the light in here."

Bloody hell, the fucking contacts, Raines thought. In all the chaos, he'd forgotten to get rid of them. *Christly stupid that was*, he thought.

"Oh that," he said, trying desperately to think of an explanation. "You're very observant. You see, I lost a contact when I first arrived and had to get a replacement set from one of those quick order places—what do they call them, Lens Builders or something? Of course, they botched the order and came up with this brown pair. Hardly matters, I suppose, except that if I'd been wearing them at dinner your level of service wouldn't have been nearly as exquisite."

"It depends on what you mean by 'level of service,'" she said, taking a drink and placing the glass on the table. Then she leaned against him and kissed him, cradling the back of his head with her left hand and running her right hand along his thigh. She tasted of both scotch and tobacco, and he kissed her back, hard. Then he placed his right hand across her back and pulled her over, so her legs straddled him. She began sliding rhythmically, back and forth along his legs, arching her back and pressing against him. He bent down and kissed her breasts, then took the bottom of the shirt and lifted it over her head as she raised her arms into the air, running his hands along her chest as he did.

"Oh, my god you feel so good," she said, rising on her knees and pressing his mouth to her breasts.

He reached down and unzipped her jeans. When he'd finished, she stood up in front of him and began sliding them off. He reached behind her with both hands, leaned forward and kissed her. She pulled his head against her.

"Graham," she groaned, softly. "Don't stop. Please don't stop. God, I want you."

He leaned back on the couch and pulled her on top of him. They kissed, wildly now, as his hands poured over her body. Her skin was astonishingly smooth, still moist from her perspiration and lotion.

She slid off the couch and knelt beside him. She ran her hand along his waist and unfastened his belt, slowly undoing his pants.

"Let's go upstairs," he said.

"No," she said, as she kissed his ear. "I want you right here."

If the outside gate slammed, he didn't hear it. But there was a knock on the door and he bolted upright. The girl looked up at him. He nodded.

"Who is it? she called.

"LAPD," came a woman's voice. "We'd like to ask you a few questions."

"Just a minute," the girl said. "I'll be right there."

They both scrambled to get dressed, although it would be obvious to even the densest officer what they had just interrupted.

"How do I look?" she asked. Her face was flushed, her hair was still wet and her nipples pressed against the thin, cotton shirt.

"Like someone who's just had a lovely orgasm," he said, as he straightened his clothes.

"Two, but who's counting," she said, leaning over and patting his crotch. "See what you can do about this. We don't want any incriminating evidence popping up—so to speak."

Moments later the girl returned to the room with two officers.

One was black, and from the looks of his uniform he was probably on motorcycle patrol. He was tall and powerfully built, and his tight-fitting uniform and highly polished black boots made him seem especially intimidating. The woman officer was short, athletically built, with cropped, badly bleached hair and a pinched, boyish face.

"I'm Officer LeBlanc of the LAPD," she said, pulling a notebook from her pocket. "This is Patrolman Cleveland of the traffic division. Are you aware of the shooting over at Riviera?"

"Yeah, we were just watching it on the news," the girl said.

"Could we have your names, please?" the woman officer asked.

"My name is Terry Gardner. I live here. This is my friend, Graham Archer."

"Have you two been here all afternoon?" the motorcycle patrolman asked.

"No, Terry was working and I was actually at the course when the shooting took place," he said. "Frightening thing. I understand the caddie died."

"We don't have that information, sir," the woman officer said. "Ms. Gardner, where do you work?"

"The Holiday Inn down on Sunset at the 405. I'm a waitress."

"You live here and work for tips at the Holiday Inn? Things must be better than when I was a waitress."

"The Seatons, who own the property, are family friends. I just kind of keep an eye on the place for them."

"The Seatons, are they out of town?" Officer LeBlanc asked. "We tried the main house but there didn't seem to be anyone around."

"They're supposed to be back tomorrow night," she answered. "Do you want me to have them call you?"

"We'll let you know," Patrolman Cleveland replied. "Did you both arrive at the same time? Did you plan to meet, say, at a certain time?"

"I actually got here a minute or two before Terry," he said. "I don't know what time it was. I was rushing to get out of the rain. I would say we've been here for 30 minutes or so. Maybe a little longer."

"And you haven't seen anyone around the property?" Cleveland asked. "Nobody suspicious?"

"No," he said.

"No," the girl agreed. "I mean we haven't actually been looking."

"Right," the patrolman said. "Listen, do you mind if we look around the property?"

"No, no, go right ahead," the girl said. "Let us know if we can help."

"We'll leave cards on your table, " said the woman officer. "If you think of anything that might help, please call."

The officers had walked just a few steps when Officer LeBlanc stopped and turned around.

"One last thing, Mr. Archer," she asked. "Do you live around here?"

"No, London. Just here on business."

"Where are you staying?" she asked.

"I checked out of the Holiday Inn this morning and thought I might drive north along the coast for a bit of sightseeing," he answered, lighting a cigarette and taking another drink of whiskey.

"When were you planning to leave, Mr. Archer?" Patrolman Cleveland asked. "Today? Tomorrow? Later in the week?"

Raines paused and inhaled on the cigarette.

"No firm plans, officer," he said. "As I say, just stealing a bit of holiday."

"Mr. Archer, if you weren't planning to leave tonight, where were you planning to stay?" Officer LeBlanc asked.

"Well...well, here, I'd hoped," he said, looking over at the girl.

"Ms. Gardner?" LeBlanc asked.

"We were going to go out for dinner and I just assumed Graham would stay here," she said.

"Ms. Gardner, how long have you two known each other?" LeBlanc asked.

"Long enough," the girl answered.

"Long enough for what?"

"Long enough for him to spend the night," the girl said, with an edge to her voice. "Do you have a problem with that?"

"No, just curious," LeBlanc replied, closing her notebook and putting it away. "We'll just be a few minutes out there."

The officers left and Raines and the girl watched as they walked around the pool, looking back along the rear wall. As they approached the pool house, Raines's stomach began to knot and beads of sweat began formed across his forehead. He stole a glance at the closet where he had hidden the waist pack containing the Glock. When the officer shined his flashlight into the darkened room, Raines felt the hair began to rise across the back of his neck. His head began to throb at the temples. He ran the last few hours back through his mind. Had he made any mistakes? Had he left any fingerprints? He held his breath.

"Graham, are you okay?" the girl asked.

"Yes, fine really," he sighed as the two officers left the pool house and headed back toward the cottage. "Still a bit stressed out, I suppose. Shall we go see if there's anything else they need?"

The two walked outside. The clouds were clearing off to the west, and the sun was breaking though. Raines felt the tension ease.

"Thank you for your help," the woman officer said. "The shooter is probably long gone by now, so you don't have anything to worry about. There'll be officers around for a while anyway, searching the area."

"The television reports said there are roadblocks set up," Raines asked. "If we wanted to go out for dinner, are we going to get caught up in traffic?"

"They should break them off by dinner time," the traffic patrolman said. "Whoever the shooter is, they ain't gonna get him at no roadblock. Not now. Thanks again. You've got our cards."

When the officers left, Raines turned and took the girl in his arms.

"What would you say to a little drive north?" he asked. "I've got some people to see in San Francisco who might be good for you to meet. We could leave first thing in the morning."

"But don't you want to see my reel first?" she asked.

"Yes," he said. "But I already know you can act."

• • •

Within minutes of the shooting, the Media Monster was in full-throated roar.

At the *New York Times*, editors scrambled to remake the early edition. The killing was teased in a box at the bottom right corner of the front page. It was the lead story in "SportsMonday," with a graphic, if restrained, AP photo. At the *Daily News* and the *Post*, it was a no-brainer. Both papers splashed the story across the front page, waiting as long as possible for the most gruesome photos the wires could move.

By the time the late editions were on press, the two papers had taken different spins on the story.

The *Post*, owned by Australian media magnate Rupert Murdoch, was quoting one of his London papers as saying the "victim, a veteran caddie named 'Speedball,' was a known drug dealer" and speculating that the killing was the result of a failed drug deal between the caddie and one of Los Angeles' notorious street gangs.

The late editions of the *Daily News* had a sidebar that quoted members of the city's black political establishment demanding an immediate investigation of what one termed "the apparent assassination attempt on our brother, Dexter Bradley." It was the spin that quickly got the biggest play as the story was dissected over the next few days.

At *Sports Illustrated*, the editors took advantage of their late Tuesday afternoon pressrun to plan their coverage. The managing editor, who in the old Time-Life tradition ruled with baronial power, ordered up all the available photos, and had alternate covers mocked up. If he wanted to, he could change the cover as late as Tuesday night. It would cost the magazine about $200,000. No one would question his decision.

The city's local television stations—like stations across the country—would follow the first and most basic rule of local television news: "If it bleeds, it leads." Naturally, viewers were warned that the footage was graphic and naturally, the more graphic the better.

At the three network morning shows—"Today," "Good Morning America", and CBS's "The Early Show"—producers scrambled to arrange interviews with players and PGA Tour officials. In the world of television news, if you had good video, you had a good story. That the shooting may have involved one of the most prominent black athletes in America, maybe the world, made it even stronger. All in all, the betting was that this would be a story with legs.

· · ·

It was just a few days later when some early morning surfers found a girl's body washed ashore at Morro Bay, halfway between Los Angeles and San Francisco. There were no signs of violence or foul play. Preliminary police reports listed the cause of death as an accidental drowning. There was no identification on the body. The only distinguishing mark was the small tattoo of a flower—a buckeye—on her left arm just above the wrist.

It took less than a week for local police to identify the body from a missing person's report filed in Los Angeles. Her name was Terry Gardner. She was 25. She was an actress.

She was also the daughter of Senator John M. Gardner of Ohio, the chairman of the Senate Intelligence Committee and one of the most powerful men in Washington.

Graham Raines had made his first big mistake.

CHAPTER FOUR

THE UPPER EAST SIDE | NEW YORK CITY | FEBRUARY

By every appearance, it was just another elegant old brownstone on a block lined with them. If it was in slightly better condition than most, it was because the building's owner had a virtually unlimited budget. The owner was the Central Intelligence Agency and the building was a throwback to the days of Allen Dulles, the Agency's first director. In those days, the Agency was like a club—a gathering place for the Ivy Leaguers who went off to World War II and came home to find that life as bankers, bond traders, and lawyers left something to be desired. This was one of their clubhouses, and its cost had always been buried in the "Black Holes"—the budgets immune from the ordinary congressional reviews.

To the schooled eye, however, it was clear this wasn't just any ordinary townhouse. The bulletproof glass in the windows was unusually thick. The fire hydrant on the sidewalk in front of the building had never been used. In fact, it wasn't attached to any water mains. It was there to create a "No Parking" zone in front of the building. It had been installed after the truck bombing of the Marine barracks in Beirut. The day after, in fact. On the roof was a collection of antennas and satellite dishes that picked up a lot more than ESPN.

The building had a variety of uses. The Agency used it for a safe house, when they had to keep assets out of view before getting them out of the country. It was a convenient place to meet with friendly members of foreign consulates and UN missions. And it was a place to do business away from Washington and Agency headquarters in Langley, Virginia where there were people who didn't need to know—but always wanted to know.

It was almost noon when Tom Quinn arrived at the front door and was immediately buzzed through to a small entranceway. After a moment, while he was checked by an unseen metal-scanning security device, he heard the lock click open on a second door and he was met by a young man.

"Mr. Quinn, it's good to see you. The Deputy Director is upstairs. May I take your coat?"

"Thanks," Quinn said. "Are the British here?"

"Arrived a few minutes ago, sir," the agent said. "Sir Owen and a woman. We've never seen her before."

"A woman?" Quinn asked. "Well, there goes the Empire."

As Tom Quinn climbed the old, curving staircase to the second floor, he thought about Sir Owen Tunnicliffe and the Deputy Director, Ladston Jackson III. Like the townhouse, they were from another time. They both came from wealthy families. "Laddie" Jackson's history ran deep in Virginia. The Jacksons pre-dated the revolution and had been one of the state's leading families for as long as anyone could remember. Laddie had been a popular and successful athlete at Princeton and likely would have become a lawyer if the war hadn't interrupted his studies. The Tunnicliffes were from Edinburgh and their fortune had been made in the woolen trade generations earlier. The two served together in the war as part of a secret organization made up of members of America's Office of Strategic Services and British Intelligence. Stories of their operations against the Nazis were legendary—if largely unreported to this day—on both sides of the Atlantic.

Following the war, they stayed in foreign intelligence work, moving steadily into influential positions. Neither man ever had sought or wanted the top job in either CIA or M.I.6, Britain's foreign intelligence service, preferring to stay out of the public eye. They shared a common if unspoken belief that close Anglo-

American cooperation was in the best interest of the world. The French and Germans were fine as far as they went, but for the most part they were meddlesome cousins who never quite measured up. The Russians were barbarians, barely a step removed from the savages that made up the so-called Third World. No, if there were to be world peace and prosperity, it would be best left to the British and the Americans.

Over the years, their friendship had been pivotal in helping the two countries over the rough spots. When the Suez Crisis broke in the '50s, they ran a back-channel operation that kept open the lines of communications between Eisenhower's staff and Whitehall, the British Foreign Office. When the Cuban Missile Crisis threatened to explode into war, Sir Owen passed along a secret proposal for a compromise from the Kennedys to an M.I.6 asset close to Khrushchev and then arranged for the Soviet's counteroffer to be made through a reliable American newsman. And when Margaret Thatcher decided to go to war with Argentina over the Falkland Islands, the British received the best and latest American intelligence—over the protests of State Department officials who disapproved of the CIA's involvement in a delicate foreign policy question.

Laddie Jackson could have cared less.

Last but not least, they shared a love of the sea and sailing. Over the years they had developed a ritual of exchanging gifts whenever they met. The gifts were always tied to the sea—paintings, scrimshaw, old model ships, that kind of thing. Occasionally they were expensive. They were always carefully—even painstakingly—selected. In an odd way it symbolized the depth of their friendship and the feelings the two men had for one another.

When Tom Quinn entered the Deputy Director's private dining room, the two men were carefully examining the small painting Sir Owen had brought from London. The painting rested on the dark, highly-polished dining room table, amid the exquisite silver, crystal, and familiar old china, eggshell white with navy trim. A woman that Tom figured was in her early 40s stood between the two men, as all three studied the painting.

"HMS Devonshire was one of the first corvettes in the fleet," Sir Owen explained, pointing out details with the stem of his pipe. "Gloriously fast ship, smaller than a frigate but as you see she covered a lot of sail. Now here, Miss Devlin, you'll notice she had just a single tier of cannons. Not much use against the likes of the great ships of the line but useful for coastal raiding and that sort of thing. Drove the French bloody mad in the West Indies."

The woman appeared to be enthralled, like a schoolgirl visiting her two favorite—if slightly eccentric—uncles. Tom had taken just a few steps into the room before she noticed the movement and glanced up.

Her looks were arresting. Her hair, light brown with streaks of blond, was pulled back off her face, which highlighted her blue-gray eyes and high cheekbones. Her skin had a tanned, faintly ruddy glow. Probably a pretty good athlete, he thought, or a fanatic about working out. She was dressed conservatively, in a dark wool dress that set off a single strand of pearls around her neck. The only other jewelry was a handsome gold Rolex and a small, well-worn gold signet ring. There was an awkward pause before the two old men looked up from the painting and realized Tom had arrived.

"Well, here he is now," said the Deputy Director. "How you doin' boy? Tommy, you remember Sir Owen, of course."

"Yes, nice to see you again, sir," he said, reaching over to shake the man's hand.

"And this is Miss Devlin of M.I.6," he continued. Unlike Sir Owen, whose accent could have been a model for the BBC's World Service, Laddie Jackson's was his and his alone. Sentences flowed on with a casual Southern grace, except when he was excited. Then the words would seem to jumble together. The bright, orange hair of his youth had thinned and faded, and now was largely white, but his blue eyes still sent off sparks of merriment and enthusiasm for life—particularly when there was an attractive woman in the room. "Miss Devlin, I want you to meet Tom Quinn."

"Kathryn, please," she said, extending her hand. "It's a pleasure to meet you. Sir Owen has told me a great deal about you."

"My pleasure," Tom said, shaking her hand.

Her handshake was firm but not hard, and her hands and arms were muscular. She carefully studied his face. Clearly, this was not some intelligence analyst brought over for a briefing. Unless he missed his guess, she was an operative and probably a very effective one at that.

"How was your flight?" the Deputy Director asked.

"Uneventful, sir," Tom answered.

"Well, that's at least somethin' to be thankful for these days, isn't it?" The Deputy Director checked his watch. "Would y'all like a cocktail before lunch? Miss Devlin? Don't be bashful now, 'cause you know old Owen and I are gonna have at least one."

"A scotch please, sir," she said. "With just a bit of soda."

"Wonderful, I was afraid you might be a white wine drinker or even worse, one of those Perrier drinkers," he said, at once dragging out and mangling the French pronunciation. It was classic Laddie Jackson, reflecting both his disdain for the country of origin and for people who drank the stuff. "Tom, what'll you have?"

"Scotch would be fine, sir—no soda, please," he said, deciding to save the white wine for lunch. He looked at the woman, and she gave him a small smile. At least she had appeared to have a sense of humor.

"Well, Thomas, now that you're planning to leave us for the world of high finance, I guess you better get used to a real drink at lunch every now and then," the DD said, pouring the four drinks. "This is Tom's last assignment for us," he said to Kathryn.

"Yes, and we're sorry to hear that," Sir Owen said. "Here's to your good fortune. Cheers."

A short while later, after some preliminary small talk, the four took their seats at the dining room table. Tom sat next to the Deputy Director and across from Kathryn. Within minutes, an older couple quietly entered the room and began to serve lunch— Dover sole garnished with sliced white grapes, baby peas and new red potatoes. The wine was a Bernadus Monterey County Chardonnay '94, particularly aromatic and richly flavored with excellent balance. Nothing that would overpower the delicacy of the fish.

After the couple left, discreetly shutting the heavy double doors behind them, the Deputy Director got right to the point.

"Tom, let me give you the background of this operation before we get into the details," he said. "We've been working real close with the British to help move along this damned Irish peace process. Until recently, things seemed to be going pretty well. A lot better than some of us had expected, to tell you the truth."

"But I'm afraid we've had a bit of a cock-up lately," Sir Owen said, taking a sip of wine to clear his palate. "It seems our agreement had the unintended consequence of causing a split in the IRA ranks. There's a splinter group that doesn't want any part of a peace accord—not with London, Dublin, the Unionists, or with their fellow Republicans."

"And that's what's behind the most recent bombings in London," the Deputy Director said.

"We're virtually certain of it," Sir Owen replied. The delicate clink of silver on china was the only other sound in the room. "But I'm afraid that's only the half of it. The leader of the splinter faction is a particularly fanatic old-timer named Martin McGonagle. I suspect he's quite psychopathic. Terror for the sake of terror. Can't be reasoned with. What we view as a peace process and our Irish friends view as taking the best deal possible, McGonagle sees as treachery, pure and simple. In recent weeks he's struck back, first with the bombings and then the shootings of two of the IRA moderates."

"Killings?" Tom asked.

"No, the traditional Irish favorite," Sir Owen said. "Kneecappings. Pity, they were young men, too."

He put down his knife and fork and leaned forward. "What's worse," he said, "beyond showing he can bring the war to London, we have evidence that McGonagle's vowed to bring it here, to punish the United States for your efforts in trying to bring the parties together."

"You can't be serious," Tom said.

"Quite serious, I'm afraid," Kathryn said, looking straight into Tom's eyes. "You know that shooting at a golf tournament in Los Angeles? A caddie was killed."

"Yes," Tom replied.

"What do you make of it?" she asked, focusing intently upon him.

"Well, I *don't* think it was a drug deal that went south," he said. "You don't take out a low-level guy with a high-powered rifle in front of thousands of people and half the LAPD."

"You don't think he was a dealer then?" she asked.

"He may well have been, but that's not what bought him a bullet," Tom said.

"Tom, we planted that story with a friendly British newspaperman immediately after the shooting," Sir Owen said. "Unfair to the man's family, to be sure, but we had to buy some time. What about the speculation that the black golfer was the target?"

"I doubt it," Tom said. "If someone wanted to kill him they'd be doing it to make a statement. It's been over a week and there hasn't been a peep from the usual suspects. At least there hasn't been anything credible. If there had been, the FBI would have leaked it all over town."

"Actually, we have information we believe to be rock solid that McGonagle has hired a contract assassin to kill Peter Brookes, the British golfer," Devlin explained. "Surely you're familiar with him, being a superior golfer yourself."

M.I.6 certainly does its homework, Tom thought. And isn't above a little flattery, either.

"That's news that would certainly warm all his ex-wives' hearts," Tom replied, and paused for a second. "It was Brookes's caddie that was killed. Your theory makes as much sense as anything else."

"We believe the shooter is a man named Graham Raines," Sir Owen said. "He's a freelancer. A Londoner. As best we can tell, he's dropped from sight. Neither M.I.5 nor Scotland Yard can find hide nor hair of him."

"Surely he's left the country by now," the Deputy Director said.

"We don't think so, sir," Kathryn Devlin said, taking a thick manila envelope from her shoulder bag and sliding it across the table to Tom. "McGonagle has considerable resources. He can make it well worth Raines's while to try again. And Raines will simply take this as an even greater challenge. We've worked up a complete dossier for you. His psychological profile, history, tendencies and so on. This is not a man to be taken at all lightly."

"But why would McGonagle want to kill Peter Brookes?" Tom asked as he opened the envelope and pulled out its contents.

"For starters," Kathryn said, "it didn't help that at last year's Irish Open, he told a local newspaperman that he—and I quote directly—'didn't understand why the bloody Boggies couldn't get over it and get along with each other like the rest of the civilized world.'"

"So he's stupid," Tom replied. "The last time I looked, death wasn't the punishment for stupidity."

Sir Owen's growing exasperation was obvious.

"Good God, Tom, he's the best athlete we've produced in decades, perhaps since the war. America turns out champions like Hershey bars. They're nothing special here. Why, just last year Brookes received the OBE. It was huge news. If the IRA can reach across the Atlantic and kill our most popular athlete, well, you can see what a frightening message that sends."

The Deputy Director leaned back in his chair, sighed, and removed his old, half-moon reading glasses. "All seen by tens of millions of people on television around the world," he said. "God, you've got to admire their audacity. It's brilliant. Terrifying, but brilliant."

Sir Owen looked squarely at his old friend, as he had so often before in times of crisis.

"Laddie, as I told you when we spoke earlier, Raines must be stopped, however that's done," he said. "The English people are weary of this bloodshed. So are our Irish cousins, truly. With your country's help in brokering this peace effort, we have played what could possibly be our last, best trick in the awful hand we've been dealt by history. We dare not fail now. What McGonagle has done is nothing short of declaring war for the heart and soul of the IRA. If he succeeds—if Raines kills Brookes and McGonagle can finally destroy the peace initiative—all our work will be for naught, and the cycle of violence will be one hundred times worse than ever before. But like you, we cannot have our fingerprints upon this. Discretion is everything. I shall leave that to your good judgment."

"Owen, you know this is going to need a very high clearance," Laddie Jackson said. "I've given a strong recommendation to the Director. Whether he takes it any higher is up to him."

"If he does, what's your read?" Sir Owen asked.

"The White House has invested a lot in the peace process," the Deputy Director said. "They need a big foreign policy win going into the off-year elections. If it has to go to the Senate Select Committee on Intelligence, it could be a tougher sell. This kind of thing makes the chairman, Senator Gardner, very nervous. He's been burned before. And as a Republican, he's not inclined to do any favors for the President this close to the elections. But right now though, I'd put the odds in our favor. I'll call the Director this afternoon and try to push him for approval."

"Fine, thank you," Sir Owen said. "Gentlemen, Miss Devlin here knows more about Raines than anyone in the world. I have her service record here. I assure you it is impeccable. Assuming we receive approval for this operation, it is my strongest request that she be allowed to work with you. Further, you know our admiration for Tom. I should think they'd be a formidable team."

The Deputy Director turned and looked at Tom. He felt Sir Owen's gaze on him as well.

"Tom, this is your call," the Deputy Director said. "Win or lose, it's going to be a hell of a way for you to go out the door."

Tom didn't kid himself for a second that this was his call. Once the Deputy Director and Sir Owen had come this far down the road, Tom knew he and Kathryn were in this together, for better or worse, no matter what he thought. He looked dead into her eyes. They betrayed not even the slightest emotion.

"Welcome to America," he said, after a moment.

"Thank you," she said, nodding slightly. "This shall be exciting."

"Let's just hope it's not too exciting," Tom said. "Tell me more about your shooter."

"Graham Raines had, at one point, a most promising future in the Special Air Service which, as you know, is roughly our equivalent of your Green Berets," she explained. "In the Falklands War, we had intelligence reports indicating that the Argentineans were prepared to use tactical nuclear weapons against our forces. Elite units of the SAS were sent into Argentina. Had those weapons been deployed, they had orders to neutralize certain members of the military dictatorship using whatever means necessary. Until that time, however, each five-man team had strict orders to avoid engaging the enemy. Raines violated those orders. There was a firefight. Two members of his team were killed. He was captured along with two of his men."

Sir Owen interrupted.

"The Argentineans were particularly brutal in their treatment of prisoners," he said. "Raines and his men were taken to the Navy Mechanics School in Buenos Aires. Perhaps you're familiar with it. It was where they did some of their most hellish work during their so-called 'Dirty War.' Killed 30,000 of their own people. A favorite trick was to take prisoners up in military aircraft and threaten to push them out over the Atlantic."

"So Raines was given a VIP flight on Air Junta," Tom said. "I can't say that I blame the poor bastard for folding."

"No one did, but the revelation that we had assassination teams in Argentina caused a serious diplomatic problem," Sir Owen continued. "We were only lucky that the war was short-lived or it could have been much worse. When Raines returned to England he was quietly court-martialed for violating orders and needlessly endangering the lives of his men. He was found guilty and dismissed from the service."

"Whether it was the torture or the humiliation of the court-martial, Raines seemed to snap," Kathryn explained. "We began getting information that he was for hire. We know of two killings he committed in South Africa alone, and are certain there are others. Most likely he was involved in the killings by the E.T.A., the Basque separatists, in Spain last year. He's also been kept busy in the Middle East, as you might expect. He's totally nonpolitical. It's strictly business with him."

"How can you be sure he's the shooter in Los Angeles?" Tom asked.

"We have intercepts of McGonagle's telephone calls," Devlin said. "The electronic voiceprints on some of the calls match Raines's voice. They're both too smart, of course, to say anything that's directly incriminating, but it's not too difficult to make the connection. Also, the details of the shooting point to him. It would take someone very skilled and very confident to attempt something so difficult. It fits his profile."

"And you think his ego will lead him to try again?" Tom asked.

"In a perverse way, it's not so much his ego as his need to rebuild his ego," she explained. "Prior to the incident in Argentina he saw himself as an elite within an elite. Suddenly, that was shattered. The fact that he's one of the most highly regarded mercenaries in the world—however deplorable one might find that—provides a certain reaffirmation."

"Why not just get Brookes to lie low for a while, until Raines surfaces?" Tom asked.

"We believe it's important to get Raines now," Sir Owen said. "If it's known within the IRA that Brookes has been forced into hiding, it might still be seen as a victory for McGonagle and a potential blow to the peace process."

"What if Brookes doesn't see it that way?" Tom asked.

"Yes, well we're not sure that telling him right now is the proper strategy for just that reason," Sir Owen said. "If he continues to play, we believe he will eventually draw Raines out into the open, and probably sooner rather than later."

"That's why we brought you in, Tom," the Deputy Director said. "We need someone who can fit in on the Tour. You're totally familiar with the game and that, coupled with your previous dealings with counterterrorism, gives you a certain unique expertise."

"Does the Tour know about any of this?" Tom asked.

"Not yet," the Deputy Director said. "Again, we'd like to play this as close to the vest as possible. Any leaks could drive off Raines. Right now the Tour is a spin machine. They want desperately to knock down the story that this was an attempt on Dexter Bradley's life. The longer that story stays alive, the better for us. If, in fact, Raines is our man he won't suspect we're on to him. Maybe we'll get lucky and he'll get careless."

"That's counting on a lot of luck," Tom said. "What's the next step?"

"The Tour is in San Diego next week," the Deputy Director said. "Brookes took this week off and is scheduled to play for the first time since the shooting. Assuming we get approval from Langley, you two should plan to fly out as soon as possible. While you're there, why don't you drive on up to Los Angeles and see what you can learn about the shooting. We'll arrange for press credentials for both of you. That will get you whatever access you need."

The Deputy Director sat back in his chair and smiled at Tom. "In a way, the golf connection is somehow appropriate. Your last assignment brings you full circle."

"Well, I just hope I have more success this time around," Tom said. "All that first year taught me was that I wasn't as good as I thought I was."

"Sometimes that's a very good lesson to learn early on in life," Sir Owen said. "Good luck to both of you. And Godspeed."

CHAPTER FIVE

Anyone relying upon Sir Owen Tunnicliffe's description of Martin McGonagle would have been hard-pressed to pick him from among the patrons of the Lock-Keeper's Inn in this small dot on the map 20 miles southwest of Belfast.

The man who sat alone, sipping tea at a table in a rear corner of the pub, looked for all the world like a retired accountant. A small man, McGonagle's thinning white hair was neatly trimmed and the soft pink skin of his face looked as though it had never been touched by a razor. Indeed, far from appearing to be a criminal fanatic, the man who sat reading the afternoon paper seemed utterly at peace with himself and his world.

But the truth was that Martin McGonagle had rarely known anything approaching tranquility. For as long as he could remember, his life had been consumed by the struggle against the Protestant majority, its British protectors, and all those who would bring their so-called peace to his homeland. The fight had cost him a son. It had occasionally cost him his freedom. And now, with his health slowly fading, it had cost him a chance to quietly live out his final days.

Even as a child, Martin McGonagle had been fascinated by numbers. He loved the discipline and precision that came with mathematics. Things either added up or they didn't. The numbers provided his private escape from the grinding poverty of Derry, and in the end they became the route he would take to university and an engineering career that was successful beyond any of his childhood dreams.

But for all his love of logic and order, he had a particular genius for understanding and navigating the murky waters of Irish—and Irish Republican Army—politics, where the first and only firm rule was that there were no rules. As a leader in Sinn Fein, the political arm of the IRA, he had studied the American civil rights movement and learned his lessons well, organizing massive peaceful protests and seizing the moral high ground against the Protestants and the British government. By the late 1960s, as improbable as it may have seemed, McGonagle's strategy was succeeding, and putting enormous pressures on the ruling Unionists in and around Belfast and their British brethren.

It would be a mistake—and a mistake that many of his enemies made at the time—to think that McGonagle had somehow gone soft or had sworn off the gun and the bomb. Nothing could be further from the truth. By the time the bloody "Battle of the Bogside" spread through Northern Ireland in 1969, McGonagle and his fellow Provisionals had plotted to take back the IRA from the Marxist/Leninist/Trotskyites that had taken over the organization in its fallow period, when the joke was that IRA stood for little more than "I'll Run Away." The Communists loved to discuss political theory endlessly and go on about their "Solidarity" with the other oppressed people of the world. For McGonagle and his followers, the time for talking was over. The bombings would begin.

For the next three years, McGonagle's Provisional IRA would plant no fewer than 150 bombs in Belfast alone. West Belfast was in such a state of civil collapse that it became known as "The Wild, Wild West." In 1973, the British began their hated "Internment," a policy that allowed them to jail suspected IRA members without trial. The IRA responded by killing 40 people by the end of the year. The British met force with force while reaching out to the Provisionals with the offer of secret peace talks. Still, in a country where hatreds went back generations, even centuries, any movement toward reconciliation was painfully slow.

McGonagle, then in his 50s, was receptive to the British overtures. He knew the Unionists had been weakened and now was the time for the IRA to press its advantage with a Labour government. McGonagle figured, correctly as it turned out, that the weakened Labourites would soon be forced to call a general election, and instead of negotiating with James Callaghan, the IRA could well be facing a far more formidable foe in the Tory leader, Margaret Thatcher.

All that changed, however, when his only son, Sean, was killed one evening as he returned home with his wife and small daughter. No one was ever charged in the shooting. The British assured McGonagle that it was the work of his opponents within the IRA. Nobody else thought anyone in the IRA would be foolish enough to strike at Martin McGonagle in such a treacherous way. Not then. Not when he was at the height of his power. And no one was surprised when a few months later the IRA struck back with their most daring single act of violence: the 1979 assassination of Lord Louis Mountbatten, the 1st Earl of Burma and a cousin of Queen Elizabeth II.

McGonagle may have been alone at the table but he was far from alone in the pub when his visitors arrived. Two men were posted on either side of the door. One sat near McGonagle at the bar. One waited outside with his car. All were heavily armed.

Two of the men that joined McGonagle at his table that night at the Lock-Keeper's Inn were still teenagers when the bombs went off that killed Lord Mountbatten. They were of a generation that had regarded the old man with a respect bordering on reverence. The third man was one of McGonagle's oldest friends, Eamon O'Shea. None of them looked forward to the confrontation they knew awaited them.

McGonagle was never one for small talk, even under the best of circumstances, and since he knew what lay at the heart of this meeting he was anxious to get on with it.

"Martin, you look very well," O'Shea said, as he gently took McGonagle's hand. "This wet weather must be hell on your arthritis."

"Gentlemen, my health is fine, my family is fine, and the weather is fine," he said, in a voice that was quiet but firm. He paused as the barman brought over a round of drinks. "What's not fine is my mood and unless I very much miss my guess, it's not going to get a bit better as this evening wears on, so let's get down to business."

"Martin, we've been asked to make one last effort to get you to understand our position," O'Shea said. "You and yours are the last holdouts and the clock is ticking."

"But it's not that I don't understand your position, Eamon," McGonagle said, clasping his hands under the table to hide the twitches—the slow, steady shaking that evidenced his advancing Parkinson's disease. "In fact, I understand it far better than any of you do. The point is that I disagree with it. It's a disastrous policy. You can dress up surrender and call it a peace, but at the end of the evening, you're still a beaten man."

"But sir," one of the young men said. "This time it's different. This time we have the backing of the Americans..."

McGonagle turned and dismissed him with a wave of his arm. As he did, his fading eyesight caught the glimpse of light reflecting off an expensive watch and the gold chain around the man's neck. Such a garish display of newfound wealth only served to heighten the old man's suspicions

"The Too-ra-loo-ra-loo-ras," McGonagle hissed. "The once-a-year Irish. Give them a funny hat and a free beer and they're your friends for life."

"Martin, that's being a bit harsh now," O'Shea said. "They've invested a lot in this process. It's in their interest to see that investment pay off."

"Investment," McGonagle said. "It's interesting that you should use that word. I don't suppose that any of you read in the paper about the lovely visit the American Secretary of the Treasury made to The City of London the other day?"

McGonagle looked at each of the men seated around the table. Clearly, none had seen the story.

"Well, if you'd read more than the racing charts you might learn something," McGonagle said, dismissively. "The Yank went on in his way about the so-called 'Special Relationship' between London and Washington. You would have thought Roosevelt and that murdering bastard Churchill were saints sent down from Heaven. But tucked away in the fine print was the *real* special relationship between the two countries. The facts are that the Yanks are the biggest foreign investors in the U.K. and the Brits are the biggest investors in the States. They're joined at the purse like Siamese twins. Don't talk to me about their commitment to the peace process. They're committed to their money and their money alone. And if you think any differently, you're as dumb as that door over there."

"Martin," O'Shea said. "You've been removed from the talks— by your own hand, I might add. Truly, things are different this time 'round. If you'd involve yourself you'd see that."

"Eamon, you of all people should know better," McGonagle said. Under the table, his hands shook violently as he grew angrier. "The actors change. The words change. But the play remains the same. I wouldn't so much as step in the same room with the bastards and if your so-called leaders continue with this disgrace, then they're fools or traitors or both."

One of the young men slammed both fists down on the table, rose, and leaned toward McGonagle. As he did, the men at the door and at the bar moved toward the table, their hands reaching for their guns.

"We came here as a courtesy but we don't have to listen to this from you," he said, his face twisted in rage. "Your day is done. You're a relic, you and your boyos running about the countryside like banshees. The boat is leaving the dock. You can be on it or be left behind with your memories and not much else."

McGonagle and the man stared at one another. There wasn't a sound in the room.

"Come on," the man said. "We're wasting our time here." He reached into his pocket, removed a large handful of bills, and threw a few down on the table to cover the drinks.

"This is our treat," he said. "I don't want to feel that we owe you a thing."

The two younger men walked toward the door. As they did, McGonagle's men watched their every move and followed them outside.

"I'm sorry, Martin," O'Shea said. "There's a lot of frustration about. People say things they don't really mean. We genuinely believe this is for the best."

"Then go back and read your history," McGonagle said, with resignation in his voice. "While you're at it, read up on your Bible. Matthew 26.14."

O'Shea rose and clasped his friend's shoulder.

"I'm afraid I'm not much up on the Bible these days," O'Shea said. "It's been a long time since my days with the sisters at St. Bridget's."

"Just read it and you'll recognize it," McGonagle said. "One last thing, Eamon. Tell your friends there won't be any boat leaving the dock. A boat can't leave if it's burned to the waterline."

CHAPTER SIX

Their flight on an Agency Lear jet was somewhere over the Rockies when Tom finished the M.I.6 report on Graham Raines. Everything you could possibly want to know about the man was in the report, including some things that were frightening to learn. He was every bit as dangerous as Kathryn Devlin had said, possibly even more so.

But for all the information about Raines, some questions stilled nagged at Tom. There were things about this assignment that didn't make any sense.

For starters, if Peter Brookes was the biggest thing in Britain since Churchill, why was M.I.6 willing to dangle him out there as bait? If Raines was as good as he seemed on paper, he wouldn't go 0-for-2.

And why get the CIA involved? It's against the law for the Agency to operate in America. Everyone knows that. If this thing blew up, heads would roll from one end of Pennsylvania Avenue to the other. Why not let the FBI take over? Or at least help out? The only possible answer was that M.I.6 and the CIA were desperate to keep this as quiet as possible and the FBI was notorious for grabbing headlines. It was what J. Edgar Hoover did best, and the tradition lived on.

As he gazed out the window toward the snow-covered mountains below, his thoughts were interrupted by Kathryn in the seat across from him.

"What I want to know is how you managed to make your first assignment with the Agency a jaunt around the world playing in golf tournaments?" she asked.

He turned to look at her.

"It was really sort of ingenious. I had been planning to play in Europe with a friend of mine, Pres Elliott. When I mentioned that to the people who recruited me into the agency, you could see the wheels turning. I actually started out as sort of a glorified courier but it was a perfect cover. No one ever suspected a golfer would be doing anything but playing in tournaments and sightseeing, let alone anything that might require even the smallest amount of thought. I could meet with our people and if there was any material that we needed to get back to the States, we had ways of doing that, too. It worked so well in Europe that I did it for a while in the Caribbean and in South America. It was a great education, it was fun, and it got golf out of my system."

"So by the time you were through, you'd decided to quit golf?" she asked.

"No, but I realized I couldn't make a living at it," Tom said. "Actually, it wasn't a hard decision to make. I was paired in the first round of a tournament in Scotland with a guy named Lanny Wadkins. It was a brutally tough course and I played as well as I possibly could. Better than I knew how, really. I shot a 69, which was three under par. Lanny shot a 67 and was steaming. He absolutely believed he should birdie every hole. He was just that much better than me. Forget guys like Nicklaus. They're gods. But Lanny back then was so much better than me that it kind of shocked me back to reality. I'm glad I gave it a shot, but it was a real wake-up call."

"So now you're moving on to a career in finance," Kathryn said. "I'm surprised, frankly. It sounds dreadfully boring."

"Call it a midlife crisis," Tom said. "Some guys toss over their wives for younger women. Other guys buy expensive sports cars. I don't have a wife and I can't afford a Porsche, so this is the next best thing. Besides, I'm not sure you ever completely quit the

Agency. Like my friend Pres says, it's a 'Hotel California' job. You can check out anytime you like, but you can never leave."

"And you were married once, right?" she asked.

"Sure, happily married for three years," Tom said. "Unfortunately we were married for five. It wasn't anyone's fault, really. My work seemed romantic and exciting at first, but the reality was that I was gone a lot. She wanted kids, and for me to settle down. Ironically, she wanted me to do what I'm going to do now—quit the Agency and get a real job. Maybe she was right and I'm just a slow learner. Anyway, it was a long time ago. What about you? How did you wind up at M.I.6?"

"Rather the opposite of you," she said. "I read for economics at university. After graduation I worked in the City for a time, then joined M.I.6, doing economic analysis. After a bit of that, I became bored and moved into operations. Did a stint in South Africa as a political attaché, then moved back to Europe when the Soviet Union began to break up. For the past year or so I've been assigned to our work in Northern Ireland."

"How's it going?" Tom asked.

"Frustrating as hell," she said. "Every time we have a cease-fire the relief and joy is palpable. But then it starts all over again. The truth is a few small groups have their little slices of power and they won't give them up. I honestly believe it's no longer about the British staying or leaving or Ulster joining the Republic. It's about holding on to power, saving face, and settling old scores. Unfortunately, they've all got so many weapons stashed away—both the IRA and the Ulstermen—that even the slightest disagreement leads to violence and the cycle begins anew."

"Tell me about McGonagle," Tom said. "How does he fit in all this?"

"He's a throwback to the old IRA," she said. "His father was active in the IRA and like most Catholics in the north, he experienced his fair share of problems with the Protestant majority. Like everyone else he probably sees the writing on the wall. There's too much support for peace for the madness to continue indefinitely. But McGonagle won't accept that. He's a true believer. He and his cadre will fight on and oppose anyone willing to compromise. In his mind, they're traitors to the cause, pure and simple. I should think he's the wild card in the entire process. In an odd way, I almost respect him. At least he actually believes in something. He's not a street punk or a would-be Trotskyite like so many of the dregs in the IRA now."

"Have your intercepts picked up any contact between Raines and McGonagle since the shooting?" Tom asked.

"No, but our surveillance of the airports hasn't picked Raines up either," she said. "It's a safe bet he's still here."

Tom stared out the window for a moment. In the reflection, he could see Kathryn looking at him.

"I've arranged for a video of the shooting to be delivered to the hotel," Tom said. "It should be there when we check in. Tomorrow, let's head over to the course. We'll pick up our credentials and look around. Langley has arranged for a confidential briefing by a senior Los Angeles police official. Our story is that we believe the shooting was connected to Mexican drug cartels. That at least gives us a pretext for CIA involvement. Obviously, we can't mention M.I.6."

"That's fine," Kathryn said. "I'm still a bit jet-lagged. I think I'll try to steal a nap."

She reached up and turned off the overhead light, then eased her seat back and closed her eyes. Tom glanced at her briefly then looked back out the window. The sun was starting to set, casting the Rockies in a soft, purplish glow. Kathryn Devlin was very bright, he thought. And very beautiful. But most of all he wondered what secrets she knew.

• • •

Naturally, there was a screwup when they tried to check in at the Sheraton Hotel at Torrey Pines. The clerk had a reservation for Tom but none for Kathryn Devlin.

"I'm very sorry," the young man said. "We understood that you were staying together."

"Nice try," Kathryn said, turning to Tom and rolling her eyes.

"Budget constraints," Tom said.

To make up for their mistake, the hotel upgraded her to a suite on the top floor, with a view of the Pacific out over the cliffs of La Jolla—a vista that was considerably better than Tom's view of a parking lot. As they finished registering, Tom asked the clerk if there had been a FedEx delivery for him. The man went into the back and returned in a moment.

"I'm sorry, there's nothing back there, but FedEx doesn't deliver on Sunday," the clerk said. "They usually come by around 10 in the morning. I'll leave a note for the front desk to call your room as soon as the package arrives."

The next morning, when they left the hotel to walk over to the golf course, there was a small but loud line of protesters demanding that the Tour increase its security for Dexter Bradley. The local television stations were covering the protest as part of their morning news shows.

"I thought you said Dexter Bradley wasn't playing this week," Kathryn said, as they made their way around the protesters. "I was looking forward to seeing him play after all I've heard about him."

"He's not, but why ruin a good protest," Tom said, turning to look back at the hotel. "Four floors. Not much of a risk there. A shooter couldn't get enough elevation. Just to be on the safe side, when we get back to the hotel, take a couple photos of Raines and leave them with the front desk and the bell stand. Tell them he's an old boyfriend you want to surprise. Say there's a 50 in it for anyone who sees him and calls you. Maybe we'll catch a break."

After picking up their press credentials, they headed out to look at the golf courses. The North and South courses at Torrey Pines were owned by the City of San Diego and while they might not be as great as Pebble Beach or Cypress Point, they were fiercely defended civic institutions. The South course, which was the stronger of the two, would see play for all four rounds, so they decided to walk that one first. As they headed toward the ocean, the sun began to warm the air and burn off some of the morning fog. It wasn't quite 9:30 but there were already hang gliders sailing off the cliffs, riding the gentle morning winds that swept in off the water and up over the beach. By the time they had reached the fifth tee, they had a spectacular view of the Pacific, stretching as a backdrop for the fourth green. Not far offshore, migrating whales swam by. All in all, it was about as good as California gets which, as people from California are quick to point out, is about as good as life gets.

When they had finished walking both courses, it was early in the afternoon and they had decided that if you tried to pick a difficult place for a shooting, you couldn't find one more problematic than Torrey Pines. There were no tall buildings to speak of. The ocean and the cliffs blocked off the courses to one side. Access, particularly during a tournament, was restricted. No, while Kathryn might be right and the odds on Raines trying again might be good, the chances of him trying at Torrey Pines were virtually nil. Not unless he was desperate or mad or suicidal—and he was clearly none of the three as far as Tom could tell.

After a quick lunch at the course, they returned to the hotel. Tom picked up the FedEx package at the front desk, and they took the elevator to Kathryn's suite. It was the third time Tom had watched tapes of the shooting and it was no less gruesome this time around. At the moment when the caddie was shot and tumbled over, Tom stole a glance at Kathryn. She stared straight at the screen. Her expression never changed, never betraying even the slightest emotion. She was cold, clinical, and completely detached, like a surgeon observing a particularly difficult and dangerous operation.

Toward the end of the tape, there was footage taken from the blimp as it passed over the golf course. Because of the storm, the images were shaky but the blimp was flying lower than usual, trying to stay out of the strong winds. Tom watched the footage play out, then rewound the tape and watched it again, this time sitting very close to the television.

"What are you looking for?" Kathryn asked.

"I'm not sure, really," Tom said. "But there are things about this shooting that don't make any sense, no matter how many times I watch it. Look, a guy gets shot but no one sees anything suspicious? No one sees the shooter coming or going with anything that looks like a gun? And how does the shooter escape? The roads are all blocked off and the place is crawling with cops. Where'd the shooter go? I just thought I might see something in those overheads that would give us a clue."

"But there's not," Kathryn said.

"Not on this tape but there must be other footage that never got on-air, right?" Tom said. "Some of those overheads were recorded at the beginning of the day, before the storm hit."

"How do you know?" Kathryn asked.

"Because the weather was almost perfect when those were

shot," Tom said. "Think back. The pictures were spectacular. Everything was bright and sunny but off in the distance, over the ocean, they showed storm clouds and the announcer said they were expecting some weather. Remember that?"

"Right," she said. "But by the time the telecast started, the weather was already quite ominous."

"Exactly, so if they recorded all that footage, maybe the tapes are still available," Tom said. "Better yet, maybe the police seized them as evidence. We have that meeting in Los Angeles tomorrow. I'll call and see if they have the tapes. If they do, let's take a look and see what turns up."

They were in luck. The police had impounded all the tapes right after the shooting and would have them available for screening the next day.

The meeting was moved to a small video production company in Santa Monica, in part so they could screen the tapes, in part because Captain of Detectives L.C. Edwards didn't want anyone in the department wondering who these two people were and why they were looking at potential evidence. The studio was set in a side street off Santa Monica Boulevard, in an old stucco building. If it was a little rundown on the outside, the inside was state of the art. The furniture in the reception area was covered with dark, expensive leather and the lighting was subdued. A reel of some of the company's work ran continuously on a large Sony monitor. A receptionist led them to a small, windowless conference room at the end of a hallway, where Edwards was waiting.

Edwards was short and wiry, with closely trimmed hair and gold wire-rimmed glasses. He was probably in his late-40s and his voice still carried the traces of a Haitian or Jamaican accent. He was very businesslike, even formal, and after the introductions got right to the point.

"First of all, I am very happy to help you as much as possible, but you must understand that this is a very high-profile case and my people are extremely nervous," he said. "There's a lot of pressure to break it quickly and we don't have much to work with. Is it your understanding that this is somehow connected with Mexican drug cartels?"

"We think so," Tom said. "Although we're a long way from making a specific connection. That's why we need your help. The trail has gone very cold very fast. We think the shooter may already be back across the border."

"So you don't think the perp was aiming at Dexter Bradley?" Edwards asked.

"I don't," Tom said. "But let me ask you what you've heard. Anyone claiming credit?"

"Frankly no, except for about the usual number of crank calls you always get in something like this," Edwards said. "That's one reason we're leaning toward your theory. It's the only one that seems to make sense, unless you buy into the theory that Brookes, the British golfer, was the target."

"Who would want to shoot him?" Kathryn asked.

"Exactly," Edwards said.

"What do you have so far?" Tom asked.

"Not much, I'm afraid," Edwards said, leaning back in his chair. "Ballistics told us where the shot came from. It was a house on Capri owned by a family named"—he paused to find the name on a report—"Cunningham. They were away for the weekend. Came back late Monday night. Their maid was supposed to have been there but no one can find her. Probably an illegal. They usually disappear at the first sign of trouble. There was no indication she was injured and the only sign of a struggle were some pieces of duct tape that were probably used to bind her hands and feet. It wouldn't have taken much time or effort to work out of those."

"What about the weapon? Anything there?" Kathryn asked.

"No, except that whoever is the shooter, he knows what he's doing," Edwards said. "The bullet was a dum-dum. You only use those when you mean to kill. That kid was damned near dead by the time he hit the ground. And this guy is good. We went all through that house and never found a thing. Not a shred of evidence that we can pin on anyone."

"How'd he get away?" Tom asked. "We watched the tape. You had guys all over the place. It was textbook."

"He went into thin air, man," Edwards said, shaking his head. "We had people going door-to-door. Roadblocks. We didn't turn a thing."

"What about the house, the Cunningham house?" Kathryn asked. "When did you get in there?"

"We had guys over the fence right after the shooting but the doors were locked and no one came to the door when they knocked. They just figured the place was empty and moved on. We got a warrant right after the crime scene unit made their preliminary report but we came up empty."

"And the Cunninghams have no idea where their maid is?"

"No, like I said, around here the chances are she's an illegal," Edwards explained. "She'd arrive by bus on Monday morning and leave Friday night. It was probably just a fluke if she was there over the weekend. She was paid in cash. Hell, I don't even think they know her last name. She's just dear old Rosa to them."

"That's it, then?" Kathryn said.

"I'm afraid that's all we've got," Edwards said. "That and a lot of heat. Anything you can turn up, I'd appreciate. Here's my beeper number. If you need to reach me, use that. The tapes you wanted are in those boxes. I don't know what you expect to find but I hope you've got a lot of time to look 'cause there's a lot of tapes. When you finish, call me and I'll arrange to have them picked up."

Edwards left and a few minutes later the receptionist arrived with a half-dozen take-out menus from local restaurants, a tray of Cokes and a staggering assortment of bottled waters. She took their orders and left. There must have been at least 25 cassettes in the first box, which meant that there might be as many as 100 cassettes in all.

"We'll be here for a month," Tom said, picking up one of the tapes.

"Maybe not, most of these are marked," Kathryn said, going through a second box. "Let's see if there are any marked 'Blimp' or 'Overheads.'"

They found three that looked promising and were just beginning to review them when the receptionist returned with their food.

"Are you going to watch all these tapes?" the woman asked.

"No, we're looking for some specific shots," Tom said. "We're just not sure where they are."

"Well, what you should do is hit the preview button and then hit fast-forward," she said. "With these Beta machines you can screen tapes really fast. When you get to something you're interested in, just hit the play button and it will run the tape at a normal speed."

It was incredibly boring work. The room was cold and after a while watching the flickering, high-speed images began to give Tom a headache. By 6 o'clock, they had gone through all "Blimp" cassettes in slow motion and hadn't seen a thing. They had previewed at least 30 other tapes and come up empty. Frustration was beginning to set in.

"Let's get out of here and get some fresh air," Kathryn said. "This air-conditioning has chilled me to the bone."

"Hey, wait a second. Let's take a look at this," Tom said. "It's marked 'Beauty 1.' Let's see what's on it."

He slid the cassette into the machine. It made a humming noise and swallowed the tape. There was a click and a series of color bars appeared on screen. The image quivered slightly and then the top of the Riviera clubhouse appeared. People around the clubhouse looked up and waved toward the camera. The blimp was heading west, toward the ocean. As it floated along, people on the street and in small groups in houses on the hillside looked up. The camera panned along the 18th hole, then rose slowly for a panoramic shot out toward the ocean. Then the screen went black. Tom reached over to hit the rewind button and, just as he did, the image returned. This time it was back panning along the street. The tape ran on for a few more seconds, 10 maybe at the most, before it went to black.

"Damn, that's it," Tom said. "C'mon let's get out of here."

He ejected the tape, put it on the table, turned off the machine, and they headed out the door, walking down the hall. He told the receptionist they'd be back in an hour or so and they made their way down the street onto Santa Monica Boulevard. They had walked for about a quarter-mile when he suddenly stopped.

"Let's go," he said. He ran as hard as he could, and she kept up, dodging people on the sidewalk as they did. When they reached the production house, he burst through the front door and ran past the startled receptionist. He entered the conference room, flicked on the light, and searched the table for the tape they'd just watched. A few seconds later Kathryn entered the room and shut the door behind her.

"What is it?" she asked.

He jammed the cassette into the machine. Once again, there

was the shot of the people at the clubhouse and the beauty shots of the golf course and the ocean.

"C'mon, c'mon," Tom said, leaning toward the screen, his face less than a foot away. The images flowed across the screen. Suddenly he hit the pause button. The picture froze on the screen. It was a man dressed in dark clothes carrying a long, white box with orange and blue type. Tom pressed the slow-motion button and the man with the box walked for a few steps then looked up at the camera. Tom froze the image.

"Who is that guy?" Tom asked, pointing to the figure on the screen.

Kathryn looked closely.

"A delivery man of some sort," she said, leaning forward. "Federal Express, I think.

"That's right," Tom said. "And when we checked into the hotel the other night, what did the clerk say about my package?"

"That FedEx didn't deliver on Sundays," she said.

"So either this guy is the most conscientious delivery man in the world or..."

"Or it's Graham Raines," she said.

"Let's get it off to Langley and run it through the magic show," Tom said. "By the time they finish with it, we'll be able to count the freckles on the guy's face."

CHAPTER SEVEN

"This place is so American," Kathryn Devlin said, as she and Tom stood in the Deputy Director's outer office, waiting to be called in for their meeting.

"How do you mean?" Quinn said.

"Here you have the largest, most sophisticated, intelligence agency in the world and you make it as conspicuous as Disney World," she said. "Signs all over the highway. It's probably on the tourist maps of Washington. Come see Spyland! Bloody amazing."

Before Tom could respond, the Deputy Director's longtime secretary (and she was adamant that she was his secretary and not his assistant), Mary Dwyer, put down the phone and motioned to them.

"Tommy, you're up," she said. "He's just finishing up a call with Senator Gardner. Wasn't that terrible news about his daughter? And such a nice girl, too. Mr. Jackson was very fond of her. God rest her soul."

The news of Terry Gardner's death in California had hit official Washington hard. Senator John Gardner was popular and respected on both sides of the aisle, with the press, and at the White House, no matter which party was in power. Around Langley he was known as a wise and loyal ally for the Agency, and he and Laddie Jackson were especially close, both socially and professionally—which was, in no small part, why Laddie was so valuable to the Agency. When it needed help—or cover—he could go to his friend and be brutally candid. Over the years, the CIA had made its share of mistakes, and Jack Gardner was always there to do what he could to help limit the damage.

Mary Dwyer showed them into Jackson's office, and as they sat in the leather armchairs facing his old, ornately carved wooden desk, Laddie nodded to them briefly and then removed his reading glasses and slowly massaged his forehead. Tom thought his eyes looked vacant. Clearly, the news of Terry Gardner's death and this conversation with her father was very painful for him.

"Well, Jack, I'm just as sorry as I can be...She was a wonderful girl and I can't imagine what you and Susie are going through...I know you are...Well, we send all our love and let us know if there's anything any of us can do...I will...You're in our prayers. You take care now...okay, goodbye."

Jackson leaned forward and hung up the phone.

"How's the Senator doing?" Tom asked.

"About as well as you can, I suppose," he said. "He was mad about that girl. She could be headstrong, like all kids, and he wasn't happy about her being in the movies and all, but they had finally got tired of butting heads. Now this. I swear, sometimes this life just keeps you nailed to the foot of the cross."

"Was the death accidental?" Tom asked.

"They won't know until the autopsy, and maybe not even then," the Deputy Director said. "She washed ashore north of Los Angeles, a place called Morro Bay. There were no signs of foul play. We'll know more this week."

Jackson slid on his glasses and picked up a folder from his desk.

"Miss Devlin, it's nice to see you again," he said. "Are you enjoying your time here in the States?"

"Yes, very much, sir," she said. "California is far more pleasant than London at this time of the year."

The room was quiet as Jackson leaned back in his chair and studied the contents of the folder, slowing turning the pages until he found the photographic enhancements of the videotape they had sent to Langley.

"That was real nice work out there in Los Angeles," Jackson

said. "London is confident that Graham Raines is the man on the videotape..."

"And FedEx has no record of any delivery anywhere in the area on Sunday," Tom said.

"That's the good news," Jackson said, turning back to the file. "The bad news is that our boy Graham seems to have disappeared off the face of the Christly earth. He hasn't turned up on any of the intercepts we're running on McGonagle."

"Maybe he spooked and returned to England," Tom offered.

"Too cautious for that, I expect," Kathryn said. "The Caribbean would be more to form, although my money says he's still in the States."

"To try again?" the Deputy Director asked.

"Hard to tell, but if he hasn't been called off the chase, he'll likely stick with it," she said. "That fits his profile more closely. And since we haven't picked up any conversations between him and McGonagle, we should assume he's still at it."

Jackson rose from his chair and walked to the windows with their view of the northern Virginia countryside. He paused and spread his arms on the sill, leaning forward, lost in thought. Then he turned and leaned back against the windows, his arms crossed.

"One thing's for sure, and it's that nothing has cooled a bit over in Ireland," he said. "That crazy son of a bitch McGonagle is still going at it full bore. There were two more shootings last week. Two IRA boys, according to M.I.6. Maybe if we wait long enough, they'll just all kill themselves off anyway, the silly bastards. Now, what's our friend Peter Brookes been up to?"

"Well, you know he pulled out of the San Diego tournament and wasn't scheduled to play again until next week, at Bay Hill in Orlando," Tom said. "In that sense, we caught a break."

"Except that it gives Raines the luxury of making his plans without any pressure," Kathryn said. "If he's still in the game, as I believe he almost certainly is, we need to get him to show himself."

M.I.6's insistence on keeping Brookes a target had bothered Tom from the first, and made him somewhat uncomfortable with the entire operation. He genuinely liked Kathryn—more and more as time went by—but didn't have the sense he was being told the full story. Maybe Jackson wasn't either, but there wasn't much he could do about that.

Or maybe there was.

"I think we should keep Brookes tucked away for a while," Tom said, leaning back in the armchair and crossing his legs. "There isn't a tournament he really wouldn't miss until The Players Championship in mid-March. That's three weeks away. That should give us time to find out where Raines is and what he plans to do."

"But, Tom…" Kathryn said.

"Hold on a second, now," Laddie said. "Tom, that's not a bad idea. But where do we put the boy? We can't exactly ask him to just take some time off without giving him a reason, and we can't exactly give him a reason. It's not like we can say, 'Excuse us, dear boy, but could you take a bit of a holiday so you don't get your head blown off.'"

"Precisely," Kathryn said. "We can't go skittish on this."

"No, but we can't drag him around like bait off a shark boat, either," Tom said, with a purposeful edge to his voice. "I know exactly where we can stick him. Don't our friends in Morocco owe us one?"

"More than one," Laddie said. "But why Morocco?"

"The old King, Hassan II, was crazy about golf," Tom said. "He used to have a caddie that did nothing but follow him around and hold his cigarettes with a pair of tongs when it was the King's turn to play. I played in his tournament one year. He spared no expense. His son, the new king, could care less about the game but I'd bet he'd love to have Mr. Peter Brookes over for a week's worth of private lessons for his relatives," Tom said. "And he'd be more than willing to pay handsomely for the privilege. Christ, if he could teach them to just get out of a bunker they'd make him an honorary prince. Besides, it would be a small price to pay for keeping his relatives out of his hair for a while."

"I'm sorry, Tom, but I must disagree," Kathryn said. "With Brookes out of the picture, we'll never force Raines aboveground. I say it's worth the risk."

In the short time they had been working together, Tom had been impressed by both Kathryn's intelligence and her ability to control her feelings and emotions. But now, for the first time, he sensed a trace of anger and frustration. Her face flushed slightly, and she began to worry her worn, gold signet ring.

Laddie Jackson removed his reading glasses, leaned back in his chair, and gently tapped his front teeth with the glasses.

"I'm sorry, Miss Devlin, but I think Tom's right," he said. "Let me see what I can do about getting Brookes out of the country for a week or so. Maybe by then, Raines will surface, either here or someplace else. We'll keep up the surveillance, both on our end and yours in London. He can't lie low forever. In the meantime, the talks look like they're moving forward, so that's at least somewhat encouraging."

The Deputy Director put his glasses back on and picked up a second folder from his desk.

"What was the name of that detective that helped you out in Los Angeles?" he asked, thumbing through the papers in the file.

"Edwards," Tom said. "Captain L.C. Edwards."

"Do me a favor and give him a call," Laddie said. "Find out if they have anything on Terry Gardner's death. She was living in L.A. at the time. I'd like to give the senator whatever information I can."

With that, he stood and walked around from behind his desk.

"Thanks very much for coming by," he said, shaking hands with both of them. "Let's just try to be a little patient. These things always take time."

"I'm afraid time is what we're lacking, sir," Kathryn said sternly.

"We might just have a bit more than you think," Laddie Jackson said, showing them to the door. "Y'all take care now."

As the door shut behind them, they walked by Mary Dwyer's desk. Tom paused and scooped a handful of candies from the bowl next to the telephone. He offered some to Kathryn, but her expression made it clear she wasn't in the mood—either for candy or for the idea of shipping Peter Brookes halfway around the world. For the first time, there was a crack in this particular Anglo-American alliance.

"Now will the two of you be around for a bit or are you off?" Mary Dwyer asked.

"Hard to tell, Mary," Tom said.

"Well, when you become a big-shot banker, don't forget your old friends," she said.

"I'll send you a toaster," Tom said as they walked out of the office.

Nothing was said between the two as they made their way

down the hall to a bank of elevators. The silence continued as they made their way to Tom's office and the door was shut behind them.

"What the hell is the matter with you?" he asked.

"You know perfectly well what's the matter with me," Kathryn said, her eyes riveted on his, flashing with anger. "We're supposed to be partners in this lunacy. You act like this is some great game of hide and seek. I'll remind you that we're dealing with madmen here. McGonagle is stark raving mad and Raines is pathological. And never mind that there is that nagging matter of a peace process that hangs in the bloody fucking balance. And what do you propose? Shipping our only means of settling this over to the far side of the world. And to make matters worse, you set me up."

"I didn't set you up," Tom said. "You and I disagree. Big deal. It's not the last time that's going to happen. Get over it. It might help if you spent a little less time being pissed off and a little more time thinking clearly. If Raines can't tag Brookes then it gives the negotiators just that little bit more time to nail this peace plan down—not that I'm wildly optimistic that this plan or any plan has a snowball's chance in hell."

"And why is that?"

"Because it comes with the territory," he said.

"CIA?" she asked.

"No, being Irish," he said. "You know the definition of Irish Alzheimer's don't you?"

"I'm afraid not," she said coldly.

"It's when you hate someone but can't remember why," he said. "That's why this so-called peace plan is doomed—and it has nothing to do with McGonagle, Raines, or any of the rest of them."

. . .

The following day, Quinn placed a call to Detective L.C. Edwards. It would be another day before his call was returned—and the news he received cast an entirely new light on the challenge he and Kathryn Devlin faced.

When Edwards called, Tom asked for any information on Terry Gardner's death.

"It's interesting you should ask," Edwards said. "This is totally off the record. If you quote me, I'll deny it, but when the news of the girl's death broke, one of our people—an officer LeBlanc— remembered that she had interviewed the girl right after the shooting. She lived in a guest cottage in the area. There was something about the girl and the man she was with that didn't sit quite right with her and it sort of stuck in the back of her mind."

"What about them?" Tom asked.

"Nothing she could put her finger on, but we got a warrant and went back and checked the cottage. We found a slip of paper with the name 'Graham Archer, BBC/London' in what we assumed was the girl's writing."

"And..."

"And no one by that name has ever worked at the BBC. The other thing that's interesting is that they told the officers that they were planning to go up to San Francisco on business. Morro Bay is on the coast highway."

Quinn sensed his pulse quickening. He hesitated before he asked the next question, fearing it might tip his hand.

"Any prints?"

"We got the girl's and what we assume are his off a glass," Captain Edwards said. "The FBI didn't have anything in their computers."

"Captain, would you mind if we took a run at them?" Quinn asked

"Not at all," Edwards said.

Within 24 hours, M.I.6 confirmed that the man with Terry Gardner on the evening of the shooting—and the most probable suspect in her death—was Graham Raines.

Now it was time to go pay a visit to her father.

CHAPTER EIGHT

Jack Kennedy once famously observed that Washington was a city of "northern charm and southern efficiency" and this was never truer than when snow fell upon the nation's capital. Even on the best of days, the city's municipal services were marginal. If anything more than a dusting of the white stuff fell, D.C. was up for disaster relief status.

Tom had driven in from his home in Bethesda, not far from Congressional, Burning Tree, and the TPC at Avenel. The storm that came up the coast hit Washington around midnight and three inches had fallen by the morning rush hour. Of course, Washington being Washington, it might as well have been a bomb that hit the city for all the chaos it caused. The abandoned cars that filled the streets would have made snowplowing a nightmare—if the snowplows had ever made it to the streets. Instead, the funds set aside for snow removal somehow disappeared into one of the city's notorious sinkholes of corruption, leaving the locals stranded and their leaders blathering on about how this wouldn't happen if they had statehood.

He had planned to take Connecticut Avenue to Dupont Circle, and then swing onto Massachusetts Avenue and park near the capitol building. But the traffic was a nightmare, so he turned off on 8th Street and parked near Pennsylvania Avenue. It would be faster to walk down the Mall. Besides, it would give him time to clear his mind before his meeting with Senator Gardner—a meeting he most definitely was not looking forward to.

The capitol building was unusually quiet. Because of the weather, the government had declared that only "essential" employees were required to come into work. This, of course, was one of those great Washington paradoxes: In a city where absolutely everyone considers themselves of the greatest importance, all it takes is a couple inches of snow to remind them how truly unessential they really are. Even the tourists decided to stay away. The effect was an eerie silence as he made his way to the Senator's private office off the Senate floor, a hideaway that was one of the perks of seniority.

He entered the office, where he was met by the Deputy Director and Kathryn, who Laddie had picked up at her hotel en route from his home in the fashionable Dumbarton Oaks section of the city. With them was the Senator's senior and most trusted assistant, Briggs McPhee. He and Tom had known each other for years. Like Tom, McPhee had been recruited by the Agency in his senior year at Dartmouth. He had served as an intelligence analyst, specializing in the Soviet Union. After a while, however, the low pay coupled with the tedium of a desk job proved to be too much. He went off to law school at the University of Virginia, and following his graduation went to work for then-freshman Senator Gardner. Over the years Briggs had become the Senator's alter ego, and was the key staffer on the Senate Intelligence Committee

"Good to see you, Tom," McPhee said. "How have you been?"

"Not bad, Briggs, thanks," Tom said, shaking McPhee's hand. "I wish we were meeting under happier circumstances. How's the Senator?"

"It's been pretty tough," McPhee said. "Of all the kids, she was the most like him, which is probably why they had more than their share of battles over the years. She was as stubborn and hardheaded as he is. But they both softened in the past year. The Senator was scheduled to go to Mexico in May for a fact-finding visit and Terry was going to join him. He was really looking forward to it. She was talking about giving up acting and leaving L.A. and he was actually encouraging her to stick it out. And now this..."

Just then the door opened and Senator Gardner entered. Tom was momentarily taken aback by his appearance. Usually erect, powerful, and robust, his shoulders were slumped and he moved slowly. His face was drawn and ashen, and his eyes seemed lost and distant, sunken behind the dark circles that manifested the depths of his heartache and despair.

There was an awkward silence as Laddie rose from a couch and the two old friends embraced. Tom could tell from the Deputy Director's expression that he was as stunned by the Senator's demeanor as he had been.

"Thank you for meeting with us, Jack," Laddie said. "We know this isn't easy for you and we wouldn't have asked if it weren't a matter of some urgency."

"I understand, Laddie," the Senator said. "Thank you for the flowers you and Elizabeth sent over. It meant a lot to Susie and me and the kids."

"How are they doing?" Laddie asked.

"It's rough," the Senator said, slowly removing his topcoat and draping it over the back of a chair. "We were looking forward to having her back for a bit this summer. We were looking forward to having her home...."

The Senator's voice trailed off and tears began to well up in his eyes.

"I'm so sorry, Jack," Laddie said, clasping the Senator on the arm and breaking the silence that hung like a shroud over the ornate old room. "We all are. Jack, I believe you know Tom Quinn."

The Senator looked over at Tom and extended his hand.

"Yes, of course," he said, shaking Tom's hand softly, unlike the firm handshake remembered from other meetings. "How have you been, Tom?"

"I'm well, thank you, sir," Tom said. "You and your family are in my prayers."

"Thank you," the Senator said.

"And Senator, this is Kathryn Devlin of M.I.6," Laddie said. "She is working with us."

Kathryn rose smoothly from her chair and extended her hand to the Senator, her eyes looking into his softly and consolingly.

"Senator," Kathryn said. "Sir Owen sends his profound condolences and sympathies."

"Thank you, Miss Devlin," the Senator said, placing both of his hands on hers. "I received a very thoughtful note from him. Please express my appreciation. Now, should we get down to business?"

The Senator led them into a larger, adjacent room where they took their places around a conference table. The room had a spectacular view down the Mall, toward the Washington Monument, past the Reflecting Pool, to the Lincoln Memorial, and across the Potomac to the hillside of Arlington National Cemetery.

A staffer arrived with coffee and tea, and then left the room, closing the heavy wooden door behind her.

For the next 45 minutes, Laddie explained in detail McGonagle's plans and efforts to disrupt the peace process. When he finished, Kathryn gave Gardner and McPhee an equally detailed briefing on Graham Raines and the evidence she, Tom, CIA, and M.I.6 had gathered that pointed to Raines as the lead suspect in the Riviera shooting. As they were being briefed, Tom noticed that McPhee took most of the notes, while the Senator seemed to struggle to remain focused on the briefing. Periodically, he would seem to drift off, lost in his thoughts. He would gaze out the windows, down the Mall, and off into snowy distance.

When Kathryn finished, Laddie turned his attention directly to the Senator.

"Jack, if this was all we had to discuss with you, it would be serious enough but it could have waited," Laddie said, leaning forward and locking his gaze on the Senator. "I'm afraid that what we have to tell you now will be very difficult for you. It's damned hard for us to come to you with it, but you need to know before it gets into the news."

"Go ahead," the Senator said.

The Deputy Director nodded to Tom, who opened his file and looked briefly across the table toward Kathryn. She gave him a discreet nod of support and encouragement. He took a sip of water and began.

"Senator, we believe your daughter may have been involved with Graham Raines," Tom said, focusing intently on the Senator, trying to gauge his reaction. What little color had been in Gardner's face drained away, and his shoulders slumped. "We do not believe she was in any way involved in the murder, at least not with her knowledge. In fact, we're confident that she believed that the man she was with was a BBC executive named Graham Archer."

"Dear God..." the Senator said softly, almost inaudibly, before moving his outstretched hands gently to his face and shaking his head slowly from side to side.

The room was silent for what seemed like minutes while the Senator gathered himself. Tom looked at both McPhee and the Deputy Director, and could see the profound pain reflected in their faces. Kathryn was also moved, but when he looked at her, he knew exactly what she was thinking: *No time to go skittish now, Tom. Press on.*

"I'm sorry, Tom," the Senator said, his voice cracking as he struggled to maintain his composure. "Please go on."

For the next 20 minutes, he laid out the evidence the LAPD had developed, including the note Terry Gardner had written that connected her with Archer, Raines's fingerprints from the glass, and the officers' notes following the shooting that indicated the two had planned to head north toward San Francisco. As he made his case, he thought the Senator grew increasingly engaged and focused. He began jotting down notes and occasionally asked questions.

Now came the hard part.

"Senator," Tom said, referring to some papers from his file. "This is a copy of the autopsy report on your daughter. It hasn't been released. We got it from a source at the LAPD who has been helping us."

He paused to sip some water and looked directly at the Senator, who was now fully and completely focused on him.

"Senator, the report shows that your daughter did drown," Tom said. "However, there were no signs of trauma, so the medical examiner has ruled out the possibility that she was somehow knocked unconscious, which might have led to her death. She had a moderate amount of alcohol in her system, perhaps two or three glasses of wine. Probably not enough to lead to her drowning, especially since—as the Deputy Director told us—she was a good, strong swimmer. However, the report does show that she had trace elements of Diamorphine in her system."

"What is that?" the Senator asked.

Tom looked at Kathryn.

"Senator," she said "it's a powerful muscle relaxant. It isn't a drug that you would take casually, since when taken in even small doses and combined with alcohol, it can be deadly. Raines knows this from first-hand experience. As I told you, he was badly wounded in the Falklands War and used this medication for a number of years. If it is any comfort, none of your daughter's friends said she was prone to drug use. In fact, quite the opposite. I'm afraid our conclusion is that Raines slipped the drug into your daughter's wine, waited until she fell asleep, and then took her out into the Pacific and drowned her. There is no other reasonable explanation."

The Senator looked down the table toward the Deputy Director.

"Laddie?" he asked.

"I'm sorry, Jack, but we're in agreement. Nothing else makes sense."

Once again, silence hung over the room as everyone awaited the Senator's reaction.

"What do you need from me?" the Senator asked, to no one in particular.

"Cover," said the Deputy Director. "And we may need a lot of it. I don't have to tell you the risks we run having both CIA and M.I.6 involved in this. If this blows up in our faces, there'll be hell to pay on the Hill and in the media."

"Why not let the FBI run with it?" Briggs McPhee asked.

"They leak like a sieve and we need to keep this quiet," Jackson explained. "If this gets out, the peace initiative will be history. There's no way it will hold together. Beyond that, on a practical level, we stand a better chance of stopping Raines if we go it alone. Miss Devlin knows the guy inside and out. If we bring the FBI into this and Raines finds out we're onto him, he'll bolt. We're virtually certain of that. From a purely pragmatic point of view, this is our best chance to take Raines out of play."

The Senator rose from his chair and walked to the windows. He leaned forward and gazed down the Mall. The snow had stopped and the sun was starting to break though the clouds. After a few moments, he turned and looked at the Deputy Director.

"Laddie, I don't have to tell you how much I want you to nail this guy," the Senator said. "I'll give you as much support as I can.

If necessary, I'll go to the President himself. But you're going to have to move fast. The longer this plays out, the greater the risk it will leak."

"Senator, I think it would be wise to take this up with the committee," Briggs McPhee said. "They'll be at least some safety in numbers if this gets out."

"Maybe," said Senator Gardner. "But there are also leaks in numbers. I'll sit down with Senator Larkin. She's the ranking member and if she thinks she can hold the Democrats on the committee together, I'll hold off on consulting with the entire committee. If not, we'll have to take our chances. Again, I want to stress how important speed is in all this. Good luck and keep us in the loop."

The Senator gathered his papers and made his way to the door, pausing to shake hands with Tom, Kathryn, and Laddie Jackson. Briggs McPhee handed him his overcoat and the two men left the office, their footsteps echoing as they walked down the long corridor.

"Jesus, that was brutal," Tom said. "I thought he was going to lose it."

"He'll be alright," Laddie said. "He's a tough guy. Let's just hope he doesn't have to take this to his committee. There are a couple of loose cannons there that I wouldn't trust with the recipe to my wife's chocolate chip cookies."

The Deputy Director looked at his watch.

"It's getting late," he said. "Can I give either of you a ride?"

"No thanks," Tom said. "My car is parked just down the Mall."

"Thank you, no," Kathryn said. "I think I could stand a bit of a walk. Need to clear my head."

As soon as they stepped outside the capitol, the strong, cold west winds hit them. They made their way up the Mall without speaking. After several minutes, Kathryn made what he thought was an excellent suggestion.

"Christ, I'm desperate for a drink," she said. "How about you?"

"At *least* one," Tom said.

They left the Mall, crossed Constitution Avenue near the Internal Revenue Service building, and went down 10th Street until they reached Pennsylvania Avenue. After walking up the avenue for a couple blocks they ducked into a bar on one of the side streets. It felt good to get out of the wind, and after checking their coats, they took seats at the bar and ordered double scotches.

From the first time he met her in New York, Tom had been struck by her looks, but in the soft light of the bar, she looked even more beautiful. Her face was flushed by the cold, and her hair was tousled by the winds. She took a sip of the scotch, shook her head, and ran her fingers through her hair.

"I thought you were brilliant with the Senator," she said. "Truly. That couldn't have been easy. My heart broke for him."

"He's a good man," Tom said.

"So are you," she said, turning to look at him. As she did, her legs brushed against his. "I want desperately to get Raines, now more than ever. Seeing the photos of the Senator's daughter in his office brought a face to his madness."

Tom stared into her eyes, but as he did he saw her glance over his shoulder.

"Oh, dear God..." she said. "It's London."

Tom turned and looked at the television set mounted over the side of the bar. It was tuned to CNN, and the images were horrifying. He asked the bartender to turn up the volume.

"London was rocked by a series of bomb blasts during the evening rush hour today," the anchor said. "Initial police officials' reports indicate that at least four people were killed in the explosions, and dozens were injured. The largest number of casualties occurred outside Harrods, the landmark department store in the heart of the British capital."

As the anchorman spoke, live video captured a scene of utter chaos. Bodies littered the street outside Harrods. Police and medical teams treated the injured, and survivors gathered in small groups, stunned by the tragedy.

"McGonagle," Kathryn said. "Bloody McGonagle."

• • •

The bombings made front-page news in all the major newspapers, both in the United States and Europe. The tabloids were quick to call it the "St. Patrick's Day Massacre" and while both sides in the peace talks were quick to condemn the terrorism, what was more noteworthy was that McGonagle's faction of the IRA declined comment—neither claiming nor denying responsibility.

That's not to say that there was much doubt about who was behind the bombings. M.I.5's informants had warned that McGonagle's people had actions planned for St. Patrick's Day, but few expected anything so horrific or audacious. The death toll stood at 12, including five children who were visiting Harrods as part of a school trip. The death of the children particularly inflamed public outrage. The usual politicians and editorial writers were calling for dramatic action, but more importantly, so were influential and powerful religious leaders of every denomination.

McGonagle had raised the stakes—and may also have done what decades, even centuries, of debates and discussions and deals had failed to do: unite the Catholics and Protestants, the English, Irish, and Anglo-Irish in a sincere effort at a peaceful settlement of the Troubles.

In the days following the bombings, the volume of intercepts conducted by the National Security Agency, the CIA, M.I.5 and M.I.6 was enormous. As was usually the case, the vast majority of information picked up was of little value, but one was of enormous importance: It was brief, terse conversation between McGonagle and Graham Raines—the first since the failed assassination attempt almost a month earlier.

"Belfast Trading," were the first words on the tape.

"Bit of bad luck, I'm afraid," said a second voice.

"I'm not interested in luck," said the voice of an older man, muffled somewhat. "Are you still about the chase?"

"Very much so..." some of the words were lost, drowned out by what sounded like a car going past with its radio very loud.

"When can I expect results?" said the first voice.

"Soon," said the second voice. "Within the month, possibly within a week's time."

"I hope so," said the older man, before hanging up the receiver.

The analyst stopped the tape and began to rewind it.

"The voiceprints match up with McGonagle and your guy Raines, there's no question about that," she said. "The intercept was made three days ago, but with all the activity after the London bombings, it took a while to sort through everything. Sorry."

"No problem," Tom said. "I don't suppose you got lucky and were able to nail down where Raines called from."

"Yes and no," she said. "He probably was on a cell phone, so that's difficult to trace. But we were able to enhance that section where the conversation was lost momentarily. Listen closely."

She reached across the console and cued up the tape until she found the point she was listening for "...very much so..." Raines's voice was distorted by the slow speed of the tape. Then came the sound of the car and the words "...enter for your free TPC tick..."

"Does that mean anything to you?"

Tom smiled.

"You bet it does," he said. "It means our guy just came to the surface."

CHAPTER NINE

It had been some 20 years since Tom had been in Jacksonville Beach and the area's transformation was remarkable, almost unbelievable.

What had basically been a beach town for sailors at the U.S. Navy base at Mayport had been transformed into a vibrant, upscale, and wealthy community. If there were any justice, the civic fathers would fall on their knees every evening and thank God for the Atlantic Ocean and Deane Beman. The Atlantic had been a constant, attracting people to the long, beautiful beach. But it was Beman who put the place on the map in 1979 when, as the commissioner of the PGA Tour, he moved its headquarters to Ponte Vedra Beach. Three years later, when Jerry Pate won the Tournament Players Championship at the controversial new Tournament Players Club at Sawgrass, the area's transformation was well underway.

Love the TPC's Stadium course or hate it, Beman's decision was a stroke of genius. It set his tournament apart and got people talking about it and the course where it was played. Today, the tournament ranks just below the four professional Majors in terms of prestige, and the course, after much fine-tuning, is considered one of the finest tests of shotmaking in the game.

As Tom and Kathryn drove down A1A, the main coast route, on their way to the Sawgrass Marriott, they passed the Ponte Vedra Inn and Club, which brought back a cascade of memories for Tom—both good and bad.

Twenty years earlier, Tom, Pres, and their wives came down for a week in late April. Tom had just returned from a posting in Berlin and Pres had set up a series of matches with two friends of his from Seminole. They were both good players, and Tom had been looking forward to teaming up with Pres again. But there was more to the trip than just golf. He had hoped it might save a marriage that he knew, in his heart of hearts, was all but over.

Tom's wife, Becca, and Annie Elliott had gone to Concord Academy together and then headed off for college, Becca at Smith and Annie at Wellesley. Pres and Annie began dating when Pres was a sophomore at Harvard and she was a freshman, and married a few months after she graduated.

From the first, Annie had been like a kid sister to Tom, and she had always believed that he and Becca Bowen would be a good fit—and for a time they were. God knows she was beautiful, and while she was quiet, she had a nice, ironic sense of humor that appealed to Tom. She was also artistic, and would often join him during an early evening round of golf, not to play, simply to sketch or take photographs. Even now, all these years after the divorce, some of her work was scattered around his house.

The Bowens were very close, which made the divorce particularly difficult, because they had always been very good to Tom. Both her parents came from money—Pres used to joke that when they got married the story was bumped from the society pages to the business section under the headline "Two Old Boston Firms Merge: Financial Colossus Formed." But the family was completely unpretentious. Their houses, both in Chestnut Hill and on Nantucket, looked comfortably lived in—the kind of places Ralph Lauren would like you to believe you could live in if the money in your bank account had come over on the Mayflower. In fact, when Tom once joked about their ancestors coming over on the Mayflower, Mr. Bowen protested that it was totally untrue.

"We did not come over on that first voyage," he said, with mock outrage. "We sent the servants so they could prepare the summer cottage for the season."

Unlike Becca, who was never comfortable with Tom's CIA involvement, Mr. Bowen reveled in the stories, intrigues, and gossip Tom would share with him. In the early years of Tom and Becca's marriage, as she grew increasingly frustrated by his unwillingness to even consider leaving the Agency, her father counseled patience. But the rising level of revelations about previous CIA failures and misdeeds that came out in the late 1970s only stiffened her resolve that something had to go — either the Agency or the marriage.

They had been married for just over three years when Tom was assigned to the American embassy in West Berlin as a political officer in the spring of 1978. Berlin was a gray and depressing place then, and it was still very much at the center of the U.S. and Soviet conflict. In fact, it probably attracted more CIA and KGB attention than any other major city in the world.

Becca hated it from the first. She found the atmosphere bizarre and repressive and thought the Germans were cold and detached. Her photography from the period reflected her despair and frustration, and the fact that Tom was working impossible hours only made things worse.

If all that weren't enough, there was the overarching question of kids. Becca wanted to start a family but even then, Tom had his doubts about the marriage and resisted having children. This made the divide between them all but insurmountable. By the time Thanksgiving approached, she had given him an ultimatum: either try to start a family, or she was heading back to Boston for good.

Thanksgiving had always been Tom's favorite holiday, even more so since he began spending it with the Bowens at their rambling house overlooking the Atlantic on Nantucket. The family would gather for the long weekend and, with any luck, the weather would still be warm enough to go sailing, which was the family's great passion.

Coming back for the holiday revitalized Becca and seemed to mend the marriage, at least for a time. She was happier and Tom felt less defensive about the Agency, kids, about everything. They went for long walks along the beach at Surfside, on the south side of the island. They strolled around town, visiting the shops and wandering down the side streets, looking at the old houses tucked away down alleyways. They even paused at a few real estate offices and looked at the photos of houses for sale displayed in the windows.

Late in the afternoon on Sunday, the day before they had to go off-island, they walked down to the town dock, their arms around each other. The lowering sun cast a soft, orange glow and the deep blue water sparkled. As they reached the end of the dock, she stopped, reached up and put her arms around Tom's neck.

"Tom," she said, running a hand through the hair on the back of his head. "I'm so glad we came. I know we can make this work. I honestly believe we can and I want to more than anything else. This wouldn't be such a bad life you know."

Tom reached his arm around her shoulders and held her close. In the distance, he saw the ferry leaving for Woods Hole on the Cape.

The ship was leaving. It was time to make a decision.

"I know we can, Becca," he said. "And I know you're right. I love you. Don't ever forget that."

Then he lifted her face to his, kissed her softly, looked in her eyes and smiled.

She believed him. Maybe he actually believed it too.

. . .

It didn't take long for the dreadful, dreary Berlin winter to erase the magic of that Thanksgiving. By Christmas, her unhappiness and his frustration had returned, and it soon became clear that nothing short of his resignation from the Agency would save the marriage. If there were any doubts, they were erased over the Christmas holiday when Becca returned to Boston. She had only been home for a few days, when the phone calls began, first from Pres, then from her father.

The calls were virtually identical—concern for both Tom and the marriage, plus the offer of attractive jobs. No pressure, mind you. We just want you to think about it.

Instead, in the evenings when Becca was gone, he began to wonder just how much he really loved Rebecca Bowen Quinn—and how much he loved the promise of a future in the great Bowen tradition of comfortable wealth and no heavy lifting.

The ship was sailing.

CHAPTER TEN

Martin McGonagle had always been a creature of habit, and this became increasingly true as he grew older. He would awaken early, eat a small, almost Spartan breakfast, and read the morning papers. Then, without fail, he would make his way to the neighborhood church for morning Mass.

On this, the last day of his life, a soft, steady rain hung over Belfast. McGonagle, dressed in a dark suit and tie, finished his toast and jam, took a sip of tea, and neatly stacked the dishes in the sink for the housekeeper. Then he made his way to the small front parlor of his house, where his driver/bodyguard waited, just as he did every morning.

It was just a short drive to the church, and until his arthritis became too advanced, McGonagle had always enjoyed his walk through the quiet side streets to the old stone building. It gave him a chance to visit with neighbors and listen to the latest gossip or news of British outrage.

The inside of the church was dark, more so than usual because of the rain and the Lenten season. There were only a few, elderly parishioners inside, all regular communicants like McGonagle. For all the talk of Catholics and Protestants and their troubles, the truth was that the Church had begun to lose its grip on the young.

Pope John Paul's traditional conservatism had grown at odds with a modern and increasingly fashionable Ireland.

After slowly escorting McGonagle to his pew near the altar and the rows of votive candles, his bodyguard went to the back of the church, near the large, double wooden doors. The service was short, maybe just a half-hour or so, and when communion was served, the priest left the altar and walked down the center aisle, bringing the sacraments to the elderly in the pews. During the service, McGonagle would quietly say a rosary, his old, gnarled fingers struggling to work the beads.

At the close of the service, as the other parishioners slowly made their way out of the church, McGonagle went to the altar and gingerly knelt before the votive candles. He reached into his pants pocket and pulled out a handful of coins. He labored to pick out a couple of coins and put them in the collection box. Then he took a match and lit a candle in memory of his son, long since gone. He lingered for a moment, saying a quiet prayer, and dabbing a tear from his face. Then he carefully raised himself up from the altar, took the arm of his driver, and together they began to walk toward the rear of the church.

As they did, the priest, who had been extinguishing the candles on the altar, approached the two men.

"Martin," he said, taking one of the old man's hands in his. "I wanted to thank you for your kind gift to the diocese. I just learned of it from the bishop. You know that such generosity will be rewarded."

"Thank you, father," McGonagle said. "At my age, I've nothing better to do with my money. I'm too old to chase the girls or travel much beyond my own shadow."

"Well, Martin, I think you've still got a bit of time left on your clock," the priest said. "Many's the widows and their children that will remember you in their prayers for your kindness. God bless, now."

McGonagle still liked to visit the building on the outskirts of Belfast that was the headquarters of his old engineering firm. He had sold it years ago, but maintained an office there. Even into his 80s he remained fascinated by the challenge of solving complicated, mathematical problems. Indeed, he was held in so much respect by his fellow engineers that they welcomed the visits by the old man.

From his earliest days in the IRA, McGonagle had a sure understanding of the dangers involved in taking on both the British and the Unionists. He had seen many of his friends and neighbors killed or maimed over the long decades, and while he didn't think of himself as particularly brave in the usual sense of the word, neither was he foolhardy, especially now when he also had so many former allies aligned against him. The IRA was turning on itself, and McGonagle knew that the fratricide would only get worse before it got better—all in the name of peace.

One of his few concessions to his own security, however, was varying the route he took to and from his old office. He had a cabby's knowledge of the city's streets, and he wouldn't share his chosen route of the day with anyone, not even his driver, until the last possible minute.

"I think we'll take the Lough route today," McGonagle said. "It's a bit longer but perhaps the skies will clear a bit and we'll have a pleasant view for ourselves."

As the car wound its way through the city, McGonagle was struck yet again by the murals painted on walls and the sides of buildings. Most celebrated the IRA and the struggle for independence. Many had been there for decades. But increasingly, the paintings and graffiti reflected the chasms that had grown between the two factions of the IRA. To McGonagle's dismay, the phrases "Peace Now" and "End the Violence" were appearing with increasing regularity. Like the Church, McGonagle knew the IRA was losing the battle for the hearts and souls of the young people of his country.

As they approached the highway that ran out along the water, they slowed. Barricades blocked the road and signs directed traffic to an alternate route.

"What's the problem, officer?" McGonagle's driver asked one of the policemen directing traffic.

"Emergency construction," he said. "Move along now, please. We can't be backing up traffic all the way into the city."

If McGonagle or his driver had checked in the rearview mirror as they turned onto the detour, they might have noticed the policeman talking into the microphone attached to his sweater. And, moments later, they might have noticed the dark, nondescript sedan that was directed by a policeman into the line of traffic just behind their car.

McGonagle's car wound through the city, eventually making its way to the secondary road that led to his office. About two miles from the office, in a stretch of road bordered by open fields, they slowed for another police roadblock. They were the sixth, maybe seventh vehicle, in the line of cars that were being checked by police and heavily armed British troops.

Minutes later, a policeman approached the driver's side of the car. Two British soldiers stood, automatic rifles at the ready, on the other side of the car.

"Excuse me, sir," the policeman said. "May I see your papers, please?"

The driver reached into the glove compartment, retrieved the registration, and gave it and his license to the officer.

"What's the problem, officer?"

"Routine search," the policeman said. "After the London bombings, we're on a bit of an alert. Want to make sure the boyos don't start blowing up Belfast all over again. Could you pop the boot for us, please?"

The driver pulled the latch near his seat and the car's trunk popped open. As the policeman reviewed the car's registration, the two soldiers moved to the rear of the car and checked the trunk. The hood blocked the view from inside the car, and one of the soldiers discreetly pulled a small box from his jacket and placed it in the trunk. Then he closed the trunk and nodded to the policeman.

"Very well, sir," the policeman said. "Everything is in order. Sorry for the delay. Move along, now."

McGonagle's car drove off, followed closely by the dark sedan. As they made their way around a bend in the road, the sedan accelerated and pulled closer to help ensure the remote-controlled triggering device would explode the bomb concealed in the trunk of McGonagle's car. The driver looked in the rearview mirror and instinctively accelerated, downshifting into third gear.

It was too late...

The explosion turned McGonagle's car into a roaring, tangled pile of crushed metal. The gas tank exploded seconds later. The dark sedan slowed down briefly, and then sped off before any possible witnesses had a chance to identify it.

The peace process, and the Troubles that spawned it, had claimed two more victims.

•••

McGonagle's assassination was front-page news in Ireland and throughout the British Isles. The BBC's Home Service led its newscasts with the story. The *New York Times* teased the story in a box on the front page and then ran it, along with an analysis of its impact on the peace talks, on page four. The *Times*, like its London namesake, reasoned that McGonagle's death was a serious, perhaps fatal blow, to opponents of the peace plan. Neither paper mentioned that, to ensure this was the case, teams of British and Royal Ulster military and police forces swept through Belfast following the explosion, rounding up McGonagle's associates—names and addresses generously supplied by members of the regular IRA.

In London, 10 Downing Street issued a statement condemning the violence and urging both sides in the negotiations to "redouble their valiant efforts to bring an end to the bloodshed and finally bring peace to all the Irish people."

At his regular afternoon briefing, the White House press secretary said the president and the State Department were "closely monitoring the situation and deeply regretted the killings," but didn't disagree when a reporter pointed out that the fact that the IRA and Unionist negotiators blamed one another for the bombing didn't seem promising news.

"There is always an ebb and flow to delicate negotiations such as these," the spokesman said. "The United States stands ready to offer whatever assistance we can in these vitally important talks. The president is personally committed to finding a fair, peaceful, and timely resolution to these negotiations."

Meanwhile, in Belfast, the Catholic community readied itself for McGonagle's funeral mass and the hero's funeral procession down the Falls Road.

So did the police and military, just in case Martin McGonagle proved as troublesome in death as he had been in life.

In the end, however, Martin McGonagle's funeral—while large—was respectful and peaceful. Whatever lingering passions remained in the Catholic community had finally been spent after all the years of hatred and fear and violence.

The peace process was moving on.

CHAPTER ELEVEN

THE PLAYERS CHAMPIONSHIP | PONTE VEDRA BEACH, FLORIDA | MARCH

If there had been a seismograph that measured the impact of news events on the PGA Tour, the death of Martin McGonagle wouldn't have raised a blip.

While the *New York Times*, the *Washington Post*, and National Public Radio carefully read the political tea leaves to determine the impact of the assassination, it barely rated a mention in the Tour's unofficial newspaper of record—*USA Today*. There's a saying in journalism that "the people who run the country read the *Wall Street Journal*; those who know who run the country read the *New York Times*; and those who either don't have a clue or could care less read *USA Today*."

For the most part, if a paper carries the sports scores and standings, covers the stock markets (prices only, little in-depth analysis, thank you), weather forecasts and airport delays, it's just about perfect for the players on any of the Tours. That *USA Today* is frequently delivered to hotel rooms free of charge is just an added bonus.

Even the handful of players from Great Britain and Ireland who were in town for The Players Championship were seemingly unaffected by McGonagle's murder. An enterprising young writer from *Golf World* surveyed several of the players, and most predictably allowed that they "were golfers, not politicians." The lone exception was—not surprisingly—Peter Brookes, just back from his trip to Morocco.

According to the writer, he approached Brookes and asked for his reaction to the killings of the two men.

"Only two?" Brookes said. "Pity."

Tom Quinn learned of the killings when he returned to his hotel room after his morning run along the beach. It had been a perfect morning for a jog. Northeast Florida can be windy and cold in March, but the temperature was already in the 60s when he began running along the wide beach. The tide was just turning, so he ran down close to the waterline, where the sand was firmer and easier to run on. The sun was shimmering just over the horizon, and lines of pelicans were already skimming just above the surface of the water in search of the first meal of the day. The only downside was the faint, acrid odor caused by the nearby paper mills that occasionally hung over the area on still days. That aside, the weather was perfect.

He ran several miles, almost to the Ponte Vedra Inn and Club. By the time he turned and headed back to the hotel, there were more runners out on the beach, and the first surfers of the day were arriving. After several minutes he could see his hotel, and he began lengthening his stride. He sprinted the last 100 or so yards, his knees aching and his lungs burning. All in all, not bad for an old guy, he thought.

When he returned to his room, the message light was flashing on the phone. The first message was from the Agency's headquarters in Virginia asking him to call the Deputy Director's office immediately. The second message was from Kathryn.

He called Langley and was patched through to Mary Dwyer. Moments later, Laddie Jackson was on the phone.

"Have you seen the news this morning, Tom?" he asked.

"No, sir," Tom said, reaching across the bed and grabbing the television's remote control. He turned on the set and flicked to NBC and "Today."

"Martin McGonagle was killed late this morning Belfast time," the Deputy Director said. "A car bomb killed him and his driver. No one is claiming responsibility for the bombing."

"What does M.I.6 think?" Tom asked.

"Too early to tell," Jackson said. "I've got a call scheduled for Sir Owen later today, once we have more information."

"What does this mean for our operation?" Tom asked. "This should take care of things on our end, right?"

As Tom talked, NBC was showing a tape of the wreckage, as well as footage from the St. Patrick's Day bombings in London. The network was also interviewing people on the streets of Belfast, but he couldn't make out what they were saying—not that it mattered particularly.

"I imagine, but let's wait until I speak with Owen," the Deputy Director said. "I can't imagine our boy is going to stay around to finish the job now that McGonagle is gone, but who knows? I'd plan to be down there a few more days anyway. I can think of worse places to be and worse people to be there with. We'll be in touch."

Next, Tom called Kathryn's room. She had been awakened by a call from M.I.6's headquarters but she didn't have anything to add to what Tom had learned from the Deputy Director. They agreed that until they learned otherwise, they should proceed as though Graham Raines was still very much on the hunt. That being the case, they'd go to the golf course later in the morning and look for locations where Raines might make another attempt at shooting Peter Brookes. For his part, Tom thought it was time to wrap this up and get on with his life—still, he faced that possibility with mixed emotions. On the one hand, there was a sense of relief that Brookes hadn't been killed or injured. He was also pleased to be moving back to Boston and a new career. However, he had enjoyed the challenge of trying to track down and stop Raines and doubted that anything his future had to offer would match that rush.

Then there was also the matter of Kathryn Devlin. They had grown closer in their time together. There was a clear physical attraction, to be sure, but there was more than that at work between them. There was a certain emotional closeness—the beginnings of a bond that went beyond the friendship that had developed. They were kindred spirits and he felt very protective of her, maybe because he sensed there was a hurt deep inside her—a pain she wouldn't or couldn't share.

• • •

Graham Raines received the news of McGonagle's murder with a detachment that bordered on indifference. He had never met the man. Instead, the arrangements had all been made through a Libyan intermediary. Their few phone conversations had been brusque and to the point. His first attempt at killing Peter Brookes had been difficult at best, and all the complications only made it more so. But this time would be different—or at least would have been, if McGonagle hadn't been assassinated.

Disguised with a new beard, Raines had arrived in Florida weeks earlier and had traveled to Orlando, only to learn that Brookes had withdrawn from the tournament. With time on his hands, he headed north to Ponte Vedra Beach and made his way to the Tournament Players Club at Sawgrass, the site of The Players Championship the following week.

When he reached the course, he parked near the large, sprawling clubhouse that sat on a rise overlooking the course and its practice facilities. He was gathering up his binoculars and windcheater when a security guard approached his car.

"I'm sorry, sir, but the course is closed," the man said. "It's always closed just before the start of the tournament."

"Really?" said Raines. "Well, yes I suppose it would be. Actually, you see, I'm just here from England on a bit of a holiday and some friends told me that you have the most astonishing variety of bird species nesting here at this time of year. I'm a bit of a birder, you see. Not professional, mind you. I suppose you could say it's rather a hobby of mine. I was hoping to have a bit of a look about. Lovely grounds, aren't they?"

The guard glanced into Raines's car and then looked around the area.

"Yes sir, it is," he said. "Hell of a lot prettier than the old swamp they filled in to build this place. Folks in these parts are mighty proud of all this. Sir, you just go on out there and look around for birds to your heart's content. Just do me a favor and y'all stay off the course itself. Just walk on the paths. They's mighty particular about this place around tournament time, and I wouldn't want you to get anyone upset."

Raines extended his arm through the car window and shook hands with the guard.

"Officer, you have my word that I won't so much as harm a

blade of your magnificent grass," Raines said. "Could you direct me to the clubhouse? I'd like to purchase a map of the course."

"Right over yonder," the guard said, pointing up the hill. "Just follow that pathway up the hill, go in the front door there, and turn right. You can't miss it. Good luck with your birds now."

Raines found his way to the golf shop and picked out a wide-brimmed straw hat to keep the sun off his face. Even in March, it was intensely hot. The hat, along with his sunglasses, would have the benefit of partially hiding his face. He went to the sales counter and asked the woman working there for a map of the course.

"We have this yardage book," she said. "It has details of all the holes plus an overall map of the course."

"Brilliant," Raines said. "I'll take one and this hat as well. I imagine this is the calm before the storm for you people."

"Oh yes, sir," she said. "Come this time next week you won't be able to hear yourself think around here. It just gets busier and busier each and every year. The Players is just about the biggest deal in this area."

Raines paged through the book as the woman rang up the sale.

"If I read this correctly, the first hole should be right down there," he said, pointing back toward the entrance.

"Just go right out the front door and head down the driveway," she said. "It'll be right there on your left. You can't miss it. Have a nice day."

By the time he reached the fifth hole, Raines was struck by how quiet and peaceful the course was. Indeed, except for the noise made by the workers out on the course, it was very nearly pastoral—so much so, in fact, that Raines was having a difficult time focusing on the job at hand.

Increasingly, in the weeks following the shooting in Los Angeles, he had been thinking about making this his last assignment. The killing of the caddie was unfortunate—"collateral damage" as he had been taught to think of it during his training in the Special Air Service—but the killing of the young girl occasionally weighed on his mind. He well knew it was necessary, of course. She had begun to doubt his BBC cover story and it was just a question of time before her suspicions would intensify. It was a risk he couldn't take.

Still...

The cold reality of his life, however, was simply that he was being paid and paid handsomely to do this one job. Once it was done, he would be wealthy enough to live comfortably on some quiet Caribbean island, which was his preference. One more killing was a matter of complete indifference to him. He had made his peace with his faith after his first mission with the SAS. In his mind, killing was killing, whether for God, Queen, and Country or for hire. It was a fine line he'd leave for the theologians to walk, for he was far beyond that now, and had been for some time.

The afternoon sun was still high in the sky when he finished walking the front nine, so Raines decided to go back into the clubhouse to have a drink and cool off in the air-conditioning before walking the second nine. The clubhouse bar was nearly empty and he took a seat toward the end of the bar.

"What can I get you?" the bartender asked, putting a coaster on the bar. "Would you like to see a menu or will it be just something to drink?"

Raines scanned the array of bottles behind the bartender.

"I think a vodka and tonic sounds about right," Raines said.

"Stoli?" the bartender asked.

"You read my mind," Raines said. "Very little ice and a lemon twist, please. Is smoking allowed?"

The bartender gazed around the room.

"I don't see any of the smoke police, so you're safe for now," he said.

Moments later, the man returned with the vodka and tonic and placed it on the bar.

"You from England?" the bartender asked.

"Yes, but I'm afraid I haven't been there for quite some time," Raines said, taking a sip of the drink.

"Did you hear the news?" the bartender asked.

"No," Raines said. "I'm afraid to ask. What did the Royals do this time?"

"I wish," the bartender said. "They said on TV that the leader of one of those Irish groups was murdered—what are they called?"

"The IRA?" Raines replied, taking another deep drink.

"That's the group," the bartender said. "Guy named McGlonahey or something. Got blown up in his car along with his bodyguard. I think your country's gone soft, my friend. First kids being blown up in London and now this. You need to find another tough guy like Churchill. He'd know how to deal with these creeps."

"Quite so," Raines said, taking $5 from his billfold and sliding it across the bar to the man. Then he drained his glass. "Old Winnie knew how to cope with murderous bastards."

Raines picked his hat off the bar and walked back outside, pausing to look out across the course.

Perfect fools is more like it, he thought. The irony that he was part of the same deadly enterprise was utterly lost on him.

He made his way back out onto the course and by the time he reached the 12th green, the sun had begun to lower slightly and the temperature had begun to cool. When he reached the 13th tee, he looked to his left and could scarcely believe his eyes. Off in the distance, just a few hundred yards away over a lagoon, was the hotel he'd passed on the way to the course.

Raines walked to the back of the last set of tees and looked back at the hotel through his binoculars. From the top floor of the hotel, he would have a clear shot from almost any room on that side of the hotel. The roof would be better yet, since it gave him a better angle. There were two large structures on either side of the roof. Air-conditioning units, he thought. Surely you must be able to get inside those to service them. If he could somehow do that, he could dispatch Brookes with a single, clear shot, escape down the stairwells or elevators, and be well down the highway before the police could set up roadblocks. Compared to the nightmarish scenario he faced in Los Angeles, this was child's play.

Raines was so certain he had found the ideal location that he returned to his car without even bothering to look at the final five holes. He was unlocking the door on the driver's side when the security guard he had met earlier cruised up in a golf cart.

"Well professor, how'd you make out?" The guard asked.

"Bloody bonanza," Raines said. "This place is a paradise."

"You come back anytime," the guard said, as he started to drive off.

"Just a moment, officer," Raines said. "I thought that I might like to come out to watch a bit of the tournament next weekend. Is traffic a problem?"

"If you're coming from the city, but if you're coming up from

St. Augustine way, it's not bad at all," the guard said. "Good luck to you. I hope we see you back again."

When the guard left, Raines pulled the map from the glove compartment and traced the routes south. If he could get onto A1A before the police blocked it off, he had a straight shot to Route 1 in St. Augustine and then onto Route 95. From there, he figured he could make it to Orlando in under three hours. With any luck, he could catch a flight and be out of the country by midnight.

Raines carefully folded the map, started the car, and drove out of the lot, slowing to wave to the guard as he drove by. The guard tipped his cap and waved.

Marvelous country, Raines thought. *Friendliest people in the bloody world. Gullible as hell, but still friendly.*

· · ·

Tom and Kathryn arrived at the course late on the morning of the first round, but Tom felt no particular sense of urgency. In fact, he felt no urgency at all. As far as he was concerned, Graham Raines was probably long gone, off to Africa or South America or some other Third World hellhole to whack another in a long line of third-rate despots who will simply be replaced by more of the same. It never changed. Peter Brookes was in more danger of getting sunstroke than getting killed.

On top of that, he had his doubts about the news coverage that reported McGonagle had been killed by elements of either the provisional IRA or the Protestants. Something that Laddie Jackson had said to Kathryn—that we might have "more time"—to run down Raines had stuck in his mind from the moment he learned of the assassination. This was far too well organized for the boyos. This had the fine, soft, fingerprints of either M.I.6 or the Agency or—as he believed—both, all over it.

Still, Kathryn was adamant about the danger that Raines still posed. It was as if she were possessed by the man and his mission. After they picked up their press credentials, they decided to head out to the course to watch Brookes finish his round. He had teed off early and Tom figured that if they walked back from the 18th green they could pick him up in time to see him play the last few holes.

It was one of those Chamber of Commerce days in Jacksonville Beach. Plenty of sun. Light winds off the Atlantic. Almost no humidity. They walked down the right side of the 18th fairway, paused to watch Billy Andrade, Jeff Sluman, and Brad Faxon hit their approach shots into the green on the par 4, and then continued walking toward the 18th tee. When they reached the tee, Tom looked into the lake that ran the entire left side of the hole, and spotted an alligator just off shore.

"Look over there," he said to Kathryn, pointing to the lake.

"Is that really an alligator?" she said. "Do they bring them in just for this tournament? What brilliant theater! They really do think of everything."

"You haven't seen anything yet," Tom said.

They turned and walked toward the 17th hole, the infamous par 3 with its island green. Even though it was a Thursday, the area to the left of the hole was already filling with people, who were busy filling themselves with beer.

The 17th might be the most notorious par 3 in the world. It certainly is one of the most recognizable. When Deane Beman, then the commissioner of the PGA Tour, hired Pete Dye to design the Stadium course, he wanted to ensure that the holes would be visually stunning for television viewers and—more importantly—that the closing holes would ensure a dramatic finish. No hole came to symbolize this to a greater degree than the 17th. At around 132 yards, for most players it is usually just a 7-, 8-, or 9-iron into a fairly generous green. The problem is that the hole is virtually surrounded by water. Complicating matters are the winds, which tend to gust and swirl, making club selection complicated. Then there is the simple matter of trying to make a good swing under almost inconceivable pressure for the leaders on Sunday.

Tom looked at his watch.

"Let's stay here for a while," he said. "We've got plenty of time to catch up with our man Brookes."

They found an open spot on the hillside to the left of the green and as luck would have it, the first player they watched found the water. His ball carried far enough to reach the green, but just as he hit it Tom felt a gust of wind from the left, off the lake bordering the 18th hole. The ball seemed to balloon in the air as it was hit by the wind, and then it drifted to the right. The ball landed on a wooden piling and careened into the air before splashing into the lake. A collective moan went up from the gallery. Back on the tee, the player reached down, picked up some grass and tossed it into the air. It drifted straight to the ground. The player just shook his head and held out his hand to his caddie for another ball.

"What does he do now?" Kathryn asked.

"Hit it again, either from there or from that circled spot closer to the green," Tom explained.

"Bloody torture," she said. "This is like one of those silly automobile races where everyone sits around like vultures waiting for the drivers to crash and burn. We don't have things like this in Britain, do we?"

"No, you've got cricket," Tom said. "It's just as deadly, but it's more of a slow death."

"*Touché*," Kathryn said.

They watched players move through the 17th for about a half hour, but by then the midday sun had become too intense to just stay in one spot. They walked in the shade down the left side of the 16th hole, cut across to the 15th, and then down the right side of the 14th.

"Not that I mind the company, Kathryn, but I think we're wasting our time," Tom said. "With McGonagle gone, Raines isn't going to hang around and he's certainly not going to risk his life taking a whack at Brookes. You said it yourself. He doesn't have any emotional investment in this. It's just a job and the guy who hired him is history. For that matter, so is most of his group. He's already gotten whatever money he's going to get. I'll bet you anything he's long gone."

They walked along in silence for a few moments before Kathryn spoke.

"Perhaps you're right," she said. "I mean, I know that's the logical way to look at all this. But don't you see that this is all so illogical on its face? Suppose, for example, that Raines looks at McGonagle's killing as simply part of a greater challenge. Wouldn't he then be inclined to make one last effort?"

"For what?" Tom said.

Kathryn started to answer, but he touched his finger to his lips and then pointed to the tee where a player was getting ready to hit his drive. The player hit and the group left the tee.

"Simply for the...I don't know, not the thrill necessarily," she said. "Perhaps the challenge of it all."

"What are you saying, that our guy is a psychopath?" Tom said. "You said something snapped back there in Argentina. You didn't say it was his mainspring."

"Well, you can scarcely think he's perfectly normal, Thomas," she said, an air of disbelief in her voice. "I mean, Christ almighty, the man is a bloody murderer. Let's not lose sight of that, shall we?"

They walked a bit further, approaching the green on the par-3 13th.

"Okay, even if he is way the hell over the edge, look around this place," Tom said. "Where would you take a shot at a guy from? How would you escape? The more I think about it, the more I think that Riviera was a fluke. The location made it his one-in-a-million chance. There's nothing here but trees and swamp."

"Oh, really?" Kathryn said, pointing toward the tee...and the hotel that loomed in the distance behind it.

• • •

The Sawgrass Marriott reflected the enormous change that the PGA Tour brought to the area when it moved its headquarters to Ponte Vedra Beach in the 1970s. With the exception of the old Ponte Vedra Inn and Club, the local hotels were nondescript mediocrities whose idea of an amenity was a working Coke machine down the hall. But with the construction of the Tournament Players Club at Sawgrass and its sister, the Valley course, the area had been transformed into an upscale golf destination rivaling any in the country.

Tom and Kathryn made their way though the lobby, past the reception desk, to a bank of elevators that took them to the top floor of the hotel, where they could look out across to the 13th tee.

"We can rule out anything lower than this floor," Tom said. "He needs at least this much elevation for a clean shot."

"And we can rule out most of the rooms on the left wing," Kathryn said. "It's almost an impossible angle."

She turned and looked at the room listings posted near the elevators.

"That leaves 10, maybe 12, rooms," she said. "The odds are pretty slim."

"Or the roof," Tom said. "Let's take a look."

They walked down the hallway until they reached the stairwell. Tom opened the door slowly and they paused, listening for footsteps or voices. After several seconds, they entered and Kathryn shut the door softly behind them. They climbed the stairs until they reached the top, and then opened the door to the outside. It took a moment for their eyes to adjust to the bright sunlight that reflected off the light beige paint. Tom checked to make sure that the door wasn't locked from the inside, and then they walked out onto the roof.

"If he weren't so exposed, this would be quite the ideal location," Kathryn said. "It's a perfect sightline, and this would give him at least some cover."

"But how much time would he really need?" Tom said. "If he knew when Brookes was going to arrive on the tee, he'd only have to be up here for five minutes, tops. And he'd be out of the hotel before anyone realized what had happened. Still, it's awfully long odds."

The breeze had died and in the still air, the heat coming off the roof was intense.

"Let's get out of here before we're reduced to two puddles," Kathryn said.

They walked down the stairwell, and as they reached the landing for the top floor, one of the housekeepers opened the door. Kathryn reacted quickly, putting her arms around Tom and kissing him.

"Oh, I sorry..." the woman said, with a Caribbean accent.

"Newlyweds on our honeymoon," Kathryn said. "I simply can't get enough of him."

"*Bon chance*," the woman said, smiling.

Tom and Kathryn walked through the door into the hallway.

"Quick thinking," Tom said.

"Anything for Queen and Country," Kathryn said.

They took the elevator to the ground level, and then walked out by the swimming pools to the outside bar, where they ordered a couple of beers. Across the lagoon, they could hear the cheers of the gallery.

"We need a plan that can guarantee us access to the roof on the weekend," Tom said. "We can't plan to just camp out up there without approval from whoever runs this place. And that's assuming Brookes even makes the cut."

"Do you think there's a chance that he won't?" Kathryn asked.

"I don't know," Tom said. "It's a tough golf course. You can sky to some big numbers pretty easily. Plus, he hasn't been playing very much, at least not competitively. It would make our life a hell of a lot easier of he shot himself out of town for the weekend."

Kathryn lifted the Heineken bottle to her lips and took a long drink. She put the bottle down on the bar and slowly began peeling off the wet label.

"I've got these credentials," she said. "What if we told them that we wanted to take some photos from the roof? Or perhaps make some paintings. They couldn't mind, could they?"

"It's worth a try," Tom said. "We'll finish these and then go find the general manager."

Tom's pager buzzed, and he checked the number.

"Langley," he said. "Let me call and see what's up."

He walked a short distance away from the bar and called the Deputy Director's number. Mary Dwyer answered and put him directly through.

"Tom, how's it going down there?" Laddie Jackson asked.

"If I were going to pick a spot for our guy Raines, this wouldn't be it, sir," Tom said. "As far as we can tell, there's only one possible place he could work from and we're trying to isolate that right now. Is surveillance picking anything up?"

"Nothing," said the Deputy Director. "My bet is that he's long gone. I'm for pulling the plug on all this, but Sir Owen is urging us to keep on and so is Senator Gardner. I don't blame them, but this is starting to feel like a wild goose chase."

"I agree," Tom said, looking over at Kathryn, who was watching him intently. "Kathryn insists that Raines won't give up. I don't know."

"Well, let's give it through the weekend and then talk on Monday," said Laddie Jackson.

"That's fine, sir," Tom said. "I'll call you then."

Tom returned to the bar and took a drink of beer.

"Well?" Kathryn said. "Any news?"

"Nothing on their end," Tom said. "The DD is giving us through the weekend and if nothing turns up, I think he's ready to call it quits."

"That would be a frightful mistake," Kathryn said.

"Maybe, but I don't see that we have much choice," Tom said. "Let's drain these and go see if we can find the general manager."

Tom reached for his wallet.

"My treat," said Kathryn, reaching into her bag and removing her wallet. As she did, a man sitting nearby stood and walked over to where they were seated.

"Excuse me," he said. "Would you pass me that ash tray? Lucky to find one of those things nowadays."

Kathryn pulled out a credit card and placed her billfold on the bar, then slid the ashtray toward the man, looking briefly in his direction.

"Thank you," he said, glancing at her card and billfold.

"Certainly," she said, handing her American Express card to the bartender. After signing the sales slip, they walked back toward the hotel. As they did, the man at the bar motioned to the bartender.

"The woman who just left here looks terribly familiar," he said, discreetly sliding a $20 bill to the bartender. "Could you tell me her name?"

The bartender looked around and then read the name off the American Express slip.

"Kathryn Devlin," he whispered to the man.

He thanked the bartender and followed Tom and Kathryn at a discreet distance, watching as they moved through the crowded lobby. With his beard and sunglasses, and the large straw hat pulled low on his forehead, Graham Raines was confident he wouldn't be recognized. Now he was sure of it and sure of something else as well.

The game was still very much on.

• • •

Tom and Kathryn went to the front desk and asked to meet with the general manager. They explained their request and minutes later were escorted by one of the bellman to the executive offices.

"Use all your charm," Tom said quietly, as they approached his office.

"Feminine or British?" she asked.

"Whatever you think will work best," Tom said. "But my money's on the feminine. Half the people in this state can't find England on a map."

The hotel's general manager, Eric Perry, was very polite, if somewhat distracted, which certainly made sense given that this was his week from hell.

"What can we do for you, Ms..."

"Devlin, Kathryn Devlin," she said, handing him her press credential. "This is my partner, Tom Quinn. We're here on assignment to cover the tournament. I'm to paint some watercolors of the tournament and I thought that if we might paint one or two from the roof of your hotel, back across the water, they would be simply smashing panoramas. Has anyone ever painted from there?"

"Not as far as I know," he said. "Would it be just one day?"

"I suppose that depends a lot on the weather and lighting," she said. "Dicey stuff, that. But we'd work as quickly as possible and promise to be most discreet."

"I don't suppose your paintings might include some of our property?" he said.

"It certainly could if you'd like," Kathryn said. "In fact, if there's anything in particular you'd like me to paint I'd be happy to help out," she added.

Eric Perry leaned back in his chair and stared up at the ceiling. Then he looked back down at Kathryn.

"I'll be here through the weekend," he said. "Here is my card. It has my direct extension. Please let me know when you want to come over and I will arrange to have someone help you out."

He rose out of his chair and extended his hand to Kathryn.

"Thank you very much, Mr. Perry," she said, shaking his hand. Tom shook his hand as well.

"Just out of curiosity," he said. "I don't suppose it would be possible for us to get a room would it? The place we're staying in down on the beach is like a dungeon compared to your hotel."

"I'm afraid not," Perry said. "Between the players and media and everyone else, we're completely booked months in advance. It's easily our biggest week of the year."

"Pity," said Kathryn, playing to his ego. "It's a lovely facility. You must be very proud."

"Thank you, we are," he said, glancing at his watch. "It's a bit early, but if you'd like I think I can get you into the Augustine Grille. It's our finest restaurant. I'm sure you'll enjoy it. Like every other place around here this week, it will be jammed later on."

Kathryn looked over at Tom.

"That will be lovely," she said. "You're most kind."

"Fine, I'll call over there and set you up," the general manager said. "It's just through the lobby. Try the Chilean Sea Bass. It's particularly good. One of the chef's favorites."

• • •

It was just after six when they entered the restaurant and although the atmosphere was quiet and restrained, it was already beginning to fill. The maitre d' checked off their names in the reservation book and escorted them to a small banquette off to the left side of the room, where the lighting was softer. As he lit the candle in the center of the table, a waiter approached with menus and a chilled bottle of mineral water.

"Enjoy your meal," the maitre d' said.

"Good evening," the waiter said, as his poured the water into their glasses. "My name is Chad and I'll be your waiter this evening. May I get you anything to drink?"

Tom looked over at Kathryn.

"Dewars with just a splash of soda," she said.

"Just over ice for me," Tom said.

"Well, that certainly went smoothly with our new best friend, Mr. Perry," Kathryn said.

"If you'll excuse me for being a sexist scum, it didn't hurt that you kept crossing and recrossing your legs," Tom said. "I thought the poor bastard was going to come flying across his desk at any minute."

"You give me too much credit," Kathryn said.

"You don't give your legs enough credit," Tom said.

"You're too kind," she said. "Thank God for sexist scum."

"Thank God for human nature," Tom said. "At least we can be pretty sure Raines didn't get a room with a nice view of the golf course."

Chad the waiter placed the drinks on the table and they ordered. Kathryn had the sea bass. Tom ordered grilled prawns.

"Here's to good luck," she said, raising her glass in a toast.

"Good luck to you and to us," Tom said.

The Dewars stung the back of his throat. He thought of Kathryn and how, if—as he expected—this weekend were going to mark the end of their partnership, he would miss her. He thought of how she had looked in the bar in Washington, on the snowy afternoon after their meeting with Senator Gardner. And he thought of the kiss in the stairwell earlier that day.

Kathryn swirled the ice in her glass with her fingers and then took another drink.

"Tom, if we are finished after this weekend, when will you be moving to Boston?" she asked. "I'd like very much to stay in touch. Perhaps I could come visit or you could see me if you come to London. I'd love to show you around. We could go to Scotland. You could play golf and I could slog around in the horrible weather."

He studied her face. The sun and the scotch had added color to her cheeks, and the candlelight was reflected in her eyes. Without any makeup, he could see the line of light freckles that ran across her nose and along the top line of her cheeks. At that moment, he thought she was one of the most beautiful women he had ever seen.

"Probably in the summer," he said. "It will take some time to finish up with the Agency. It would be great if you came in the fall. That's the most magical time of the year. It's so beautiful that it hurts."

"What do you mean, it hurts?" she asked.

"It hurts because you know it has to end," Tom said.

Kathryn leaned over and kissed him gently on his cheek.

"I know the feeling," she said.

• • •

The meals were delicious. The prawns were browned but not blackened. The sea bass was positively sublime and the wine, a Stag's Leap Chardonnay from the Napa Valley, was a nice, subtle wine with light oak traces.

They were just finishing their meals when their waiter approached with another bottle of wine, this time a red.

"You must have been more charming that I thought," Tom said. "It seems Mr. Eric Perry is smitten."

"Ms. Devlin, one of your admirers from Argentina sends his regards," the waiter said.

"Oh, my God..." Kathryn said, her voiced edged with a cold anger. "That man, where is he?"

"I don't know," the waiter said. "He came right to the maitre d's stand, pointed to your table, and asked if we could send you a bottle of wine from Argentina. He said to tell you it was from an old friend from Argentina. You're in luck. We had a few bottles of Trapiche left over from a tasting last month."

"How long ago?" she asked.

"I don't know, 10, maybe 15 minutes," the waiter said. "It took us a while to find the bottles. Trapiche isn't exactly a big seller around here."

"Bloody hell," she said. "Bloody damned hell. What did the man look like?"

"I don't know, kind of normal," the waiter said. "About average height. In his 40s. A beard—a brown beard. He was wearing a hat and sunglasses. He kind of pretty much looked like a lot of the people you see around here during The Players, except he was a little more sober. It was sort of busy and I really didn't pay that much attention. Sorry."

"Could you please get us the check? Thank you," she said.

"I don't understand," Tom said. "What's this all about?"

"It's Raines," she said. "I'll explain later. He's the only person it could possibly be."

They paid the check and walked out into the lobby. The crowds had thinned and there was no one who evenly remotely fit the description the waiter had given them.

"Tom, we need to talk," Kathryn said.

"You bet we need to talk, and you need to tell me exactly what the hell is going on," he said, more frustrated than angry.

"Can we go to the beach?" she asked.

• • •

Even though it was high tide, the wind off the Atlantic was gentle. They walked south, above the line of waves. When they were in a secluded spot near the Sawgrass Beach Club, they sat with their backs against the dunes.

"I want you to know that everything I've told you about Raines is the truth," Kathryn said, looking directly into Tom's eyes. "But I haven't told you everything that I now realize you need to know."

"I can't wait," Tom said, with more than a trace of sarcasm in his voice.

"I don't blame you for being angry, truly I don't," she said. "You have every right to feel betrayed. But I hope once I explain everything, you will understand why I needed to keep some information from you."

"I doubt it, but go ahead," Tom said.

"You know that Raines and his SAS team was captured in Argentina during the Falklands War," Kathryn said. "What you don't know is that one of the soldiers who was killed was my husband, James Devlin. We had been married for just over a year. I was working in London and this was to be his last posting. In fact, if the war hadn't broken out, James would have resigned his commission and returned to university. He planned to read for the law."

Tom said nothing, his anger overwhelming whatever sympathy he felt.

"I was devastated," Kathryn said. "James was the great love of my life. For the longest time I didn't think I could go on. It was dreadful. But in the end, I suppose, even the most grievous wounds heal. Working in the City had completely lost its appeal, and every street corner brought back the most painful memories. That's why I tested for M.I.6. I was hoping to get a foreign posting. It didn't matter where. Just anyplace that would get me well away from England."

"When did you cross paths with Raines?" Tom asked. "It seems like an awfully big coincidence."

Kathryn paused and brushed her hair back off her face.

"I had worked in Great Britain for several years, but my first foreign posting was in Pretoria, which was terribly exciting," she said. "Mandela was emerging as the great leader and apartheid was being dismantled. de Klerk was trying to work out the power sharing with the ANC, but as you can imagine, there were oceans of tension on both sides. Whitehall was most anxious to see that the transition went as smoothly as possible. At least that was the official position. To that end, M.I.6 was terribly active behind the scenes. We began to get intelligence reports indicating that elements of the more radical white separatist groups had hired Raines to assassinate members of the ANC leadership. Our great fear was, of course, that his target was Mandela. This would have been a catastrophe of a colossal scale. The entire subcontinent might well have imploded. The violence would have been unimaginable. Our embassy was given priority orders to find Raines and neutralize him—whatever that required."

"You said this was the Foreign Office's official position," Tom said. "Was there some division?"

"Quite," Kathryn said. "This is where matters began to get truly bollixed up, if you will. There was still a residue of old boys in Whitehall that were appalled by the idea of the kaffirs taking over South Africa lock, stock, and barrel. They worked in back channels to thwart de Klerk and Mandela. To further complicate matters, there remained elements in M.I.6 and SAS that felt strongly that Raines had been made the scapegoat for what was, in truth, Mrs. Thatcher's quite explicit policy. There's no doubt that if there had even been so much as a hint that the Woggies planned to go nuclear, she wouldn't have hesitated for a second to unleash the SAS teams. Hell, the old bat might well have leveled Buenos Aires.

"I learned of the connection between Raines and James quite by accident," she continued. "When we had finally established that he was in South Africa, I was given his dossier to prep up on. If anyone had made the connection between Raines and myself, it certainly didn't concern them in the least. When I read the transcript of his court-martial, I was appalled—stupefied, really—by just how cavalier he was about the failure of his mission. He had simply overstepped the bounds of his orders and yet he showed no remorse whatsoever. I don't think I was naïve, but I had never experienced such utter arrogance."

Kathryn drew her legs up to her chest and wrapped her arms around them, lowering her forehead onto her knees.

"Getting a bit chilly," she said.

"The wind has turned from the north," Tom said, removing his jacket and placing it over her shoulders. "Here, take this."

Kathryn pulled the collar of the jacket up over her neck, and leaned lightly against Tom.

"And so you wanted revenge?" Tom asked.

"No, oddly enough, not in the least," Kathryn said. "I was more intrigued than anything else. I wanted to find out what James's last days had been like and take measure of the man, that sort of thing. Of course, that wouldn't have been possible, given the circumstances."

"How did it finally play out?" Tom asked.

"As badly as possible," she said. "It turned out to be a classic double-cross. We had turned one of the collaborators, and learned of a meeting they had planned with Raines. Our plan was to seize him and return him to England on a clandestine RAF flight. Unfortunately, he learned of our plans in the final moments. We always suspected someone in M.I.6 but could never determine who that person or persons was. At any rate, it went very badly. Our people arrived as Raines was fleeing the meeting. He shot and killed one of our senior operatives. It wasn't just that he killed him. He had wounded him and could have still made his escape. Instead, he finished him with a shot to the head from close range. It was murder, pure and simple."

"Were you there?" Tom asked.

"No," Kathryn said. "I was with the backup squad. We were there to escort him to the RAF flight. I will never forget the carnage. We were all quite in shock. From that day forward, M.I.6 has resolved to bring Raines to justice, one way or the other."

"So this isn't about the peace process after all," Tom said.

"Oh, no, that's where you're quite wrong," she said. "It's very much about trying to salvage that. But given the chance to bring down Raines at the same time only increased the urgency of our efforts. That's why I've been so adamant about not backing off on our quest. We simply believed that this was too great an opportunity to let pass by. Your skepticism was a problem, I concede, but we felt confident we could persevere."

"Does the Deputy Director know all this?" Tom asked.

"I can't say with certainty, but I suspect he does," Kathryn said. "There are a lot of secrets in this business but I don't think he and Sir Owen keep many from one another. At least, not if they don't have to. They both understand the danger that Raines and people like him pose. It's in neither country's interests to have them about, plying their hideous trade."

Tom stood up, took Kathryn's hand, and lifted her from the sand.

"C'mon, let's head back, it's going to get cold pretty quickly when that wind picks up," Tom said.

They walked north along the beach, the lights of the hotels shining in the dark ahead of them.

"How do you figure in all this?" he asked.

"How do you mean?" Kathryn asked.

"I mean, is Raines your project?" he asked.

"Not at all," Kathryn said. "It was coincidental that after my posting in South Africa I was transferred to Spain. There was an assassination of a government official that E.T.A, the Basque separatist organization, claimed credit for. Our information pointed to Raines, and that brought me back into the picture. Then it was just a matter of luck or fortunate timing that I was assigned to Ulster when the Peace Process began to unravel and McGonagle set about his business. When we linked up Raines with the old man, Sir Owen dropped it in my lap."

They walked for a while in silence. The only sounds were the waves washing ashore and the winds coming down along the beach.

"I don't believe in luck and timing," he said. "And I'm not sure I believe that it was fate that every time Raines surfaces, you happen to be stationed there. That's just too great a coincidence. And I don't believe for one minute that this isn't personal—especially after tonight. I think it's personal for both of you—very personal—and that makes me more than a little nervous. When things get personal in this business, people make mistakes, and when people make mistakes, people get hurt—or worse. I don't want to see that happen to you. "

"Then all I can do is ask you to take me at my word," she said. "I think I've earned that much. If I haven't, we can part ways right now. I'll go on my own. I know now, surer than ever before, that this is the time and the place when Graham Raines must and will be stopped. If not now, then soon. He will be the one who makes the mistakes. I'm certain of it. What a supreme act of egotism tonight was. Don't you see that?"

"Oh, I don't know," Tom said, stopping and facing Kathryn. "From where I stand, there's more than enough egotism to go around. Look, I don't blame you at all for wanting to bring this guy down. He's responsible for your husband's death. He murdered one of your people and God knows how many other people, some of whom probably deserved it, as far as I can tell. But to think that you can bring him down on your own..."

"On *our* own," Kathryn interrupted, her eyes narrowed with anger and her lips pursed. "On *our* own, Thomas. We're a team, or have you forgotten that? I certainly haven't. I couldn't have come nearly this far without you. Don't you think I know that? Don't you think that the Deputy Director and Sir Owen knew that when they selected you for this job? Do you want to quit? Then quit, damn you. Quit right this second and go back to your beloved Boston and become a banker with your pal Pres or Biff or whatever his name is. You'll be miserable in a week. No, make that suicidal. I've worked with his type. I've actually even fucked a few."

"Oh, congratulations," Tom snapped. "Was it good for you?"

"No, it was an out-of-body experience," she said. "I believe you call it sport fucking."

"A mercy fuck would be more like it," Tom said.

"Call it what you'd like. Look, the point is if you want to just piss bloody off, go right ahead and quit."

"Fuck you," he said.

Kathryn applauded sarcastically.

"Brilliant," she said. "The soul of wit—or at least brevity. I'll give you that much. Well, what is it going to be? Stay or go. Make up your mind."

Tom paused for a second and stared into her eyes. The anger he had seen minutes earlier had softened.

"Well?" she said.

He put his arms around her waist and kissed her. She kissed him back, softly and tentatively at first, and then firmly and put her arms around his neck. They kissed and then kissed again. She pressed her body against his and then buried her face against his neck.

"Don't go," she said

He pulled away from her slightly, and brushed the hair off her face. He leaned forward and kissed her gently on the forehead.

"No, I'll stay," he said.

"Thank you," she said.

"At least for tonight," Tom said, and put his arm over her shoulders and began to walk back up the beach.

"Oh, really?" she said. "And who's being an egotistical bastard now?"

• • •

Kathryn was gone when Tom awoke in her room. She had left the complimentary copy of *USA Today* near the television. Tom flipped on the "Today" show, then pulled out the sports section and found the scores for the first round of The Players Championship. The good news was that when it came to Peter Brookes, he should have started at the bottom of the list, with the DQs, WDs, and guys who cranked out rounds in the 80s. Brookes wasn't quite that bad, but on a day when the conditions set up to produce some low scores, he scraped it around with a 76. That meant that unless he went low today, he'd be gone for the weekend and so, with any luck, would Graham Raines.

Of course, true to form, Brookes had a ready explanation for his poor play—an explanation that had virtually nothing to do with him.

"I want to congratulate the Tour for hiring the mentally unbalanced," he was quoted in the paper. "Whoever set the pins for today's round was quite clearly psychotic."

Never mind that four players shared the lead with five-under-par 67s, cutting Brookes by nine strokes and forcing him to come up with a miracle today if he was going to be around for the weekend—and the forecast wasn't exactly made-to-order for miracles. The winds, which had turned from the north when they were on the beach the previous evening, were now blowing steadily harder, and the temperatures had dropped overnight into the 50s and weren't expected to get out of the 60s all day.

He heard the door open and Kathryn entered, carrying two coffees from Starbucks and a copy of the *New York Times*.

"Look," she said. "Just like being in America."

"Don't kid yourself," Tom said. "*This* is America. New York, L.A., and Washington. Those aren't the real America.

He looked over at the television, where the "Today" show cameras were panning the crowd gathered around Rockefeller Center. The people were screaming and yelling, jumping up and down, holding up signs saying hello to Matt and Katie, and hoping against hope to get on camera so the folks back home in Des Moines would see what fun The Big City really is.

"See that?" he said, pointing to the television. "*That's* America. And they couldn't care less about whether your Peace Process succeeds or fails. They're bored with the insanity between the Israelis and the Arabs, and if you gave them a map of the Balkans, they couldn't find any of the countries if you gave them a clue, a one-hand head start, and a $1 million prize. Even the blacks think Africa is a wasteland, except for the usual suspects."

"Here you go, Thomas, have some coffee," Kathryn said. "You seem a bit sluggish this morning. Last night must have taken too much out of you. "

"Don't get me started," he said.

"I'm afraid I have, somehow," Kathryn said, walking over to where he laid back against the headboard, sat down and kissed him gently on the forehead.

"Well then, since we're here in *your* magnificently isolationist—not to mention irrationally xenophobic—America, what are the plans for today?" Kathryn asked.

"We may have caught a break," he said, opening the paper to the tournament scores. "Brookes shot a 76 yesterday, which means he has to play his ass off today just to make the cut. If he doesn't, he's out of here and so are we."

"After I played *my* ass off last night," she said, "I didn't think you'd consider leaving such a great break."

"You know what I mean," he said. "I think the best plan is for you to get over to the Marriott by noon. Brookes has a 10:30 starting time, which means he should get to 13 around 1:00 or 1:30. I'm going to pick him up at the turn and stick with him on the back nine. Do you think Raines will try anything today?"

"I suspect not," Kathryn said. "He's likely to go for the big play, as you say, on the weekend. Besides, I don't fancy his chances if these winds keep up—at least not from any distance, unless he has a bloody elephant gun."

"Just to be on the safe side, I think you should carry your

Beretta," Tom said.

"Right," she said. "And you?"

"Sure," Tom said. "After last night, I think we should both be armed."

"I suppose that depends on which part of last evening you're referring to," Kathryn said, rising from the bed and walking toward the bathroom, pulling her turtleneck off over her head and tossing it over her shoulder toward Tom.

· · ·

Tom's phone call to the Deputy Director was, to use the language of diplomacy, frank and candid. He told him that he was certain that Raines was in the area but voiced his concerns that, based on Kathryn's revelations about the South African shooting and her involvement, this entire operation extended far beyond the need to preserve the peace plan.

"I think we're being played on this one," he told the Deputy Director. "M.I.6 has a much broader agenda. This is about revenge, both for them and for Kathryn."

"Be that as it may, Tom, but we've got an agenda of our own," the Deputy Director said. "Believe me, it's very much in our own interest to see that Raines is neutralized. He's connected with groups far more dangerous to our interests than our Irish friends. Trust me, this is a very high priority."

· · ·

At the same time, Kathryn placed a call to Sir Owen in London.

"I'm afraid my friend is going a bit wobbly on us," she said. "I don't think he fully grasps the gravity of the situation. It might be good to contact your friend in Washington and buy us a bit of support. I think we're very close to terminating our problem once and for all."

"I understand," said Sir Owen. "It will be taken care of immediately."

· · ·

Tom reached the course just after noon. Because of the strong, cold winds and the threat of showers, the galleries were smaller than they had been on Thursday. Even though he was wearing a sweater and a rainproof jacket, when the sun went behind the clouds it was uncomfortable. The wind just seemed to cut through the clothing. He walked down the cart path, past the 18th green, toward the 9th green, where David Duval's group was just putting out. Brookes, in the next group, was preparing to hit his third shot into the green.

The pin was cut to the left side of the putting surface, a tough placement because that side of the green was protected by a deep bunker. Brookes had played a smart second shot, however, down the right side of the fairway, leaving himself with a good angle into the pin. The wind was blowing from his right-to-left, and Brookes hit a sand wedge that started at the right side of the green and was pushed back toward the pin by the wind. The ball hit in the middle of the green, checked, and spun left toward the hole, coming to rest 10 feet from the flagstick, drawing applause from the gallery. Brookes acknowledged the applause with a slight wave, and began walking toward the green.

Brookes was the last to putt, and as he lined up his attempt, Tom scanned the gallery. Certainly no one even remotely suspicious there, unless Raines was such a master of disguise that he could pass himself off as a retiree or a kid skipping a day of school to watch a little golf.

Brookes took one more look at his putt, and then stood over his ball. He took two practice strokes and one final look at the hole, tracing the line of his putt back to the ball with his eyes. Just as he pulled the putter back from the ball, a gust of wind blew across the green. To his credit, Brookes had the discipline to stop in midstroke and back away from the ball. Then he walked back behind the ball and went through his routine again.

"Hit it, you plodder," said a man with a British accent standing with his friends near Tom. "Brilliant player, Brookes is, but he'll be out here until the Second Coming."

Brookes was methodical, but he had been correct to step away and start over. He hit a good putt, but it rimmed out of the hole, leaving himself a tough three-footer to save par. He jammed it into the hole and walked off the green with a two-under par 34, a particularly good score on a day that saw the leaders begin to move back to the rest of the field. Still, Brookes had his work cut out for him on the back nine if he was going to have any chance of being around on the weekend. Looking at the scoring, Tom figured he'd have to get to at least even par, and possibly one-under.

The Englishman got off to a good start, ripping a 3-wood down the right side of the 415-yard, par-4 10th. But his 9-iron second shot ballooned into the wind and came up short, in the bunker guarding the front-right quarter of the green. Brookes watched the result with a look of disbelief, then took his sand wedge from his caddie and headed down the fairway.

The bunker shot Brookes faced was not easy, since the pin was cut just 12 paces from the edge of the green nearest to the bunker. He took his stance, working his feet into the sand and setting most of his weight to his left side. He set his hands behind the ball at address, took the club away with a quick cocking of his wrists, and then slid the club under the ball. When Tom heard the "thud" of the club hitting the sand, he knew it was a good shot. The ball landed in the fringe and rolled to within inches of the hole, leaving Brookes with a tap-in for his par.

Walking to the tee on the 529-yard, par-5 11th, Tom wondered how Brookes would attack the hole, knowing that he had to get at least a couple birdies on the back nine. The hole offers players a variety of options. Given the proper conditions, they can drive down the right side of the fairway and gamble on an approach over a water hazard and a long bunker to a green that slopes away from them. A large bunker divides the fairway, along with a smaller bunker and a water hazard, and players who decide to lay up with the second shots must decide which side of the fairway to play to. Much of their decision is based upon the winds and the pin position. A pin cut to the back left favors an approach from the right side of the fairway, while any placement on the right half of the green is easier to reach from the left half of the fairway.

Brookes hit a fine drive but Tom doubted he'd gamble on trying to reach the green in two. He wasn't particularly long, and while he was very good with his fairway woods and long irons, this was a tough green to hit in the gusting winds. True, he needed a four, but he couldn't afford a six, and the other par 5 on this side was the 16th, which was very reachable and offered a much more realistic chance for a four—or even a three, if Brookes got lucky.

After Brookes and his caddie reached his ball, they studied the yardage book. The caddie checked the tops of the trees and indicated that the wind was quartering from right-to-left and slightly against. The hole was cut in the narrowest part of the green, the front, making an approach from the right side of the fairway much more difficult than one from the left side, where you'd be shooting right into the deepest part of the green.

Brookes pulled out an iron—it looked from where Tom stood like a 6- or 7-iron—and hit his second shot safely into the fairway. It was a good, smart play. And while he wasn't rewarded with a birdie, he came away with a par on a very difficult hole, and as Tom knew, on a course this treacherous, patience is more than a virtue—it's a requirement. With the short, par-4 12th coming up, perhaps he would pick up a stroke there.

The 12th was only 353 yards long, but it was a classic "risk-reward" short par 4, the kind of hole that has enjoyed a revival of popularity thanks to designers like Pete Dye and Tom Weiskopf. A bunker guards the right side of the hole, but it offers the best approach into the small green, which is protected by a series of grass and sand bunkers. The left side of the fairway has grass bunkers and mounds, although the mounds were much less severe than they were originally, when Tom played the course just after it opened.

Brookes hit a long iron from the tee, and the ball came to rest in the center of the fairway, about 125 yards from the hole. Standing in the fairway, Brookes could feel the wind coming strongly from his left, but as he and his caddie discussed the shot he faced, he pointed to the green, where the flag was barely fluttering.

Brookes took a 9-iron and set the ball back in his stance. He hit the shot softly, because the nine was plenty of club and he wanted to keep the ball under the tree line, where it wouldn't be hit by the wind.

He played the shot beautifully. The ball landed on the front of the green, skipped twice, and then settled and began to roll toward the hole, which was cut in the back left of the green. It came to rest four feet from the hole.

As they approached the green, the putt looked fairly simple—if such a putt exists on this course—but in fact, it turned out to be very difficult. It was downhill, with a right-to-left break at the end.

If he hit it gently and tried to die it at the hole, it would break sharply. But if he tried to play it firmly and take the break out of the putt, he ran the risk of spinning it out of the hole and leaving himself a tough par putt. In the end, Brookes decided to try and finesse the ball into the hole. He barely touched the ball, and it trickled toward the hole. Inches from the cup it looked like it was going in, but as it lost speed it moved to the left and rolled right across the front of the hole, coming to rest on the edge.

As he walked through the trees toward the 13th tee, Tom thought that while Brookes might well be a world-class pain in the ass, he had to be respected for the quality of his play and how well he thought his way around a golf course. For such a tall man, his swing was very tight and controlled, with very few extraneous movements. His positions at every point in the swing were textbook. No funny angles and no compensations for flawed fundamentals. His ball striking was very solid—so solid, in fact, the winds didn't seem to affect his shots as much as those of the other players. But what really impressed Tom was the fact that Brookes seldom seemed to make a mental error. Whatever shot he hit seemed to be the right shot at just that moment. Sure, he occasionally missed shots. Everyone does. But Brookes seemed to have a keen sense of when to gamble and when to play safe. And he also had that rarest of abilities that all the great players had—the ability to elevate their game when they needed to take it to another level in order to win. Tom was also impressed by his attitude. He seemed to be constantly in control of his emotions. There were no real highs or lows in his attitude, no matter what was happening in his round. Tom had never seen Ben Hogan play, but as he reached the tee, he thought that it must have been very much like watching Peter Brookes take apart a golf course.

The 13th hole is a 172-yard par 3, with water running down the entire left side of the hole. The green is divided into three tiers, with the front tier being the highest, followed by the back right and then the left, which is the section of the green that really brings the water into play and traditionally provides the most drama during Sunday's final round.

The pin was cut in the back-right portion of the green, which was a safe pin placement but not an easy one to get to, since the wind was coming from the right side of the hole.

Brookes pulled a 6-iron from his bag and aimed for the center of the green, playing for a cut that he could hold against the wind. Even though he had missed a good birdie chance on the previous hole, he resisted the temptation to try to make up for it on this difficult one.

He opened his stance slightly at address and cut across the ball at impact, keeping his hands moving through the hitting area slightly ahead of the clubface. The ball headed for the center of the green and then began to drift slightly back toward the pin. The ball landed safely on the putting surface, leaving him with a 20-foot birdie putt.

When Brookes and his group left for the green, Tom moved to the far end of the tee and called Kathryn on his cell phone. There was a slight delay in making the connection, and then she picked up on the third ring.

"I could see you perfectly from here," she said.

"How is it up there?" he asked.

"I'm positively freezing," she said. "Fortunately my new best friend, Bianca, is keeping me amply fortified with hot tea or I might simply turn into a block of ice."

"Anything suspicious?" he asked.

"Not a thing," Kathryn said. "Now that your group has gone through, I'm going to go downstairs and try to warm up, although I may be past what mere brandy can do medicinally. I will meet you back here in the lobby in a couple of hours."

She put her phone back in her bag, gathered up her paints and brushes, and put those away as well, and then walked over to the door leading to the stairwell. As she opened the door, she heard footsteps from a nearby floor echoing in the darkened stairwell. After a few moments, the noise stopped.

"Bianca?" Kathryn called. "Is that you?"

There was no response. Kathryn reached into her bag and removed the Beretta, clicking off the safety and slowly and quietly loading a round into the chamber.

She stood motionless and listened but there wasn't a sound. She edged over to the railing and looked down. There was no light from the landing on the next floor. She searched in the darkness for movement, and when she didn't see anyone, she edged down the stairs, constantly looking over the side of the stairway. When she was just steps away from reaching the landing for the next floor, she gently laid her bags down and held the pistol in front of her, with her left hand under her right. She paused, took another deep breath, and then spun to her right with her arms out-stretched in front of her. She frantically looked around the landing, the gun tracing the movement of her eyes. Seconds later, when she realized she was alone, she leaned against the wall, clicked on the safety, and then slid down and sat on a step.

Perhaps a minute or two passed before she walked quietly over to the exit door and opened it slowly, the pistol off to the side so if anyone was in the hallway, they wouldn't see it. The hall was empty, except for the supply carts used by the housekeeper. With the light from the hall coming through the doorway, she checked the light bulb. After a slight turn, the bulb was illuminated. She paused, and then eased the door shut. As she did, she heard another door close, several floors below. She waited and listened, but there were no other sounds, so she retrieved her bags and put the Beretta away.

Riding in the elevator to the lobby, she told herself that it was probably nothing. A housekeeper or possibly some kids. She was probably overreacting. Maybe. Or maybe not.

• • •

Tom caught up with Brookes in time to see him sink his par putt and head for the tee on the 455-yard, par-4 14th. He looked at a leader board and knew that Brookes was running out of time. He needed at least two birdies, and the chances that he would make one on this hole weren't very good at all.

The hole had water and a narrow bunker that ran down the left side of the fairway. Even if Brookes hit the fairway on the left, he could still be in trouble because a stand of tall oaks block the green from that side, and a large bunker protects that side of the green as well. But there's no bailout on the right side of the land-ing area, as rough and mounds come into play for drives lost to the right.

With the pin set in the far left side of the green, the ideal drive would favor the right side of the landing area, but Brooks, trying to hit a fade, came over the top and hit his drive left of center in the fairway. He was slightly blocked out by the trees but had hit his drive far enough that Tom thought he could go at the green with a 5-iron or maybe a 6.

Watching him prepare to hit his shot, Tom thought that this is where Brookes's height is an advantage. When other players would have had to hit a hard, sweeping hook that could easily get away from them, Brookes could hit the ball high enough to take it over the trees with a draw, allowing him to get the ball back to the pin.

The shot Brookes played was perfect, bordering on the majestic—one of the finest shots Tom had ever seen. The ball tore off the clubface, rising swiftly and easily clearing the oaks. At the height of its trajectory, it began to curve to the left and landed just on the front edge of the green, rolling to a stop within four feet of the hole. The gallery gathered by the green applauded and Tom could hear the cheers back in the landing area. But Brookes took it all in stride, barely acknowledging the gallery and walking purposefully toward the green.

Watching Brookes brought back memories of Tom's old teacher, Bruce Codding, who helped forge his game as a junior. Once, when he was playing in one of his first statewide championships, Tom had hit a spectacular 4-iron approach to the 18th green at The Country Club in Brookline. The hole was cut close to the front of the green, just past the bunkers. Tom hit a very high approach that stopped just inches from the hole, nailing down his victory. When he saw the ball land by the hole, Tom fell over on his back. After the match, his pro—an old Yankee—took him aside in the locker room.

"When you hit a great shot, do yourself a favor," Codding said. "Don't act surprised."

Tom thought that at some point in Peter Brookes's career, someone had told him the same thing.

Tom always thought that the 15th hole, a 440-yard par 4, was sort of the sleeper on the back nine. The 16th, 17th, and 18th get all the attention, but a lot of tournaments have been lost on the 15th over the years. It's a tough driving hole. Players tee off through a chute of trees to a landing area protected by a large bunker down the right side and trees along the left. A long, large bunker sits to the left of the green, along with grass bunkers that are scattered around the green. To top things off, the green is bisected by a swale that makes it imperative that approach shots wind up in the proper section of the green.

Brookes, coming off his birdie on 14, decided to play conservatively and took a fairway wood from the tee, starting the ball down the left side of the hole and cutting it back into the center of the fairway. The hole was in the back right of the green, a difficult pin to attack because of the two bunkers that guarded that side of the putting surface.

With 143 yards to the front of the green, Brookes took an 8-iron and started it at the center of the green and cut it back toward the hole. The ball landed on the front edge, ran up the swale, and then turned and rolled back toward the hole, coming to rest six feet from the pin.

Brookes knew this was a crucial putt. If he could make a birdie here and then make at least a four on the 16th, he had an excellent chance to be in contention going into the weekend—if he could keep the ball dry on 17 and 18.

There was no question the putt was going to move from left to right. The key was matching the right speed to the correct line. He decided to try to just get the ball to the hole, and read about six inches of break as the ball came off the swale. As soon as he hit it, Brookes was sure it was going to go. Sure enough, the ball was barely rolling when it fell into the center of the cup for his third three in three holes. He was finally at even par, but more importantly, the leaders had stumbled to three-under, and Brookes was right back in the game.

Like the 13th at Augusta National, the 497-yard, par-5 16th at the Stadium course is a dramatic hole because it offers so much potential reward, balanced by great danger for the player willing to take a gamble. When the course was being designed, Deane Beman insisted that the hole give players fighting for the lead a chance to gamble on making a four or even a three, while making it risky for the leader to play the hole conservatively to protect his lead. The 16th does this beautifully.

Brookes hit a big drive, a powerful draw that left him with 210 yards to the front of the green. More importantly, however, he was in the center of the fairway. Drives hit to the right required players trying to hit the green in two to flirt with the pond on the right side of the green. Bailing out to the left from the tee brings the trees near the green into play, as well as the thick rough.

There was never any doubt that Brooke was going for the green in two. He had a perfect angle to carry the ball onto the front edge and let it feed back toward the pin. His biggest concern was that he might overclub downwind and put the ball in the water behind the green.

Brookes was between a 4-iron and a 5, and decided to play safe with the 5. He hit another solid iron shot, and watched as it landed safely in the center of the green, leaving a 25-footer to the hole cut on the front right of the green. By now, there was almost a sense of inevitability about Brookes's round. No one seemed surprised when he made the putt—least of all Peter Brookes.

For the first time in the championship, Peter Brookes was in red figures and on the first page of the leader board. But he knew better than anyone how quickly that could disappear on the last two holes.

If the 16th was a tough place to protect a lead, the 17th was all but impossible. At 135 yards, it was usually something between a 7-iron and a pitching wedge, depending on the winds and the pin placement. Friday's placement was among the easiest on the green, on the front side of the ridge that runs across the green. The problem was the wind, which swirled and gusted, making club selection difficult.

Brookes would hit first. That was good because he wouldn't have to watch if his fellow competitors ahead of him found the water. The down side was that he wouldn't get to see what the other players hit, and take a read off their club selection.

Brookes tossed some grass into the air and checked the treetops to try to gauge the wind. On the tee it seemed to be in his face, yet the flag and the trees behind the green showed a wind quartering from the left.

"We've got 121 to carry the water plus eight to the hole," said his caddie. "It's a good pitching wedge."

Brookes studied the shot, his hand alternating between the pitching wedge and his 9-iron. After a few moments, he pulled the 9.

"Just a good, smooth swing," his caddie said, as he pulled the bag away from the ball.

Brookes addressed the ball, choking down slightly on the grip and positioning the ball back slightly in his stance. He made a good, three-quarter swing, and watched as the ball carried over the flag, landed softly, and rolled up the swale. Just as it reached the top and looked like it might stay there, leaving a difficult putt, the ball paused and then slowly began to trickle back down the slope toward the hole. As it did, the roar from the crowd increased. Brookes dropped his club and began motioning for the ball to keep rolling toward him. The gallery loved it.

The ball finally came to rest just over five feet from the hole. It was a dead straight putt and it seemed all but certain that Brookes would pick up another stroke. Maybe it was because it was such an easy putt, or because his string of good fortune had finally run out, Brookes missed. The ball never threatened the hole, and when he tapped in for his par, Tom wondered how it would affect him on the final hole. Would he become deflated or would he shake it off and make one last birdie?

When Brookes reached the tee of the 440-yard par 4, his caddie took the headcover off his driver and started to pull the club from the bag. Brookes shook him off and held up three fingers. *Smart play*, Tom thought. He ran the risk of blowing the ball through the fairway with his driver, leaving himself with no option but to pitch the ball back into the fairway to try to salvage his par.

Instead, Brookes took the 3-wood, started the ball down the right rough, and turned it back into the center of the fairway. With the hole exposed to the wind, Brookes had 211 yards to the front edge of the green and 227 to the hole. Tom didn't expect Brookes would try to force the ball back to the hole. Instead, he thought Brookes would play for the center of the green and let the ball feed back toward the hole. His biggest concern was not losing the ball to the left, into either the bunker or, worse, the water.

Brookes took a long iron from his bag, and his caddie flashed four fingers to the nearby cameraman. By hitting a 4-iron, Brookes was taking any trouble behind the green out of play. Another smart play. He'd be better off pitching from short of the green than trying to play from the deep rough or the bunkers.

If Brookes was tiring or disappointed by his failure to birdie the 17th, it didn't show in his approach shot. It bore through the wind, landing some 10 feet on the front of the green and releasing toward the flag. It came to rest pin-high, 12 feet from the hole. The putt was fairly straight, with perhaps just a couple inches of break from left to right.

Brookes put a beautiful stroke on the ball, and the perfect speed helped it hold the line. As it left the putter, an enormous roar began to build in the grandstands to the right of the green. When the ball began to take the break halfway to the hole, Brookes raised his putter in the air with his left hand and began to walk toward the hole. When the ball fell from sight, he stopped and shot his arms in the air, shaking them in celebration. The cheering continued until Brookes motioned to the gallery to settle down so his fellow players could finish off their rounds. When they did, they both congratulated Brookes on one of the most remarkable finishes anyone had seen at Sawgrass in a very long time. Six straight threes on one of the world's most demanding courses. By shooting a seven-under-par 65 under brutal conditions, Peter Brookes had not only kept himself around on the weekend, but he had played himself very much into contention.

The gallery resumed cheering as Brookes left the green and went into the scoring tent. The roar was so enormous that the group back in the fairway waited to hit their second shots. Finally, Brookes stepped from the tent and waved to the gallery like Yaz being called out of the dugout at Fenway for one long, last goodbye.

Tom followed Brookes to the media center on the far side of the clubhouse. He was surrounded by people, mostly kids seeking autographs, but they were largely blocked by police and private security. The few that did manage to get an autograph got that and no more. No eye contact. Not even the briefest word of thanks or acknowledgment that they were anything more than a necessary inconvenience as he tried to get from here to there. They were the human equivalent of a bunker or a water hazard.

The interview area was jammed with writers, photographers, and television crews, but unlike the adoring galleries, they didn't seem particularly thrilled to be in the presence of Mr. Peter Brookes. It didn't take long to figure out why.

Brookes began the interview session by going over his scorecard, hole-by-hole.

"Driver, pitching wedge to 12 feet, two putts; 3-wood, 8-iron to six feet, one putt" and so on.

After he finished, the Tour's media official opened the floor for questions. The first came from a young woman writer.

"How did you find the course today?" she asked.

"It was quite easy, actually," Brookes said. "I simply got in my car, took a left out of the hotel and then another left at the Tour offices. I kept driving quite intently and, to my astonishment, it was right there."

A few of the writers groaned. The woman blushed and stared down at her notebook.

"What an asshole," said one of the writers standing near Tom.

"All-world, all the time," said another nearby writer.

After a few mundane questions and answers, Brookes reverted to form.

"What was the difference between yesterday's round and today's," another writer asked.

"Eleven strokes," he said.

The interview droned on for several more minutes until Brookes came up with an answer that was actually pretty good, but didn't amuse the Tour's media official.

"Peter, coming off your victory in last year's Open championship, how would you compare this tournament to the Open?" a British writer asked.

"There is no comparison," Brookes said.

"What's the difference?"

"One hundred years," said Brookes.

Laughter erupted in the room.

"Okay, does everyone have what they need?" the media guy asked, not waiting for a response. "Thank you, Peter."

Giving credit where it is due, Brookes had given everyone their lead for the next day's stories.

Tom found his car in the media lot and returned to the Marriott. The lobby was already crowded and it took him a while to finally find Kathryn, who was standing near the lobby bar. She seemed to be staring intently at the man standing next to her, but when she spotted Tom approaching, she waved and a look of relief came over her face.

"Tom, this is...I'm sorry, tell me your name again," she said.

"Ouelette, Lou Ouelette," he said, extending his hand to Tom.

"Oh, yes, that's right," Kathryn said. "Everyone calls him

'Frenchy,' though, because he's from Montreal. Isn't that just divinely clever?"

Tom looked at Kathryn as though she had recently misplaced her mind.

"Really?" Tom said. "Are you here for the tournament?"

"No, my trade group is here for a convention," he said "We just came over for the afternoon. We followed that Brookes. I don't know much about golf, but he's a beaut, eh? Made those other fellows look like they didn't know if they were going side by each."

"Oh, what line of business are you in?" Kathryn asked.

"I work for a company that grinds specialty optical lenses," he said, reaching into his shirt pocket and handing each of them a business card.

"That must be why you're making a spectacle out of yourself, Frenchy," Kathryn said.

Before you could say "Sacre bleu," Mr. Lou "Frenchy" Ouelette of the Montreal Ouelettes, was gone in search of easier prey.

"Good Lord, what a bore," Kathryn said, taking a sip of her brandy. "Thank God you finally got here. If he had oozed any more Gaelic charm, I would have needed to shower off. Where were you? Brookes finished quite a while ago."

"I stayed and watched our guy try to charm and impress the writers," he said.

"How'd it go?" she asked.

"I'd say it was a huge success," Tom said. "No one had punched him out by the time I left. How many of those have you had?"

"Two large, but I earned it," she said.

Kathryn waited until Tom ordered a beer and then began telling him the story about the footsteps in the stairwell and the light bulb that had been tampered with. Neither of them noticed the two police officers approaching through the crowd.

"Ma'am, I'm Sgt. Giles of the Jacksonville Police Department," the tall, muscular officer said in a hushed voice. "This is Patrolman Oakley. We'd like you to come with us."

"Whatever for?" Kathryn said.

"Is there a problem, Sergeant?" Tom asked.

"Are you together?" the sergeant asked.

"Yes," Tom said.

"Would you please both come with us then?" he said. "We'd like you to come quietly. We'd prefer to attract as little attention as possible."

"Fine," Kathryn said. "Let me just get my bags."

"Actually, we'll get them, ma'am," the female officer said. "Just point them out, please."

"That won't be necessary," Kathryn said. "I'm perfectly capable of carrying them."

"Yes ma'am, we're sure you are," the sergeant said. "But I'm afraid we have to insist."

"Very well, then," Kathryn said, pointing to the bags. "They're right there."

The woman officer picked up the bags and the four walked through the crowd, which had suddenly grown quiet. Every eye seemed to follow them as they made their way through the lobby. When they reached the reception area they were joined by a member of the front desk staff. The man led them to an empty conference room, and then left, shutting the large wooden doors behind him.

"What's this all about, Sergeant?" Tom asked.

"Ma'am, we'd like your permission to check your belongings," the sergeant said. "You don't have to allow us to, but if you don't, we have the authority to perform such a search. Do you understand that?"

"Yes, of course," Kathryn said.

The female officer began methodically searching Kathryn's bags. As she did, Kathryn looked impassively at Tom, who returned her gaze. The officer pulled out her address book. Then reached back into the bag.

"Bingo," she said, pulling the Beretta from the bag, checking to make sure the safety was in place before handing it to the sergeant, who ejected the round from the chamber and released the clip. He laid the pistol and the clip on the table.

"Ma'am, I surely hope you have a license for this," the sergeant said. "Would you please stand up and step away from the table so Officer Oakley can make sure you don't have another one of these little beauties hidden someplace."

"Sergeant, that won't be necessary, if you'll let us explain," Tom said, placing his hands palms down on the table. "For starters, you can just reach under my jacket—right there," he said, motioning to his left shoulder with his head—"and remove mine as well."

The sergeant reached over and unzipped Tom's wind jacket, then removed the pistol from his shoulder holster. Just as he had done with Kathryn's Beretta, he removed the clip and then checked to make sure the chamber of Tom's pistol was empty as well.

"I'm with the Central Intelligence Agency and Ms. Devlin is from British Intelligence," Tom said. "M.I.6."

"And I assume you have some sort of identification," the Sergeant said.

"Yes, right here," Kathryn said, starting to reach for her bag.

"Uh-uh," the officer said, sliding the bag away from Kathryn. "Just tell us where it is and I'll get it for you."

"In my wallet, along with the permit to carry the gun from the Commonwealth of Virginia," Kathryn said.

The woman officer searched through the bag and found the wallet. She handed it to Kathryn, who produced both her M.I.6 identification as well has her British passport and handed them to the officer.

"They look legitimate," the female officer said, handing them to the sergeant.

"Your turn," the Sergeant said, looking at Tom. "Slowly."

Tom reached into his jacket, unzipped a pocket and pulled out his billfold. He handed his documents to the sergeant, who looked at them closely before handing them back to the officer.

"Call those permits in and have them checked out," the sergeant said.

The officer walked to the far side of the room and Tom could overhear her calling in the request to headquarters.

"Well, what is it that brings you to our fair city and what makes you think that you need to be packing?" the Sergeant asked.

Kathryn looked over at Tom.

"We'd rather not get into that right now," Tom said. "It's a matter of national security."

"Really? Isn't everything?" the sergeant said. "Well, this isn't Beirut, so why do the CIA and the Brits care about us enough to send two spooks with guns down for a visit?"

"Can't tell you," Tom said.

"Might have to," the sergeant said.

"I doubt it," Tom said. Out of the corner of his eye, he saw the officer approaching.

"They're clean," she said. "The licenses check out."

"Okay, you're free to go," the sergeant said. "Although Ma'am, if I could give you one piece of advice, I wouldn't go around with one in the chamber. Safety or no safety, that's a good way to get yourself seriously dead."

"Thank you, Sergeant," Kathryn said, with more than a trace of annoyance in her voice. "I'll keep that in mind. There's nothing worse than being seriously dead. That's one of the first things we learn in spy school."

"Sergeant, let me ask you a question," Tom said, sliding the clip back into the pistol and slipping it back into his holster. "Just how was it that you knew Kathryn had a gun in her bag. It's not like she left it open in plain view."

"Someone from the hotel called it in," he said. "The report was that one of the guests had seen a pistol in her bag. They gave downtown a description that fit Ms. Devlin and we got the call."

"Do you have the name of the person who called it in?" Kathryn said.

The officer checked her notes.

"The general manager, a Mr. Perry," she said. "Eric Perry."

"Oh, Christ," Kathryn said.

"Would you come with us to see Mr. Perry," Tom asked. "We need to try to determine just who dropped the dime on us."

Tom, Kathryn, and the two officers walked to the front desk and were taken back to the general manager's office, where he met them at the door.

"Ms. Devlin," he said. "What's this all about?"

"Mr. Perry, can we go into your office?" she said.

"Certainly, certainly," he said, ushering them in. "Officer, does this concern the call we received about the gun?"

"Mr. Perry, I need you to think very hard about this," Tom said. "Who saw the gun, do you have a name?"

"I don't think so," Perry said "The call came into the front desk and we called the police immediately. You can never be too sure these days, right, Sergeant?"

"Absolutely," the sergeant said.

"Who took the call?" Kathryn asked.

Perry looked down at the notes on his desk.

"Um, Angela did," he said. "Angela Bascom. She's new here but very good."

"Could you ask her to come in?" Tom said.

Perry called the front desk and a few minutes later, a nervous Angela Bascom arrived. She was barely in her 20s and was trying desperately to control herself.

"Angela, could you tell us about the phone call you received this afternoon about the guest with a gun," the general manager asked.

"It was just a call saying that there was a woman in the lobby bar that had a gun in her bag," Angela said. "The man said she was—actually, he said she was dressed just like you."

Kathryn smiled, hoping to calm the girl's nerves.

"Angela," Kathryn said. "You're sure it was a man's voice."

"Yes, well, I mean I'm pretty sure," she said. "He did have sort of an accent though."

"What kind of accent?" Kathryn said. "Was it a southern accent? A New York accent?"

"No, classy, like yours," she said. "He sounded kind of like Hugh Grant, you know, the famous actor. Did I do something wrong?"

"Not at all," Kathryn said. "You did brilliantly. Thank you."

"Can I go now?" the girl said. "We're pretty busy up front."

"In a minute," Tom said. "We can't stress enough how important it is that all this be kept as quiet as possible. As I'm sure the officers will tell you, it was all part of a prank—actually an attempt to embarrass Ms. Devlin by a former lover who is carrying a grudge against her for breaking off their engagement."

"Carrying the torch a bit too far, I'm afraid," Kathryn sighed, picking up on Tom's lead. "Men..."

"Oh, well that's a relief," Eric Perry said. "We had quite a scare there for a while."

"Well, nothing to worry about now," Kathryn said. "What is it they say? Dreams die hard."

Tom and Kathryn rose from their chairs, followed by the police officers.

"Thank you, Mr. Perry and Ms. Bascom" Tom said.

The general manager walked them to his office door.

"By the way, Ms. Devlin," he said. "How's your painting coming?"

"Waiting for the muse to strike, Mr. Perry," Kathryn said.

Kathryn and Tom walked the two officers to their car, which

was parked in the driveway in front of the hotel's entrance.

"Thanks for helping in there," Tom said. "I know you have to make your report, but anything you could do to help keep a lid on this would be a huge help."

"Right," said Sergeant Giles, as he got into the car and drove off.

. . .

If either Tom or Kathryn thought that Raines had played his last card, they were in for a surprise when they awoke Saturday morning to the headline on the front page of the *Florida Times-Union*.

Death Threat Rocks Players Championship; Britain's Brookes Believed Target

"Jesus, look at this," Tom said, walking over to the bed and handing the newspaper to Kathryn. Then he picked up the remote and flicked on the television, looking for a local station that might be covering the story. After flicking past infomercials for miracle diets, exercise machines that guarantee abs of steel, and ministers promising redemption if you'll just send money away, he switched to a station that had a reporter broadcasting from the tournament.

"...Tour officials refused to comment on today's story in the *Florida Times-Union* that reported that the Tour had received a telephone threat on the life of Peter Brookes, the world's top-ranked golfer. The paper also reported that they had received a similar call late yesterday afternoon, following Brooke's round. Privately, a member of the Tour staff confirmed that a telephone threat had been received and that the Tour was taking it very seriously in light of the shooting death of Brookes's caddie earlier this year in Los Angeles. Additional police presence had been requested, according to that source, and Brookes was notified by the Tour. The *Florida Times-Union* also reported that Jacksonville police had detained a woman in the lobby of the Sawgrass Marriott yesterday and charged her with possession of an unlicensed handgun. A spokesman for the Jacksonville police confirmed that they responded to a call at the hotel yesterday, but said that no arrests were made at that time. A source at the newspaper said the information came from an unidentified person who witnessed police escorting a couple from the hotel lobby late yesterday afternoon. No one at the hotel was available for comment as of this morning."

"Jim, has there been any reaction from Peter Brookes?" the news anchor asked.

"No," the reporter said. "He has a 1:45 starting time today and isn't expected to arrive at the course until early this afternoon. My source at the Tour did say that no one expected him to withdraw from the tournament. It's worth noting that no suspects have been arrested in February's shooting at a Tour event in Los Angeles, but many leaders in the African-American community here in Jacksonville and across the country suspected that Dexter Bradley may have been the intended target and that the shooting was racially motivated. Since that time, the Tour has reportedly increased security for Bradley."

"Has security become a bigger issue for the Tour in recent years?" the anchor asked.

"Probably," the reporter said, "although they are reluctant to discuss it. Galleries have gotten bigger and the nature of golf fans has changed since the game has become more popular. Part of the game's appeal is that you can get so close to the players. It's not like football or baseball where you're watching the action from 25 rows up. For that reason, the Tour has a delicate balancing act they have to perform. The bottom line is that golf is a microcosm of life, and it attracts good people and people who aren't so good."

"Why did I know that was coming?" Tom said. "Golf is like life? Golf is *much* tougher than life."

Kathryn got out of bed and pulled one of Tom's golf shirts on over her head.

"Raines is bloody mad," she said, walking to the sliding glass door and looking out at the Atlantic. The winds had died down and the forecast was for a bright, sunny and warm day.

"He might be mad, but this is brilliant," Tom said, opening the door and stepping out onto the balcony.

"How do you figure?" Kathryn said, joining him "How does calling attention to yourself make any sense whatsoever?"

"Because I didn't think trying to get Brookes here was doable," Tom said. "He might have pulled it off if he could have gotten into a room but I'm pretty sure that wasn't going to happen. The roof shot was a possibility, but let's assume that it was Raines in the stairwell yesterday. He must have known that we had that option closed off, one way or another. What other choices did he have?"

"Okay, let's say you're right," Kathryn said, moving behind Tom and rubbing his shoulders. "Why go to all the bother of calling in the death threat?"

"Two phone calls aren't all that much bother," Tom said

"You know what I mean," she said.

"Well, for starters, it forces our hand, doesn't it?" Tom said.

"How?" Kathryn said.

"Because now we have to go to the Tour and tell them what we know," Tom explained. "That means that from now on, everything we do will have to be coordinated with them and with local cops. It may even mean bringing in the FBI, which is not going to make anyone at the Agency very happy."

"Why do we have to go to the Tour?" Kathryn said. "I mean, I pretty much agree with you that even Raines isn't mad enough to try to take out Brookes here—especially now, since this place is going to look like a police convention."

Tom turned and leaned against the railing.

"Let's play worst-case scenario," he said. "Let's say that he does try to pop Brookes and the word gets out that CIA and M.I.6 knew about it and didn't alert the Tour. How's that going to play out in the papers?"

"Point well taken," Kathryn said. "We'd be crucified."

"Now play things out one step further," Tom said. "Brookes is going to have better security than the President from now until he flies out of here Sunday night. That's a huge bonus for Raines because it gives him two entire days to see exactly what the Tour will be doing to increase security and then he can plan accordingly. But it's also inevitable that there'll be less security next week and even less in the tournaments that follow. If you're right about Raines—and I'm increasingly convinced you are, after all this— then he's got nothing but time. Money apparently isn't an issue. He can wait a week or a month or even six months. There's no more pressure from McGonagle. And let's face it, the longer he waits, the faster the clock is going to run out on us. At some point, CIA and M.I.6 are going to pull the plug on this operation. Raines almost certainly realizes that."

"So what's your plan?" Kathryn asked.

"I'm not sure," Tom said. "I guess find out who we need to meet with at the Tour and get with them as soon as possible."

"But that creates an entirely new set of problems." Kathryn argued.

"How?" Tom asked.

"Well, unless we keep a very snug lid on our involvement, it's bound to leak out that CIA and M.I.6 are up to their necks in all this," Kathryn said. "I imagine that would produce a precious little uproar, especially among your more troublesome members of the Congress."

Tom heard The Players Championship mentioned on television, and they went back into the room. NBC, which was televising the championship, was reporting on the death threat during the "Today" show.

"That should help the ratings for the tournament," Tom said, sarcastically. "Tune in and see if the best player in the world gets his head blown off on the infamous island green. Details and videotape at 11. Jesus, what a nightmare."

"I think we should get Sir Owen and the Deputy Director to sign off on this before we talk with anyone," Kathryn said, picking her Rolex up off the table next to the bed. "It's 2:30 in London. He's probably at his country house, but I'll have the call routed through Thamesside so they can connect with him on a secure line."

While Kathryn called London, Tom showered and shaved. As he did, he tried to think through all the possibilities as logically as possible. The first and most important thing he had to do was find a way to limit the amount of exposure CIA and M.I.6 had if all this blew up in their face. That meant reducing the number of people at the Tour that would have to be kept in the loop. Next, he had to come up with a way to force Raines's hand.

He came back into the room just as Kathryn was ending her conversation with Sir Owen.

"He's quite well," she said. "We're getting along splendidly. He insists that's still his plan although I think it's a lot of rot. I'd trust him with my life but not my checking account. I will, sir. Good-bye."

"Sir Owen sends his regards," she said. "He'd like you to brief the Deputy Director as soon as possible and then they'll discuss what our course of action should be. He's very concerned about limiting our risk of exposure on this. Apparently there's been a bit of a dustup involving one of our operations in Angola and he expects it to become public in a matter of days. Apparently the BBC is already onto the story. The Foreign Secretary is trying to block them by citing the Official Secrets Act, but Sir Owen believes it's just a question of time before the story breaks. Any reports of our involvement here in the States would only complicate matters."

Tom's pager went off and he checked the message.

"Apparently Laddie just flicked on the morning news," Tom said. "I hope he didn't choke on his English muffins."

"Good luck," Kathryn said, heading for the shower.

Tom called CIA headquarters, identified himself, and the call was routed to the Deputy Director's house.

"Glad we caught up with you," Jackson said. "What the hell is going on down there? I thought you had everything under control."

"Before yesterday, yes," Tom said. "The good news is that neither Kathryn nor I think he's going to make a move down here. The odds were long to begin with and my guess is that he's just going spend the weekend seeing how they try to protect Brookes. Whether he gives it one more try or just packs it in, that's a different matter. I'll give him this much: He may be fucking nuts, but he's good. He's very good. He checks us at every move we make."

"What do you suggest we do next, Tom?" Jackson asked.

"I think we need to go to the Tour and give them the fullest possible briefing," Tom said. "The problem is I don't want to run through the entire bureaucracy down here. I looked through their media guide yesterday, trying to figure out who we needed to get to. I don't have a clue. It looks like even the assistants have assistants."

"Why don't you just go right to the top?" Laddie asked.

"He might be tough to reach, especially this week, but that would make the most sense," Tom said.

"What if I called him?" The Deputy Director asked.

"I was thinking of someone that might give a little more cover," Tom said. "All the warning lights would go off down here if word got around that the Deputy Director of the CIA was calling the commissioner of the PGA Tour—especially given the coverage of the threat on Brookes. They'd probably figure out pretty quickly that you weren't calling about a spot in the next pro-am."

"What do you have in mind?" he asked.

"Senator Gardner is on the Finance Committee isn't he?" Tom asked.

"That's right," Jackson said.

"Well, surely the commissioner would go out of his way to talk with a senator on that committee," Tom said.

"I believe you might be right," Laddie said. "I'll try to reach him this morning. What do you want him do?"

"I want him to arrange a private meeting for Kathryn and myself with the commissioner," Tom said. "No assistants or vice-presidents or anyone else. We can do it wherever he wants, but the sooner the better. The senator should also stress as firmly as possible that he needs to keep this to himself."

"Alright," the Deputy Director said. "That sounds good. I'll let you know what develops."

"Okay, "Tom said. "Thanks. Also, Kathryn spoke with Sir Owen this morning. He'd like you to give him a call to make sure we're all on the same page with this."

"I'll call him before I speak with the senator," Laddie said, and then hung up.

• • •

No one could accuse the Tour or the police officials of not taking the threat seriously. The security on Saturday was extraordinary. Police were stationed at every entrance to the course, as well as at the off-site parking lots, where they checked the bags of people entering the shuttle buses. Writers entering the media center had their bags checked as well, and as an added precaution, anyone making a purchase at the golf shop was given a claim check that allowed them to pick up any packages upon their exit from the course.

Police with binoculars and—Tom assumed—high-powered rifles equipped with sniper scopes, were positioned atop the clubhouse, which offered the best view of the golf course and practice area. They were also posted on the roof of the Marriott and in the hallways of the top two floors.

A cordon of police was assigned to Peter Brookes, and would surround him as he walked from a green to the next tee. In addition, units of undercover officers leapfrogged between the hole Brookes was playing and the next hole.

The police offered to provide the caddies in Brookes's group with lightweight bulletproof vests, and the volunteers assigned to the group were given the option of being replaced. Only one scorer accepted the offer.

Over at the NBC Sports production unit, members of the Jacksonville Police Department's SWAT team sat with directors in the production trucks, carefully scanning the monitors. The cameramen had been told that, whenever possible, they should scan the galleries, with the hope that one of the officers in the trucks might spot any suspicious individuals or behavior. An officer with powerful binoculars was also stationed in the blimp, which was ordered to fly lower than usual. Finally, a pair of helicopters were assigned to periodically fly over the course, although neither low enough nor frequently enough to disrupt play.

Brookes made the short trip from the Marriott to the clubhouse in a police Suburban with tinted windows. As he changed his shoes in the locker room, members of the bomb squad and their German shepherd checked Brookes's bag and the bags of the other players in his group for explosives.

The atmosphere in the locker room was tense and subdued. The police had restricted entry to players, Tour officials, and employees. There was a brief incident when a writer from one of the British tabloids demanded entry and was finally taken out of the building and down to the media center, where he was threatened with losing his press credential and being escorted off the property by the police. Several players paused by Brookes's locker and offered support. Brookes thanked them, but didn't try to minimize the threat. He didn't seem nervous or frightened, possibly just a bit more determined and focused than usual.

When he was ready to leave, a police officer stationed at the entrance to the locker room motioned to a second officer stationed near the front door of the clubhouse and the squad of officers assigned to escort Brookes formed at the door. When Brookes came out the door, they formed a wedge around him and headed for the practice range. A second group of officers kept the gallery back.

When Brookes and his caddie reached the practice tee, the gallery broke into loud, sustained applause of support, which he briefly acknowledged. Brookes was directed to a spot next to a large white tent, rather than at the far end of the tee, which would increase his exposure. A line of especially large, muscular officers formed in a line behind Brookes. As he began hitting some soft wedge shots, several players stopped by on their way off the tee to wish him luck. He thanked them, but quickly went back to work. Never one for small talk anyway, he was understandably even less inclined under the circumstances.

As Brookes warmed up, uniformed police and officers in plain clothes carefully scanned the gallery gathered behind the tee. Any sudden or unusual movement drew their attention. At one point, a man wearing a long, old, raincoat in the warm weather was approached by two policemen who asked if he would open it so they could check for a possible weapon. It turned out that he didn't have a gun but did have poor circulation—as well as a small bottle of Cutty Sark, for medicinal reasons, he claimed. The police took the scotch.

If Brookes was nervous, it didn't show on the practice tee. His ball-striking was crisp and pure as he worked his way through the bag methodically. He ended by hitting his driver, first some fades and then some draws that rose up against the clear blue sky, turned gently, and dropped down on his target. When he finished, the gallery again gave him a long, loud roar of approval and support. He gave them a quick, small wave and then was enveloped by the cordon of police, which escorted him to the nearby practice green.

Brookes hit practice putts for about five minutes, and then motioned to his caddie that it was time to head for the first tee.

"Don't stay very close to me," he said to his caddie as he handed him his putter. "After I make my club selection, stand away. And don't walk near me between shots."

"You let me worry about me," the caddie said. "You worry about hitting the shots. Let's go."

A steady applause accompanied Brookes, his caddie, and their police protection as they walked along the pathway that led from the practice area to the 1st tee. It reached its crescendo as they arrived on the tee. As they did, the police spread out around the perimeter.

The two other players in Brookes's group, approached him, shook his hand, and wished him luck.

"I wish I knew you were also wearing a blue shirt today," one said, trying to break the tension. "I would have changed."

Brookes gave a small laugh.

"I told my caddie not to stand near me unless it's necessary," Brookes said. "The same is true for you."

"Don't worry about us, we'll be fine," the second player said. "Good luck. Play well."

"Good luck to you," Brookes said.

Brookes took three Titleists from his caddie and carefully marked each ball with a pencil dot on either side of the number one—the only number he used in competition.

"Now on the tee," the nearby announcer said loudly, "the number one ranked player in the world. From London, England, Peter Brookes."

Again, the large gallery burst into a loud, sustained applause, which Brookes acknowledged with a tip of his cap. He handed two of the balls to his caddie and took his driver.

As Brookes bent down to tee his ball, the ovation subsided. As he addressed the ball and prepared to hit his drive, a total, eerie, silence came over the tee. Brookes set up over the ball, waggled the club once and then looked down the fairway. He waggled the club again, looked back toward the landing area, and then hit a drive that started out over the water guarding the right side of the fairway, carried the fairway bunker, and landed in perfect position to hit his approach at the pin tucked on the left side of the green.

As soon as the ball landed, the gallery again burst into applause. Brookes gave a small wave, and then walked to the side of the tee to watch the two other players hit their drives. When they did, he strode off the tee almost defiantly it seemed, with his police escort nearby but at a comfortable distance.

Brookes reached his ball and checked the yardage with his caddie before pulling a pitching wedge from his bag. Once he did, the caddie took three strides back away from the ball. Brookes looked at him and gave him a small, subtle wave, motioning him to move farther back. The caddie shook his head.

"Get it close," the caddie said. "Remember, it's going to go left when it releases."

Brookes took a couple smooth practice swings, ran the club-face along the sole of his shoe to clean off the grass, and then set the club down behind the ball. He looked at his target, and then hit a beautiful shot. The ball landed on the green, skipped once, then checked up and trickled to the left, near the hole. It came to rest six feet from the cup.

Brookes arrived at the green to more applause, marked his ball and flipped it to his caddie. When it was his turn to putt, he carefully replaced the ball and lined up his putt with his caddie.

"I've got it two balls outside the hole, dying at the cup," Brookes said.

"Maybe not quite that much," the caddie said. "The greens start to slow down just a little this time of day."

Brookes got set up, made two practice strokes, and then settled over the putt. Again, there wasn't a sound from the gallery.

Brookes made a good stroke, the ball began to break left as it lost speed, but hung on the right edge of the cup. The caddie had been right. Brookes shook his head and then looked over at his caddie.

"Good read," he said.

"We'll get the next one," the caddie said, taking the putter from Brookes.

As they walked off the green, they were again surrounded by police as they made their way through the gallery. Ahead of them, people ran to get a good vantage point. If the gallery was worried about being in the line of fire, it certainly didn't show.

On the par-5 2nd hole, Brookes again hit a good drive. He laid up with his second shot, and then hit a delicate little sand wedge into the green, leaving himself an eight-footer for birdie. Just as he had done on the previous hole, he hit a good putt but not quite good enough.

The 1st and 2nd holes largely mirrored his play that day. He hit the ball solidly and avoided mistakes, but hurt himself on the greens. He took 35 putts, well above his average, and it showed in his scoring. He shot a two-under-par 70 that included a chip-in birdie on the 11th hole. Maybe it was his nerves or maybe he was just due for a bad putting round. Either way, all things considered, it was a solid round that left him in contention on Sunday, four strokes out of the lead on a course where disaster waited on almost every hole.

From a security standpoint, the round was marred by just one minor incident. On the 17th hole, Brookes and his group had just arrived on the tee when a group of teenagers gathered around a trash container, lit a cherry bomb, and dropped it in the bag. When the firework exploded, police immediately surrounded Brookes. A few people in the gallery pointed to the boys and they were immediately seized by police, placed in two patrol cars, and taken off the course. If Brookes was shaken, he hid it well. He hit a fine 9-iron from the tee that settled in the middle of the green, and then two-putted for his par.

Tom and Kathryn had followed Brookes for much of his round, nursing the vague and unrealistic hope that Graham Raines, in his sheer arrogance, might show up as well. They both knew, of course, that even if he did, the chances of recognizing him were slim, even with the photo taken off the video from the blimp in Los Angeles and the knowledge that he had grown a beard.

Following the round, they went to the media center to listen to Brookes's post-round interview. The interview area was jammed when they arrived and there was a loud, collective groan that went up from the press when a Tour official announced that Brookes had decided to go to the practice green before meeting with the reporters.

For his part, Tom thought it revealed volumes about the man. Death threat or no death threat, his game was of paramount importance. If that meant that an army of police and a room filled with writers on deadline had to be inconvenienced, so be it. It was all for the greater good of Peter Brookes, and Tom was starting to respect him—if not like him—for it.

When Brookes finally arrived for his interview with the press, he seemed like a different man than he had been the day before. He was less belligerent, for one thing, less willing to spar with the writers. Perhaps it was the effects of the death threat, but Tom's sense was that he had been moved by the reaction of his fellow players and the support of the galleries.

After going through his round, hole by hole, the first question from a writer was whether he had considered withdrawing from the tournament.

"No, not seriously," Brookes said. "At the end of the day, what can you do, really? If someone is willing to trade their life for yours, that's simply fate or a very big dose of bad luck."

"So you're in favor of the death penalty?" was the next question.

"As it pertains to me, yes," he said, drawing a laugh from a few of the writers.

After a few innocuous questions, a British writer asked the question that Tom had been expecting.

"Peter, do you think this sort of thing reflects the rather cowboy culture in the United States?" he asked. "You know, a gun for every man and every man for his gun?"

A groan went up from many of the American writers.

"If I remember my history, we British have reason to be bloody thankful in this century that Americans knew how to use guns and were willing to use them in defense of our culture and values," Brookes said. "Personally, I think that's a rather foolish question. Beyond that, I can think back to playing in my own backyard when there were concerns about possible terrorism and the like. So in answer to your daft question, not at all. I think the person—if there is, in fact, someone who plans to do something beyond making a few phone calls—is someone who is slightly off the bubble."

"So you're not frightened?" the writer persisted.

"Oh, yes, this is a frightening golf course," Brookes said. "There are any number of things about being out here that are frightening, beginning with that terrifying 17th hole and the holes on either side of it. But am I concerning myself with the threat? No, and if I was I certainly wouldn't share it with you or anyone else."

When Brookes was asked about the galleries and the police, his attitude softened considerably.

"The police have been magnificent in every regard, and I cannot possibly thank them enough," he said. "As for the galleries, their many kindnesses toward me today were quite moving. The people here in America have always been most supportive and gracious, and today was simply the most dramatic example of what I have been lucky enough to enjoy throughout my career."

The interview session went on for 20 minutes or so and writers were starting to leave their seats to file their stories. The Tour's media official that was conducting the interview session called for one last question.

"Could you tell us, please, what was your reaction when the fireworks exploded on the 17th hole?" a writer asked.

"My first reaction was the hope that somebody at the Tour's headquarters had finally come to their senses and decided to blow up that green," Brookes said. "When I saw that, alas, to my great disappointment that wasn't the case, I simply assumed that the July 4th holiday celebrating the victory of our English-speaking peoples over King George and his Hessians had been moved up."

Having given the press a lecture on his historical and political views—with a little golf tossed in on the side—Brookes left the interview area and the media center with his police escort.

"I actually find him rather refreshing," Kathryn said.

"You caught him on a good day," Tom said.

. . .

The meeting with the commissioner was set for 7:30 Saturday night at his office in the Tour's headquarters building. There were just a couple of cars in the parking lot in front of the one-story wood building. The lights were on in the lobby and as they approached the entrance, a security guard opened the door and escorted them back to the commissioner's office.

Ted Malloy had been the Tour's commissioner for just over a year, leaving the International Management Group where he had worked in their golf division.

"After fighting the Tour all these years, I decided to join them," he joked when his appointment was announced.

Malloy had served in the Marines in Vietnam and had a pleasant, if no-nonsense, manner about him. A photo of him with some fellow Marines in fatigues sat on the bookcase behind his desk, along with photos of his family. Golf course photos hung on his office walls. An unopened box of Hogan Apex irons rested against the wall in one corner of his office.

Malloy was just the fourth commissioner in the Tour's history. The previous three had brought distinctly different qualities to the job. Joe Dey, the first commissioner, had been the executive director of the United States Golf Association and one of the most widely respected members of the world golf community. He brought instant credibility to the Tour following its break with the PGA of America. Dey's successor was Deane Beman, who had been one of the country's best amateurs in the 1960s and had played the Tour before becoming commissioner. Beman was a visionary and an intensely competitive person. He brought the Tour—often kicking and screaming—into the modern era of high-powered sports. If he managed to make a few enemies along the way, it didn't seem to bother him in the least as long as the Tour benefited from the fight. Tim Finchem followed Beman's reign and, like Beman, was the right man at the right time. A Washington lawyer before he joined the Tour, he was more inclined to finesse the issues facing the Tour than Beman, and was successful in steering the Tour through the legal and political shoals it increasingly faced as it grew. Malloy's strength was marketing, and his charge was making the Tour a truly worldwide franchise.

"Thank you for meeting with us on such short notice," Tom said, as they shook hands.

"You have very persuasive friends," Malloy said. "Please sit down. Can I get you anything to drink?"

"No, thanks," Tom said. "Mr. Malloy, this is Kathryn Devlin. She's from Britain's M.I.6."

"So I understand," the commissioner said. "And you're with the CIA. Senator Gardner gave me an overview and told me that you'd fill in the details. I have to tell you, if I knew this job meant dealing with spies and assassins, I would have stayed at IMG doing clothing deals for our millionaires."

"We're not so bad," Kathryn said.

"The spies or the assassins?" Malloy said, joking.

Kathryn briefed the commissioner on Graham Raines and Tom explained their theory on the assassination attempt in Los Angeles, and how they believed Raines had killed the senator's daughter.

"So Dexter Bradley wasn't really the target?" the commissioner said. "I wish we had known that earlier. It would have solved a lot of our PR problems."

"We couldn't let anyone know because we really weren't sure ourselves," Kathryn said. "Raines disappeared after the shooting and we weren't even sure he was still in the States. We couldn't take any chances, though. That's why we arranged for the royal family in Morocco to hire Peter Brookes. We needed to get him out of the country and they were very generous."

"Not all of my people were pleased about that," the commissioner said. "Losing the top-ranked player in the world plays hell with the ratings."

"I'm afraid it couldn't be helped," Kathryn said.

"And you think Raines is here?"

"We're certain he was here, but I doubt if he's still around," Tom said.

"So the threat was a hoax?" the commissioner said.

"We're sure it was Raines," Kathryn said. "Everything points to him and nothing else makes sense. How many of these sort of things do you get?"

"Not many, thank God," Malloy said. "Every now and then one of the black players will get a threat if they're in the lead. It depends where we're playing. Sometimes a foreign player will get one, but that's pretty rare. We usually just alert the police and they step in and handle it very discreetly. The problem is, as the Tour grows and becomes more popular, it naturally attracts more attention and more nuts like your guy. In truth, there isn't a lot we can do."

"In a case like this, when there's so much publicity, do you get copycats?" Kathryn asked.

"Occasionally," the commissioner said. "We really haven't had anything comparable to this, though. The media monster is in a feeding frenzy. We're trying to keep a lid on it but as you can see, we haven't had much success. A story like this takes on a life force of its own."

"Well, let's just hope we don't get too many," Tom said. "It will only make things more complicated."

"Do you really think Raines will make another attempt?" the commissioner asked, leaning forward and resting his elbows on his desk.

"Kathryn is sure he'll make one last try," Tom said. "I'm less sure, but it can't be ruled out. We don't think he'll try here, though."

"Since Raines knows we're on to him," Kathryn said, "it only increases the challenge as he sees it. My feeling is that he'll try it just to prove that he can outwit M.I.6. Whether he knows CIA is involved really doesn't matter."

Malloy rose from his chair and began walking around behind his desk.

"What would you like us to do?" he asked.

"First, we need you to restrict this information to as few people as possible," Kathryn said. "If it gets out that we are involved in this, the repercussions will be enormous. I'm sure you can appreciate that."

"Certainly," said the commissioner. "I think I'll need to have you brief our director of communications, in case we get any questions from the press, as well as our legal guy, so we can determine what our responsibilities and liabilities are. I'd also like to include our chief of operations. You can coordinate anything you need through him. That should do it, at least for now."

"How soon can we meet with them?" Tom asked. "Obviously, the sooner we get everyone in the loop, the better."

"I'll call them tonight and set it up for tomorrow morning," Malloy said. "Is 8:00 alright for you?"

"That's fine," Tom said, writing on a notepad on the commissioner's desk. "Here's the number where we can be reached if that changes. We'd also like you to set up a meeting with Brookes for tomorrow morning. Do you know his playing schedule after this week?"

"No, but I could check the player commitments and let you know," the commissioner said. "The Masters is in two weeks. I'm sure he'll play there. Beyond that, I don't know."

"Ideally, we'd be best off if he simply withdrew from any Tour events for the next month or so, or went and played overseas," Kathryn said. "By that time, I'm certain even Raines would give up the ghost."

"I'm afraid it would take more than the threat of death for Peter to skip the Masters," the commissioner said.

"Yes, and I'm afraid Augusta is the ideal spot from Raines's point of view," Tom said. "A major championship with television coverage around the world. To Raines's way of thinking, it's a perfect stage. Could you arrange for us to meet with the chairman of Augusta National? We're going to need his cooperation as well."

"I'll call him first thing Monday," the commissioner said. "Let me try Brookes now."

The commissioner opened a phone book, found the number for the Sawgrass Marriott, and was connected with Brookes's room.

"Peter, this is Ted Malloy," he said. "How are you bearing up? Very good. Listen, I'm here in my office with two representatives from the British and United States governments. We've been discussing some information pertaining to the death threat and I think it would be very useful for everyone concerned if you met with them as well. I'm trying to arrange a meeting with some of my senior staff here in my office tomorrow morning at eight. Would you be able to attend? Fine. Peter, I have to ask you to keep all of this to yourself. Please don't mention any of this to anyone. Thank you. I know you will. We'll see you tomorrow then."

The commissioner hung up the phone.

"We're all set," he said. "I'll see you tomorrow at eight."

Tom and Kathryn rose and shook the commissioner's hand.

"Thank you," Tom said.

"Thank you," the commissioner said. "I hope you're wrong."

"So do we," said Kathryn. "Sometimes wrong is a very good thing to be."

• • •

Twelve hours later, Tom and Kathryn were back at the Tour's headquarters. Everyone was seated around a large table in a conference room, waiting for Peter Brookes, who was running a few minutes late. When he walked into the room, the commissioner introduced him. When they shook hands, Tom was surprised by the size and strength of Brookes's hands, and how Brookes looked intently at him, as though he were sizing him up, just as he would an opponent on the golf course.

During the 30-minute meeting, Tom and Kathryn laid out in detail the events dating back to the shooting in Los Angeles and the background on Graham Raines. There were no interruptions except when Kathryn explained that Brookes had been targeted by the IRA.

"Was it something I said?" he joked, prompting a few nervous laughs from around the table.

Following their briefing, they answered a variety of questions but none from Brookes, which struck Tom as strange. Finally, he turned and faced Brookes.

"Obviously, we're going to need your cooperation," Tom said. "Can you tell me your tournament schedule for the next month to six weeks?"

"I'm committed to Atlanta next week, then the Masters and Hilton Head the following week. After that, I'm skipping Greensboro and New Orleans, but playing the Byron Nelson, Colonial and probably Jack's tournament."

"Ideally, we'd like you to withdraw from all of them," Kathryn said.

Brookes was incredulous. "Well yes, but ideally I wouldn't have to deal with this madman and this insanity," he said. "I can't simply crawl into a hole because of all this."

"Maybe you don't have to," Tom said. "Maybe you just have to announce that you plan to."

"I'm afraid I don't understand," Brookes said.

"Would you be willing to skip Atlanta?" Tom asked.

"I suppose," he said. "I don't really favor the course."

"What if we plant a rumor that because of the threats on your life, you plan to withdraw from Atlanta and go to Augusta for some extra practice rounds. You'll play in Augusta but after that you're returning to England, possibly to play some events on the European Tour."

"If that's what we decide to do," the commissioner said to the Tour's public relations man, "we should get the story out to some of the friendlier writers this morning. That way it's sure to come up in Peter's post-round interviews."

"No problem," the man said, nodding. "They're dying for anything on this story. Or we could just set up an interview with Peter on TV. If we move fast, we could probably get it on one of the morning news shows."

"Can you live with that, Peter?" Tom asked.

"Just so long as I'm given proper time to warm up," Brookes said. "I don't need any further distractions today. It's a bloody zoo out there."

"And you're in the cage," Kathryn said.

Brookes stared at her.

"That's just how I feel," he said.

"Any other questions?" the commissioner asked. "Okay, then. Tom and Kathryn, you know how to reach us."

"Actually, Peter, is there a number where we can reach you once you leave Jacksonville?"

Brookes took a card from his wallet and wrote a number on the back.

"Here's my agent's number at IMG," he said, sliding the business card to Tom. "And my cell phone number is on the back. Is there a reward if this Raines character is captured?"

"I don't really know," Kathryn said. "Why?"

"Because IMG will want 20 percent," Brookes joked, rising from the table and shaking Tom's hand. When Brookes opened the door to the conference room, there were two very large and very serious Jacksonville policemen waiting in the hallway. "Alright, lads, off we go."

. . .

A series of headlines in the *New York Times* on Monday neatly summed up the predicament Tom and Kathryn faced. The first, on the front page above the fold, read:

U.S. Envoy Reports Dramatic Breakthrough in Irish Peace Talks

The next, also on the front page, in the lower left-hand corner, was for a news analysis piece:

Death Threat Stuns Cozy World of Professional Golf

The third was for a story on page A4, by the paper's London Bureau Chief:

M.I.6 Blunder in Angola Tests Official Secrets Act

The final headline led the sports section:

Brookes Wins Players Championship in Play-off; Threat Prompts Cutback in Schedule

Apparently, the *Times* arrived early in the offices of M.I.6 and the CIA. It was just after ten in the morning when Tom received a message on his pager to call the Deputy Director. After seeing the day's headlines, Tom wasn't surprised by the call or by the conversation he had with Laddie Jackson.

"You've seen the morning papers?" the Deputy Director asked.

"Just the *Times*," Tom said.

"That's enough," Jackson said. "I just got off the phone with Sir Owen and they are more than a little skittish about their potential exposure on this whole Peter Brookes business. They want Kathryn recalled to London immediately. Their thinking is that Raines no longer poses a threat to the peace process, so they don't want to run the risk of having this thing blow up in their face. I can't say I disagree. I'm of the same opinion on our end. We can hand it off to the FBI."

"With all due respect, sir, I disagree," Tom said. "It would take weeks for the FBI to get up to speed on this and by then it could be too late. Give us two weeks. Brookes is sitting out this week, so there's no danger there. That leaves the Masters, which is the most attractive site for Raines in terms of international media coverage. If we can get past that, I really believe we're home free. Besides all that, I feel strongly that we have a moral obligation to Brookes. We certainly knew enough weeks ago to warrant warning him. We played God with his life. I think we owe him this much."

"I'm not prepared to discuss playing the role of God with someone trained by the good Jesuits of Boston College," the Deputy Director said. "Why don't you and Kathryn come on up here and we'll thrash this thing out once and for all."

"Is it worth having Sir Owen fly over as well?" Tom asked. "No one has a better handle on Raines than Kathryn does. She's been right at every turn. I hate to say this, but if she's called back to London we're going to lose a huge advantage."

"Well, let me see what I can do," the Deputy Director said. "If I were in his shoes with this Angola mess, I just might want to get my ass out of the country anyway. I'll have Operations send a plane down to bring you back. Good luck."

CHAPTER TWELVE

Tom and Kathryn's flight arrived in Washington late on Monday afternoon and when he called the Deputy Director's office, Mary Dwyer informed him that Sir Owen Tunnicliffe was arriving Tuesday and that Laddie Jackson would host a dinner Tuesday evening at his Dumbarton Oaks residence to discuss their plans.

"Well, if they're going to give us the hook, they're going to do it in style," Tom said to Kathryn after hanging up the receiver. "Cocktails and dinner at seven tomorrow night at the Jackson mansion."

"Just the three of us?" Kathryn asked.

"No, Sir Owen is flying over for a guest appearance," Tom said. "The opportunity for an elegant dinner and a chance to dodge his many admirers on Fleet Street and in Parliament was too much to pass up."

· · ·

The Dumbarton Oaks section of the city is among the most beautiful and wealthy sections of Washington, and of all the area's elegant old residences, the Jacksons' was one of the most admired.

The house was an old, rambling, red brick and slate-roofed mansion that sat at the end of a long, winding pea stone driveway. The view from the street was blocked by a high brick wall and tall, thick, flowering shrubs. Mrs. Jackson was born and raised in Charleston, South Carolina, where her family dated back to the revolution and had made a fortune in the rice trade. Her passion was gardening and, fortunately, her marriage to Laddie Jackson had given her more than enough resources to indulge it. Tom wished that it had been another month or two into the year so Kathryn could have seen the gardens that had been featured in magazines like *Town and Country* and *Architectural Digest*—surely the only high-ranking intelligence agency official to have that sort of coverage. Her annual spring garden party raised tens of thousands of dollars for AIDS research, and she was more than happy to use her position as a power broker in Washington society to also lobby for millions of additional dollars to find a cure for the disease that claimed their only son, Ladston Jackson IV—"Lads."

Heavy metal gates blocked the entrance from the road—only the most visible element of the elaborate security that guarded the Deputy Director's residence. Tom and Kathryn were buzzed through and as they drove out from underneath the canopy of trees that lined the driveway, the house was bathed in the soft, slanting, late afternoon light of early spring in Washington.

"My God, this is glorious," Kathryn said. "Positively exquisite. It's like something out of a dream."

Tom parked the Jeep and as they approached the front entrance, he saw their reflection in one of the large windows. Kathryn was stunning. She had gotten a tan in Florida and it set off her blue eyes and sandy blond hair. She was wearing a pale yellow cashmere sweater, a dark green skirt, and a pair of green leather high heels. Tom wore a navy blue pinstripe suit he'd had made during a posting in Hong Kong, a crisp white shirt, and a tie Kathryn had bought him so he'd own "something that didn't have stripes."

Tom rang the buzzer and an older woman opened the door.

"Good evening, Mr. Quinn," the woman said, with the traces of a lilting Irish accent.

"Hello, Francis," Tom said. "Francis, this is Kathryn Devlin. Francis has been running this place forever."

"I came with the mortgage," the woman said. "Come this way, please. The others are on the patio."

They followed her out of the foyer and down a hall hung with family portraits and paintings of the Carolina low country. They turned left and walked through the dining room onto the patio that overlooked a small pond and the formal gardens that were particularly lush in the fading light.

"Mr. Jackson, your guests are here," Francis said.

"Tom, good to see you," Laddie Jackson said. "And you as well, Kathryn. Tom, you remember Sir Owen, of course."

Everyone shook hands, and Tom noticed that Sir Owen seemed to have aged since their last meeting. Apparently the scandal rocking M.I.6 was taking its toll on him.

"What would you like to drink?" the Deputy Director asked. "Still a scotch drinker, Kathryn?"

"That would be lovely," she said. "With just a bit of soda."

"Tom?" Jackson asked.

"Scotch would be fine, thank you," Tom said. "No soda, though."

"Your house is spectacular, Mr. Jackson," Kathryn said "And these gardens are simply beyond words. Tom had told me how beautiful it would be, but I'm afraid he didn't do it justice."

"Y'all call me Laddie now, remember?" said the Deputy Director, who had never been above flattery from a beautiful woman. "It's all Libby's doing. She just has a way with all these flowers and trees and what not. I swear that woman could make a rose bloom in the desert."

"Will she be joining us for dinner?" Tom asked.

"No, she's down beautifying the Bermuda house," Jackson said. "Been down there a week. I don't know what she's up to. Won't know 'til the bills arrive."

Francis arrived with their drinks. Waterford crystal glasses on a silver tray. *First boat all the way*, Tom thought.

"May I get anything else for anyone?" Francis asked.

"I believe Sir Owen and I could use a refill when you have a minute," the Deputy Director said. "And next time, dear, not so much water with my scotch. If I wanted that much water I'd go take a damn bath."

Francis rolled her eyes theatrically and left.

"Owen was just telling me about the Angola business," the Deputy Director said. "It sounds like a tough one."

"I'm afraid the times have slipped past old dinosaurs like us," Sir Owen said with a note of resignation in his voice. "I fear that it will be increasingly difficult to ply our trade in the future."

"What happened precisely, sir?" Kathryn asked.

"Well, the political infrastructure of the country is going to bloody hell, just as it is across the entire continent," Sir Owen said. "We have considerable economic interests to protect there and were acting to replace the present gang of savages running the government with people more attuned to our thinking. Things got a bit out of hand as they sometimes do when you're dealing with these sorts of people. Now the usual harpies in Parliament are screaming bloody murder about the government's colonial meddling. If the truth be told, the entire miserable continent would be better off if they were still colonies. It's just a bomb running off a very short fuse and when it *does* explode, we'll be powerless to do anything about it."

"Now Owen, remember that you're in America," Laddie joked. "You can't talk like that. It's politically incorrect."

"Stuff political correctness," Sir Owen harrumphed. "That's precisely the sort of thing that got us into this quagmire in the first place. We should stop worrying about what the rest of the world thinks and get about our business."

Sir Owen was just building up a nice rhetorical head of steam when Francis arrived with a second round of drinks. Jackson took his and held it up to the floodlights shining onto the patio.

"Now that's much better Francis," he said. "You should never be able to see through your drink."

"I thought you had invoked the Official Secrets Act," Kathryn said.

"It's worthless, a mere scrap of paper," Sir Owen said. "It's absolutely porous. With all this cable and satellite technology, we simply can't control the press to any degree whatsoever. Pity."

"But the good news is that the bad guys can't either," Tom said.

"Yes, except they aren't bound by the rules of democracy," the Deputy Director said. "It doesn't matter what the masses know if they're powerless to do anything about it. It's a delusion. It's the great delusion of our time."

Francis reappeared on the patio and announced that dinner was served in the dining room. They left the patio and walked back through the French doors. The lights in the dining room had been dimmed slightly, accenting the flame burning in the fireplace and the flickering of the candles on the table and the mantle. A soft light shone on the painting that hung over the fireplace. It was a Winslow Homer depicting a scene somewhere along the north shore of Massachusetts—Rockport, Tom thought, or possibly Gloucester. A bowl of fresh flowers sat at the center of the dark, heavily polished mahogany table, which was set with silverware engraved with Mrs. Jackson's initials, and elegant china settings.

Jackson pulled out a chair for Kathryn, who was seated across the table from Tom, then sat at the head of the table, opposite Sir Owen. Francis poured wine from one of the two bottles of Clos du Val on the sideboard. When she had finished pouring the wine, she served rich lobster bisque from a silver tureen and quietly left the room, the door to the kitchen swinging shut behind her. Classical music played discreetly in the background.

"The bisque is divine," Kathryn said.

"Try just a splash of that sherry in it," Laddie Jackson said. "Libby swears by it. Drives Francis crazy. She prides herself in her bisque and doesn't think anyone should fiddle around with it."

The conversation during the soup course centered around Laddie's plans to take Sir Owen sailing on the Chesapeake tomorrow if the weather held. It was something both men looked forward to doing every time Sir Owen came to Washington, and while the conversation and retelling of tales by the two old friends was interesting enough, Tom was anxious to get down to the matter at hand—the hunt for Graham Raines. He knew Kathryn was, as well. Tom knew, however, that protocol required that either the Deputy Director or Sir Owen would have to be the first to bring up the Raines operation.

With a timing that reflected her years of experience, Francis discreetly entered the room, pausing briefly in the doorway to make sure she wasn't interrupting any sensitive conversations. She cleared the soup bowls and spoons, and filled the wine glasses, then served the evening's main course—medallions of beef tenderloin, fresh asparagus, and baby red potatoes. She placed two small, silver gravy boats filled with béarnaise sauce on the table.

"Will there be anything else?" she asked before leaving the room.

"No, thank you, Francis," Laddie Jackson said. "Everything looks wonderful."

Indeed, everything was wonderful. The beef was remarkably tender and medium-rare. The thin asparagus retained a certain crispness and the potatoes had been browned slightly after they were boiled, giving them a slight crust and an interesting texture. The béarnaise was a sublime accompaniment to the meal.

As the meal continued, Tom was becoming increasingly frustrated by the apparent unwillingness of either man to discuss Graham Raines. The conversation shifted from sailing to old war stories to the inside politics and gossip of Washington and London. If it bothered Kathryn, though, she was putting up a good front. She seemed fascinated by the two old friends and they were utterly charmed by her—which Tom hoped might help when push inevitably came to shove.

Tom was also concerned about the small, subtle changes he saw in Sir Owen. His earlier rant about Africa was nothing new. He was a product of his generation and his place in the British social structure, and as such, fairly articulated their views. You could have replaced Africa with South America or the Middle East or the Balkans—or Ireland for that matter—and gotten pretty much the same screed.

But what concerned Tom was the bitter edge he sensed about the old man. Perhaps it was the pressure of the Angola scandal, but Tom doubted it. Sir Owen and M.I.6 had withstood worse over the decades, and with the Tories in office, they weren't likely to get anything worse than a slap on their political wrists.

The closer he observed Sir Owen during dinner, the more Tom thought he seemed distracted. He had always had a razor's edge to him—a sharp, insightful and quick intelligence and a knack for cutting to the root of any problem and staying on focus. Now his mind seemed to wander, if ever so briefly, and it was as though he was losing interest, or at the very least, enthusiasm, for any topic of discussion. At one point, he dropped his knife and it landed on his plate with a *clank* that startled the others at the table.

It wasn't until after they had finished dessert—a tart with raspberries, blueberries and blackberries—and retired to Laddie Jackson's den/office, that the conversation finally turned to Graham Raines.

The room had dark green walls and wood paneling. There was a handsome, old wooden desk and two small couches separated by a coffee table. Francis had lit a fire in the fireplace as dinner began to wind down. There were two phones on the desk, one of them a secure line to the communications center at Langley.

When they entered the room, Tom and Kathryn sat on one couch, Sir Owen sat on the other, and Laddie Jackson poured brandy into the four snifters Francis had left on the table. When he finished, he sat next to Sir Owen and leaned back on the couch.

"First of all, Sir Owen and I want to congratulate both of you on your work thus far," the Deputy Director said, after taking a sip of his brandy. "But we need to make a decision on where we go from here. Owen believes we should terminate the operation, or at least Kathryn's role in it. I'm inclined to agree but wanted to hear your thinking before we make any decision."

Sir Owen placed his snifter on the table.

"With this Angola business hanging over our heads," he said, "we believe it is vital that we limit our exposure in this Raines matter. If it were discovered that we had an operative working in America at this time, the fallout would be calamitous, to say the least."

Kathryn leaned forward, resting her elbows on her knees and cradling the glass in both hands. She swirled the brandy in the glass for a moment, pondering how she wanted to respond.

"Tom and I believe that we need just two more weeks," she said. "We're 100 percent convinced that Raines was in Jacksonville and was targeting Peter Brookes. Of that we're certain and united. We can't be sure that he will make one final attempt at the Masters tournament, but we believe there is a very good chance of it. Give us this two-week window and then, one way or another, we'll cease the operation."

"Suppose nothing happens at the Masters," the Deputy Director said. "How can you be sure he won't simply wait until another tournament?"

"Because as far as he or anyone else knows, Brookes has no plans to play in America for months after the Masters," Tom explained. "According to all the press reports, he's planning to return to England for an indeterminate stay."

"I'm still not convinced *he* is even in this country," Sir Owen said, looking directly at Kathryn. "And every day *you* are raises the risks that M.I.6 will be exposed."

"We don't know that he's here, either," Kathryn replied. "But failing any evidence that he's someplace else, I think the prudent course is to assume that he is here."

"But why not let the authorities in Augusta handle things from now on?" the Deputy Director argued. "We've alerted them. Now it's their problem."

"Two reasons," Tom said. "First, no one knows Raines as completely as Kathryn. She knows how he thinks and how he acts. Next, while we're worrying about the public relations concerns of all this, think how it will play out if Brookes is shot and it turns out that we washed our hands of the matter at this crucial moment. Never mind the ramifications of knowing for months that he was the target of an assassination plot and not bothering to inform either him or anyone else. To me, those considerations trump Sir Owen's concerns, no matter how valid."

"Can you be sure that your roles in this will be kept under the radar screen?" Jackson asked.

"Confident but not sure," Kathryn said. "The people we met with in Florida assured us that they would make every effort, and I think we have to take them at their word."

"It's not in their interest for this to leak out," Tom added.

"I also think we have a moral obligation to Peter Brookes," Kathryn added. "As Tom said, we did keep all this from him for a very long time."

"Miss Devlin, we deal in a world of moral uncertainties, or has that escaped you," Sir Owen said peevishly, as though he were lecturing a schoolgirl. Kathryn seemed briefly taken aback by his tone.

"No, sir, it hasn't," she said in a measured voice. "I'm simply suggesting that it is an additional consideration."

Sir Owen waved off her answer dismissively. Tom looked briefly toward Laddie Jackson for a reaction, but there was none.

Tom took another sip of brandy and when he glanced at Sir Owen, he noticed that the old man's right hand was shaking ever so slightly.

"There is another consideration that we haven't discussed," Tom said.

"Go ahead," the Deputy Director said.

"Do you want to be the person who tells Senator Gardner that we're walking away from this operation just at the time when we believe we might be just days away from getting the man who killed his daughter?" Tom said. "I don't think that will be a very pleasant conversation, do you?"

The Deputy Director rose from the couch and poured more brandy into each of the four glasses. Then he paced around the room for a few moments, finally leaning against his desk.

"That would be as rough as a cob," he said, tapping his forefinger against his front teeth. "That could have serious repercussions for us, Owen, and possibly M.I.6 as well. I don't have to tell you how powerful he is. He's been calling me weekly to find out where we stand with this operation. Between his position on the Senate's Intelligence Committee and the Finance Committee, he's got us by the balls."

"Politics, politics, I'm bloody sick of it," Sir Owen said. "Why don't we just hold off until tomorrow before we make any decisions. I have a blinding headache. I'd like to go to sleep."

Sir Owen rose somewhat unsteadily from the couch, placed his snifter on the table, shook hands, and left.

"I'll have Francis check in on you," Jackson said.

"That won't be necessary," Sir Owen said, opening the door to the hallway. "I'm going straight off to sleep."

After Sir Owen left, Jackson sat back down on the couch.

"I'm afraid this Angola business is bothering him more than he's letting on," the Deputy Director said. "Downing Street is getting a lot of pressure to make some heads roll. Owen represents the bad old days for a lot of the opposition in Parliament and in the press. With the Prime Minister expected to call an election in the next few weeks, that's a bad combination."

"He did seem distracted," Kathryn said.

"Yes, and I was surprised when he snapped at you," the Deputy Director said. "That's very out of character. He's very fond of you and often mentioned how pleased he is that you two are getting on so well."

Tom glanced at Kathryn and saw a trace of red rise in her cheeks.

"No sacrifice is too great for Queen and Country, right Kathryn?" Tom joked. "We'd better be going. We'll check with you in the morning. I'd like to get down to Augusta as soon as possible."

"That's fine," said the Deputy Director. "I still have some very real reservations about going forward with this but you make a good point about Jack Gardner. I'm pretty damn sure I don't want him all over my ass."

The Deputy Director escorted Tom and Kathryn to the door and said good night. The door had barely shut behind them when they heard Francis calling from the top of the stairway.

"Mr. Jackson, come quickly!" she cried. "It's Sir Owen! Hurry!"

Tom and Kathryn opened the door in time to see Laddie Jackson race up the stairs, two at a time. As he did, he pushed a button on a small black transmitter he always carried in his pocket. Within what seemed to be just seconds, two men ran to the front door. One was the Deputy Director's driver and body-guard and the other was part of the security detail assigned to the house when the Deputy Director was home. They followed Tom and Kathryn up the long staircase.

When they reached the guest room they saw Laddie Jackson leaning over Sir Owen, who was lying on the floor, still fully dressed. He was conscious but unable to speak.

"Owen, can you hear me?" Jackson asked. "Can you understand what I'm saying?"

Tom instinctively reached for the phone and dialed 911. He gave the address and told the operator to inform the EMS crew that they were probably going to be dealing with a stroke victim.

"Francis, bring me some aspirin and a glass of water," Kathryn said. "Hurry, please."

Tom took two pillows off the bed and placed them under Sir Owen's head. The old man was trying desperately to speak but all he could manage were some grunting sounds. He could make some slight movements with his arms, but Tom suspected that there was substantial paralysis. The fear was evident in Sir Owen's eyes.

Francis returned with the aspirin and the water, and handed them to Kathryn. Tom and the Deputy Director gingerly lifted Sir Owen into a sitting position and Kathryn knelt down beside the stricken man. She gently pried open his mouth and placed one of the aspirins on his tongue, then she lifted the glass of water to his lips and leaned his head back. Sir Owen gagged slightly but managed to get the aspirin down. She repeated the process two more times and then softly ran her fingers over his face to dry the water that had spilled.

In the distance came the sounds of the sirens. As they came closer, Laddie Jackson's bodyguard went downstairs to direct the EMS crew to the guest bedroom. At the same time, the second agent called Langley to alert the duty officer in charge.

"Kathryn," the Deputy Director said calmly, "you better call your person at the embassy. We'll take him to Bethesda Naval Hospital. It's more secure. Have someone from the embassy meet us there."

The EMS crew came into the room and immediately began checking Sir Owen's vital signs. One of the technicians removed Sir Owen's jacket and cut the shirtsleeve back from his left arm. As he did this, the second technician prepared a disposable syringe.

"You should know we gave him three aspirins as soon as we discovered him," Kathryn said.

"Had he complained of dizziness or headaches?" one of the technicians asked. "Did he have any numbness or tingling in his hands or arms?"

"He complained of a very bad headache just before he came upstairs," Kathryn said.

"He also dropped his knife during dinner, but he didn't say anything about a numbness or tingling," Tom said.

The technician tied a piece of rubber tubing around Sir Owen's upper arm and as soon as the veins began to swell, he tapped one of the large veins with the tip his finger, wiped the area with a cotton ball soaked with alcohol, and injected the drug D5W, a dextrose mixture.

"Okay, let's go," said one of the technicians.

They gently lifted Sir Owen onto a stretcher and stabilized his body with straps across his chest and thighs.

"This gentleman is an important member of the British government," the Deputy Director said to the EMS crew. "It's very important for security reasons that he be taken to Bethesda Naval Hospital. Can you arrange that?"

"Georgetown University Hospital would be closer but his vital signs are stable and we've got two police cars downstairs to escort us," one of the technicians said, as they began to roll the stretcher out of the room. "Bethesda should be fine."

The EMS crew carried the stretcher down the stairs, rolled it through the foyer, and slid it into the van, locking it into place. The doors shut and it pulled down the driveway, following the police cars, their sirens cutting through the still night air.

"May I use your secure line to call the embassy?" Kathryn asked the Deputy Director.

"Certainly, it's the green phone on my desk," he said. "It will connect you with Langley and they'll patch you right through to the embassy."

"What do you think?" Tom asked the Deputy Director.

"We got to him quickly and that's crucial," he said. "It's still a crapshoot with these things, though. My father died from a stroke. He was a tough old bird, though. He lingered for a long time but he was pretty much a vegetable toward the end. I sure as hell hope that doesn't happen to Owen."

"I guess these new drugs are pretty remarkable," Tom said. "Those guys were good. That's another one in the plus column."

"Well, if you can will yourself to beat one of these things, my money's on Owen," the Deputy Director said.

Kathryn returned and joined the two men in the driveway.

"The ambassador has been informed and wishes to be kept abreast of any developments," Kathryn said. "He is sending a member of his staff to the hospital and will contact London. He has requested that until more is known about Sir Owen's condition, we do what we can to keep it out of the media."

"That's one reason I had him sent to Bethesda," the Deputy Director said. "We have a better chance of keeping a lid on this there than we would at Georgetown."

· · ·

Sir Owen was admitted to the hospital under an assumed name, in an attempt to keep word of his stroke from leaking out. Tom, Kathryn and the Deputy Director went to the hospital, but Sir Owen had undergone an extensive examination and it was two in the morning before they were briefed by the attending physician, Dr. Jeanne Fahey, in her office.

"Mr. Tunnicliffe has had a moderate to serious stroke," she said. "The next 48 to 72 hours are crucial. Until then, we won't know the extent of the damage or how much of a recovery we can reasonably expect. In fact, there's a very good chance his condition might actually worsen. He owes a great deal of thanks to whoever administered the aspirin. That was very quick thinking and might well have, if not saved his life, at least minimized the damage. Right now, he is experiencing some paralysis, particularly on his left side. That's not unusual in a case like this. The paralysis also extends to his facial muscles, which is why he's having difficulty speaking. Again, this isn't unusual in a stroke of this severity, but again, it's not irreversible either, which is the good news. Right now, he's under sedation and will remain so for at least the next 12 hours."

"When would he be able to have visitors?" the Deputy Director asked.

"Well, at least not until his condition fully stabilizes," the doctor said. " At least 24 to 48 hours at a minimum."

"Doctor, Mr. Tunnicliffe is a high-ranking member of the British government," the Deputy Director explained. "The nature and severity of his affliction is a matter of considerable political sensitivity."

"I understand," the doctor said.

"We would appreciate a private suite and it's vitally important that his identity is restricted to people on a need-to-know basis only," the Deputy Director said. "We would also like to provide some security—very low key, of course."

"Certainly," the doctor said. "I will arrange it with the appropriate administrators in the morning."

"Is he in any pain?" Kathryn asked.

"He probably experienced some but he's fine now," the doctor said. "Right now the best course of action is rest and medication. He'll remain in the critical care unit for the next several days, so he can be closely monitored. As I said, we'll know more in the next few days."

"If you had to speculate on his chances, what would you think?" Tom asked.

"It's just so hard to tell," the doctor. "He received very good treatment very early in the episode, and we have him on anticoagulants, which is all to the good. On the other hand, I have to be candid with you and warn you that his age works against him. Any recovery from a stroke of this severity is going to be lengthy at best."

"And if you had to set odds..." Tom asked.

"A significant recovery?" the doctor said. "Maybe 50-50. I don't realistically think you should hold out much hope for a complete recovery at his age. I'm sorry, but that's my best opinion at this time. Having said that, people never cease to surprise me. But I'm afraid that's the best I can offer you."

. . .

It was just a short drive to Tom's house in Bethesda. It was a two-bedroom stone cottage that had been part of a large estate that was broken up and sold in the early 1980s, when Tom bought it for what now seemed an absurdly low price. The rooms had exposed, dark wooden beams and white walls. There was a fireplace in the main room and also in Tom's bedroom and a deck off the kitchen that overlooked a small field and a stream.

Neither Tom nor Kathryn spoke during the 10-minute drive. When they reached Tom's house, they went straight to his bedroom. Kathryn went into the bathroom to wash her face, while Tom put on a pair of pajama bottoms and got into bed. He had almost fallen asleep when Kathryn came into the bedroom, removed her clothes, and got into bed. She pressed against him, running her hand softly over his chest. Then she leaned over and kissed him gently.

"I love you, "she said.

Tom turned slightly and embraced her.

"Try to get some sleep," he said.

Tom woke up early after just a few hours of sleep. The morning had dawned bright and clear, but cool. He slowly closed the windows and pulled the covers back over Kathryn's shoulders. She moved slightly, but didn't awaken. He pulled on a sweater and left the room, gently shutting the door behind him. He made some coffee and then walked down to the end of the dirt driveway and picked up the *Washington Post*. As he walked back to his cottage, he scanned the paper. There was no news of Sir Owen, at least in this edition, and when he reached the house, he turned on the television, and was relieved that there was nothing on either the national or local news programs.

Tom poured some coffee, dumped in some sugar, turned up the television and went out on to the deck. He started reading the paper, but kept thinking back to the night before—not Sir Owen's stroke, but what Kathryn had said just before she went to sleep and how he had responded.

The truth was that he *did* love her. She was bright and beautiful and clever and she needed him and maybe that, after all these years, was what worried him. He had made a commitment once and knew that he hadn't lived up to his end of the bargain. He had hurt Becca and hurt her badly and none of it was really her fault.

There had been plenty of women in his life since then, but none of them touched Tom the way that Kathryn did. But what if the plug was pulled on their operation and she went back to London? What would they do? Mixing business with emotions was a bad idea in this life, and he had let it happen almost from the start. As much as he had grown to trust her and, yes, even love her, he couldn't escape the small and nagging suspicion that he and the Agency were being played by the Brits—or maybe just *he* was being played and the Deputy Director was in on it. He put down the paper and looked out across the field, to the mist rising off the stream, and wondered if all the secrecy and cynicism had finally taken too much out of him after all these years.

Or maybe it was just that all the years of being alone had finally caught up with him.

As he stared down across the field, he watched as some ducks swept in low across the stream and splashed gracefully into the water.

"Penny for your thoughts?" Kathryn said, as she walked over and kissed him lightly on his forehead. "Did you sleep well?"

"Pretty well," Tom said. "The day was just too beautiful to stay in bed."

"I won't take that as a compliment," she said, sitting down on the lounge chair next to him.

"Sorry," Tom said, and he should have been. The morning sun hit her face as it slanted through the trees and Tom was again struck by how pure her beauty was, not in the way Hollywood portrays glamour, but in a simple, classic sense. Of course, it didn't hurt that she was wearing one of his golf shirts and nothing else.

"Any news?" she asked.

"Not in the *Post* or on TV," Tom said. "It's probably too soon for the news to leak out, even in Washington."

"How'd your beloved Red Sox do?" she asked.

Tom turned to the sports section and scanned the scores.

"They beat the Yankees but it's still early," Tom said. "There's still months to go before their inevitable collapse. Give them at least until the All-Star break."

"Hope springs eternal," Kathryn said, taking a sip of her coffee. "God, this is beautiful out here. Why would you ever leave?"

"Because it's a hellhole in the summer and Boston has an ocean," Tom said, turning to the editorial page to see what was outraging the great, cosmic, save-the-world thinkers at the *Post* on this particular day.

"The flimsiest of all possible excuses," Kathryn said. "If you dive into it, you'll disintegrate before you drown."

Tom was about to explain how Tip O'Neill and Teddy Kennedy had been environmental miracle workers when Kathryn grew serious.

"Look Tom, I'm sorry about last night," she said, running her hand lightly over his face. "I was feeling very vulnerable and sad. It just slipped out and I'm sorry, but it's true and I want you to know that. No pressure. No strings. Nothing attached. I'm just very pleased that all this brought us together—no matter how it all ends up."

Tom took her hands in his.

"We'll just have to take it one day at a time," he said. "You might be on a flight to London by the end of the week. What do we do then?"

"Do you really think that will happen?" she asked.

"I don't know," Tom said. "All I'm saying is, what if?"

"Then we'll have to make some decisions, won't we?" she said. "But I prefer to be an optimist about all this. All I know for certain is that I haven't felt this way for a very long time and I thank you for that."

Tom pulled her toward him and pressed her head against his chest.

"I feel the same way," he said. "Whatever happens, we'll work it out."

Tom leaned over and kissed her forehead. As he did the phone rang.

"I believe that's the sound of the world not going away," he said.

The call was from the Deputy Director's assistant, asking them to come to the Agency's headquarters for a 2 P.M. meeting.

"We'll be there," Tom said. "Any word on Sir Owen's condition?"

"We spoke with the attending physician a few minutes ago," Mary Dwyer said. "He's still in critical care. His condition is listed as serious but stable. His doctor said that the good news was that there hasn't been any worsening of his condition, so at least he's stabilized."

"How's the DD taking it?" Tom asked.

"You know, he just keeps plowing ahead," she said. "I think he's planning to go out to the hospital later this afternoon unless there's a dramatic change in Sir Owen's condition."

"Would you tell him that Kathryn and I would like to join him?" Tom said.

"I think he was planning on it," Mary Dwyer said. "We'll see you at two."

"Two o'clock at Langley," Tom said to Kathryn. "No real change in Sir Owen's condition. We'll probably go over to the hospital late this afternoon with the Deputy Director."

He flipped her the television remote from the kitchen table.

"I'm going to take a shower," Tom said. "See if there's anything that amuses you."

"I've already found something that amuses me," she said.

. . .

Tom and Kathryn arrived at the Deputy Director's office slightly before two and Mary Dwyer escorted them immediately into the meeting. Laddie Jackson was in the room, along with Briggs McPhee of Senator Gardner's staff.

"Any word on Sir Owen?" Tom asked the Deputy Director.

"No change," Laddie Jackson said. "He's holding his own but that's about it. You remember Briggs McPhee."

"Yes, good to see you again," Kathryn said, shaking his hand.

"I spoke with Senator Gardner this morning and brought him up to speed on your operation," the Deputy Director said. "I relayed the concerns of Sir Owen and M.I.6 and while he is sympathetic, he was very insistent that you continue. He agrees with your assessment that Raines will probably make an attempt at the Masters, so we've decided to give you approval to continue through that tournament. After that, it's going to be tough sledding. As you know, I have reservations about this, but I'm persuaded by your arguments and those of Senator Gardner."

"What about Sir Owen?" Kathryn asked.

"Obviously, we haven't been able to consult with him," the Deputy Director said. "In light of the circumstances, we've decided to go ahead and then brief him when his condition improves."

"What about London?" Kathryn asked. "Have you advised Thamesside?"

"Frankly, given the political situation there, we've decided to adapt a 'Don't ask, don't tell' position," the Deputy Director said. "There was no formal decision or request to terminate your operation. Sir Owen was here to discuss it, and since that isn't possible, we've decided to simply proceed. Briggs, anything you want to add?"

"I just want everyone in this room to understand that the senator is willing to spend every bit of political capital he has to support you and this operation," Briggs McPhee said. "He discussed it with Senator Larkin, the ranking member, this morning and she's on board. They both have a lot of respect on the committee and will give the Agency as much cover as they can. The important thing is that you get this guy."

"Thank you," Tom said. "We appreciate that."

"It goes without saying that any resources the Agency can offer will be made available to you," the Deputy Director said.

"We're going to have to wing it," Tom said. "We'll go Augusta tomorrow and meet with the people there and with the Tour staff. Let's be honest, we lost a couple of days that we couldn't afford to lose. The good news is that the Masters probably has the best organization and security of any tournament in the world. They're the lords of the universe down there. They say 'jump' and everyone says 'how high?'"

"And the bad news?" Briggs McPhee asked.

"The bad news is that this guy is very good and this is the greatest stage in golf," Tom said. "It gets huge ratings and it's broadcast all over the world. If Kathryn has read this guy right, then he's going to make one last attempt and it's going to be at Augusta."

"Realistically, what are your chances of stopping him, Kathryn?" McPhee asked.

"It's like anything else: if he's willing to trade his life for Brookes's, then it will be very difficult," she said. "There's nothing in the psychological profile that M.I.6 has done up that indicates he's suicidal—pathological, certainly, but not suicidal. The best we can hope for is that we establish as much security around Brookes as possible, both obvious and otherwise, and hope it scares him off."

"How is Augusta as a location?" the Deputy Director asked.

"We won't know for sure until we get there," Tom said. "I think it might work in our favor, though. My recollection from watching the Masters is that there are no tall buildings or hillsides near the course. In that sense, Riviera was really a fluke, since the course runs along the bottom of a canyon. There were any number of places he could have fired from."

The phone on the Deputy Director's desk buzzed once and he picked up the receiver.

"Yes," he said. "How long ago?" he asked. "Did they give any indication of the severity?" He glanced at Tom, then looked down at his desk. "Alright," he said. "Have my car brought around. Thank you." Laddie hung up the phone.

"Owen has had another episode, as they call it," the Deputy Director said. "They're monitoring his condition to judge how bad it was, but the doctor suggested we come right over. It doesn't sound good, though. Let's go."

• • •

The agent from the security detail met them at the doorway to Sir Owen's room.

"Any word on his condition?" Tom asked.

"No, but when the bells and whistles went off, this place exploded with people," the agent said. "If he doesn't make it, no one can blame the staff here."

The door opened and two nurses walked out followed by Dr. Fahey, who asked them to join her in Sir Owen's room. The old man seemed to be sleeping peacefully. He had intravenous drips in his arm and tubes carrying oxygen were inserted into his nostrils. A bank of screens tracking his vital signs was placed near his bed, where a young doctor carefully monitored the lines and blips and numbers, occasionally making notes on a clipboard. Except for an occasional beeping from the monitors, the room was eerily quiet.

"Your friend has had another stroke," Dr. Fahey said, breaking the silence that hung over the room. "It wasn't as severe as his first one and these things aren't entirely unexpected, particularly in a man of his age."

"How much damage has he suffered?" the Deputy Director asked.

"We've taken CAT scans and an MRI and while there is some scarring, it doesn't seem as severe as we feared," the doctor said. "The danger is that even with the fairly significant doses of the anticoagulant medications, he did have this second episode. What we have to hope is that these don't presage a series of CVAs."

"I'm sorry," Kathryn said. "CVAs?"

"Cerebral Vascular Accidents," the doctor said. "If that's the case, which is not uncommon in people of his age, then his condition will simply deteriorate over a matter of months or perhaps years. At any rate, his quality of life would be significantly lessened."

"And he's not in any pain?" Kathryn asked.

"No, none at all," the doctor said. "He's just in a very deep, peaceful sleep."

"Well, that's at least some comfort," Kathryn said.

"It doesn't look like there's anything else for us to do here," the Deputy Director said. "I'd like to be kept informed of any changes immediately."

"I understand," the doctor said.

"Might I just say goodbye to him?" Kathryn asked.

"Certainly," the doctor said. "Although I don't believe he will be aware of you or anything you might say."

"I'm sure that's true, but it will mean a great deal to me," Kathryn said.

She walked over to the side of Sir Owen's bed and took one of his hands in hers. Then she gently ran her finger along the top of his head, smoothing his hair back into place. Then she leaned over and whispered in his ear. Finally, she kissed him lightly on his forehead and gave his hand one final squeeze. Before she turned to walk away, she wiped a tear from her eye.

"Are you okay?" Tom asked.

"Yes," Kathryn said. "I just wanted to wish him Godspeed, because I'm afraid I shall never see him or his like again."

CHAPTER THIRTEEN

It is a joke of almost cosmic proportions that to get to the most elegant and historic entranceway of any golf club in the world, Augusta National's Magnolia Lane, you have to first drive down one of the most unrelentingly tacky streets in America, Washington Road. For 51 weeks a year, it is a stretch of road lined with every conceivable fast food outlet, convenience store, and gas station known to man. For the other week, the week of the Masters, it is a virtual parking lot dotted with people selling tickets, parking spaces, and some of the most astonishingly tasteless souvenirs imaginable. To date, no one has been seen selling paintings on velvet of Arnold Palmer, Jack Nicklaus, and Elvis—the Blessed Trinity of life in Augusta—but then, like the Red Sox, there's always next year.

In some respects, the difference between Magnolia Lane and Washington Road symbolizes the city of Augusta itself. The old part of the city is elegant and steeped in the rich history of the South. The new parts of the city, in developments like West Lake, represent the modern South, where business reigns supreme, life is good, and everyone is a Georgia Bulldog at heart. Then there is the poorest part of the city, a ramshackle reminder of the bad old days, where it is painfully difficult to discern that the Civil Rights movement and the dramatic days of the 1960s ever actually occurred at all.

But through the years, almost since its founding in 1931, when the rest of the world thinks of Augusta, Georgia, they think of the Augusta National Golf Club—although for much of its early years, its survival, never mind its success, was a damn close thing.

Following his retirement from competitive golf in 1930 at age 28, Bobby Jones expressed a desire to build a golf course in his native Georgia that would be the equal of Merion, Winged Foot, the Old Course at St. Andrews, or any of the other places where he had won championships. His friend Clifford Roberts, a successful financier, helped in the search for the right piece of property and they eventually found it at the Fruitland Nurseries in Augusta, which was owned by the Berckmans family.

Augusta was 150 miles from Jones's home in Atlanta, which made it convenient for many of the potential members. It also was farther south, right on the South Carolina border, which meant that the climate was considerably better in the winter months when the club would attract most of its play.

When Jones first walked the property, he declared it ideally suited for a golf course. It had dramatic changes in elevations, Rae's Creek, which ran through what would eventually become much of the back nine, tall pines and, of course, a seemingly endless variety of flowering plants that the nursery was famous for and which would come to serve as a harbinger of spring for golfers across the country.

While Jones played a significant role in the design of the course, the architect of record was the esteemed Dr. Alister MacKenzie. Jones had been an admirer of MacKenzie's work since he played Cypress Point in California following his early loss in the 1929 U.S. Amateur at Pebble Beach.

While he was initially baffled and frustrated by the Old Course at St. Andrews, Jones had come to revere it and that reverence was reflected in the design of Augusta National. The fairways are generous and generally lacking in penal rough and the greens are large, but a premium is placed on hitting drives and approach shots to the proper places on the course. It can fairly be said that both St. Andrews and Augusta reward those players who are best able to think their way around a course.

It can also fairly be said that no great golf course has undergone more changes than Augusta National. For starters, the nines were flopped very early on, and any number of architects including Robert Trent Jones, Tom Fazio, and Jack Nicklaus have been brought in to oversee changes over the years.

In an early effort to create some publicity (and attract desperately needed members), Jones and Roberts courted the United States Golf Association, hoping to become the first course south of the Mason-Dixon line to host either a U.S. Open or Amateur. The course was barely six months old when Prescott S. Bush, the father of President George H.W. Bush and at the time the chairman of the USGA's tournament committee, visited the course and played two rounds. He was suitably impressed and promised to approach the USGA's powerful Executive Committee with the idea. That it had the support of Bobby Jones was no small consideration.

In the end, the USGA elected not to offer the 1934 Open to Augusta National, in no small part because it would have meant moving the date of the championship from June to late March or early April, which would have created havoc with the sectional qualifying.

Jones and Roberts were disappointed by the USGA's decision, but Roberts came up with an alternative: they would run a tournament of their own. The Augusta National Invitation Tournament debuted in 1934 and was won by Horton Smith. Jones, who hadn't played a competitive round since winning the 1930 U.S. Amateur, finished 13th, largely because of mediocre play around the greens. Still, the tournament had attracted most of the top sportswriters who stopped on their way north following spring training to watch Bob Jones and a select gathering of his friends—who also happened to be the best players in the world.

For all intents and purposes, the tournament—which didn't become known as the Masters Tournament until 1939 because Jones found the name pretentious—became a "Major" championship on a par with the Open in 1935 when Gene Sarazen holed his 4-wood approach to the par-5 15th hole in the final round. His double eagle allowed him to tie Craig Wood, who he beat in a playoff the following day.

Over the years, there have been occasional criticisms of the course or the changes made to it, but if it's true that great courses produce great champions, then Augusta National certainly qualifies as one of the premier tests in the game. From its earliest days, the winners of the Masters reads like a Who's Who of Golf—Sarazen, Byron Nelson, Sam Snead, Ben Hogan, Jimmy Demaret, Doc Middlecoff, Arnold Palmer, Jack Nicklaus, Billy Casper, Gary Player, Raymond Floyd, Tom Watson, Seve Ballesteros, Ben Crenshaw, Nick Faldo, and Tiger Woods, just to name a handful of the great players who won at Augusta.

· · ·

Tom had never been to Augusta and was looking forward to seeing in person the course he had seen so often on television. He and Kathryn arrived in Augusta the following morning and were driving along the Bobby Jones Expressway on their way to the course.

"Isn't that nice," Kathryn said as they turned onto the expressway. "They named a road after him."

"It's horrible," Tom said. "They should name highways after congressmen that beat indictments, not gods."

"Oh," Kathryn said. "So much to learn about America and so little time."

The ride from the airport took about a half hour and when they turned onto Washington Road, neither of them could quite believe their eyes. It was Krispy Kremes and Taco Bells and every other fast food joint known to man for as far as the eye could see.

"Good God," Kathryn said. "This makes Jacksonville Beach look like the bloody Cotswolds."

"Want to stop for lunch?" Tom asked.

"I may never eat again," Kathryn said.

Mercifully, there wasn't much traffic and in a few minutes they were at the entrance to Augusta National. They stopped at the gate and were cleared through by the security guard.

The drive down Magnolia Lane was majestic. No description Tom had ever read had managed to do it justice except Gary Player's, who said that Augusta is the only place where you begin choking when you drive into the place. Ancient magnolias lined both sides of the roadway, with practice fields off on either side. As they drove down the lane, the large, white antebellum mansion that is the clubhouse came into view, and as they approached it they came to a large circle of deep green grass with a map of the United States formed by bright yellow pansies. Behind the flowers stood a tall white flagpole with the flags of the United States and Augusta National waving against a cloudless blue sky.

"This isn't a golf course, it's a movie set," Kathryn said. "Any second now Scarlett O'Hara is going to appear on the porch and invite us in for mint julips. What a place."

They turned to the right and parked in a small lot. For a place that was less than a week away from hosting one of the biggest sporting events in the world, it was surprisingly quiet. A few players were on the practice tee and some members of the grounds crew were tending to the plantings along the front of the clubhouse, but the general feeling was that it was just another weekday at the club—albeit one of the most exclusive clubs in the world.

As they approached the clubhouse they were greeted by a tall, older man with white hair who opened the door for them.

"Welcome to the Augusta National," he said. "May I help you?"

"We have an appointment with the chairman," Tom said.

"Just go on in and announce yourself to the lady at the reception desk there on your right," the man said. "She'll take good care of you. Y'all have a nice visit now."

They entered the clubhouse and introduced themselves to the attractive, well-dressed woman, who called the chairman's office and told his assistant that they had arrived. Moments later, she handed the phone to Tom.

"Please hold for Mr. Franklin," she said. "He'll be with you presently."

The chairman came on the line and asked if they'd eaten lunch yet. Tom told him no and the chairman said that he'd meet them in the clubhouse in a few minutes.

"Just have yourself a look around and I'll be right along," he said.

Tom was surprised by how small, even intimate, the interior of the clubhouse was, but what caught his eye was a painting of Bob Jones that hung on one of the walls. It had been given to the club by the R & A and it captured Jones at the height of his career, but what struck Tom was the look in his eyes. It was as though the penetrating gaze captured the sheer intelligence and intensity of the man. It was also a vivid reminder of just how much Jones continued to profoundly influence this place and this tournament—even the game itself—all these years after his death.

They were studying some of the other artwork when the club's chairman, Charles Franklin approached.

"Mr. Quinn, Miss Devlin, I'm Charlie Franklin," he said. "Welcome to Augusta National."

"Nice to meet you, Mr. Franklin," Tom said. "Thank you for agreeing to meet with us so quickly."

"I wish you were visiting us under more pleasant circumstances," he said. "And please, call me Charlie. It's such a beautiful day, should we eat outside?"

"That would be lovely, thank you," said Kathryn.

They walked outside and saw one of the most stunning and beautiful sights in the world of golf. To the left were dozens of wrought iron tables and chairs, shaded by green and white umbrellas. To the right was a vast expanse of lawn that stretched out under enormous, wisteria-entwined trees. But it was the vision of the golf course and the towering pines that was breathtaking. The ocean of green began at the clubhouse with the first and 10th tees and the 9th and 18th greens, and then cascaded down the hill to the holes that ran along Rae's Creek. Tom had watched God knows how many Masters telecasts, but television didn't do justice to the scale of the course and its overpowering beauty. There might indeed be better courses than Augusta National, he thought, but surely there are none that are more magnificent and pleasing to the eye.

"My word, look at all this," Kathryn said. "My mum would be delirious."

"Is she a golfer?" the chairman asked.

"Not at all, but she's passionate about gardening," Kathryn said. "This would be heaven for her."

"Well, Miss Devlin, you tell her that if she ever comes to the States to give us a visit," the chairman said. "Where would you like to sit?"

"Someplace with some privacy would probably be best," Tom said.

The chairman motioned to one of the waiters.

"We've got a little business to discuss here so I'd appreciate it if you didn't seat anyone too nearby," he said.

"Yes sir," the waiter said. "Can I get you anything to drink, sir?

"Miss Devlin?" the chairman asked. "How about some iced tea?"

Tom wondered if Kathyrn would gag at the prospect.

"Thank you, no," she said. "Perhaps just some water. And please call me Kathryn."

"And you, Mr. Quinn?" the chairman asked.

"Tom, please," he said. "Iced tea would be fine."

"Two iced teas and some water then," the chairman said.

Charlie Franklin was in his mid-60s, with a round, almost cherubic face, made all the more so by his slight sunburn. He was polite, even courtly, and his accent was reminiscent of Laddie Jackson's with its traces of a Tidewater drawl. Like the Deputy Director, he tended to stretch words out and then run them together a bit. Tom knew from his discussions with Ted Malloy at the Tour, that once you got past all that charm, Charlie Franklin was one tough guy. He had taken a small, family-owned bank in North Carolina and turned it into a financial powerhouse. He was just the kind of person that made up so large a part of Augusta National's membership. He was successful, but more important than that, he was a self-made man.

Tom also knew that the chairmanship at Augusta National was as close to a benevolent dictatorship as you were likely to find. It had always been that way, beginning with Clifford Roberts who, at least according to legend, was occasionally less than benevolent when it came to his club and its tournament. To one degree or another, the chairmen who followed Roberts were cut from the same cloth.

The chairman opened his menu and Tom and Kathryn followed suit.

"The strip steak is very popular, although I'm partial to the cheeseburgers," the chairman said. "Plays hell with my cholesterol but I've gotten to the point where I can't stand the sight of either fish or chicken."

Tom looked at Kathryn.

"I think I'll just have a salad," she said. "I'm off red meat for a bit, I'm afraid."

After they ordered, a man about Tom's age approached the table.

"This is Ken Rice, he's our general manager," the chairman said. "He'll be the person you're coordinating with. I included him in my briefings from the man Ted Malloy sent up from the Tour so we're both pretty much up to speed, unless you have any additional information you need to share with us."

Rice had barely taken his seat when a waiter arrived for his order. Say what you want about southern efficiency, Tom thought, but the waiters here seem remarkably on the ball—at least when the chairman is around.

"We'll give you any assistance you require," Rice said. "Both we and the Tour are taking this very seriously. We're prepared to ask the state and local law enforcement agencies to provide us with an increased presence if you feel that's necessary. We can also bring in more Pinkertons."

"Thank you," Tom said. "Right now, I think the first thing we should do is go around the course. I'd like to see what we have to deal with in terms of possible places a shooter might make an attempt from."

"I anticipated that, and frankly, I can't think of anyplace out on the course," Rice said. "We can arrange for you to take a cart out right after lunch if you'd like."

The waiter arrived with the food, and there was a pause in the conversation until he left.

"Ken served in the Special Forces during Vietnam," the chairman said. "His experience should be helpful."

"Absolutely," Tom said. "That's great. The next thing, and this is crucial, is that we need to keep this as quiet as possible. If the press gets wind of this it will be a nightmare for everyone involved. And it's particularly important that there's not even a hint of CIA or M.I.6 involvement."

"We understand completely," the chairman said.

"Should that happen, we'd like to have some deniability," Tom said.

"Such as?" the chairman asked.

"If worse came to worse and the story leaked, would you be willing to tell the press that we're here as consultants to the club?" Tom asked.

"I don't see why not," the chairman said.

There was another pause in the conversation as a member, who appeared to be about the same age as the chairman, walked over to the table with a woman in her 20s—at the most—on his arm.

"Sorry to interrupt Charlie, but I just got down and wanted to introduce you to the new bride," he said. "Honey, say hello to Charlie Franklin. He's the chairman here and this is Ken Rice, our general manager."

Both men stood and shook her hands.

"These are friends of ours just down for their first visit to Augusta," the chairman said. "Tom Quinn and Kathryn Devlin."

After a few moments of small talk, the loving couple left, holding hands.

"Damn fool," the chairman said, chuckling. "A girl that age will kill him. He'll need a pacemaker the size of a car battery."

"We understand that getting a pass for the tournament is almost impossible," Kathryn said. "How difficult would it be for our man to get in here?"

"In theory, very," Ken Rice said. "In reality it's like anything else. You can get a day pass out on Washington Road. A pass that will get you access to the clubhouse or get you in for the entire tournament is considerably harder to get, but if you have the money, anything is possible. We go to great pains to guard against counterfeit badges, but again, if your man is resourceful enough, it's possible."

"I don't think we have to worry about him going that route," Tom said. "There probably isn't enough time. However, there is some technology we could bring in that might be helpful."

"What is it?" the chairman asked.

"I'd like to set up some surveillance cameras at every gate," Tom said. "This is very sophisticated stuff. Each camera feeds an image into a computer that is programmed with 80 facial reference points. If the computer recognizes 12 or more matches with our man, then we could pull that person aside."

"How intrusive is it?" the chairman asked.

"Not very," Tom said. "The cameras would be visible but most people won't think anything of it. We'd need to find a place to put the equipment and have someone assigned to monitor it, but they wouldn't need to know who they were looking for or why. Beyond that, you already have guards at the gates I assume."

"Yes," the chairman said. "How long will it take to get the equipment down here?"

"I can call Langley today and arrange it," Tom said. "We could have it installed over the weekend."

"Do it," the chairman said.

Lunch was winding down and Tom was anxious to get out onto the golf course, but he had two more questions.

"Charlie, would it be possible for you to arrange a very discreet meeting with whoever runs the television coverage?" Tom asked. "They can be very helpful."

"Certainly, I'll set it up for tomorrow morning in my office," the chairman said.

"Finally, what's that room at the top, under the cupola?" Tom asked. "Is it used during the tournament?"

"We call it the Crow's Nest," the chairman said. "It's got four beds and a small bathroom. The amateurs usually stay there during the tournament. Ken can take you up there after lunch if you'd like."

"It must offer the best view of this entire area, right?" Tom asked.

"Not really," the chairman said. "The windows are too high."

"It would be very useful for us if we could put a man in there with some powerful binoculars," Tom said. "What if we put some scaffolding in there to get him high enough to see out the windows? It will be an ideal location."

"A sharpshooter?" Ken Rice asked.

"Precisely," Tom said.

"Let me worry that one just a bit," the chairman said. "I'm afraid that might just be a shade beyond my comfort level. But y'all go on up there anyway. I don't believe there's anyone staying there just yet."

The waiter came by with a check, which the chairman signed.

"We will have badges for you this afternoon that give you complete access to the club," the chairman asked. "Is there anything else we can do for you?"

"There is one thing," Kathryn said. "We came down on very short notice and we haven't made any reservations. It must be nightmarish finding a room at this late date."

"We'll take care of that this afternoon as well," Ken Rice said. "Come with me down to the golf shop and we'll get you a cart."

• • •

For the next several hours, they rode around the golf course, beginning at the first hole and finishing on No. 18. They drove down the service roads that cut through the woods and along the borders of the course. It was clear that this was a far more dangerous site than the Stadium course, which was essentially flat and surrounded by swamps and low-lying areas.

Augusta, on the other hand, was cut through thick stands of trees, largely pines, as well as dense shrubbery. This was especially true along the 11th, 12th and 13th holes—"Amen Corner"—which were laid out along the lowest part of the course. These holes were particularly dangerous since they bordered the Augusta Country Club. If Raines could somehow park there it would make his escape much easier.

"I think we need to have canine units up there," Tom told Kathryn, pointing to the ridge that ran along behind the 11th and 12th greens and the 13th tee. "If we have one patrol ahead of Brookes and one with him, we might have a decent chance of scaring off Raines. We should also arrange to have the perimeter of the course patrolled at all times."

They drove past one of the television towers and Kathryn suggested putting security in those as well.

"We have that meeting tomorrow," Tom said. "I'm sure they'll go along with whatever the club wants but I'm afraid it will raise suspicions. It will be pretty hard to explain away."

They returned to the clubhouse, dropping the cart off at the golf shop and walking over to Ken Rice's office near the reception area. He gave them their badges and directions for the house he rented for them at West Lake.

"Here are the directions, plus a back route that will save you some time once the tournaments starts," he said. "Pick up the house keys at the security gate. We've arranged for food to be delivered and there's a number to call if you need anything else. The meeting with the television people is set for ten in the morning at the chairman's office. Go left out the front door and just follow the driveway. It's down past the public pro shop and the media center. You can't miss it."

Tom thanked him and they walked over to the parking lot near the practice tee. The sun was beginning to set and there was just one player left on the tee in the fading light: Peter Brookes.

. . .

Tom liked Jake O'Banion right from the start. He was smart and tough, but charming and polished. He arrived for the meeting at the chairman's office right on time, dressed in a pale blue, Irish linen shirt, a lightweight navy blue blazer, gray slacks and expensive Gucci loafers that he wore without socks.

After the introductions were made, he shared a little Tour gossip with the chairman, and Tom was pretty sure there would have been more—and more involving women—if Kathryn hadn't been in the room. But once they got down to business, he proved to have a quick and analytical mind. He grasped the political ramifications early on and since one of the most important elements of his job was keeping the good people at Augusta National—which basically meant Charlie Franklin—happy, he instinctively picked up on the club's position and pretty much echoed it at every turn in the conversation.

The Masters is one of the crown jewels of sport and no one knows that better than the people at Augusta National. For as long as anyone could remember, the club's relationship with the network has been based on a series of one-year contracts, which gives Augusta National unprecedented power and leverage. The club knows that executives from the other networks would sell their mothers, wives, and daughters into a life in the brothels of Calcutta if it meant getting a shot at the Masters—and the people at CBS know they know it, too. Every year, the Green Jackets—as they're known—offer "suggestions" about how the television coverage could be improved, and every year the people at the network regard this as Moses coming down from the Mount with the 10 Commandments.

Not that they are intimidated or anything.

But while he was appropriately differential toward the chairman, he was far from sycophantic. In fact, he was more candid that Tom had expected. Clearly the two men liked and respected one another, which would make the days ahead infinitely easier.

By the end of the meeting, which took a little over an hour,

O'Banion had agreed to let Tom sit with him in the production truck to watch the wall of monitors. He had also agreed to bring in some extra crew and hand-held cameras to scan the galleries on the holes Brookes was playing as well as the preceding holes. They had also had a discussion about putting people in the announcer's towers on the back nine. The elevation would give them an advantage in scanning the galleries.

"What am I supposed to tell the announcers?" O'Banion asked.

"Pretend you're talking to the suits in New York about your budget," the chairman said. "Tell them anything you want but just don't tell them the truth."

It was quickly decided that there would be security personnel in the announcer's towers, and the camera towers as well, over the weekend. The chairman also told them that the Crow's Nest would be closed to the amateurs and handed them a release that would be issued to the press early in the week of the tournament.

It is part of the tradition of the Masters Tournament that the amateur invitees are welcome to stay in the "Crow's Nest" in the clubhouse. While the club cherishes this tradition as part of our long-standing commitment to amateur golfers dating back to Bob Jones and Clifford Roberts, we have been informed that asbestos has been found in that area, and as a health precaution, the club has arranged for housing for the amateurs in an area convenient to Augusta National. We plan to resume our tradition of housing the amateurs in the Crow's Nest at next year's Masters Tournament.

"This should work, don't you think?" the chairman asked. "It would explain why we'll have the scaffolding in there."

"I can't see anyone questioning it" Tom said. "This kind of thing is in the papers every day."

"I'll agree to having people in there as a spotters, but under no circumstances will they have permission to use their weapons," the chairman said. "This place is a sea of people during the tournament and it's just too dangerous."

• • •

By the time the players and writers began to arrive early in the week of the tournament, all the planning and coordination with the state and local police officials was complete. To the extent it would be possible to protect Peter Brookes, Tom felt confident that they had done everything possible.

The surveillance cameras were in place at all the general admission gates and the banks of video screens were installed in an office in the club's administration building. The manufacturer of the equipment was supplying technicians to monitor the screens. In the case of a match, they would be in direct contact with the guards posted at the gate, who were instructed to pull the person aside for a check of their admissions badge.

Working through the Agency's military liaison staff in Langley, Tom had arranged for special military police canine units from Ft. Benning to patrol the perimeters of the course, concentrating on the 11th, 12th and 13th holes. In addition, the army had detached a two-man special operations team—a spotter and a shooter—that would be stationed in the Crow's Nest. They would be unarmed— at least for the time being. The army had also provided three veteran Special Forces officers. Their job was to position themselves in an announcer or camera tower either on the hole Brookes was playing or the two upcoming holes. They would leapfrog each other in the course of the round. Finally, there would be a cordon of uniformed and plainclothes police walking with Brookes any time he was on the property.

Tom would coordinate the operation from the network's production truck, where he would also have the best view of the different camera feeds, while Kathryn would walk in Brookes's gallery, watching for Raines.

The chairman had initially resisted the involvement of the army, preferring to use local police and Pinkerton security, but Tom finally convinced him that this offered the best chance of preventing leaks.

A meeting was arranged with Brookes, the chairman, Ken Rice, Tom and Kathryn in the chairman's office on Wednesday, between Brookes's final practice round and his starting time in the annual Par 3 Tournament.

By the time of the meeting, Brookes and the club's officials had done everything they could to downplay the media's interest in the death threats at The Players Championship and the possibility that he was at risk during the Masters.

As one of the tournament favorites, Brookes had been brought to the press building early in the week for a pretournament interview where he was, as usual, in part charming and in equal parts dismissive and condescending. At any rate, after several questions about the death threats, he simply said he wasn't concerned and felt the press had blown the entire business totally out of proportion.

"Am I worried?" he said in response to a question. "Certainly. I'm worried about the speed of the greens, several of the hole placements, and a few of the changes that have been made. Am I worried about whether I may or may not be at risk from some lunatic who, for all I know, doesn't even exist? Not a bit."

The chairman also did his part during his annual press interview. He enjoyed the writers and they cut him a lot of slack, mostly because they found him to be a sort of charming rogue who didn't take himself all that seriously.

"Charlie," one writer asked, "could you tell us if you've increased security in light of the threat on Peter Brookes?"

"No," the chairman said.

"No you haven't or no you can't tell us?" the writer asked.

"Just plain old no," the chairman said, to a smattering a laughter from the crowded room. "Just N for N and O for O. No."

"Could you describe the club's standard security arrangements?" a second writer asked.

"Beyond keeping an eye on you boys?" the chairman replied. "We do try to keep a count on the pimento cheese sandwiches. We don't want y'all taking them home to your friends and relatives. We're on a budget here you know."

Having sidestepped the security question, the interview moved on to the usual questions such as drainage down in Amen Corner, the club's mysterious membership policies, and whether the bar near the Champions locker room would be named after Jimmy Demaret, the first three-time winner of the Masters. This final question prompted applause from the Texas writers.

"It would certainly be a fitting honor," the chairman said. "We'll take it under advisement. Will the golf writers pay for the plaque?"

• • •

Brookes arrived for the meeting and listened calmly and carefully as Tom ran through the arrangements that had been made.

"Do you know if this Raines fellow is even in the area?" he asked.

"No," Kathryn said. "But we have no reports of him being anyplace else, either."

"Well it sounds as though you've done all you can do," Brookes said, rising from his chair. "Now I've just got to get about my business. I do want to thank you for your efforts."

"Good luck this afternoon," Kathryn said.

"Not too much luck," Brookes said. "No one has ever won the Par 3 tournament and the Masters in the same year. I'd prefer to use up my luck in some other fashion."

After Brookes left, Tom just shook his head.

"He's an interesting guy," he said. "In a lot of ways I admire him but he seems to have an awful big chip on his shoulder. He's almost a Jekyll and Hyde personality."

"He's been burned a few times by the press," Charlie Franklin said. "The British writers can be tough. It's not like the old days, when the writers wrote about the players but didn't get into their personal lives. Now everyone and everything is fair game. Brookes isn't that much different in his feelings about the press than most of the players, I imagine. He just likes to get in their face."

"He's also a very bright and thoughtful guy," the chairman said. "Occasionally, we'll get a letter from him suggesting changes on the course or the way the tournament is run that are very good. And unlike some players who take their criticisms to the press without bothering to discuss them with us, Brookes invariably communicates directly with the club. If we accept his suggestions, fine. If we don't, that's fine, too. Either way, we don't read about it. We appreciate that."

Tom and Kathryn left the chairman's office and went to the clubhouse for lunch. It was another perfect spring day and they decided to eat outside. The verandah was roped off, and hundreds of spectators without passes that would get them inside the ropes were lined up, hoping to catch a glimpse of their favorite players and possibly an autograph. The effect was a little like eating lunch on stage.

As Tom suspected, the service slowed considerably if you weren't dining with the chairman. In fact, it was positively glacial for nonmembers. They finally ordered, and while they waited for their food to arrive, Kathryn asked him why, if Brookes was such a great player, he'd never won the Masters.

"It takes luck to win any tournament," Tom explained. "Sometimes it's good luck on your part. Sometimes it's bad luck on some other guy's part. That's especially true here. The course is so difficult and the margin for error is so small that the slightest mistake at the wrong time can blow you out of the water. There's probably no other tournament where there's so much potential for disaster. Brookes has probably had three or four good chances to win. Sometimes he made some wrong decisions or hit a poor shot and it cost him, especially when he was younger. Other times, guys just out and out beat him. That happens."

"What do you think his chances are this week?" she asked.

"Without this stuff hanging over his head, I'd say they're excellent," Tom said. "Who knows at this point?"

"He seems pretty calm about the whole thing," Kathryn said.

"He's either a great actor or the most fatalistic person I've ever met," Tom said. "I'm just not sure which it is."

When their meals finally arrived, Tom couldn't resist commenting on Kathryn's fruit salad.

"Still boycotting red meat?" he asked.

"Yes, and if I see one more grotesquely overweight person—what do you call them? Bubbas?—with one of those Krispy Kremey things attached to their face, I shall also be swearing off all pastries forever. Honestly, how do they manage to walk around this place without having a coronary?"

"It's a mystery but doctors suspect that Krispy Kremes, when washed down with beer, form an anticlotting agent," Tom said. "For people in this part of the country, they also form two of the four key elements in the essential food group."

"What are the others?" Kathryn asked, in mock seriousness. "Though I shudder to ask."

"Marlboros and barbeque," Tom said.

• • •

Until he encountered Kathryn Devlin at The Players Championship, Graham Raines had decided to leave America and spend a few months laying low in the Caribbean. In the days since Martin McGonagle's death—and Raines had no doubt it was an M.I.6 assassination—Raines hadn't had any contact with any members of McGonagle's organization. He assumed correctly that most of the members had been arrested or, failing any concrete evidence, at least detained indefinitely. When it came to the IRA, the British took a diminished view of the niceties of civil rights. The gloves had come off a very long time ago.

But with Kathryn Devlin in the picture, his thinking changed dramatically. Since their first encounter in South Africa, she and M.I.6 had hunted him with singular purpose and he had come to both respect and despise her in equal measures. Now, with her in the States, he resolved once and for all to best her and be done with it.

He knew all too well not to underestimate Kathryn Devlin. He still bore the scar on his shoulder as a reminder of how ruthless and effective she truly was, and there were a great many nights when he lay awake recalling how lucky he was to escape from South Africa, not only with his freedom, but also his life—no thanks to Kathryn Devlin.

The South African affair had been botched almost from the start. The right-wing opposition to Mandela and the African National Congress that hired him had plenty of money but it had been thoroughly infiltrated by M.I.6 and the CIA, as well as elements of the South African security apparatus. For his part, Raines rather admired Mandela and regarded his opponents as neofascist dinosaurs desperate to hold onto power—not that it mattered a bit to Raines.

Raines had been hired to assassinate one of Mandela's closest associates, thereby intimidating Mandela into accepting a compromise, power-sharing arrangement much more accommodating to the entrenched and powerful white minority.

But he had barely arrived in Cape Town when every one of Raines's instincts told him to get out of South Africa. The political situation was extremely fluid and volatile and with every passing day he became increasingly unsure of his chances for success. He had reluctantly agreed to meet with a group of rogue army intelligence officers, and it was at that meeting that the shootout with M.I.6 agents occurred.

Raines shot one agent, seriously wounding him and then killing him when the man struggled to get off one last shot. He was racing down a side street to rendezvous with a waiting car when a second wave of M.I.6 agents arrived as a backup unit. Among them was Kathryn Devlin, and as Raines sprinted toward the car, she emerged from the shadows and ordered him to stop. He turned in her direction and raised his pistol. As he did, she coolly squeezed off one round from her automatic. The bullet slammed into his shoulder, the impact throwing him back against the car. He managed to open the door and dove across the backseat as the Mercedes sped off. As it did, Kathryn Devlin stood her ground, firing three more rounds through the windshield, barely missing the driver.

The surgery to remove the bullet was done in a safe house but the damage had been extensive, leaving a large, purplish scar.

It wasn't until a few years later that a sympathetic member of M.I.6 informed Raines that Kathryn Devlin was the widow of one of the men from his unit killed in Argentina, and that she had been assigned to lead the team of agents charged with tracking him down and, if necessary, eliminating him. From that moment on, the two had engaged in a deadly serious game of cat and mouse that had taken them to Spain, the Caribbean and the hellhole that is Haiti, back to Africa and now, finally, the States. None of their encounters had been as close as their first, but now he was determined to outwit her on this very large and public stage.

By the time he left The Players Championship, Raines had set into motion his plan to kill Peter Brookes at the Masters.

First, he rented every video he could find about the tournament. It didn't take long for him to realize that an attempt similar to the one he had made in Los Angeles was probably out of the question. Security would be too tight, for one thing. The element of surprise was gone. For another, as far as he could tell the course didn't lend itself to a shooting from a distance that would allow him a reasonable chance of success and escape.

The next step was to secure credentials. Newspapers advertised tickets for sale, but Raines's plans called for something far more difficult to arrange: a photographer's badge that would give him access to virtually the entire course. After speaking with some of the photographers at The Players Championship, he knew that the Masters guarded these passes like the crown jewels.

But Graham Raines knew something else as well: money talks.

Before The Players Championship had even ended, Raines had made a phone call to a contact in London, a former member of M.I.5, the British domestic intelligence agency, who had moved onto a considerably more lucrative line of work.

"How quickly can you secure a photographer's credential for the Masters?" Raines asked.

"Very dicey stuff, that," the man replied. "And expensive as well."

"I'm sure," Raines said.

"I'll need to work with one of our American friends who specializes in this sort of thing," the man said. "A chap whose name contains a great many vowels, if you will."

"Fine, but you must act as the cutout," Raines said. "I want everything to go through you. It cannot, under any circumstances, be traced to me."

"Understood," the man said.

Organized crime in America is good at a great many things, counterfeiting being one of them. A discreetly placed bribe to an employee of the company that manufactures the various badges for the Masters and other sporting events secured a badge for just long enough to make a perfect counterfeit version that was undetectable. By the time Raines arrived in Augusta, the badge had been shipped from New York to London and on to Raines.

Finally, there was the matter of the explosive device that Raines planned to use to kill Peter Brookes, should he completely rule out a shooting. Graham Raines had a plan in mind, but it would have to wait until he got to Augusta National before he would be able to finalize it.

• • •

When Raines arrived at the main gate on Wednesday for the Par 3 Tournament he saw the security cameras and the long lines. People were being asked to remove hats and dark glasses. Raines wasn't particularly surprised. In fact, he rather expected such an increase in security and had taken the necessary precautions. He had dyed his hair and eyebrows a dark brown and was wearing the dark contact lenses he had worn in Los Angeles. As an added pre-caution, he had applied some latex patches around his eyes and placed some wads of tissue between his cheeks and gums. Taken together, he was confident it would be enough to throw off any computer scanning equipment, no matter how sophisticated.

Raines arrived at the Par 3 course a few minutes before Brookes was scheduled to tee off. The galleries were enormous, and seemed even larger because unlike the main course, they were compressed into a much smaller area.

Brookes finished warming up on the small practice green, and as soon as he headed for the nearby first tee he was surrounded by police who guided him through the gallery that was eight or ten people deep in spots. In addition, there were police positioned along the ropes running from the tee to the green. Even given Brookes's height, it was difficult to see anything but the top of his head as he stood on the tee preparing to play.

When Brookes was announced on the tee, he received a tremendous ovation, which he acknowledged with a theatrical bow that delighted the gallery. His tee shot landed safely on the green and ran back to within 10 feet of the hole. Again, the gallery erupted in applause as he walked from the tee toward the green.

There was a carnival atmosphere to the Par 3 Tournament. The players didn't take it very seriously and it was a good chance to watch them without the pressure of tournament competition. One of the beauties of the Par 3 Tournament was that so many of the older Masters Champions competed and the gallery was both supportive and appreciative of their efforts.

At one point, Raines had decided to see how close he could get to Brookes. He quickly discovered that the answer was: not very. As Brookes walked from a green to the next tee, Raines thrust a pairing sheet and a pen toward him and asked for an autograph. Two policemen closed ranks between the two men and politely but firmly moved Raines aside. For his part, Brookes never even looked at Raines, keeping his eyes focused on the next tee, not looking to either side.

After watching Brookes for several holes, Raines decided to walk back out onto the big course. The practice rounds had been completed and the course was closed to play as the grounds crews made their final preparations. Raines left the Par 3 course and turned left, down behind the line of handsome white cabins that sat along the left side of the 10th hole. As he started down the heavily wooded hillside Raines was stopped by a very large and very serious Georgia state policeman.

"I'm sorry sir, you'll have to go back up the hill and cross behind the tee," the officer said. "No one is allowed down this side of the hole."

"Is that just for today or for the entire tournament?" Raines asked.

"All week," the officer said. "Besides, the view is a lot better from the other side."

Raines walked down the 10th hole, past the green set back in the trees, and then alongside the 11th as it played downhill toward the green, which was protected by water on the left. The course was virtually deserted except for people from the grounds crew and a smattering of spectators simply taking in the scenery. When he reached the corner formed by the 11th, 12th and 13th holes, Raines trained his binoculars into the heavily wooded areas bordering those holes. If he could somehow get in there, he would have a clear shot at Brookes on any of those three holes. The question was, how would he get in there? And the larger question was, how would he make his escape?

Both questions became moot on Thursday morning, when two college students tried to sneak onto the golf course by scaling the fence separating Augusta National from the Augusta Country Club. They had barely made it onto Augusta National's property when they were tracked down and taken into custody by two of the canine patrols from Fort Benning. The students were taken to an isolated area near the television production compound, where they were arrested by Augusta police, charged with trespassing, and escorted off the grounds. The problem was a writer from the Augusta *Chronicle*, who was leaving the compound after interviewing Jake O'Banion, spotted the military police and the arrest. By noontime, the story had swept through the media center and writers were asking club officials whether army personnel were involved in the security arrangements for the tournament. Finally, Ken Rice went down to meet with the press.

"Ken, can you either confirm or deny that the army is supplying soldiers for the tournament?" a writer asked.

"As a matter of longstanding club policy, we don't discuss specific elements of our security policies, but it's fair to say that from time to time over the years they have been helpful," Rice said.

"Is this part of an increased security presence because of the threats on Peter Brookes's life following the shooting at Riviera?" another writer asked.

"As far as I know, there has only been the one threat down at The Players Championship," Rice said. "We have not received word of any additional threats, but as a general rule, yes, we have increased security over the years as the tournament has grown larger. I think that's true for every tournament."

"Can you tell us if the club has taken any other extraordinary steps to increase security?" a radio reporter asked.

"I don't believe I've confirmed anything that I would consider extraordinary," Rice said.

"You don't think having army troops here at Augusta is extraordinary?" the radio guy asked.

"I didn't confirm that," Rice said.

"Do you deny it?" the man persisted.

"No, I can't confirm it or deny it because we don't discuss those arrangements," Rice said.

"Well, if some of us went down to that area along Amen Corner, what would we find?" the reporter asked.

"This is Georgia," Rice said. "There's all kinds of things you might find down there in those woods. But one thing you'll almost certainly find is a very large police officer who will be more than willing to point you back in the direction of the golf course. Are there any other questions?"

• • •

To no one's surprise, a source in the Augusta Police Department confirmed that teams from Fort Benning were, in fact, involved in patrolling the perimeter of the course. The story made the front page of the local papers and was played prominently on the local television news shows. On Friday, the *New York Times* ran it in their notes column and *USA Today* treated it as a sidebar to the main story, which was Peter Brookes taking the first round lead with a 67.

By the time the story broke, however, Raines had abandoned the idea of shooting Brookes as far too risky. Even if he could manage to get into position for a clear shot, the traffic situation, the heightened security, and the large galleries made any reasonable chance of escape unlikely.

Raines had become increasingly frustrated. He had been checkmated and this only increased his determination to prove to M.I.6 and their American counterparts that he could not and would not be deterred, even by their best efforts. His alternate plan was infinitely riskier and more complicated, and more deadly as well, but if there had to be some degree of collateral damage, so be it.

When he was at Riviera, Raines observed that when a player was teeing off, the other players and caddies generally stood very near to the tee markers on the right side of the tee, making any shot from that direction difficult. At Augusta, the markers were pieces of logs roughly a foot or so long and six inches wide.

As part of his training for the Special Air Service, Raines had received instruction in the use of explosives. His plan was to somehow get his hands on one of those tee markers—or failing that, try to have one made—hollow out a small section of the wood and fill it with C-4, a putty-like plastic explosive that was extremely powerful and could be detonated from a safe distance using a remote device. He had planned to use the C-4 as a possible diversion. It would not be a diversion now.

The first complication was figuring out how to get his hands on one of the tee markers. He had hoped that the grounds crew simply left them on the tees overnight, but he soon discovered that this wasn't the case. After the final group had finished playing on a hole, the tee markers and flagsticks were removed and returned to the maintenance building, which was located out on the west side of the course, near the second hole.

At one point he struck up a conversation with a member of the grounds crew.

"This must be a terribly busy week for you fellows," he said.

"All day and most of the night," the man replied.

"Really?" Raines said. "What time do you finish for the day?"

"About dark," the man said. "We try to get as much done as we can before nightfall."

"What time do you have to be at work?" Raines asked.

"Six o'clock or when the sun comes up, whichever comes first," he said. "It's the week from hell."

"Well, you're to be congratulated," Raines said. "You perform brilliantly."

. . .

Initially, Raines planned to break into the maintenance building at night. He imagined that since it was far enough away from the main clubhouse complex, the security would be fairly light. One option was to hide out on the course until late in the evening. He had noticed thick, tall stands of bamboo on the perimeter of the Par 3 course that would make an ideal place to hide. His other option was to enter the course under the cover of darkness. The problem inherent in both options was the level of security. Raines simply had no idea how intense it would be at night, but in the end he decided it wasn't worth the risk, especially since making the bomb wasn't difficult. As Raines's SAS instructor had told him years ago, anything that an Irishman or an Arab can make can't be all that complicated.

First thing on Friday morning, be began telephoning local woodworking shops, explaining that he was a golfer from Britain over for his first Masters and was quite taken by the tee markers at Augusta National. He said that he hoped to bring a replica back with him and wondered if one could be made quickly.

The initial results were disappointing and Raines began to think he might have to revert to his original plan of breaking into the maintenance building under the cover of night. But on the fifth call, he got lucky. It was a company that made similar tee markers for other area clubs and could have one ready for Raines by the end of the day that would be identical to the markers at Augusta National.

While Raines was confident that the plan was solid, he also realized that he needed a backup in case there were complications. He knew there would be chaos when the bomb exploded, and his plan was to blend into the gallery and make his escape through the main entrance gates. But that would almost certainly be where the police would be stationed in the greatest numbers, so he decided to look for an alternative. One option was to leave by one of the other gates. Another was to simply find a place where the police wouldn't be likely to look for a suspect in a bombing.

Raines arrived at Augusta National late in the morning on Friday. It was a lovely spring day and the gallery gathered around the clubhouse area was large, although not as large as it had been on Wednesday. Raines walked past the clubhouse toward the 10th tee, and as he did, he saw two of the television announcers in their navy blue blazers walking up a small rise from a cabin across the road from the Par 3 course. As the men neared, he approached them and asked if the building was their headquarters.

"No," said one of the men, who Raines recognized from the videos as Tim Prince, the anchor of the telecasts. "That's Butler Cabin. It's where the green jacket is given to the winner at the end of the tournament."

"Oh, splendid," said Raines. "One of my assignments was to get some photos of your studio there. Do you suppose this would be a proper time?"

"Sure," said Prince. "We don't go on-air until four today. There's nothing going on down there now. The entrance is down in the back. Just don't wake anyone up. The camera guys need their beauty sleep or they get cranky."

Raines thanked him and walked down to the rear of the cabin. There was a door on the left side as he came around the corner, and a small patio, where some of the technical crew were relaxing in the warm sunshine. Raines introduced himself as a photographer from London and asked if he might take some shots of the studio.

"The talent won't be here for a couple hours," one of the men said. "There's nothing to shoot."

"No, actually that's ideal," Raines said. "It's for a story about what the Masters is like behind the scenes. I'd like to include you lads if I could."

"Do you think we should check with Jake?" a second man said. "You know how the Green Jackets can get pissy about this kind of thing."

The first man looked his watch.

"Nah, Jake's holding court up at the clubhouse," he said. "And he hates to be interrupted when the peasants are coming by to kiss his ring. Besides, even the Green Jackets can't get upset about somebody taking pictures of empty chairs. Go on in through that door over there. Hank, the stage manager, is in the studio. He'll show you around."

Raines entered the cabin through the door on the left side of the building. The first room was small, with cases and boxes on the left side and a row of computers on a table that ran along the right. Scoring sheets were scattered across the table. To the rear of the room was a small hallway and a bathroom and on the right side was a door leading to the studio.

As Raines entered the studio, there were a series of armchairs arranged in front of a brick wall and a fireplace with a series of plants around it. Cameras were placed in front of the chairs and large lights were arranged overhead. Behind the cameras was an area cluttered with equipment and other chairs, and French doors opening out to the patio. Raines introduced himself to the stage manager, a genial older man, who politely answered Raines's questions.

Raines shot several photographs as the stage manager regaled him with stories about how chaotic the studio was in the minutes leading up to the green jacket ceremony, as people waited for the new champion to arrive.

"Do you supposed I might be allowed in here to shoot it?" Raines asked. "It would be quite a coup for me."

"No, they close this place right down," the man said. "You'd have to be a friend of Jake's and even then probably not."

Raines looked around the room and noticed a door on the right side.

"What's through that door?" he asked.

"Another room," the man said. "We use it for storage and sometimes the talent will use it to get cleaned up," the stage manager said.

"Mind if I have a look?" Raines said.

"Suit yourself," the man said. "There's not much to see."

"Is there a loo in there I could use by any chance?" Raines asked.

"No, but go ahead and take a look," the man said.

Raines walked through the door into a small hallway. He opened a door to his left. It led to a set of stairs that ran to the main level of the cabin. The other room was a cluttered mess, as described, with a door leading to the patio—a possible escape route of last resort.

Raines walked back into the studio.

"Is the upstairs used for your telecast?" he asked the stage manager.

"No, one of the big investment houses or something rents the place for the week," the man said. "It's one big, loud party. When they bring the new champion down here the place goes nuts. When Nicklaus won in '86, there was so much noise I thought the cabin was going to collapse around us. Between them and the crowds that are always out on the patio, you could hardly hear yourself think."

Raines thanked the man and left. He walked across the patio and thanked the other men, and then strolled along the right rear of the building. It might—just might—make a decent escape route if the crowds were large enough.

Raines drove away from Augusta National with more confidence than when he arrived that morning. Now he had a possible backup plan, as well as an alternative escape route.

He drove down Washington Road to a nearby hardware store, where he bought a hand drill with a one-inch bit, a small saw, and some plastic wood to seal the cavity where the explosive would be placed. He returned to his hotel in time to watch some of the television coverage before heading off to pick up the tee marker.

When he returned to his hotel room he went to work building the bomb. He carefully cut a half-inch slice from one end of the marker, removed the metal spike that held the marker into the ground, and then bored a hole lengthwise into the marker, creating a cavity that would contain the C-4. He filled the hole with the explosive and the blasting cap, leaving a space he stuffed with plastic wood. Then he meticulously glued the slice of wood he had removed back onto the tee marker.

It was a simple, but deadly, device. Now the last trick was getting it to the course.

• • •

Sir Owen Tunnicliffe died at Bethesda Naval Hospital early

Saturday morning from complications following a third and ultimately fatal stroke. He was 80.

Tom and Kathryn learned of his death by a series of phone calls, first from a political officer at the British Embassy, followed almost immediately by a call from the Deputy Director and then one to Kathryn from the British Ambassador's office later in the day.

"There's to be a memorial service in Washington on Tuesday," she told Tom. "Following the service, he's to be flown back to London. I've been asked to escort his body on the flight."

There was silence as they both tried to grasp that she would be leaving in a matter of days, no matter how their assignment ended at Augusta on Sunday. They both knew the time would come when she would leave, but neither expected it would come so soon or under such sad circumstances. They both had studiously avoided talking about it but now their time together was running short.

"Will you go up for the service?" Kathryn asked.

"Of course," Tom said. "We'll fly out of here Monday. I'll arrange for a plane."

"I can't believe he's gone," Kathryn said. "In my heart of hearts, of course, I knew this day was coming. But it's still rather a shock."

Tom held her and tried to console her, but the reality was they had two days of a hard work left and he knew all along that the weekend was the time of greatest danger. If Raines was going to make his play, he wasn't going to do it when the tournament was being covered by cable. It was going to be on network television and it was going to be televised around the world. Tom knew the trap was closing. He just couldn't be sure who it was closing in on.

. . .

The grounds crew began cutting the tees and greens early on Sunday morning, just as the sun was beginning to rise. The admission gates didn't open until eight, but even at that early hour, there would be a line of people waiting to enter, so they could take up their seats at key viewing locations such as the 18th green and all down along Amen Corner. Many of these people had done this year after year. It was part of the Masters' tradition.

Raines's alarm woke him at four in the morning and he dressed quickly in nondescript clothing. He packed the bomb and the stake that would hold it into the ground in the bottom of a case designed to hold a long telephoto lens, along with a small .32 caliber automatic and the remote control signaling device that would trigger the bomb when Brookes reached the final tee.

Raines drove through the deserted streets in darkness until he reached the main parking lot off Washington Road. The gate was locked, so Raines walked down to the main entrance to the club, where a guard was on duty.

"I've come to shoot the grounds crew working in the wee hours of the day," he said to the guard, holding up his photographer's badge.

The guard studied the badge and waved him through.

By Raines's guess, it would still be a good half-hour before the sun rose, so he made his way down Magnolia Lane, past the clubhouse, and down the 10th fairway, staying close to the trees that separated the 10th and 18th holes to help avoid undue attention.

Sure enough, the sun had barely come over the trees to the east when the first crews appeared on the course. He could hear mowers back up on the 10th tee and the 18th green, and a few minutes later, from down at the holes along Rae's Creek. It took them about 15 minutes for one crew to make its way down to the 10th green, while another moved across the way to the 18th tee, on the other side of the stand of trees.

Raines watched as they finished cutting the 18th tee, placed the tee markers, and then moved to the 8th tee, to the left and down a slight hill. Over on the 14th green, another crew finished and left for the 11th hole. He marveled—and gave thanks—for their efficiency. Within 45 minutes, they had finished cutting all the tees and greens in the vicinity of the 18th tee and moved on.

Raines began moving toward the 18th tee, walking slowly and stopping often to take photographs, first at the 10th green and the 15th tee, before walking back through the trees toward the 18th tee. As he did, he saw a maintenance cart out of the corner of his eye as it came down the right side of the 10th hole. The cart stopped by the bunker just short of the green, no more than 20 yards from Raines, who continued to take photos. The worker inspected the bunker briefly, then got back in his cart and drove down the 11th hole. Raines, his heart pounding and beads of sweat forming on his forehead, waved as the man drove off.

After a few minutes, Raines was satisfied that no one was in the immediate area, and he walked to the edge of the trees nearest the 18th tee. He removed the bomb from the lens case and replaced the spike that held it into the turf. He checked one more time to ensure that no one could see him, and then walked to the right side of the tee box. Just as he had removed the right-hand tee marker from the turf, he heard a helicopter roar low over the club-house, heading down the 18th fairway toward the tee.

"Fuck," he muttered under his breath.

The helicopter was already halfway down the fairway, over the bunkers on the left side of the landing area. Raines, panicking slightly, hurriedly stuck the bomb into the turf, tossed the other marker into the trees, and then focused his camera on the heli-copter as it passed overhead.

Raines watched as the helicopter banked to the right and flew down the 11th fairway until it reached the green, where it hovered for a moment, before turning to the right again and flying over Amen Corner.

By now, the sun was up over the trees and Raines knew he had to leave the area. He worked the spike in the discarded tee marker back and forth until it was loose enough to pull out of the wood and placed both pieces in the camera case. Hugging the treeline along the left side of the 10th fairway, he found a thick patch of bamboo and ducked behind it. Once there, he discarded the pieces in the deep underbrush.

Peter Brookes, who had led the tournament after all three rounds, was due to tee off at 2:30. That meant he'd arrive on the 18th tee in just about 12 hours.

Now, Raines thought, *the game is truly on.*

• • •

The network actually began its coverage of the final round an hour before it went on-air. This gave Jake O'Banion, his crew, and the announcers time to get up to speed—not that O'Banion needed to warm up. Sitting near him in the main production truck for the past three days had been a revelation for Tom. The man was a genius, a virtuoso. He played the pictures and the announcers like a great theatrical director—except when he was running the place like General Patton.

"Listen to me, you mutts," O'Banion said, just before they went live. "This is being fed to the clubhouse and the chairman's office, so don't fuck up. You know the drill. No past champions, just champions. No mention of money. Patrons, not galleries, and never, ever, under any circumstances, no crowds or mobs. Think before you talk and then say half of what you were planning to say. Remember, we're guests here at the plantation. Have a good one."

"Two minutes to air, Jake," said Charlie Walsh.

Jake O'Banion opened his microphone so all the announcers could hear him. "Good luck, boys," he said. "Remember, there's nothing riding on all this except your careers."

· · ·

The network picked up the leaders midway through the front nine. Brookes was playing his usual intelligent, conservative game. He opened with a par, birdied the par-5 2nd hole, made a par on the short, par-4 3rd, and then bogeyed the par-3 4th when his tee shot was hit by a gust of wind and it plugged in the face of the bunker.

"Okay, Timmy and Ben, we're live in 30 seconds," O'Banion said. "Tim, you've got the opener from Butler Cabin, then we go to the chairman's taped introduction, a few highlights, and then we go live to Brookes on the fifth hole. You'll throw it to Ben for a quick comment. Head's up now, ladies, and three, two, one and—go Timmy."

The transition from the live opener to the tape piece and the highlights package and then back to the live coverage was seamless.

"Timmy, I'm really impressed by the way Brookes has played these early holes," Ben Ward said. "He doesn't need to attack the golf course. He has to let the field chase him. He's playing very smart, percentage golf. Just like another guy who did pretty well around here."

"Jack Nicklaus," said Tim Prince

"That's right," Ward said. "People think you can attack this course, but really what you've got to do is take what it will give you."

· · ·

So far, the effort to protect Brookes had been seamless as well. Except for the two college kids on Thursday, the canine patrols had been there for a stroll in the woods. The computer scanning had turned up a few matches but no one really coming close to resembling Raines. In fact, everything had gone so well that Tom worried that his people might be losing their edge.

· · ·

Brookes birdied the uphill par-5 8th hole and finished the front nine with a two-stroke lead over his playing partner, Dexter Bradley, and two other players. He hit a good drive on the 10th hole that caught the slope and chased down the hill. After following his tee shot, O'Banion called for a shot of the 18th tee.

"Okay, we've got Nicklaus here on the 18th tee," O'Banion said. "He needs a par here for a 70. Christ, the guy is unbelievable. Somebody send him a card and tell him how old he is. Let this one play out now, Timmy."

Tom watched on the monitor as Nicklaus lined up his tee shot.

"The greatest champion in Master's history needs a par here for a two-under-par round of 70," said Tim Prince.

"How many times have we seen him pull off a miracle on this hole, Timmy?" Ben Ward asked.

Nicklaus's drive started down the right side of the chute of trees just off the tee, then faded to the right, catching a few of the limbs before dropping down into the light rough. O'Banion called for a tight shot of Nicklaus. He had a puzzled look on his face, and then just shook his head.

"How many balls have we seen in those trees today?" O'Banion said. "It's like the Green Jackets added trees overnight."

Charlie Walsh opened his microphone down to the people running the scoring and statistical computers in Butler Cabin.

"Where does 18 rank in scoring today?" he asked. A moment later, he said, "You're kidding me. Jake, it's the fourth hardest hole today."

Suddenly, a terrible fear gripped Tom Quinn.

"Son of a bitch," he said under his breath. Then, quietly, he said, "Charlie, can you guys call up a shot from behind the 18th tee for me?"

"That monitor right there," Walsh said, pulling back on a switch on the console.

"Can you get a closer shot?" Tom asked.

To Tom's eye, the tee markers were set incorrectly. It looked as though the marker on the right side was set back slightly, which could cause players to aim to the right.

"Jake, can I talk with Ben Ward?" Tom asked.

O'Banion turned to Tom.

"That phone right there," he said, then he flipped a switch and spoke directly to Ward. "Ben, that phone's for you."

"Ben," Tom said. "It's Tom Quinn. Let me ask you a question and I need you to keep this to yourself. Who sets the tee markers?"

"The committee sets them, but they don't change very much from year to year and round to round except on the three pars," Ward said.

"Okay, but who actually, physically sets them into the tee?" Tom asked.

"The committee marks the spot with a dot of spray paint, just like they mark the hole locations," Ward said. "The crew places them after they cut the tees in the morning."

"When do they do that?" Tom asked.

"Early," he said. "Usually six or seven in the morning."

"Okay, hang on," Tom said. "Jake, can we get that shot of 18 tee from that monitor to Ben Ward on 18?"

"Done," O'Banion said.

"Ben," Tom said, "look carefully at your monitor and tell me if those tee markers look like they're aimed to the right side of the hole."

"It's hard to tell for sure from this angle, but yeah, the one on the right side of the tee does look a little bit off," Ward said.

"Thanks," Tom said, hanging up the phone.

"I'll be right back," Tom said.

Tom left the truck and called Kathryn on the walkie-talkie.

"Is our guy a bomber?" Tom asked.

"Negative," Kathryn said.

"Does he have the training?" Tom said.

"SAS, sure," Kathryn said. "Not very sophisticated, though."

"We're not talking about building a rocket," Tom said. "Where are you now?"

"With Brookes. What's going on?" she asked.

"Meet me by the 18th tee," Tom said. "Just wait there. I'll be right up."

"But what about Brookes?" she asked.

"Don't worry about him right now," Tom said.

Next, Tom called the officer in charge of the canine patrols.

"Are any of your dogs trained for bomb detection?" Tom asked.

When he learned that one of the dogs was, he told the officer to bring the dog and his handler to the network's compound immediately.

His next call was to the captain coordinating the various police agencies.

"How many people can you get to the area around the 18th tee in 30 minutes?" Tom asked.

"Twenty-five or so, more if we pull them off the Brookes detail," the captain said.

"No, leave them in place," Tom said. "Check your watch. At exactly 5:35, I want as many as you can get to appear there in force. I want to see as many uniforms as you can find. I want everyone in that area to know something is going on. If you want to march them in there like a parade, that's fine with me."

"What do you want them to do when they get there?" the captain asked.

"Get right in the face of every middle-aged white guy you can find," Tom said. "Don't roust anyone, just pay careful attention to them and make sure they know it."

The canine team emerged from the woods. The soldier and his commanding officer were in combat fatigues. His dog was a large German shepherd. Tom quickly told the two men of his suspicion that one of the tee markers contained explosives.

"Will the dog accept commands from anyone or just you?" Tom asked the soldier.

"No, sir," the soldier said. "Heidi will only act on my commands."

Tom looked at the sharp teeth and powerful body and thought that Heidi was one hell of a name for a dog like this.

"Explain exactly how she will act if there is a bomb up there," Tom asked.

"On command, she will begin to sniff around any objects in the area," the officer said. "If she detects an explosive, she will immediately sit next to the object and won't budge until she's ordered to move."

"What about any distractions?" Tom asked. "There are hundreds of people up there."

"Sir, nothing will distract her," the soldier said.

Tom looked at his watch and then looked the soldier squarely in the eye.

"Okay, here's the deal," Tom said. "We don't have time to call in the bomb squad. I'm not sure this town would even have one. If there's a bomb up there, we need to get it out of there. There's a lot of risk involved."

The soldier looked at his officer.

"Your call," the officer reiterated.

"Let's go, sir," the soldier said.

"Good," Tom said. "Thanks. The first thing we need to do is get you out of those clothes."

He thought for a moment.

"How would you like to become a member of Augusta National?" he asked.

Tom called Ken Rice at his office in the clubhouse and explained his fears that Raines had placed a bomb in one of the tee markers.

"Ken, can you get us a change of clothes and two green jackets?" he asked. "A couple of 42s or 44s should do it. We'll meet you in your office in a few minutes."

"Captain, thanks very much," Tom said, shaking the officer's hand. "Wait for us here."

"Good luck," the officer said.

By the time Tom and the soldier—Corporal Logan—arrived at the clubhouse, Ken Rice had the green jackets and the change of clothes in his office. As Logan changed, Tom explained his plan to Rice.

"We need to be able to get the corporal and his dog onto the tee without attracting the kind of attention it would if he appeared in uniform," Tom said. "If I'm right about the bomb, Raines will explode it on the spot. But I'm hoping that by flooding the area with police, it might scare him off long enough for us to determine if there's a bomb there and remove it. Remember, he's not interested in what happens at that tee until Brookes arrives."

"Why the green jackets?" Rice asked.

"He's not likely to be suspicious if two members show up on the tee," Tom explained. "At least not initially, and especially if he believes one of the men is blind."

"Which explains the dog," Rice said.

"Exactly," Tom said.

"But what if he's there and panics?" Rice asked.

"That's the worst case scenario and we don't have time to deal with that," Tom said.

"Sir, could I ask a question?" Corporal Logan said.

"Go ahead," Tom said.

"Sir, how do you plan to get the bomb out of there?" the corporal said.

"Just grab it and go," Tom said. "We don't have any other choice."

"Actually, sir, we do," the soldier said. "Heidi is trained to remove a bomb on command. If it's small enough for her to hold in her mouth, she'll run off with it until she hears my whistle. Then she'll drop it and return to my side."

"Excellent," Tom said. "Thanks, corporal."

Tom checked his watch.

"We've got to go," he said. "Ken, let me borrow your sunglasses."

Tom, Corporal Logan and Heidi drove in their cart down the vast triangle of grass that separated the 9th, 8th and 18th holes and past the 17th green, where a group was approaching from the fairway. As they did, he checked the scoreboard and saw that Brookes had just completed the 12th hole and still had a two-stroke lead. He parked the cart as near to the right side of the 18th tee as possible and called Jake O'Banion.

"Jake, do me a favor and don't show any shots from the 18th tee until you hear from me," Tom said. "It will just be a few minutes."

Just as they arrived, the police were spreading out into the gallery around the tee. A murmur went through the crowd and just as Tom had requested, the officers were paying particular attention to middle-aged white men.

"Ready?" Tom said to Corporal Logan.

"Let's do it," the soldier said, rubbing his hand along the dog's neck. "Let's go, girl."

The corporal played the part of a blind man beautifully. He took Tom's arm and held the leash with the other. The gallery separated as they made their way to an opening in the gallery ropes. The dog was oblivious to the large gallery and when they reached the right side of the tee box, Tom spotted Kathryn and motioned for her to come over.

"This is my friend Mr. Logan," he said, loud enough for anyone standing nearby to hear.

Then he leaned across the ropes and whispered to Kathryn.

"I think Raines may have planted a bomb here," Tom said. "We're going to find out. I want you to get out among the gallery. Take a policeman with you. If you see anyone who even looks remotely like Raines, confront him. If he reaches for anything in his pockets, put him on the ground and make your apologies later."

"Tom, are you sure..." Kathryn said.

"Just do it," Tom said.

Kathryn stared at him for a moment.

"Let's go," Tom said to the corporal.

The three walked over to a bench where there was a container of water. The dog sniffed all around. Nothing. Then they walked to the tee marker on the left side of the tee. The same thing. But when they reached the right side of the tee, the dog immediately sat next to the marker.

"Come girl," the corporal said, giving a slight tug on the leash.

The dog remained motionless.

"Right there," the corporal said softly to Tom.

Tom immediately moved closer to the marker and loosened it with his foot. As he did, he noticed that Raines had placed the spike a good four or five inches behind the paint spot.

"Go ahead," he said to the corporal.

The corporal dropped the leash.

"Heidi, fetch," he said, quietly

The dog immediately picked up the tee marker in her mouth and looked at the soldier.

"Heidi, go," he said, subtly, almost imperceptibly, pointing to the woods on the left side of the 10th fairway.

The dog ran off at full speed toward the 10th hole. The gallery around the tee erupted into laughter.

"Let's get out of here," Tom said to the soldier.

They left the tee, got in the cart, and raced down the right side of the 18th hole, through the trees, and across to the 10th hole where they stopped. The soldier pulled a silver dog whistle from his pocket and blew into it. It didn't make a sound, but seconds later, the dog ran out from the trees.

"Can you disarm the bomb?" Tom asked Corporal Logan.

"If it's not too complicated," Logan said. "My guess is that it's fairly straightforward."

The soldier took the leash and gave Heidi another fetch command. They followed her into the trees and she led them right to the tee marker. As Tom watched to make sure they didn't get any visitors, Logan examined the marker. He quickly found the seam where the two pieces had been glued together, and separated them with the large service knife he had brought along. He carefully cut out the plug of plastic wood and removed the blasting cap, and then cut out a piece of the explosive.

"Plastique," Logan said. "Probably C-4. It's pretty common stuff. It's harmless now."

They got back in their cart and drove past the cottages and down the maintenance road toward the television compound. When they returned to the television trucks the army captain was waiting for them.

"This is one damn good man, captain," Tom said. "And one damn good dog. Thank you both."

"Thank you, sir," Corporal Logan said. "Anytime."

"I don't plan to make a habit of this," Tom said.

"One last thing, sir," the corporal said. "Can I keep the green jacket?"

"Sure," Tom said, laughing. "Tell all your friends you won it at a member-guest."

• • •

Tom had guessed right. Raines had been in the gallery behind the 18th tee, but when the police arrived in force, he grew suspicious and walked down the 17th fairway, where the gallery had begun to swell as the last groups played through the back nine. As the police fanned out, he worked his way through the crowd, which was as many as 10 people deep in places, until he was so far into the gallery that he would be difficult to spot. He knew that as the final pairing approached the 17th and 18th holes, the size of the gallery crowding into this relatively small area would be enormous. That was good for him...and bad for them.

. . .

Kathryn felt a tremendous sense of relief when she watched Tom drive safely away, but she had an awful sense of foreboding as she scanned the gallery. It would be nearly impossible to spot Raines. It would be an act of colossal good fortune, but even if she did, how could he be stopped without a risk of injury to innocent bystanders? She was certain he would be armed and, at this stage of the game, quite desperate.

. . .

After thanking the soldiers, Tom called Ken Rice and told him about the bomb.

"Where is it now?" Rice asked.

"I've got it tucked away for safekeeping," Tom said. "It's been disarmed. How does Brookes stand?"

"He's got a two-stroke lead and he's in the middle of the 17th fairway," Rice said.

"Okay, tell me exactly what will happen once he leaves the 18th green," Tom said.

"If he wins, he signs his scorecard and then we take him by cart through the galleries down to the Butler Cabin studio," Rice explained. "He does the green jacket ceremony down there, and then we bring him up to the practice green for the public ceremony. Then he goes to the media center, followed by a small dinner in his honor."

"Okay, I want to be down in Butler Cabin, just in case," Tom said.

"Just let Jake O'Banion know so they'll let you in," Rice said.

Tom ducked into the production truck, where O'Banion was railing against Brookes.

"Hit it, you slow-playing sonofabitch," O'Banion said, looking at the wall of monitors "They ought to slap two on you just to make this goddamned tournament interesting. Our ratings are going to be lower than the fucking 'Early Show.'"

Tom leaned over and whispered to O'Banion.

"Jake, we're clear on 18," Tom said.

"What the hell was going on up there with the Green Jackets?" O'Banion asked. "The Plantation is the only place in the world where they use blind members to set tee markers in the middle of a goddamned tournament."

"You don't want to know," Tom said. "Look, I want to be in the Butler Cabin studio when Brookes comes in. Will you tell them?"

"Charlie, let them know that our friend the Mick is on his way up to help the chairman with the green jacket ceremony," Jake said.

"Thanks for everything," Tom said, patting O'Banion on the back.

"Get the fuck out of here," O'Banion said. "I've got Masterpiece Theater to produce here..."

As Tom slipped out of the truck, he heard O'Banion in full roar.

"Will you p-l-e-a-s-e hit the fucking ball, you lousy limey bastard?"

. . .

By the time Brookes left the 17th green, Raines had made his way to the stand of large trees that stood to the right and rear of the 18th tee, running back to the right side of the 15th tee. He stopped behind one that was thick enough to block any effects of the blast. He watched as Brookes's caddie walked to the right side of the tee. Brookes joined him a moment later and pulled a club from his bag. Raines reached into his jacket pocket, found the button that would detonate the bomb, leaned against the tree and pushed the button, closing his eyes in anticipation of the explosion.

Nothing.

He tried again.

Nothing. He discreetly pulled the device from his pocket. It seemed undamaged.

Brookes hit a tremendous drive, starting out at the fairway

bunkers and cutting back into the center of the fairway.

Raines tried a third time to no avail. He felt a rage well up inside him. His head began to pound.

"Bloody M.I.6," he said under his breath.

• • •

While Brookes was making his way to the 18th tee, Kathryn desperately searched the crowd, looking for anyone who even remotely resembled Raines. It was madness. Brookes finally reached the tee to enormous applause from the gallery. Droves of people were moving toward the clubhouse, alongside the 18th and 10th fairways.

As she scanned the gallery, she noticed a solitary man well off in the trees. She thought it was odd, since he wouldn't be able to see any of the tee shots from there. But as soon as Brookes hit his tee shot, the man began walking very quickly down the right side of the 10th fairway. He soon began jogging. It was a long shot, but maybe...

"Come with me," she said to the large, muscular state policeman who had been with her all afternoon. "See that bearded man? Let's keep an eye on him."

• • •

Tom reached Butler Cabin and made his way through the press of people gathered in the back patio and all along the left side of the building. He entered the door at the left rear of the building. Above, in the main part of the cabin, there was an enormous party going on, yet it was amazingly quiet downstairs. In the small anteroom, people sat at computers that provided scoring information. A young woman motioned for him to follow her. She stopped at the white door to her right, listened to make sure no one was on-air, and then ushered him in.

"You need to go around the back, behind the cameras, and be very quiet," she said.

There were five chairs arranged in front of a fireplace. The chairman sat in one of the two chairs to the viewer's right. When he saw Tom, he gave him a nod of recognition. The chair next to him was empty, awaiting the arrival of Tim Prince, who would host the ceremony as soon has he finished announcing play on the 18th.

Seated across from the chairman were the defending champion, who would place the green jacket on Brookes, and the low amateur. Brookes would fill the third chair.

Tom stood behind the cameras. There were several monitors in the room, and on them he could see Brookes walking toward the final green as the gallery gave him a standing ovation.

"I've been coming to this tournament for a long time, Tim," Ben Ward said from the tower on 18, "and I don't think I've ever seen a player more in control of his emotions and his game."

"This has been a tough few weeks for Peter Brookes, but he's come through it like a true champion," Prince said. "The patrons here at the Masters certainly respect him for it."

• • •

As Kathryn and the state policeman followed the man she believed was Raines, she called Tom.

"I think we've got him," she said, her words interrupted by deep breaths as they hurried to keep Raines in sight. "We picked him up behind the 18th tee, just after Brookes hit. He's got a beard and he's wearing a big straw hat pulled down over his forehead, but he's raced off after Brookes. He's heading for the clubhouse."

"Can you catch him?" Tom asked. "Can you cut him off?"

"Not before he reaches the top of the hill. And then he'll lose himself in the crowd," Kathryn said.

"Stay with him for as long as you can," Tom said.

Tom paused for a moment to collect his thoughts. If Raines could manage to get off just one shot, there'd be such chaos he'd have a chance of escaping—a very good chance. Tom only had one play and it was a long shot—literally. He called the sniper team positioned in the Crow's Nest in the clubhouse.

"We have a possible suspect," he said. "Bearded man, middle age, wearing a large straw hat pulled low on his face. He should be running up the hill on eighteen toward the clubhouse. Can you pick him up?"

"We're looking but nothing yet, sir," one of the soldiers said, scanning the area with binoculars. "Even if we spot him in this crowd ..."

"Never mind that," Tom said sharply. "Just keep looking."

The sharpshooter, scanning the area through the scope on his rifle motioned to his partner. "There, over by that right-hand bunker by the green. Near 10 tee. See him?"

"We have him, sir," the spotter said. "He's headed toward the putting green. Sir, we don't really have a clean shot. Too many civilians."

Tom was silent. He knew that they would get just one shot – one chance to stop Raines and save Brookes's life. He also knew the risks, and they were enormous. They didn't have permission to use the sniper team to take out Raines, and if there were innocents wounded or, God forbid, even killed, there would be endless hell to pay.

"Sir...?" the spotter called, awaiting Tom's instructions.

There was silence as Tom calculated the options. They were tumbling in front of him like cards falling from a deck, but with perfect clarity. He exhaled slowly and closed his eyes.

"Listen carefully," Tom said. "I want you to put the button on him. Put that laser right in his eyes. I want him to know he's targeted. As soon as you hit him with the laser, I want you to tell me how he reacts. Exactly how he reacts. But do not shoot without my orders. Do you understand?"

"Yes, sir," the spotter said.

Tom was betting that if the guy was an innocent spectator, he'd be confused by the light and would look around for the source. But if it was Raines, he'd instantly realize that a sniper had him in his sights and his instinctive reaction would be to flee. If he did, they'd have him. Finally.

Graham Raines made his way up to the clubhouse and saw the crowds gathered to the side of Butler Cabin.

"Is this the best place to see the new champion?" he said to a group of people near the practice green, where chairs had been arranged for the ceremony honoring Brookes. "I'd fancy a close-up look at him. He's quite popular in my country."

"He'll go right past here, and down behind Butler Cabin there," one of the people said.

"I see," said Raines, pointing toward the cabin. "Is that a private party or can anyone sufficiently drunk get in?"

"Private as hell," one of the women said. "That's why they have the Rent-a-Cop guarding the door."

Raines was walking toward Butler Cabin when he heard a roar from the 18th green. He turned and looked. As he did, the light from the sniper's laser hit him squarely in the eyes. Instinctively, he raised his arm to block the intense flash. He looked toward the clubhouse roof and saw the light coming through an open window. He could also make out at least one figure, possibly two. In that instant, he knew he had to get into the crowd as fast as he possibly could.

"Sir, he's moving," the spotter said to Tom.

"He knew he was in your sights?" Tom asked. "You're sure?"

"No doubt, sir," the spotter replied. "He took one look up here and bolted. He knew exactly what was going on, sir."

"Do you have a shot?"

The spotter looked over at the shooter, who slowly shook his head.

"Negative," the spotter said. "Too many civilians."

The shooter kept his rifle trained on Raines, who was deep into the large gallery.

"Lock it down," Tom said. "But keep him in sight. Let me know if you lose him."

"Kathryn," Tom said, "he's our man."

"Right, then," Kathryn said.

As Raines turned away toward the clubhouse, he caught a glimpse of Kathryn Devlin, coming through the crowd with the state policeman clearing the way. He had to get into the cabin, blend in with the crowd and make his escape down the back stairway, out of danger from the shooters on the roof. Before, the cabin had only been one option. Now it was the only option. As he got closer, two young women came out of the front door, looking none too steady after an afternoon of intense hospitality.

"Could you help me?" he asked them. "I was in the party earlier but left my bag. My host left to catch an early flight back to New York and I have neither the time nor the energy to deal with J. Edgar Hoover there. Could you do me a huge favor and escort me back inside. I'd be eternally grateful."

The girls looked at Raines and then one another.

"A roadie can't hurt," one said.

"Never has," the other woman said.

The women walked Raines past the guard at the front door. Once they were inside, he pretended to look around for a minute or so, then asked directions for the bathroom and walked away from the women, promising to meet them at one of the bars.

Kathryn thought she caught a glimpse of Raines as he entered Butler Cabin. She and the police officer ran toward the building, dodging spectators as they did. At the same time, to their right, Brookes was being driven to the Butler Cabin studio, through the hundreds of people who had gathered to cheer him. As the crowd in the cabin and those gathered in the rear saw him, an enormous roar went up. Brookes smiled and waved as the police escort struggled to keep the gallery back.

"Tom," she said into her walkie-talkie, "Raines is in Butler Cabin. He's just gone through the front door. We're going in now."

Tom asked one of the cameramen if there was any way to get to the studio from the main level of the cabin.

"Through that door," he said, pointing to his right. "There's a stairway on your left but we keep it locked when we're on the air."

Kathryn and the policeman reached the front door and brushed past the guard. They entered the main part of the cabin and were immediately engulfed by the crowd. They both frantically scanned the room for a glimpse of Raines. Kathryn reached into her bag and discreetly clicked off the safety of her Beretta. The policeman undid the strap holding his pistol in the holster.

"You go around to the right," Kathryn said. "I'll go this way."

• • •

Raines walked around to the rear of the room and saw the doorway leading to a set of stairs that ran down to the lower floor of the cabin. The doorway was blocked by a second guard.

"Are those the stairs that lead to the television studio?" Raines said to the guard.

"Yes, but no one's allowed down there during the telecast," the guard said.

"Yes, well you see Peter Brookes is my cousin and I was told by his agent to come this way so that I might avoid the crowds," Raines said. As he did, he saw Kathryn Devlin to one side and the policeman making his way through the crowd.

"I'm sorry but those are my orders…"

"Blast your orders, " Raines said, pushing past the guard.

"Hey, you can't…!"

Both Kathryn and the policeman looked over in time to see Raines disappear down the stairwell. They pushed through the people and reached the head of the stairs. The officer grabbed the hapless guard and shoved him aside. Raines was struggling with the locked door at the foot of the stairs, frantically turning the doorknob.

"It's finished, Raines," Kathryn said in a loud but calm voice, taking dead aim at the center of his back.

"You're under arrest," the state policeman shouted, his gun pointed down the stairwell.

Raines turned to his right and as he did, he pulled the .32 from inside his jacket.

Kathryn fired once. The round crashed into the right side of his chest, just below his collarbone. The shot slammed Raines up and back against the door. He grabbed his shoulder with his left hand and his gun hand dropped to his side.

Kathryn and the state policeman both leveled their guns at Raines. The inside of the cabin was a scene of chaos. People screamed and tried to run from the room. Others fell to the floor or huddled in corners.

"Let the gun drop slowly to the ground," Kathryn said. Her Beretta was now aimed at the center of Raines's chest.

"Put it down, now!" the policeman yelled.

Raines locked eyes with Kathryn but didn't move. He said nothing, but leaned his head back against the door and slumped ever so slightly. Blood was gushing from the wound, pouring over his hand.

"Don't be a fool," Kathryn said.

Raines smiled grimly. "You've won," he said.

Before they could react, Raines lifted his gun to his head and fired one round. Blood exploded all over the small stairwell and the door. He was dead by the time his body collapsed against the door in a grotesque sprawl.

Both Kathryn and the officer kept their guns trained on the body. Neither moved.

. . .

In the studio, Peter Brookes had just taken his seat and a technician had finished placing a mike under his shirt, attaching it to his
collar as Tom left to make sure Raines didn't try to reach the studio.

"Alright, 30 seconds to air," he heard Jake O'Banion say over
the speaker. "Good playing, Peter. Fish and chips at next year's
Champion's Dinner?"

"Just some Mad Cow burgers," Brookes said.

Tom heard a thudding as he approached the door to the stairway, followed by the sounds of someone turning the doorknob.
Just as he reached the door, he heard a single gunshot, followed
just seconds later by a second, louder, shot.

"Stay with Brookes," he said to a policeman who had suddenly
appeared in the hallway.

Tom pulled out his pistol and clicked off the safety. He
unlocked the door, stood off to the left, and then swung the door
open. As he did, he pointed his gun in the stairwell. Raines's body
tumbled onto the floor at his feet. He looked to the top of the
stairs and saw Kathryn and a policeman. She was still in a shooter's
crouch, her gun pointing at Raines. The policeman stood behind
her and off slightly to the right.

Tom reached down to check Raines's pulse, but he knew from
the massive head wound that he was already dead. He picked up
Raines's gun, released the clip, and ejected the round that was in
the chamber.

"Are you okay?" he called up to Kathryn.

"Yes, I think so," she said.

"Officer, how 'bout you?"

"Yes, sir, " he said, sliding his pistol back in its holster. Then he
placed his large, muscular arm around Kathryn and gently took
the pistol from her hand. "You best let me have that, ma'am."

"Kathyrn, stay up there with the officer," Tom said. "I'll be right
up. And get those people the hell away from the door. Just shut it."

Tom took a deep breath, placed his pistol back in its holster,
and looked around. He spotted a large piece of canvas and covered
Raines and the pool of blood that was spreading across the floor.

. . .

As soon as Tim Price heard the gunshot, he motioned into the cameras to get Jake O'Banion's attention.

"Jake, you better stay in commercial, we've had something happen here," Prince said.

"Jake, did you hear Timmy?" the stage manager said into his direct line with the truck.

"What's going on?" O'Banion said over the speaker.

"We think there was a gunshot, maybe two," Prince said. "One of the cops has Brookes tucked away somewhere in the back."

. . .

Tom called the officer coordinating the police coverage.

"The suspect is dead," he said. "There are no other injuries. He's on the first floor of Butler Cabin. One of your officers witnessed the shooting. He's also in the cabin, along with Kathryn Devlin. They were both involved. Send an ambulance to the back entrance of the cabin and you'd better get some more of your people up here for crowd control."

Next, Tom thought he'd better alert the chairman and Jake O'Banion. He walked to a back doorway, spotted an officer, and motioned him into the cabin.

"This is a crime scene," Tom said. "Keep everyone the hell out of here and especially the press. There's an ambulance on the way."

"Who are you?" the officer asked.

"Never mind who I am," Tom said. "Just do it."

Then he left and went back into the studio. Every eye in the place was on him.

"Mr. Franklin, can I see you?" he said. "Where's Brookes?"

"The cop has him," the stage manager said. "He's fine."

He took the chairman to the far back corner of the room, where they both got on a direct line with Jake O'Banion.

"Raines is dead," Tom said. "I don't know the details. He was in Butler Cabin trying to get into the studio and was shot. Brookes is fine."

Tom saw some movement outside the French doors and watched as the EMTs rolled a stretcher toward the door on the far side of the cabin. The large crowd grew completely quiet.

As soon as the EMTs removed Raines's body, Tom went

upstairs and found Kathryn. She and the policeman had been taken to one of the bedrooms, where they were waiting to be interviewed by detectives. Tom asked if he could have a few minutes alone with her. The police left the room, closing the door behind them.

"Tom, he killed himself," she said. "We had him cornered in the stairwell. He turned and I fired once, hitting him here. It wouldn't have been fatal, I swear. Then he turned and stared into my eyes. I will never forget that. Then he gave me the most eerie smile and shot himself. He said I'd won, as though this was some sort of bloody game. It was ghastly."

Tom pressed her head close to him and stroked her hair.

"Okay, it's over now," he said. "It's finally all over. And you *did* win."

CHAPTER FOURTEEN

St. John's Episcopal Church stands opposite the White House on the north side of Lafayette Square. It is known as the "Church of the Presidents," and rightly so. It was established in 1815 specifically to serve as the place of worship for the occupants of the White House and their families. President James Madison was the first presidential communicant and almost every president since then is believed to have attended services there, either regularly or occasionally.

The Greek revival building was designed by Benjamin Henry Latrobe, best known for his restoration of both the White House and the capitol building after the British burned them during the War of 1812.

The church was already half-filled for Sir Owen's memorial service when Tom and Kathryn arrived at 9:45. She was still badly shaken by Graham Raines's suicide and was also upset about Sir Owen's death and the prospect of returning to England.

They took their seats next to the Deputy Director and his wife and Mary Dwyer. Across the aisle were Senator Gardner, his wife, Susie, and Briggs McPhee. There was a delegation from the State Department as well as the British embassy, and the President's National Security Advisor headed the representatives from the

White House. Just before 10 A.M., a series of middle-aged and older men filtered in and sat in the back of the church. Tom didn't have to look around to know they were veterans of the Agency coming to pay their last respects to a comrade they deeply respected.

The bright spring sunlight filtered into the church through the ornate stained glass windows that in some cases dated back to the mid-1800s. Many of them commemorate the lives and deeds of past American political leaders. Every pew was filled save one: No. 54, the President's Pew.

At precisely 10, the organist began playing Bach's *Jesu, Joy of Man's Desiring* and a military honor guard entered the church carrying Sir Owen's coffin, draped by a Union Jack. When they reached the altar they placed it upon a simple wood bier. Then they turned as one to their left and stoically marched to the rear of the church.

The service began with a simple Collect led by the Rector.

"O God, whose mercies cannot be numbered, accept our prayers on behalf of your servant Sir Owen Tunnicliffe, and grant him an entrance into the land of light and joy, in the fellowship of thy saints, through Jesus Christ thy son our Lord, who liveth and reigneth with thee and the Holy Spirit, one God now and forever. Amen."

"Amen," answered the congregation.

A reading of Psalm 121 was followed by a hymn, *O God, Our Help in Ages Past*.

Then it was time for Kathryn to go to the altar for the first reading. She squeezed Tom's hand and brushed back a tear. She had selected Revelation 21:2-7 from the New Testament. She delivered it with a clear strong voice that carried across the hushed chamber, and carried herself with great dignity as she returned to her seat next to Tom. When she sat down, she looked over and gave him a rueful smile as tears filled her eyes. Tom took her hands in his.

"Good job," he said softly.

Another hymn, *For the Beauty of the Earth*, followed. Then Laddie Jackson walked to the altar and reflected on his old friend.

"We are gathered together today to celebrate the life of a great man," the Deputy Director said. "And make no mistake, Sir Owen Tunnicliffe was truly both a great and good man. He loved his friends and family and he loved his country. He was devoted to the fight for freedom and liberty. His was not a fight played out in the headlines. He did not live for glory. He was not perfect, for none of us are. But he lived his life with courage and dignity; grace and good humor; love and loyalty. He treasured and celebrated America and all that our two nations stand for. Owen Tunnicliffe fought the good fight and we are the better for it. I will miss him. Godspeed, old friend."

As Laddie Jackson walked back to the pew, the sound of muffled sobbing could be heard.

The final hymn was Tom's favorite, number 608, *The Navy Hymn*. It always brought back memories of watching President Kennedy's funeral when he was a boy, but as he sang it he thought it was particularly appropriate for this service.

The Rector led the congregation in the Lord's Prayer and closed the service with a blessing. Then the Honor Guard marched back down the aisle and took their places on either side of the casket. Without any verbal command, they pivoted to their left. As they did, the organist began playing the most fitting possible melody: In America, it is the music to *My Country 'Tis of Thee*. In Great Britain, it is the music for *God Save the Queen*. They carried Sir Owen out of the church and into the waiting hearse for the trip to Dulles Airport, where it would be loaded into a British Airways plane for the flight home to London.

The motorcade drove slowly from the church, pausing briefly near the White House before proceeding along Pennsylvania Avenue, past the the capitol, then along the Mall past the Washington Monument and the Lincoln Memorial.

When the motorcade reached Dulles Airport in the Virginia suburbs, it was given a police escort onto the tarmac, where the British Airways plane waited, gleaming in the sunlight.

The cars emptied, and people gathered by the side of the plane as the Honor Guard took the casket from the hearse and carried it to the rear of the plane. They placed it on a gurney draped in black cloth, and then the Honor Guard removed the Union Jack and crisply and precisely folded it. They handed it to the officer in charge and then saluted him. He, in turn, handed it to the British Ambassador. The Ambassador turned, walked a few yards to his right, and gave the flag to Laddie Jackson.

"Thank you, Mr. Ambassador," the Deputy Director said.

"No, Mr. Jackson," the ambassador said. "Thank *you*."

Slowly, the cars began to pull away and the moment that both Tom and Kathryn had dreaded finally arrived.

"Take your time, Tom," Laddie said.

Then he turned to Kathryn and shook her hand.

"Take care, Kathryn," he said. "I hope we see you back here in the States real soon."

"Thank you for everything," Kathryn said, embracing him and patting his back. "I hope so, too."

She turned to Tom.

"Well, it's time," she said.

They embraced and then walked toward the stairway leading to the plane's entrance. They kissed once and then she stepped onto the stairway, smiled, and ran her hand slowly across his face.

"I've heard rumors that New England is sublime in the fall," she said. "Perhaps I could come for a visit."

"I couldn't think of anything better," he said. "Unless it was a visit to London. What do you think?"

"I think that would be brilliant," Kathryn said. "Oh ,Tom, do you promise?"

"It's a deal," Tom said. "Take care of yourself until then."

They shared one more embrace and then she climbed the stairs. When she reached the top, she waved to the Jacksons and then turned, looked at Tom, and waved sadly.

Tom searched the windows hoping to get one last glance, then turned and joined the Jacksons. The Deputy Director put his arm over Tom's shoulders as they walked toward his limousine.

"Now, Thomas, let's talk about this banking business..."